I0818088

BORN UPON A CURSE

THE DARKNESS WITHIN

Book Cover by M. Dane

Paperback ISBN: 9780645520996

Hardcover ISBN: 9780975661543

eBook ISBN: 9780645520989

1st edition 2024

BORN UPON A CURSE

THE DARKNESS WITHIN

M. DANE

Chapter One

Working Friday night shifts at Taco Express in the Southern heat felt a lot like being stuck on a date with Mr. I-Don't-Believe-in-Climate-Change-Because-It's-Cold-Outside—almost torture, but unacceptably legal. Sweat poured down my back, threatening to turn the slick tiles into a slip-and-slide, while the heavy air clung to my throat in a greasy layer. As bad as it was, surviving spontaneous combustion was only part of the challenge; the real struggle was ignoring the stares thrown my way.

I wasn't strange to look at. While my auburn hair didn't match the typical Southern belle palette, it didn't scream "outcast" either. I had no missing teeth or bonus ears. Yet the folks knew that the girl with freckles was different. Dangerous. A weed that needed plucking before it spread.

I braced against the windowsill, the calm between orders offering a moment to dream of my bed and the bliss of air conditioning. Two hours to go. Work had lobotomized me enough for one night. Soon I would find peace in my solitude.

As I clung to that fleeting image of comfort, reality swooped in and snapped me back to my pitiful existence. A searing pain sliced through my stomach. I caught my breath, fingers digging into the windowsill. It was her.

"No," I breathed, the pain climbing. "Please." I forced myself upright, steeling against the familiar dread. "Don't do this."

She didn't listen.

She never listened.

She exploded through me with a force that buckled my knees. I bit my tongue, tasting the tang of blood, but refused to cry out. Unwanted attention was the last thing I needed.

The first tendrils of her being snaked into my mind, piercing my thoughts like rusty hooks. I gasped. The intensity, the power, was new and terrifying.

"Hello?" a man's voice crackled in my headset. "Did you hear me? I said I want—"

I tore it off and dropped it on the bench. My vision dimmed as I fought to bury the chaos in her cage. Her anger flared. She was tired of being locked up. She wanted out.

But she hurt people when she escaped.

My hands trembled as flashes of the times she'd stolen control burst through my mind. I'd woken in the beds of strangers too often to count, naked and ashamed of what she'd done. I fought harder, terrified of another scandal, unhooking her from my thoughts and pushing her down. Bit by bit, like water dripping down a hair-clogged drain, I squeezed her into the confines of her prison. She flared for a moment of pure frustration, then withered into the darkness and fought no more.

I slumped onto the bench, shaking like I'd sprinted a mile. Something had changed in her over the last few days. It was like she'd awoken after a long, booze-induced siesta, and was desperate to make up for lost time.

"Alina?" a voice called behind me.

I jolted, having forgotten where I was. I faked a smile and turned to find Grace, her dark skin glistening with kitchen grease.

"You okay, sweetie?" she asked.

My smile wavered. "Yeah, just a little tired is all—"

A spasm rocked me onto my heels. Fire raced through my veins as I clutched my abdomen, barely keeping upright. My breath came in short gasps as panic set in. She surged upwards in a hot fury.

Twice in one night. She'd never escaped twice in one night.

"Alina?" Grace asked, voice echoing in the distance. "What's wrong, puddin'?"

I leaped forward, sliding on the slick floor, and dashed for the restrooms. "Look after the window?" I called, not waiting for her reply.

I hurtled past the drink fridge and collided with someone, sending a tray of tacos rocketing skyward as I tumbled to the floor.

"What the hell?" bellowed Juan, a guy I worked with. He sat on his backside, glaring at me.

I cringed. "I'm so sorry . . . It was an accident—"

"You're the accident. Damn it—look at this!" He gathered the tacos, slapping them back on the tray. "You're almost twenty, but you're as useful as a guitar without strings."

I grabbed a taco and handed it to him. My hand shook from the effort of keeping a straight face while my insides were being torn to shreds. "Five-second rule?"

He snatched it from my grip and threw it with the others. "One day, you'll fall so hard you won't get up. No one will care. Get help, Alina." He stood, straightened his cap, then stormed away.

I wanted to shout after him, to point out that he was a twenty-year-old man working at Taco Express, that his life was as shot to hell as mine. But my thoughts scrambled as she penetrated my mind. I sprang to my feet and sprinted into the restroom.

The cubicle door slammed behind me as I fumbled through my pockets. I found my medicine bottle and unscrewed the lid with trembling fingers, but the bottle slipped from my grasp and fell to the ground with a clatter. My few remaining pills spilled onto the tiles.

I froze as they rolled along the floor and stopped in a puddle.

"No," I whispered, staring in horror. My mouth went dry. When was the world going to cut me some slack? I sank onto the toilet, darkness ringing the edge of my vision, and my feet began tapping while I stared unblinkingly.

In a daze, I bent forward and gathered the three white pills. Their surface was slimy, leaving a chalky residue on my fingers. It was just water. It had to be just water. I stared at them for the time it took to fill my mouth with saliva, and, grateful no one could see how pathetic I'd become, closed my eyes and placed them on my tongue. My body convulsed as an urge to retch took over. I clamped my jaw closed and swallowed. A shudder rolled through me.

I found my hip flask and took a drink, the fiery vodka burning my throat. A mental barrier quickly formed, protecting me from her influence, though I suspected this was from a belief in my impending recovery, rather than pharmaceutical intervention. I closed my eyes and waited for the blissful moment when my mind would be my own again.

Six years.

Six years, and I still fought the same battle. I'd been diagnosed with dissociative identity disorder when I was thirteen. They said it was from childhood trauma, that I'd created her to shield me away from the world. Bouncing from foster home to foster home was bound to leave a stain on anyone, as certain as a squashed bug will mark a finger. Trouble was, I was both the finger and the bug. I drained my flask with a wince.

Back then, as they'd tossed me from family to family, all I'd wanted was to belong. To stop feeling alone. Now, I was never by myself, no matter how hard I ran. I hosted this creature I'd birthed to protect me. My friends called her Machina. Alina Machina—a play on my name. She felt more like Satan.

The sharp edge of my panic dulled.

Was this what life had laid out for me? An unending battle for control, one where I slipped more and more each day? Heck . . . twice in one night? At this rate, making it through the year seemed impossible—

The restroom door burst open with a bang.

"Alina Rose?" My heart fell as I recognized the voice of my boss, Chelsea. "I know you're in here."

"Just a minute," I said, sitting straighter.

"A minute? You've had a minute. You've had three years of minutes!"

"It was an emergency—"

"It always is with you. Shit, Alina, while you're here enjoying your emergencies, other people have to pick up the slack. Don't think we don't know what you're doing in there—we smell it on you every time you come out. What's it today? Tequila?"

I rested my elbows on my legs and kneaded my eyes with my palms. "I'm sorry—"

"Why you were hired in the first place, I'll never know," she continued. "Troubled child you were, and a troubled young lady you are. But tell you what, you won't be working here much longer if you take another break tonight—"

All the pent-up anger and fear welled inside me and erupted out. I slammed my hands against the cubicle walls. "I said I need a minute!"

The lights flickered and plunged us into darkness. Instant regret washed over me. The anxiety that the pills had silenced now rushed back. A buzzing filled the room, and after a moment, the lights spluttered back to life.

"Y-you're done," Chelsea stammered. "Done. Breaking the fixtures with your childish tantrums. You may as well look for another job right now."

The door slammed shut.

I sat there for a while, staring at my hands. When I opened the door and saw the woman in the mirror, dark rings under her eyes, she was unrecognizable. At nineteen, I sure looked a lot of fifty. I dropped my gaze and made my way back into the kitchen. Chelsea hadn't officially fired me, and I didn't want to give her any more incentive.

"A bad one, huh?" Grace asked, offering me my headset.

"Worst one all week," I muttered, slipping it on like a muzzle. I'd never told Grace the details of my problems—I couldn't bear her treating me differently—but she had concluded that I suffered from chronic migraines. I let her run with it. For the last three years, she'd been a shining light in that place. Her smile could warm me more than a Chipotle in June.

She gently squeezed my shoulders with her large hands. "Chin up, dear. God don't bless just anyone with rainbow eyes. You're meant for great things, and don't I know it." She stroked my cheek, then hummed as she ambled back to her station.

I turned to the drive-thru window, sagging back into my spot of hell. I wouldn't call them rainbow eyes. One green, one blue; they were more muddy water than anything.

A car rolled up to the speaker. "Welcome to Taco Express," I mumbled. "May I take your order?"

"Yes, you can," said a voice that was too excited. "We'd love to *taco* walk on the wild side with you."

My breath caught. It couldn't be . . .

I leaned out the window and saw two people hanging out of a beat-up Honda Civic. Georgie's hair was as wild and free as she was, and Dustin sported a short-cropped bleached beard. They waved at me, huge smiles on their faces.

"Well, I'll be!" I cried into the microphone. "What're y'all doing back here?"

"We missed you!" shouted Dustin.

"A year's a long time, Lina," said Georgie.

My heart swelled. After everything I'd been through, seeing my two best friends was almost enough to make me sing. "I didn't expect you back until next week. What happened?"

"Dustin wanted to come early for the Ragin' Cajuns game," said Georgie, rolling her eyes.

"The after-party, actually," he said. "And the prospect of a little fun with some football players."

"You be careful," I said. "Trent's still fixin' to knock your lights out after the rumors you spread." How could it have been a full year since they'd moved to San Fran? They hadn't changed at all.

"Rumors? The only thing I spread was a detailed account of everything that happened after graduation."

"Come on, Lina!" Georgie urged. "Ditch this place already. We have serious catching up to do."

I hesitated. "I'm in a bit of hot water—"

"Please!" they said together.

I glanced over my shoulder and saw Juan glaring at me, arms crossed. How much longer could I work at a place that policed bathroom breaks? I chewed my bottom lip. Sure, I could use the money, but not if it killed me . . .

In a rush of rebellion, I yanked off my headset and scrambled out the window. "Well, alright, then!"

"Wait until Chelsea hears about this," Juan called after me.

I paused, then turned, and glowered at him. "Wait until your pa hears about you fooling around with his best friend." I smiled as the color drained from his face.

Georgie pulled the car up beside me, the music blasting, and I dove into the back seat. She slammed her foot onto the gas, and we raced out of the drive-thru, merging onto the road and leaving the Taco Express—and my job—in the dust.

"Buckle up, darling," Georgie said. "And in the event of a fiery crash, feel free to scream."

Dustin tossed a warm beer onto my lap. "Complimentary beverage?"

I cracked the can. "I knew I liked you." With one hand, I pulled my hair out of the bun and let the warm night breeze whip it into a wild dance. Any lingering doubts about my impromptu exit were blown away. I was alive, and, for the first time in ages, felt like I was where I belonged.

Chapter Two

We tore through the deserted streets of Breaux Bridge, Dustin's and Georgie's voices bringing back old memories. I was transported to those old sunny days when storm clouds couldn't reach us. The smell of magnolia blossoms filling the air as we rode our way to some mischief or another. I closed my eyes, savoring those simple times before my world had changed.

"Don't mind a pit stop before we hit the club, do you?" Georgie's voice brought me back.

"As long as it's not to visit one of your deadbeat exes," I said. Georgie had never found a nice guy to settle down with. She had never tried. That's what hurt the most—she was wonderful and deserved the best man walking. She could have him, too, but none of those guys came with the side of danger that hooked her.

She held a hand to her heart. "Deadbeat? My, Alina! They were outstanding gentlemen."

"I'm sure their wives would agree," I said, earning a laugh from Dustin.

"Alina brought the sass tonight!" he said, spinning in his seat to grab my hand. "I've missed you, honey. And Machina, too. Will we catch her while we're back?"

"Machina!" Georgie cried, jolting the wheel in her excitement. "I clean forgot about her. How is she? It's been a hot minute."

I watched the streetlights whizzing by, their golden trails streaking in the darkness. We were on the main highway, heading out of town. "No," I said.

"Please, honey," Dustin pressed. "Y'all remember how much fun we used to have? It wouldn't be a party without her."

I pulled out of his grip and clasped my arms around my waist. Dustin and Georgie loved enticing Machina out of her hole. They'd poke and prod until I gave up and gave in. Back then, it wasn't so bad. Machina was simply a carefree version of myself. I never let them know how much it affected me, how I wondered what Machina had that I didn't.

But things had changed. No one knew how bad it had gotten. I hadn't told them of the nights I woke up in beds that weren't my own.

"Machina doesn't come out anymore," I said. "You'll have to make do with me." The familiar twang of a country song filled the car. It was "Chicken Fried," and I was addicted. I leaned forward and turned the volume on full blast, grateful for the distraction.

Dustin slumped in his seat. "I think we've accidentally picked up a hillbilly hitcher. Country—ugh!"

The song washed away the bitter taste of my troubles, and by the time the chorus played, all three of us were screaming the lyrics with enough force to flip a turtle.

We left the outskirts of Breaux Bridge and drove a few minutes to Lake Martin's fishing pier. Though outsiders may find it eerie and unsettling, to me, it was a slice of home.

Georgie pulled into the empty parking lot beneath a towering oak tree, and we clambered out, taking in the familiar sights and sounds. The air, thick and humid, carried the croaks of frogs and the calls of insects. Tall cypress trees, their knobby knees in the murky water, jutted high above us, scratching the night sky.

"Lord, I've missed coming here," I breathed, inhaling the earthy scent of the place. It'd been a favorite hangout of ours since we started school together. I'd once kissed a boy under that same oak, and, of course, he went and told the entire school about it.

Dustin snorted. "You mean *despised* coming here, right?"

Though born and raised in Breaux Bridge, Dustin had never quite gotten the same thrill from exploring the countryside like Georgie and me. He was more of a concrete-jungle kind of kid, preferring lattes to late-night campfires.

"I've missed it," said Georgie. "It's the only place that can overpower that god-awful cologne you wear."

"Hell, Georgie," Dustin protested. "At least I don't smell like a cheap hooker."

"That's where you're going wrong," I said. "Word has it that cheap hookers attract Trent like honey to a bee."

"Well, slap your momma," Dustin said, eyes gleaming, "you'd better slather me in sweat and spritz me with poor decisions, 'cause I've got a bee to catch!"

Georgie and I fell into a fit of laughter.

Grabbing the case of beers, we made our way to the end of the pier and sat with our legs dangling over the side. Fog rolled across the lake's surface as wispy clouds danced in front of the moon.

"I've missed you," I said after a moment of silence.

Dustin reached out and squeezed my leg. "I know," he said somberly. "We feel horrible for abandoning you. Why don't you come stay with us sometime? It's a small apartment, but you'll fit. And ain't no bugs neither! I figure Georgie's snoring scares them away."

Georgie slapped his arm. "It's your hygiene routine that has them heading for the hills." She turned to me. "But numbskull's right. This swamp isn't good for you. I mean, gracious, look at your hair. You're one Taco Express shift away from looking like you fell into a deep fryer."

I finished my beer and placed it beside the case, spinning it so the label faced the lake. "I couldn't leave this place, even if I wanted to."

"Why?" asked Dustin. "Not like it's full of happy memories and unicorn rides."

I pulled another beer and cracked it. Why couldn't I go? I didn't have many friends here, and I hated the looks that shadowed me everywhere. But it was all I'd known since I was seven. Out there, in the city, I'd have to go through it all again and again. New people judging me every day. Nope. Despite everything, Breaux Bridge was home, and to leave it, to pack my bags and step out the front door, needed a lot more courage than I had.

A plop sounded nearby, likely a decent-size catfish.

Georgie wrapped her arm around me and rested her head on my shoulder. "How are you, Lina? Tell me honest."

My stomach knotted, as I knew follow-up questions were coming. "Dandy."

"You're still seeing the . . . *psychologist*?" She whispered the last word as though it had the power to sink me if any gators overheard.

"Sometimes."

"And it's helping?"

"Of course, it's not helping," Dustin groaned. "Because there's nothing to help. You're not broken, Alina. You don't need the moldy mutterings of some doctor. Listen to them long enough, and you'll catch a problem just from word of mouth—"

"Leave the girl be!" Georgie said. "If a psychologist is what she needs, it's what she needs."

"What she needs is friends," Dustin said. "And a long game of hide-the-sausage."

I snorted beer from my nose. "Dustin!"

"Finally, something we agree on," Georgie said, and dodged the playful slap I aimed at her shoulder. "Is it too much to hope that you've wrangled yourself a plaything since we left?"

Heat rose to my cheeks. I'd rather make an argument for the gender pay gap than talk about my sex life. I never understood why people felt the need to overshare personal details. But the embarrassing truth was, I'd never had anything to share in those types of conversations, anyway. Not that I didn't want some spice in my life, but I couldn't handle it, and it couldn't handle me. One night, years ago, I'd gone home with a guy from a party. We had our moment, which wasn't worth the energy to discuss, and passed out. It was Machina who woke us, rearing her ugly head, ready for another round. As I battled to control her, likely looking like I was having a fit, I'd caught sight of his expression. Shock slowly transforming into horror. He leaped out of bed, pulling his jeans over his winky, and told me I needed to leave. I did, reassuring myself that he was rubbish in the sack, and I wouldn't miss him. But the ache that found my heart after that, the burning embarrassment, would never wash away.

Machina, however, was another story. If asked about her sexual exploits, she could rattle on for hours. That was back before I learned to control her. Back when she took what she wanted and didn't give a damn about consequences. Things had changed, and now I had a way to beat her—a beautiful thing called booze.

"I'll take that as a no," said Dustin. "Which is why I accept the role—no, the responsibility—of charming you a damned-right big python. I got your back, or my name's not Dustin Hoffman."

"It's not," I pointed out.

"Yet. But don't write me off. I'm on the lookout for a sugar daddy."

Though I laughed, I feared perhaps they were right. Maybe I needed to let my hair down, to throw caution to the wind and try my luck again. To find that part of me that wasn't so brick-wall rigid. But stepping outside of my comfort zone was not something I was practiced in, especially when I had Machina to take care of. The thought of her surprising me while I was mid . . . well, while I was with a man, made me sick to the stomach.

We finished the beers by eleven, my sides hurting from laughter, and climbed back into the car, Dustin with a stumble in his step.

"You sure you're okay to drive?" I asked Georgie. "We can leave the car here tonight—"

"Not my first rodeo," she said, fumbling her keys into the ignition. "Just keep an eye out for the sheriff's boys." The car rattled to life, its headlights cutting through the dense foliage and revealing countless tiny luminescent eyes. She slammed her foot on the gas pedal, and we sped away in a cloud of dust.

"Everyone's hitting up Wrangler's tonight," Dustin said as he scrolled through his socials. Wrangler's was a bar in Lafayette, fifteen miles away. It was dark and rowdy, with plenty of nooks I could hide away in and drink with no one bothering me.

"Course, they are," said Georgie. "Who needs ID at Wrangler's?"

Before I knew it, we were already cruising down Interstate 10, the city lights flashing past. Perhaps there was an extra drop of poison in those beers because time seemed to have flown by.

A red Walgreens sign appeared ahead on the left.

"Take the next exit," I said as we approached the turnoff. "I gotta pick up a prescription real quick."

Georgie signaled and started to change lanes, but Dustin abruptly grabbed the wheel, stopping us from turning.

"Over my dead body," he said.

"What the heck!" Georgie cried. "Hands off or I'll break them."

The exit raced toward us; we were going to miss it.

"I won't be no part in murdering our best friend," Dustin said, holding on stubbornly as Georgie tried to pry his fingers free.

"Please, Dustin," I said. "It won't take a minute, I promise."

"It's not about time, it's about your health," he said. "And I ain't letting go. I can stay here all night if need be." He closed his eyes and pretended to sleep.

"You're lucky I don't deck you," Georgie said as we passed the turnoff. She looked at me in the mirror. "I'm sorry, honey. I'll come back with you tomorrow. If I'm not in jail for killing Dustin, that is."

Dustin turned and faced me. "Alina, I love you more than Grammy's grits, but I ain't about to let you live a diet of poisoned pills."

I wanted to grab his shirt and shake him. "They help me—"

"They help fill Big Pharma's pockets, and that's that," Dustin said. "They say you're sick and sell you the cure. The whole thing stinks from the head down."

"Heavens!" Georgie said. "You and your conspiracies will end us all."

"And another thing," Dustin said, ignoring her, "if you're not already sick, you best bet your sweet booty they'll build ways to make you sick. No money to be made in the healthy."

"They are *prescribed*," I insisted. "I've seen you take a lot worse."

"They would prescribe you a smack on the nose if there was money in it," he said. "I'm sorry, Lina, but drugs won't fix what you got. You want a better life? Only you can do that. Look inside yourself, you ain't got no virus, all you got is a bit of mind difficulty."

I wanted to serve him a piece of my mind, to tell him I had a professional diagnosis, to tell him I felt better just having the pills in my pocket, but when he got to running his mouth like that, it was damned near impossible to make him see reason.

"You're a real turd sometimes, you know that?" I said, resigned as Walgreens faded away. I'd just have to drink myself silly to build a barrier between anxiety and me.

"Love you, too."

The rest of the trip was silent. I had at least a few hours left before my pills wore off. If I was home by three, safely away from anyone Machina could hurt, I should be fine. But then again, with the way she'd acted lately, who knew? It was a worrying thought, but it wasn't enough to make me abandon a night out with the friends I'd not seen in so long.

Drunks crowded the club, hooting and hollering. Most of them wore the red and white of the Ragin' Cajuns and had probably spent the entire game funneling brews. I left the others and hurried to the bar, ordering four tequilas and three Stellas. I downed the first shot, savoring the burn, before carefully balancing the tray of drinks as I squeezed through the press of people, beer sloshing over the glass rims. Dustin and Georgie had claimed a table against the wall.

Dustin threw his arms open, grinning ear to ear. "Well? What do you think? One eye on the door for jocks, the other on the floor for strays."

"I think two more drinks, and your eyes will look at each other," I said, handing him a shot.

"If things work out, they just might." He clinked his glass with mine. "To a night we won't remember—"

"With the friends we'll never forget," Georgie and I finished, having used the same toast since we stole our first barley pop as kids.

It didn't take long before our table was covered in empty glasses. The football team rolled in after midnight, all swagger and boots. Dustin pulled

Georgie onto the dance floor, where they cast their lines to see who was biting. Unlike them, the thought of people watching me dance made my stomach drop.

I leaned back, smiling at their antics. Something told me they wouldn't see a lick of daylight tomorrow. Dustin's hangovers were notoriously bad, and Georgie's stomach was as strong as a cotton crop in a hurricane.

I reached for my Stella, but the sensation of being watched made me pause. I scanned the room, and spotted Jaxon, the Ragin' Cajuns' captain, eying me from near the bar. Surprised, I twisted away, blushing. Sure, he was hot as hell, but he was also hell no. He must have been looking at someone else. I took a sip of my drink, yet when I dared to sneak another glance, I found him still looking. He raised his glass and flashed a smile.

My ears caught fire. I whipped my head around, letting my hair fall over my face to hide from his attention. Was I dreaming? Jaxon could have any girl in Lafayette, so why was he looking at me? I straightened my shirt, cursing myself for not bothering to change out of my work clothes. Though I knew there was zero chance I'd go home with him, even if he wanted to, the idea of indulging in a bit of flirtation with Lafayette's most eligible bachelor was tempting.

"You're not from around here, are you?" a voice said from close to my ear.

I jerked, sloshing beer down my front. Jaxon leaned in, his white teeth gleaming in the darkness. My heart thrummed in my chest. Damn, he'd gotten hotter since last I'd seen him. "Oh, yes," I finally answered, dabbing at my shirt with a napkin. "From Breaux Bridge, but I've seen you at plenty of parties. One time you gave me a beer and said you liked my hat."

"Well, ain't that a thing," he said. "Might be that I do remember now. In any case, I saw you sitting here alone, and I figured I needed to speak to you."

Jaxon, the hottest guy in the room, wanted to talk to me? My heart went into overdrive.

"Oh?" I said. "And what did you want to talk about?"

He glanced over his shoulder, then leaned even closer and slipped something into my hand. "This."

It was a creased piece of paper. My breath caught in my throat. Out of all the things that could have happened tonight, I'd never imagined receiving a love note from Jaxon was in the cards. It was incredibly pure, endearing, and utterly—I unfolded the letter—*not for me.*

The note had a phone number and a succinct, yet graphically detailed, account of what Jaxon wanted to do with someone. Given that he couldn't possibly do such acts with a woman, I assumed the message was intended for Dustin.

I sagged into my seat, trying to appear unaffected, as if I hadn't just imagined the captain of the football team was crushing on me.

"Would you be a doll and hand that to the guy you're with?" Jaxon said, suddenly looking uneasy. "I can't exactly do it myself. You know, appearances and all." He squeezed my shoulder, then strolled back to his friends with a forced a smile.

I threw the note onto the table and watched the heaving bodies on the dance floor. How could I be so stupid? I was Alina, the crazy girl. No one wants a crazy girl.

I glanced at my phone and was wondering if it was too early to leave when a gravelly voice caught me off guard.

"His loss."

Startled, I turned to find a man I'd never seen before. His black hair fell in waves, framing a strong, angular face, and his pale complexion highlighted his striking features. The top buttons of his collared shirt were undone, revealing a colorful chest tattoo. His gray eyes locked onto mine as my jaw hit the floor. He was stunning.

The corner of his mouth twitched upward, almost mischievously, and it took a second to remember he'd said something.

"Excuse me?" I said, trying to use my words. Sure, he was the hottest guy I'd ever seen, but that was no reason to be weird.

It was easier said than done.

"His loss," he repeated. He swung a chair around and sat beside me. A whiff musky cologne with a faint hint of motor oil surged up my nose. He was older, perhaps late twenties, and held himself as a real man should: shoulders back, eye contact, and oh so confident. He extended his hand. "I'm Nester."

I hesitated a moment before placing mine in his. "Alina." His touch sent a surge of electricity through me.

"Alina," he mused, leaning back. "So, how much effort do I need to put in to prove I'm not like that tasteless guy you were just with?"

"It's about as simple as unscrambling eggs."

He laughed. "I'm always up for a challenge. Test me—ask anything, and you will have the truth."

There was something about him. More than his looks, there was a sort of magnetic pull, and I was wholly caught in it. "Alright. Why approach me? The club's full of gorgeous women. What's your game?"

He seemed amused, but then quickly masked it. He cast a casual glance around the room. "Yes, there are plenty of gorgeous women here. None are quite like you though."

Living in Georgie's shadow, I was often overlooked. It made no sense for tonight to be any different. "Now I'm certain you're drunk. Or have you lost a bet?"

"I don't gamble. But you're just underestimating yourself. You're captivating."

I raised my eyebrows. "Captivating? Not the usual pickup line."

He leaned in, eyes boring into mine. "I assure you, it's not just another line. In a world full of conformity, you stand out in the most powerful way. You're truly captivating."

I should have laughed it off, but the sincerity in his gaze made me hesitate. A huge part of me wanted to fall into his words and believe that I was special, but the gap between who I knew I was, and the person he described, was too large to bridge. I was Alina, the girl with too many voices in her head—

"Stop that," he said, gentle but firm. "That noise in your head? You need to silence it. It serves no purpose."

I blinked. "How could you possibly—"

"I see it. The internal battle, the feeling of being out of place, of not fitting in. It's like you're in a sea, struggling to breathe, and every attempt to surface just drags you under. You're not alone."

It took a few heartbeats to remember to close my mouth. Even my psychologist hadn't seen through my facade as effortlessly as he did. How could he, a stranger, understand so much? It should have worried me, but rather than being alarmed, I was intrigued. He saw me—really saw me—and he hadn't run away.

"What do you mean?" I asked, finding myself leaning in. "I'm not alone?"

He stared at his drink for a moment, a gin and tonic perhaps. "I've been there. I've walked miles in shoes like yours. Marched in them until the soles peeled off and my heels bled. And I promise, all you need to know is which path to take, and you will come out on the other side much stronger."

The blare of the music drowned out his voice, and a flash of irritation passed over his face. He leaned back, finished his drink in one, and stood.

"Let's go outside, somewhere we can hear each other," he said, extending a hand to help me up.

I took it, then glanced over at Dustin and Georgie, both dancing wildly. "I'm not sure that's a good idea."

"That's what will make it memorable." He grinned, then turned and headed for the exit.

I didn't move and felt his absence instantly. It was a terrible, lonely feeling, and it chewed at my insides. It was too much. With a final look at Dustin and Georgie, I pressed through the crowd, following this man I'd just met. I needed to hear more of what he had to say. Something inside tried to stop me, some vague warning, but I ignored it, my sight locked on his broad shoulders.

Outside, the night air was a refreshing contrast to the warmth of the club. Though it was quieter in the parking lot, Nester didn't seem satisfied. He looked around, then led me across the road to the lane beside the gas station. When he faced me, I was once again struck by the beauty of him. But then I noticed a small crease of concern on his lips, and a flicker of unease sparked in my chest.

"Alina," he began, his voice cautious. He held my hands in his. "What I'm about to tell you might sound absurd, but I need you to listen, really listen."

A prickle on the back of my neck was the first sign that I may have made a mistake.

"Okay," I said slowly. A change had come over him, and I regretted my decision to be out here alone with him almost immediately.

"You're not going crazy," he said, his gaze begging me to understand. "What you're struggling with inside you . . . it's not what you think it is—not by far. It's much, much darker."

His ominous words hung in the air. Warning bells filled my head. *Run! Escape! Flee!*

He watched me, waiting for a reaction. "Alina? Do you understand what I'm saying? You're not the person you believe you are. There's a part of you that's . . . different." He drew in a deep breath, eyes closing for a moment. "Alina, you're a demon."

The word didn't crash into me. It didn't beat me about the head with its meaning. It seeped in slowly, taking its time, enjoying the journey.

And then I understood all too well. He was on drugs. I'd seen some crazy stuff in Breaux Bridge, but Nester? He took the cake.

"Right," I said carefully. "Demon, huh? Well, this has been . . . enlightening. Thanks for the heads-up, but I need to get back to my friends now. They'll be wondering where I've gotten to." I moved to make my way back to Wrangler's.

He sidestepped into my path, blocking the way to the club. "Your friends can't save you from what's coming."

Chapter Three

Nester's gray eyes reflected the golden light of a distant streetlamp, giving him an eerie, otherworldly look. Now, far from beautiful, they held a danger that made my skin itch.

I stumbled back a step, glancing at the bar over his shoulder. It was just a dash away, yet it might as well be miles. He could outrun me in seconds, and though it wasn't as loud as inside, the pounding music could still drown out any scream I might make. With this realization came a cold dread that settled in the pit of my stomach, rooting me to the spot.

Nester's face was calm as he watched me, but his body was as tense as a spring. "I know what you're thinking. When they told me what I was, I ran, too. It's the only logical thing to do. But before you go, hear me out, okay?"

Hear him out? It wasn't like I had much choice. "Yeah, sure," I said, my voice shaky. The only hope I had was to keep him talking long enough for someone to walk by. With effort, I forced a smile to my lips and attempted to look like I wasn't trying to remember any self-defense moves I'd seen in movies. *When all else fails, aim for the cock.* "So, demons, huh? That certainly explains my thirst for blood."

"I know how it sounds," he said. "When it happened to me, when I first showed signs that I was . . . different . . . my mother thought I was ill. She spared no expense in finding me the best doctors. I swallowed all the pills and talked on all the couches. Nothing stopped what was to come. Nothing on Earth could."

My mouth was dry as powder. "Those couches will get you every time," I said. "Sofas. Love seats. Red ones and blue ones—I've been on them all. Anyway, thanks for the chat. I better get going now—"

"I'm not here to frighten you—"

"You need to work on that," I said, carefully shifting my weight onto my left leg so I could kick out if needed.

His eyes narrowed as he closed in half a step. "I'm here to give you hope. The doctors couldn't fix me because I wasn't ill—I was simply different. There was no cure, only understanding. Let me help you see. Aren't you tired of it? The fear? The anxiety? I can make it all go away." He offered his hand. "Come with me. I'll show you things you couldn't dream of."

The smell of his cologne now assaulted my senses, and before I knew it, my legs began to shake. "That's awfully kind of you, but I forgot to feed my ants. Rain check?"

His hand shot forward and clamped my wrist. "This isn't some game. You awakened fully tonight. The essence that spewed out of you was the most I've ever felt, and I've been a Collector for six years! Your power . . . it could help us win the war."

I pulled against him, but his grip was a vise. "Please—I don't care about any war," I said desperately. "Just let me go. I won't tell anyone, I promise."

"You would have felt it," he continued, reeling me in. "The magnitude of your essence left a trace for all the worlds to see."

"I didn't feel anything— *Ouch!* You're hurting me!"

"We don't have much time. They will come, and hell will come with them. We have to leave, but I need you to understand first. Earlier tonight, did you notice anything strange? A flash of lightning? A TV gone to static? A phone misbehaving?"

I looked around wildly. Where was everyone? Why wasn't there anyone around to help? "I'll scream if you don't let go—"

"Think!"

"No!" I shrieked. "There weren't any stupid TVs or phones. Just the darn toilet lights going off." I gasped, having said the last part without thinking. The memory of that light had barely registered in my mind.

A smile pulled at the edge of his mouth. "Interesting."

"No, it's not," I said, my chest now heaving. "There's nothing interesting about me."

"The more you fight, the harder it will be to accept the truth. You're in the middle of a war fought in shadows. We need your help—"

A screech of tires cut through the night air. We spun to see a black car careen wildly around the corner, its wheels spinning as it barreled down the street towards us.

"Fuck!" Nester cursed. He turned to face me, his brow creased. "You need to run. Never look back. Your old home, your old life—they're not safe anymore. Run, and for God's sake, don't let them get their hands on you."

Icy terror flooded my veins as my mind struggled to make sense of it all. Who was in the car? And why was Nester telling me to run? That wasn't exactly something a psychotic murderer would do.

The car's headlights washed over us as Nester raised my hand to his lips and kissed it. "I'll find you again, Alina. Believe that." He pivoted me, then shoved me forward down the lane. "Run, Alina. For everything you're worth, run."

And I did. Adrenaline lit a fire inside, and I dashed past the gas station and down the dark road beyond. My breathing was frantic as I sprinted into the night, feet pounding the asphalt.

Tires screeched again, followed by the slamming of doors.

"I won't let you take her!" Nester's voice rang out. "You can't control what's destined."

A flicker of doubt crept into my mind. If these people were Nester's enemies, could they somehow be my allies? Was I running away from people who wanted to help? Or what if they were social workers sent to take him back to the psychiatric hospital?

"Stop this foolishness," a stern voice answered him. "Let's not do this again."

Unable to stop myself, I glanced over my shoulder to find a woman silhouetted against the car's beams. She squared off with Nester, her black leather outfit shining. Heavy rings circled her fingers and tattoos climbed up her neck all the way to her short-cropped hair. She was older, perhaps in her forties, and was backed up by three figures who also wore black suits.

My need to flee wavered momentarily, and I stopped running. I knew it was stupid, knew I should sprint all the damned way back to Breaux

Bridge, but I needed to understand what was happening. Despite my brain screaming at me to get out of there, I crouched behind a mound of trash against the chain-link fence and watched on, praying I wouldn't be a news headline tomorrow.

Nester clenched his fists at his sides. "Foolish? No. *Foolish* is working for them. You know they're not the angels they pretend to be."

The woman shook her head sadly. "I'm not here to argue or defend them. I'm not here to fight. Let us take the girl and we'll be on our way."

"You're not here to fight," he mused. "If that were true, you would have left your lackeys behind!" He snapped his hands forward in a blur, and a shock wave exploded out of him, rippling the air like a heat haze. The woman raised a necklace pendant just before it hit her, and an invisible shield seemed to form, diverting the blast. The others weren't so quick, and the force slammed into them, knocking them off their feet and scattering them across the road.

My hands clawed around the trash bags in front of me as my mouth dropped open. *What the actual heck?* Had I had one too many drinks? Or the cocktail of booze and meds finally corrupted my head? Because what I'd just seen was impossible. I'd lost it completely.

The woman dropped her necklace and weaved her hands in a pattern, golden light trailing her fingers. A blast of light stole the darkness, and a cage of fire sprouted from thin air to encase Nester, the bars white hot and angry.

Nester roared and kicked the cage, trying to break free, but the flames grew with contact. The three he'd blasted away returned, one limping badly, and crowded the woman.

"Find the girl," she ordered, her voice carrying down the lane.

My stomach plunged into my shoes. I ducked behind the trash heap and pressed into the bags, wishing I could just vanish. Why had I stopped running? What would they do if they found me? Lock me up in a burning cage? Torture me? Sell me for parts? It took all my will power to stop from releasing the scream building inside.

The distant sounds of the city faded into the background, leaving only the deafening silence of the alleyway and the crackle of the cage. A breeze picked up and tousled my hair as something moved in one of the black bags by my shoulder, but I was too terrified to pull away.

"What'cha sitting in garbage for?" a voice said behind me.

My heart leaped to my throat. I whirled around to come face-to-face with a grinning man hanging upside down. I screamed, kicking away as my mind raced to understand what I saw. He was flying! Literally flying like some sort of genie. My hand fell on a bag, and I launched it at his head, but he knocked it away easily.

"Hardly any need for that, miss," he said. "If you'll just come with me, it'll all make sense before long." He swooped down and wrapped his arms around my waist. In a rush of wind, I left the ground screaming.

"No need for dramatics," he said in an Irish accent as he struggled to hold me while I thrashed. "We'll explain everything in the car."

"Please, let me go," I begged, squirming as we rocketed down the lane. "I haven't done anything—I don't even know Nester."

"Fine way to show you don't know a fellow by saying their name and all. But not a worry, we'll get it sorted out in short order." We streaked past the fiery cage and to the black Rolls-Royce.

As soon as my feet touched down, I tried to run, but another man, much bigger than Irish Flyer, stepped from the shadows and helped force me into the back seat. The Irish guy sat beside me, and the other climbed in behind the wheel.

"Fight, Alina!" Nester shrieked. "Fight for your life!"

I stared at him through the windshield, stunned, as a savage roar cut the night. He shot out of his prison, hair and coat ablaze, and flew ten feet into the air, smoke and cinders trailing him. He whipped his hands forward and fired a blast at the woman.

She raised her arms above her head and vanished, the attack slamming into the road. It ricocheted off the asphalt, crashing into a row of cars and flipping them onto their roofs.

The passenger door opened, and the woman dove in, sweat glistening on her brow. "Get in the damned car, Nia!" she shouted behind her.

An ear-splitting crack resounded, followed by a gut-wrenching scream of agony. The rear door exploded open and a figure tumbled in. She pressed her hands tightly against her stomach as blood seeped through her fingers in a steady flow.

"Gun it, Logan!" the woman shouted to the driver.

He stomped his foot on the gas pedal. The tires spun wildly before gaining traction and rocketing us forward, the movement slamming the last door closed.

I stared at the woman's bleeding stomach, at her trembling hands and the red river that flowed onto the seat. Something protruded from between her fingers.

Her eyes, gleaming with pain, gradually shifted to me. “I hope you’re worth it.”

Chapter Four

"She's dying!" I screamed, unable to tear my eyes away from the wound. "You have to take her to the hospital!"

The woman in the front swung her head around. "Fuck! Nia, stay with us. Hold on, we'll get you help soon. Alina, don't just sit there—do something!"

"I—what do I do?" I stammered, looking at the stern face of the tattooed woman.

She ignored me and turned to the Irish man. "Find Nester—he won't let us escape that easy."

"Rightio," he said, finger on the window button.

"And, Murphy," she added. "Don't kill him."

"Kinda taking the fun out of things," he said. "But I'll see what I can do." He gripped the back of the seat and leaned out of the car. "Um, Audrey, there's a bit of fog tonight. Can't see a ruddy thing."

"It came from nowhere," said Logan, gripping the wheel tightly.

"No," said Audrey as she leaned over the dash to look up through the windshield. "It came from him."

My head spun. The fight, the magic, the blood—everything meshed together into a numbing mess. I turned my attention back to Nia. Her eyelids had drooped and her breathing was shallow. Blood pooled on her seat.

"Damn it, Alina!" snapped Audrey. *"Help her!"*

"I—I don't know how," I stammered. It wasn't like it was a Band-Aid job. She needed a doctor.

"You'd better damn well learn!"

I racked my brain, trying to recall any medical procedures that could heal magically induced injuries. Unfortunately, the countless hours I'd spent watching reruns of ER had not prepared me for dealing with demon wounds. I took a steadying breath and tried to gently pry Nia's fingers from her stomach, but she screamed at the slightest touch.

"I'm so sorry," I choked out, tears bursting on my lips. I steeled myself, then pulled her hands away and she shrieked. The fragment of metal sticking out of her was a shard from a road sign.

An explosion shook the ground beneath us, sending the car lurching to the side. Logan wrestled with the wheel to regain control, his hands white-knuckled.

"He'll blast the damn road apart if he keeps it up!" he exclaimed. "Audrey, we need the gate, like, yesterday!"

"I've got him!" shouted Murphy, climbing in through his window and poking his head out of the sunroof. A clap of thunder tore through the night and the car rocked onto two wheels.

"Damn him!" spat Audrey, her dozen necklaces jangling around her neck. "Why's he fighting so hard for a fledgling?" She swiped at the car monitor, bringing up a map of the area.

Nia groaned. I ignored everything else and focused on her. "The good news is, it's not as bad as it looks," I lied, my voice high-pitched. "Some stitches and a lollipop should do the trick. You'll be on your feet in no time, casting magic and sprouting horns—"

"For heaven's sake," Audrey said. "This is not a meet-cute. Cut strips of this and wrap them around the shard like a donut!" She forced a serrated knife and a chamois into my hand and went back to studying the map.

Explosions came with every heartbeat, Murphy's curses echoing them. I cut the chamois into strips, doing my best to shut down the part of my brain that screamed at me to wake up from this nightmare.

"There!" Audrey cried, pointing at the map. It showed an area near the airport, Spanish Lake, and a blue gate icon was marked nearby. "Follow this highway a few miles. Don't miss the turn."

I rolled my makeshift bandages into a rough ring and eased Nia's hands away once more. She put up little resistance this time, her eyes almost closed. "Take a deep breath for me," I said, positioning the cloth around the protruding metal. In one movement, I rolled it down and applied pressure to the wound, careful not to move the shard at all.

Nia's eyes flared wide, a silent scream twisting her face, then her body gave in and she crumpled against the seat. I held the bandages, the yellow turning red, as the blood flow slowed and finally stemmed to a trickle.

An enormous blast split the air, making my ears ring.

"Christ!" Murphy exclaimed. "He's gone and blown a feckin' hole in the road."

The car spun out of control and slid on the road like it was covered in ice. Logan slammed on the brakes and yanked the wheel hard, forcing the car to face forward again before fishtailing.

"First job after the academy," he muttered darkly, "and I've got a nutter trying to kill me."

"It's his damn tattoos," said Murphy. "They won't let me create a vacuum around him."

I watched numbly as we swerved through Lafayette's outskirts. It felt surreal, like it was a scene from an action movie, not something that should happen in my life. I was just a country girl who worked at Taco Express, not a movie star caught up in some high-speed chase.

"Watch for the turnoff," Audrey said, pulling out her phone and dialing a number. "Shouldn't be much farther . . . Yes, gatekeeper! This is Alpha Romeo, requesting preparation for gate"—she read a number from the screen—"2835 to be opened. ETA, approximately three minutes. We may have company—have the FTF at the ready. Cleanup crew requested at location of pickup. Stand by."

"The Frostfire Task Force?" Logan said, glancing at Audrey. "It's late afternoon—they'll be drunk by now."

"I don't need a commentary," she said, looking up through the windshield again. "Just get us there in one piece."

"Easier said than done."

She spun to face me, and her face fell into a heavier scowl. "For heaven's sake—stop looking like a lost bunny! You do not know what we just saved you from."

I watched her thin lips move but barely heard her words. After everything that'd happened, I was teetering on the edge, my mind giving in. "I think I'm ready to go home now."

She closed her eyes and groaned. "Fuck—she's losing it." She leaned in and snapped her fingers in front of my face. "Alina, listen to me—your home isn't safe anymore. Nowhere is safe anymore. If the Reavers catch you, it's not just your life at stake, it's everyone's. I refuse to let that happen—"

"He's charging up!" warned Murphy from the sunroof. "Christ, the air's full of static! I—I can't counter it. Logan, get ready to dodge!"

The driver cursed. "Make the call, Audrey! We're running out of time."

Her eyes didn't leave mine. "Listen to me. Our mission is to help every soul on Earth. They're counting on you to stay safe and away from Nester and the faction of demons he works for. Alina—look at me—I need your permission to bring you back to the academy with us—"

A blast split the air apart. The car veered onto the shoulder of the road and my neck whipped to the side, cracking into Murphy's knee.

"Make the call, Audrey!" Logan shouted, his voice rising as he punched the wheel.

"I need your permission," Audrey said, a flicker of fear in her eyes for the first time.

The ringing in my ears grew louder. The *academy*? I grasped at the word, trying to find meaning in it. I didn't apply to any academy. "Permission . . ." I echoed slowly. They'd taken me by force, and now they wanted *permission*?

"Audrey!" Logan's voice thundered.

Audrey's fingers clenched around my hands. "Please?" Her eyes met mine in a moment of mutual terror.

My throat tightened. Nester roared furiously above, and it sparked something inside me. If I was to survive the night, I needed their help. I nodded.

"Yes! Please . . . get me out of here!"

Chapter Five

Audrey snapped the phone to her ear and swiveled back to the front. "Gatekeeper, this is Alpha Romeo—open the damned gate right now!"

The car skidded off the highway and onto a trailer park road, launching over the speed bump. Old caravans and cabins whizzed by as the smell of burning rubber stung my nostrils. A blaze of light appeared ahead, turning the windshield a deep violet. I covered my eyes from the glare and spotted an enormous disk at the end of the road, bright white with purple edges. A creeping mist drifted out along the ground. I pressed back into my seat and fumbled with the seat belt. We were heading right for it, and Logan wasn't slowing.

A shout of rage sounded above us.

"Something tells me our friend's not thrilled about us leaving early," said Murphy.

Audrey leaned forward and scanned the sky. "Shit!"

I buckled Nia's belt, then leaned back as we raced toward the gate, squeezing my eyes shut as I braced for impact.

But the crash never came.

I waited, then opened my eyes, half expecting to be staring up at the ceiling of a coffin. What I saw was even more bizarre. Brilliant sunlight poured through the windows; the night having drifted away. The trailer park had disappeared too, and we were certainly not in Louisiana anymore. Now, we sped along a gravel road enclosed by tall concrete walls.

My mind spluttered as I tried to make sense of it all. What happened to the rest of the night? Had we . . . had we crashed and died? Was this some sort of purgatory?

Logan skidded the car to a stop in front of a tall metal gate in the far wall. Soldiers poured out of hidden doors, wearing formfitting icy-blue armor that looked as tough as iron yet shimmered like frost. They surrounded us, swords pointed in our direction.

Murphy collapsed back into the seat beside me, a sheen of sweat on his skin. He was smiling. "They've locked the gate and it seems our friend has lost his invitation." He nudged me playfully on the arm. "Not a bad way to spend a Friday, hey? I wasn't expecting an awakening so close to the Choosing, to be fair."

Logan rounded in his seat and fixed Murphy with a disbelieving stare. "Not a bad way to spend a Friday? Have you gone daft from one too many pints of Guinness or something? We almost died at least a hundred times."

Murphy shrugged. "I'd guess two hundred times. But we didn't."

Logan's eyes fell on Nia. "She almost did."

A sharp knock on the driver's window made us jump. A square-jawed soldier peered in; his uniform weighed down with rows of ribbons.

"Great," Logan muttered. He pressed a button, and the window slid down.

The man's eyes lingered on Nia before meeting Logan's. "Judging by the state of our vehicle, I can only assume your mission did not go according to plan."

"I'm just here on work experience," said Logan. "Blame Audrey."

Audrey, busy on her phone, didn't look up. "We have an injured person. We're going to the medical center."

A vein appeared on the soldier's temple. "I need your report first."

"It's not a priority."

"That's what you said last time. And the time before that. I want your report—"

"Do you really want this fight?" Audrey said, meeting his gaze. "We have a dying girl in the back seat. If we lose her, her blood is on your hands. I'm not sure how well that will go for your promotion."

His eyes darted back to Nia. After a moment, his face screwed up with frustration. He straightened. "Let them out," he ordered. "I won't forget this," he said to Audrey.

"I don't care," she said, returning to her phone.

The moment the metal gate creaked open, Logan floored the gas, sending us speeding down a winding mountain road.

I glanced back to see the fortresslike complex disappear behind us. Watchtowers dotted the gray concrete walls, and an odd obelisk rose from the roof of one building, glowing the same eerie purple as the disk.

I turned my attention to Nia, hoping to distract my mind before it got to thinking. Processing everything that had happened . . . I wasn't ready for that. Her skin was clammy, but her breathing was steady. It was a small comfort amid the storm that had just swept through my life.

The forest we drove through opened up to reveal a sight that pushed the shock of battle from my mind. Below us, nestled between the curves of twin rivers and a shimmering lake, was a village like something from a Disney movie. The buildings weren't of the Breaux Bridge style but magnificent French châteaux. Sprawling lawns and vibrant gardens stretched to the woodlands climbing up the hill, and misty mountains pierced the low-lying clouds.

"Welcome to Astaroth Academy," Murphy announced.

I stared in disbelief, struggling to reconcile the stark contrast of this beauty with the horrifying events of the night. It felt as if I had stepped into a dream. "It's . . . it's beautiful."

"Some of the best years of my life were spent here," said Murphy. "You're going to love it."

"If you don't die," said Logan, speeding down the slope.

"Don't listen to him," Murphy said with a laugh. "He gets his rocks off by scaring people. Most fledglings make it through with no issues."

"Fledglings?" I asked.

The car jolted as we mounted a small timber bridge that crossed the first river, the lake to our right.

"You know, baby demons?" said Logan.

A weight pressed on my chest as that word hung in the air. *Demon.* "Are you really trying to tell me that all this . . . this stuff about demons is real? That I've been kidnapped and taken to some academy from hell?"

Audrey pocketed her phone. "No. We did not kidnap you. You asked us to come."

There was something about her that was very easy to hate. "And you've kindly obliged to bring me where, exactly? The demon-infested underworld of France?"

We stopped in front of a timber lodge marked by a red cross on its roof. Logan held his hand on the horn for a long while. Audrey waited, letting the noise linger before answering.

"No. I'm telling you I've brought you to an academy in an entirely different world. But yes, if it helps, think of it as infested with demons."

I resisted the urge to kick the back of her seat. I'd been to hell and back that night. I'd been abducted, had magic thrown at me, and been covered with more blood than a slaughterhouse floor. Was it too much to ask for her to not treat me as if I were some irritating child?

People wearing scrubs raced out of the building and hurried toward us, a gurney rolling ahead of them. Murphy stepped out and helped load Nia, who was still blissfully unconscious.

"It's been a real pleasure meeting you," he said, tipping his head before following them inside.

We sat in a tense silence until Logan cleared his throat. "Er, where to?"

"Take us to Château Michael," Audrey said. "Aran May owes me a favor. He can look after her until the Choosing."

Logan snorted as he shifted into reverse. "He'll not like that."

We drove across the lawns and onto a dirt path wedged between a cliff and a pine forest. My head throbbed as I tried to sort through the tangle of my emotions. Magic, demons, and other worlds? If this wasn't all made up in my head, then it was wildly terrifying. Breaux Bridge, as much as I despised it, was home. Everyone knew me, knew my problems, and there was a comfort in that. But now, as we moved further away from everything I knew, my stomach knotted. I wasn't equipped to handle this new reality.

The tall pines gave way to reveal an enormous château washed in the golden light of late afternoon. The honey-colored building was stunning, with its grand arches and intricate carvings. Statues stood as sentries over an infinity pool filled with floating people. Groups of young people, beers in hand, lounged on the lawns.

We rolled to a stop in front of a graffitied-over sign that read *Château Michael.* As we got out of the car, the college-age kids on the lawns paused their discussions to watch us pass. I dropped my gaze, feeling like a sewer rat in my filthy clothes.

On legs numb with fatigue, I followed Audrey up the grand staircase and into the building. The marble floors gleamed under chandeliers, and the walls were painted with detailed scenes from classical mythology. But there was another layer to it all. It was a party house, like something you would see on Jersey Shore, but much fancier. A Harry Styles song blasted from the many speakers, and empty bottles and cans littered the floor. A rowdy game of beer pong took place in the entrance hall, and a series of kegs lined the fresco of what I assumed was Zeus, with yellow Post-it notes covering his nipples.

"Animals," Audrey muttered, eying the scene disapprovingly as she made her way to the staircase. "For your sake, I hope you don't get placed here. It's the black sheep château of the campus. Anyone who doesn't enjoy drowning in alcohol will sink." She looked down her nose at me. "Though, given the state of you . . ."

I glowered at her. *Back the heck up.* I didn't need her attitude to know how bad I must look . . . how bad I must smell. They found me outside a bar, not a bakery. And if this Château Michael had earned her disapproval, then perhaps it wasn't so bad after all.

On the fourth-floor landing, we took the right corridor, and Audrey knocked on a closed door. After a moment, it swung open.

A soft gasp escaped my lips. A man, at least a foot taller than me, stood there, naked but for a towel low on his hips. His tan skin was dewy, and droplets of water traced a path down his bare chest. The peak of his abs stole the strength from my legs, and his V . . . *Mercy!*

It took all my effort not to fall on my face. I battled to keep my eyes fixed on his, but it was like trying to ignore a display at Barnes & Noble. His wet hair fell around a face that was even more beautiful than the rest of him. Striking hazel eyes laughed above a powerful jawline as a brow slowly arched.

I took a deep breath to center myself. He was just a man. A stupidly hot man. By the way he held himself, he was the type who left broken hearts in his wake. The last thing I needed was those wonderful eyes judging me after he discovered Machina. Nope. This guy was off-limits, all six-foot-whatever of him.

A small smile played at his lips, and dimples erupted on his cheeks. As his gaze flickered from Audrey to me, I felt that resolve wavering.

"Looks like someone's had a rough day," he said in an accent that melted my soul.

Chapter Six

As his words filtered through my brain and I registered them, not just his voice, a wave of heat rushed through my chest, and I crossed my arms to hide my bloodstained Taco Express shirt. Of all the times to come face-to-face with Mr. Goddamn, it had to be while I looked like I'd rolled around a butchery floor.

"Aran." Audrey's voice cut through the tension, making me jump. I'd been so caught up in him I'd forgotten she was there.

"Professor," he greeted with a nod.

"Do you remember the time you smuggled your wallaby into my runes class?"

His smile wavered as he scratched his chin. "Vaguely rings a bell. Might need to check my diary. Reckon it sounds like a good time, though—"

"She shat on my floor while you were doing end-of-term exams. I stepped in it."

He snorted, not bothering to hide his amusement. "Clean forgot about that! Thanks for the memory." He leaned in close to me. "She was my good-luck wallaby. Scored ninety-one percent."

"It would have been one hundred," Audrey said, "if I hadn't been preoccupied cleaning my boots instead of grading. Alina, this is Aran May. Aran, this is Alina Rose. She's a fledgling—"

"Welcome," said Aran.

"—and I'm leaving her in your hands to make sure she is cleaned up and delivered to the Choosing on time."

His smile vanished. "Nah, no can do, Professor. I'm about to head to the Shack for a sneaky one before the ceremony."

"Not anymore," said Audrey. "Have her there on time, or you'll spend every Saturday cleaning the tattoo guns—"

"That's flag fall time!" Aran said, taking a step forward, all trace of humor leaving his face.

"Deliver the girl, or you can kiss your silly sport goodbye." She turned and left without another word.

He looked at the ceiling and groaned. "No wonder she's single," he muttered under his breath, stepping aside and gesturing for me to enter. "Come on, let's see if we can't try to make you a little less . . . bloody."

Entering his room felt like stepping foot into a lion's den, but beneath my apprehension was a flicker of excitement. I couldn't be certain, but I felt I would follow him anywhere, even to a Scientology recruitment drive if he let me. The room had the historical elegance of the château, with its grand windows revealing the sprawling valleys below, however, Aran had added his own bachelor twist to it.

The king-size bed was hidden beneath a ghastly leopard-print comforter, and red drapes covered the chandelier, giving the room a crimson glow. An enormous TV, connected to a gaming console, dominated one wall, and beside the sofa was a glass-fronted fridge stocked with beers. But the most unusual thing in the room was a pile of animal cages near the balcony. Some were empty, but some had—

"Kangaroos, emu chicks, and, of course, wallabies with impressive bowel movements," Aran said, following my gaze. "Come on, they don't bite." He guided me forward with a hand on my lower back.

"Oh, my," I said, leaning in, guessing that the kangaroos made Aran's accent. "What do you do with them all?"

"Barbecue," he said, tickling a kangaroo through the cage bars. "Sometimes a roast."

"No, you don't!" I cried, turning to him in horror.

His dimples deepened. "Nah. Meat is too tough. I work in animal commerce. The cages are temporary." He looked at a grandfather clock in the corner. "You've an hour until the Choosing begins. I'd recommend a long shower to try to wash that delicious brewery scent from your skin."

I flushed. "Believe it or not, I don't usually look this raggedy or smell this bad."

"Don't worry about it. Kinda reminds me of that glorious hour between drunk and inebriated." He crossed the room to a closet and tossed me a rolled towel. "But it's not ideal for first impressions. The Choosing is *all* about first impressions. You don't want to get stuck in Raphael."

I wasn't exactly sure what Raphael was, but the thought of being chosen for something tightened my stomach. Why would anyone choose me for anything? I mean, I wasn't into sports, and certainly not in the top percentage of any class.

Worry must have shown on my face, because Aran's expression softened. "Don't stress about it too much—it won't get you anywhere. But see if you can do something about those doe eyes. You don't want the others to see how scared you are." He pushed open the door to a royal-size en suite, complete with spa bath and shower for two. "We leave in forty. Use any soaps you need." He closed the door, and for the first time in a long time, I was alone.

I undressed, dried blood crinkling on my clothes, then stepped into the shower. As the warm water washed over me, it brought with it a dull ache at the base of my neck. What was going to happen when they—whoever they were—found out I was just an average girl? That I had no magical tricks up my sleeve, no ability to summon wind from my fingertips or fiery cages from my necklace? Would they show me the door?

Nester and Audrey seemed convinced that Breaux Bridge wasn't safe for me anymore. That implied that, no matter what happened at the Choosing, going back wasn't an option. The only place I'd ever called home was now forever out of reach, its doors locked.

I shook my head, trying to rid myself of the worrying thoughts. I had to believe there was a reason they'd brought me here, that I had something to offer, magic or no magic.

I leaned my head against the tiles and took a shaky breath. The fear of being exposed as a fraud wasn't the only thing that had my stomach knotting. What if they were right? What if I did have some hidden power, and I was supposed to attend this academy? It wasn't like I could just stride in there with my head held high, full of confidence like Georgie and

Dustin. Before the end of term, everyone would know me as the unstable girl who battled a voice inside her head, and the whispers would follow.

As I closed my eyes, the aroma of lavender soap steaming around me, a sudden bang jolted me from my thoughts. My breath hitched as I opened my eyes to find the bathroom door had been flung open and a woman stared at me, face twisted in rage.

"Oh, hell no!" she spat, storming in and coming to a stop in front of the shower, fists clenched by her sides.

I shrank back, covering myself. "Sorry?" I said, looking around for something to defend myself and settling on the liquid soap. Before I could grab it, she slammed her palms against the glass door, startling me.

"How long after I left did you wait before slithering in?" she said. "A minute? An hour?"

"I haven't slithered anywhere—"

"Get out. *Get out!*" She grabbed the door and started to open it, but I flung myself forward to pull it closed, and we got caught in a wrestling match.

Just as the handle started to slip from my wet grasp, Aran strolled into the bathroom, biting a green apple.

"Chill, babe," he said calmly as though he'd just strolled into a conversation about dog breeds.

She rounded on him. "Don't you dare tell me to chill! Who is this . . . this . . . creature? I knew something was off when Morgan showed up without you."

He took another bite, the apple crunching in his mouth. "Punishment," he said simply. "Audrey dropped her off. I'm babysitting until the Choosing. Not even getting paid for it."

Punishment... The word echoed in my mind, and unexpectedly, it hurt. Yes, it was true, and I had only known him briefly, but he didn't have to say it like I was some chore.

The woman glanced at me. Her mouth opened, then closed. A slow grin spread across her lips. "Well . . . alright. Yes, fine, she's not really your type, is she? Gangly and awkward." She turned back to Aran. "I worry about you, you know? Women are like scavengers around here."

Awkward? What the hell did that mean? I eyed the soap, half tempted to test my aim, but getting into a bathroom battle after everything I'd been through wasn't high on my to-do list.

Aran's gaze swept over my body. "I don't know, she's a bit of alright."

My eyes widened as I remembered my nakedness, and I wrapped my arms around myself, crouching low and wishing I was back in the car chase all over again. What was next? A piano falling on my head?

"*Alright?*" the girl repeated. "What the hell does that even mean?" She faced him squarely. "You know what? I'm done. So done. Everyone told me to ditch you months ago, and it looks like they were right." Her piercing gaze flicked in my direction. "Go on then, have your little fling," she said to me. "Just pray you don't end up in Uriel, because I'll make sure you don't last a damn day before you're out on your ass." She stormed out of the room.

Aran watched her go, not flinching as the door slammed shut. He took a bite of his apple, chewing thoughtfully. "So," he said, "plan on making that shower your new home? I can work out a lease, if you like. But the Choosing won't wait for you. You have two minutes, tops, considering that whole shouting thing cost you some time."

"Two minutes? Heck! Okay, I'll be right out."

"Cool." He pushed off the vanity and left without another word.

"Great job, Alina," I muttered, squeezing shower gel into my palm and scrubbing under my arms. The lather quickly washed away the grime and blood, but the drama from my first crazy hour at the academy was much harder to rinse off. "Been here minutes, and already have some crazy girl after your blood. Typical."

As I dried myself, my mind wandered back to Aran—specifically the way he'd looked at me when I was naked. The memory of his gaze, and that smile, sparked a tiny flame of . . . of what? Longing? It didn't sound right. Back in Breaux Bridge, no one had ever really paid me much attention. And Nutjob Nester approaching me didn't count. I'd always been the "average" girl, easily overlooked and largely ignored. But Aran's words hinted at something more. He thought I was *alright*.

I smiled, even as I scolded myself for letting my thoughts drift there. Aran May was the last thing I needed. But as I finished drying off, a small part of me couldn't help but hope I'd be chosen for Château Michael—just to be closer to him. Not that I would ever let anything happen between us. But there was no denying he was very easy on the eyes.

I looked at my pile of grimy clothes with a grimace. They were covered in blood, sweat, and tears, and it took a minute of hyping myself up before I could pull them back on. With a final look in the mirror to see if there was any fixing my hair, I stepped into the bedroom and found Aran by the cages.

His eyes lingered on my stained shirt, wry grin in place. "I'd say you look as good as new, but I'm not in the habit of lying." He pushed off the cages and strode to a nearby closet, where he rummaged through its contents. He resurfaced with a flannel shirt in hand. "Here, this should help hide some of the mess. I would ask about the blood, but we really don't have time for a backstory." He watched me pull it over my Taco Express shirt, nodding with approval. "Good as secondhand. Let's get moving. We're already running late."

Aran grabbed two green cans from his beer fridge, tossed one to me, then we hurried through the now deserted château. The sun was setting outside, the clouds burning orange. I followed Aran past the pool and onto a narrow cliffside trail where we walked down the staircase carved into the rocks in silence.

My mind raced, asking questions that I couldn't answer. Demons, war, magic—all of it bounced around my head in a dizzying whirl. It was all too much to think about, and if I didn't find a distraction soon I'd go crazy.

"So . . . how are you feeling?" I asked, needing to hear his accent again.

He sighed. "Frustrated."

"I'm sorry. If there's anything I can do to help, let me know."

He took a drink from his beer. "Don't worry about it. It's not like you're the reason shadow faun are so hard to bond with."

I paused, trying to understand what he said, but no matter how hard I racked my brain, his words simply didn't make sense. "Huh?"

He halted midsip, looking at me quizzically. "What are you talking about?"

"Well, your ex . . . the breakup?"

He snorted with laughter. "That? No, don't worry about it. Sophia can be fiery at times, but she eventually cools down."

A strange and unwelcome flash of disappointment filled me. "Oh. So you're not broken up?"

"Nah, that's just a usual Friday evening for us. We're as strong as ever."

I tried to keep my face neutral but knew I failed miserably. If he called that a strong relationship, I'd love to see his definition of a dysfunctional one.

We walked in silence for a moment, but I couldn't keep my probing questions down. "You love her?"

He didn't answer immediately. "We should hurry. We've only got a few minutes left."

I wanted to tell him I didn't want to hurry anywhere; I didn't want to go to this Choosing—whatever it was—and I would appreciate someone telling me exactly what was going on. But it was clear by the way he strode ahead into the darkening world that he was done talking for the moment. Despite the flurry of questions I had about this world and the so-called demons, I found my thoughts increasingly drawn toward Aran. Where exactly was he from? How did he get his body looking so damn fine? And in an almost silly way, how would it feel to kiss him.

As we rounded an outcrop, a low hum filled the air, growing louder until it became a constant drone. We climbed the cliff stairs and emerged into a wide-open field where the source of the noise became clear. An enormous open-air stadium, divided into four bleachers and packed with thousands of people, rose out of the ground to our front. Through the gap between the stands, I spotted a large group of people huddled together on the field, looking like scared sheep.

Aran turned to face me, sweeping his arms wide. "Welcome to the Choosing!"

Chapter Seven

The enormity of the stadium, reaching high into the darkening sky, reminded me of an alligator's mouth as it waited to clamp down on any catfish that drifted too close. Towering floodlights cast a harsh glow over it all, illuminating the faces of countless teeth-like spectators as they stared down at the people standing timidly on the field.

I stumbled back a few steps on the stony path. "No," I breathed. "I—I can't go in there." The idea of standing exposed in front of such an overwhelming mass, each pair of eyes locked on me, was my definition of hell.

"Course, you can," said Aran, watching me with an amused grin. "It's not like you have to fight in the Colosseum or anything."

"You don't understand," I said, my heart fluttering like crazy. "I physically can't. It's . . . it's . . ." How could I explain the magnitude of my anxiety? Any form of public speaking or being the focal point of a crowd transformed me into a quivering mess. "It's complicated."

To my surprise, he responded with a comforting calmness. "I reckon you're a lot stronger than you give yourself credit for." He took my hand. "Honestly, it's not so bad in there. Piece of piss, really. It'll be over in no time, then we can kick off the celebrations." He tugged gently, guiding me toward the towering structure.

Helpless before him, I allowed myself to be led in, my legs wobbling beneath me. What was I doing? I didn't belong there. I belonged in Breaux Bridge, miserable, taking orders.

"Aran?"

"Just breathe."

"They're staring at me."

"Course they're not."

By the time we stepped past the bleachers and onto the field, the roar of the crowd reverberated through my bones, beating the breath from my lungs.

Aran released my hands and gently gripped my shoulders. "You'll do just fine. Remember, whatever happens, hold your chin up, your back straight, and never back down." He squeezed, then took my empty beer can and nudged me toward the field's center.

I don't know how I reached the crowd without falling flat on my face. There had to be a few hundred people in the middle, many reflecting my own fear back at me. They stared into the bleachers, ashen-faced. I glanced over my shoulder and spotted Aran chatting with a broad-shouldered man. His black tee was taut over muscles that strained with every movement. Aran pointed at me, and the man's gaze met mine. He nodded to whatever Aran was saying and jotted something down on his notepad.

"You look how I feel," a British voice said, drawing my attention. The speaker was a young woman with glossy dark skin and a glowing smile. Thick, curly black hair fell to her shoulders above a black dress, and her heels told me that she, at least, had dressed for the occasion. She was beautiful.

"Like you're giving birth to a whale?" I said, trying to smile but managing a grimace.

She laughed, then stepped in to adjust the flannel around my waist to better cover the red stains. "More like I'm a bloody mess." She gave me a once-over. "Much better. I'm CJ." Her brow raised when her gaze returned to my face. "And your eyes are stunning! Two colors for the price of one."

"Oh, they're not that special—"

"Rubbish. You're rocking them, babe."

Her energy eased some of the tension in my neck. "Thanks. I'm Alina." I glanced around the bustling stadium. "So, demons, huh?"

"I know, right? So mental. Beats a slap in the face, I suppose." She shrugged. "But I've come to terms with it over the last couple weeks."

"You found out that long ago?" I asked, surprised.

"Yeah. Sorta set my toaster on fire when my powers woke. Scared the kneecaps off my mom. But after I understood what happened, I was as chuffed as a dog with two tails. Damned if I know what this Choosing is about, though. Doesn't seem anyone else does, either. There's a poor lad over there bawling his eyes out. Can't be much older than twelve."

"Twelve?" I followed her gaze across the crowd and was struck by the range of ages. While most seemed to be in their late teens, there were a few outsiders. An awkward boy wearing an oversized yellow Pokémon shirt couldn't have been older than fifteen. And farther away was a man in his thirties, his hairline receding noticeably.

As I tried to figure it all out, a thunderous voice boomed through the air: "Ladies and gentlemen, welcome to the annual Choosing ceremony!" The crowd sprung to their feet and erupted in cheers. "To our fledglings, buckle up! You're in for a demonic delight. As for our returnees, we're thrilled to have you back. I trust you had a restful break and steered clear of any temptations from Noverna and Zephtura."

I searched for the source of the voice. A light nudge from CJ brought my attention to her, and she gestured upward. There, perched on a small floating island that somehow had escaped my notice, sat a man swinging his legs with a beer in hand.

"As your student representative at Astaroth Academy, I extend a warm welcome to all our newcomers," he said, his voice resonating through the stadium. "We are thrilled to have you join our ranks in the ongoing battle between good and evil. The full gravity of our situation may not have dawned on you yet, but know this—the dark forces of Noverna and Zephtura are tireless in their pursuit of opening the gates to Earth once more. We need your commitment now more than ever."

Unease rippled through the crowd, and I felt it, too.

"Guess they conveniently left that part out of the pamphlet," CJ muttered.

The voice carried on. "I'm certain you have questions, and they will be answered in time. For now, let me clarify how the Choosing works. The academy is organized into four châteaux: Michael, Raphael, Uriel, and Gabriel. During your six-year tenure here, these groups will serve as your family. Sorting you is simple enough. It's all based on your place in a hot-dog eating competition." The crowd's laughter shook the ground. The man took a loud slurp of his beer.

"I'm only pulling your leg, folks. Châteaux leaders, please make your way onto the field."

A hush fell over the bleachers as four figures stepped onto the grass—three women and one man. It was the same guy in the black tee that Aran had spoken with earlier.

"I want to remind the châteaux leaders that gender balance must be maintained in your selections, and you will be penalized if your choice takes longer than three seconds. Now, where are our referees—ah, there they are." A group of individuals wearing bright-yellow shirts strode onto the field. "Candidates, please proceed to your new châteaux sections in the bleachers once you've been chosen." He lifted his beer for another gulp. "I think we've covered all the bases. Château Michael, you're up first. Let the Choosing begin."

"So . . . we just stand here until someone picks us?" I asked, my voice barely audible above the buzz of the stadium.

"Sounds that way," said CJ, looking around uncertainly.

The leader of Château Michael broke away from the others and cut a path directly toward me. My breath hitched. Was he . . . was he really going to pick me first? Is that what Aran had told him?

I opened my mouth to say something as he neared, but he brushed past and grabbed CJ's hand, thrusting it into the air. *"Michael!"* he roared. A referee swooped in and guided a dazed CJ in the right direction. The leader moved on, his eyes scanning the crowd for his next choice.

As the heat of embarrassment crept up my cheeks, I drew into myself, trying to become as small as possible. How many times was I going to let men get my hopes up like that? It was pathetic.

"Uriel!" a voice cried, and a man built like a rugby player was ushered to the stands.

The châteaux leaders weaved through our ranks, sizing us up like cattle at auction. Some shot rapid-fire questions at us, and if the responses didn't meet their expectations, they moved on without a second glance. Michael's leader, in particular, seemed to have a strategy of intimidating candidates, then discarding those who didn't meet his gaze. The whole ordeal felt crudely primitive.

After what seemed hours, the number of unchosen candidates dwindled to a meager few. Unwanted memories of being picked last for high school soccer games surfaced. I tried not to show how affected I was, but my eyes prickled all the same.

Uriel's leader hurried toward me, her face lighting up with a pleasant smile. Startled, I dropped my guard—

"Run!" she screamed directly in my face. The suddenness of her outburst almost made me jump out of my shoes. Her face twisted into a grimace of disgust, and she swiftly turned her attention to the next victim.

We shrank to a small group that consisted mostly of thin, young kids. The boy in the Pokémon shirt caught my gaze, visibly shaking, and I tried to reassure him with a comforting smile.

"They'd be a fool not to choose you," I whispered, hoping to ease his worry.

He nodded meekly. "T-thanks," he stuttered. "You, too."

On cue, the leader from Château Gabriel, a robust woman, stepped forward with a sigh of resignation. She lifted the boy's hand and declared, "Gabriel," her voice lacking any enthusiasm.

His face lit up like a Christmas tree. I gave him an encouraging wink, and he tried to return it, but dropped his handheld game console in his excitement. Amid bouts of laughter from the crowd, he scurried to retrieve it and bolted to the Gabriel bleachers.

The Choosing continued, and with each announcement, my heart sank a little further. The remaining candidates were selected one by one until I was the only person left standing. It was a harsh reality check.

Upon realizing he had no choice but to choose me, Michael's leader closed his eyes. "Fuck!" he yelled. The other leaders laughed.

"Last again—the curse lives on," the woman from Uriel said, clapping his back. "No point playing flag fall this year, not with your luck."

The man set his jaw as he approached me. He clamped his hand around my wrist and tugged my arm into the air. "Michael."

A smattering of sympathetic applause echoed from the stadium, but I was too consumed by my embarrassment to pay it any mind. I trudged toward the Michael bleachers, unable to meet anyone's gaze.

CJ bounded forward and pulled me into a tight hug. "You go, babes! Don't mind them dafties, picking you last. You're a queen, and they'll see it soon enough."

A man standing nearby snorted.

"Something to say, pet?" she said, fronting him.

He looked down at me. "It's bad luck when a château gets last pick. Ruins the whole damn year." He folded his arms. "You should do Michael a favor and leave. Let Earth have you if they will take you."

CJ closed the distance between them. "When was the last time a lass *chose* you for anything? Given your face looks like a bulldog chewing wasps, I imagine you've had many lonely nights. So, how about this? How about you do everyone a favor and jog on?"

I stood there, mouth hanging open. The man's cheeks, mottled and scarred, flushed red. He opened his mouth to reply, but his friends' roaring laughter drowned his words out.

"Hudson got schooled!" one of them shouted, giving him a slap on the back.

It was the most beautiful thing I'd ever seen.

"Come on," CJ said, linking her arm through mine. "Let's go find men who know how to tie their own shoelaces." She guided me down the first row of the bleachers, leaving the Hudson—still trying to splutter a response—behind.

"Thank you," I said, on edge by how nasty he had been. "That was incredible."

She gave my arm a gentle squeeze. "No—thank you. It's not every day I get such a perfect opportunity to stick it to the patriarchy. Besides, that's what friends do—stand up for each other, right?"

"Still . . . I really appreciate it. More than you know—"

"Not bad, bloodstain," a familiar voice called from the bleachers. I looked up to find Aran making his way toward us. CJ's grip tightened on my arm.

"Oh, hey," I said, my heart quickening. "You could've mentioned that all I had to do was stand there and wait to be chosen."

"I could have," he said, with that deadly smirk of his. "But where's the fun in that?"

CJ released her hold of me and extended her hand toward Aran. "Well, aren't you a fine drink of water? I'm CJ—Alina's friend."

As he shook it, my stomach twisted strangely. With a start, I realized I was jealous. *He has a girlfriend,* I reminded myself sternly. *And you have Machina.*

"Nice to meet you, CJ—" he began, but a booming voice cut him off.

"Attention, everyone!" It was Michael's leader. He stood in front of the bleachers, hands on hips. "For those who haven't had the pleasure of meeting me yet, I'm Morgan King—your château leader. Here at Michael, we have a long-standing tradition of welcoming new members, whether or not they are wanted"—he shot me a fleeting glance—"with the most epic party you'll ever see."

Cheers erupted from the stands, and despite my initial resistance, I was caught up in the excitement. The energy of the crowd, combined with my fatigue, made me momentarily forget my worries.

"All fledglings, please stay put. I'll escort you to the château myself. Everyone else, you know the drill."

Animated conversations filled the air as everyone dispersed. Some strolled like normal people would, while others launched into the air like Nester had earlier. For the first time since I'd arrived, I considered what was possible with such power. Could I learn to fly? And what else could I do? What if there was a way to master Machina? Or annihilate her altogether? The thought left me lightheaded at the implications.

Morgan took charge and ushered us out of the stadium. "Stick together—the academy is huge, and it's easy to get lost."

We bypassed the cliff trail and crossed a broad, lush field, following Morgan like a group of stray kittens. The academy's lawns rolled gently upward toward a forest that scaled the mountain. A river ran behind us, the sound of rushing water carrying on the cool breeze.

Our group hummed with chatter as we walked. I met several people and was comforted to find that they had been just as nervous as I was. Each had their own story about the day their powers manifested, but they listened with shock when I told of the Nester and Audrey fight. I realized my mistake when they started to think I was something special, something worth fighting over. I tried to correct the idea, to manage their expectations, but failed miserably.

After passing a building shaped like a rose, we turned right at a bridge and followed a trail along the river's edge. In the heart of the woods, Morgan suddenly leaped onto a moss-covered fallen log.

"One last thing," he said, raising his arms to quieten us down. "I know you're all itching to find out more about the châteaux and what's at stake in the championship. Believe me, the rewards for victory are beyond your wildest dreams. We're talking life-changing stuff here. But"—he raised a finger— "come last, and you'll feel the repercussions forever." He swept his gaze over us. "I can't stand losing, and though it's been seven years since we've won, we haven't come last in thirty-six years. I intend to keep it that way."

CJ leaned closer to me. "The things I'd do to him," she whispered.

I muffled my laugh. She was Georgie to the bone, incapable of spotting a red flag if it whacked her on the snout.

Morgan's voice dropped lower as he continued, "This is my final year at Astaroth, and I need you all to understand how crucial it is that we win. I won't rest until Château Michael claims the championship, and I expect every single one of you to give it your all. If I see anyone slacking off, know that I won't hesitate to make you wish you'd never been born a demon." Someone laughed nervously, but quickly cut it off. "Questions?"

No one moved. No one dared to breathe.

Morgan clapped his hands together. "Excellent. Now that we've set the ground rules, let's have some fun." He hopped off the log and resumed the journey down the forested river path.

Everyone held back for a moment before slowly following him.

CJ bounced with excitement. "Damn, he's dreamy! Do you think he's single? Oh, don't give me that look. I know he's not everyone's cup of tea. But I appreciate the finer idiot on rare occasions."

We rounded a bend in the path, and a bright light erupted in the darkness. I shielded my eyes, and as my vision slowly adjusted to the intensity, the scene that unfolded left me utterly speechless.

Chapter Eight

As I stepped into the clearing, it felt like I'd discovered a hidden magical world nestled within the depths of the forest. Charming log cabins, their windows glowing with warm light, were tucked among the pines, and at the heart of the scene was a roaring campfire that cast flickering shadows over the grand rear entrance to Château Michael.

I stumbled forward, captivated by the strings of fairy lights that stretched from the château's roof to the tips of the surrounding trees, twinkling like a swarm of fireflies against the black night. A gentle breeze stirred around me, bringing the forest to life. At one end of the clearing, a DJ booth had been set up, and keg stands and coolers were scattered about. I stared at them, emotionally drained and needing a cold drink to recharge.

Morgan spun to face us and threw his arms wide. "Welcome to your new home!"

A shower of fireworks erupted from the rooftop of the château, painting the night sky in red, green, and gold. A tremendous cheer rose from Michael's residents, stealing my breath away, and I was unable to hold in my grin. What did I have to go back to in Breaux Bridge? A nonexistent job? A missing Georgie and Dustin? A life on its last legs? It paled compared to what I was seeing now. And if Astaroth held the key to finally gaining control over Machina, then I had to give it a hot go.

Students rushed forward to force plastic cups of beer into our hands. They clapped our backs and showered us with compliments for being selected by the greatest château at Astaroth. Not one of them looked at me funny. Not one of them seemed to notice the chaos inside. It was a simple moment, but one I wouldn't forget.

"You're grinning like the Cheshire cat," said CJ, threading her arm through mine as we made our way toward the warmth of the fire. "Easy to imagine why . . ." She trailed off, her eyes widening as she gaped at something in the distance.

"What's wrong?" I asked.

She closed her mouth, eyes sparkling, and grinned mischievously. "I don't want to get you all hot and bothered, but there's a pack of fit lads right there stripping down to their birthday suits."

I followed her gaze and nearly dropped my drink. Sure enough, there were several guys, their bare torsos bright against the night, getting naked by the riverbank. Even from a distance, I could tell they were in great shape, their muscles rippling as they moved. A flush crept up my neck as I watched them leap into the water.

"Good Lord," I said, tearing my gaze away, feeling suddenly very warm. "What kind of place is this?"

"Heaven," she said, unhooking her arm from mine and starting forward.

I hesitated. As much as I wanted a closer look, I couldn't just waltz up to a group of naked men. I mean, that was a Georgie thing to do. "CJ," I called, but she was as distracted as a moth around a flame.

My grip on the plastic cup tightened, spilling beer onto my hand, as I realized how alone I was without CJ.

A voice behind me made me jump. "She's trouble if I ever saw it."

I turned to see a guy standing nearby, grinning from ear to ear. His gap-toothed smile and sandals-and-socks combo gave him a quirky charm. "I'm pretty sure trouble's her middle name," I said, grateful to have someone to talk to.

"She'll fit in just fine," he said, eyes sparkling. He lowered into a sweeping bow. "I'm Zach."

A girl appeared at his side and thrust a beer into his hand. "There you are. I thought you'd gone to bed already."

Zach didn't take his eyes from me. "Ava, I'm in the middle of something. Shoo."

Ava glanced my way, and her eyebrows shot up. "Well aren't you a sight for sore eyes." She pushed back her long bangs to reveal pierced dimples that deepened with her smile.

"Oh . . . thanks?" I said awkwardly, unprepared for the compliment. "I like your nose ring."

"Don't mind Ava," Zach groaned, giving her a gentle nudge with his elbow. "She has a gift for making people uncomfortable." He looked down at her and spoke slowly. "Why don't you find someone else to torment? We're in the middle of a moment here."

She looked from me to Zach before snorting. "Oh, I see what's going on! Zach's hitting on you, right? Has he shown you his collection of teaspoons yet? Some people think it's creepy, but I think it's nice he has a hobby."

"I'm not hitting on her," Zach fired back. Then he looked at me desperately. "I'm not hitting on you, just so you know. Unless, well, you want me to hit on you."

"Oh, that's right," Ava said like she'd just remembered something. "Zach prefers women with more muscle than brain."

His fist clenched, spilling beer from his cup. "That was one time, and only because of your stupid drinking games."

"Tahlia still brags about it, you know?" she said. "In between her bicep curls. Anyway—" She grabbed my hand. "Let me give you a tour. This is my fourth year, so I know all there is to know. What's your name?"

Though being fought over by two people made me wildly uncomfortable, it was far better than being alone. "Alina," I said, as Zach hooked his elbow through my free arm.

"Pleasure to meet you," he said.

"The pleasure's all mine," Ava said.

All I could do was shake my head and try not to laugh. The day's absurdity didn't seem like ending any time soon. We passed the fire, and Ava nodded to the row of log cabins we'd walked by earlier.

"Those are the fledgling dorms—where the real magic happens."

Zach snorted. "The only 'magic' you'll find there is an assortment of body odors. Word to the wise—choose who you room with carefully. Nothing worse than bunking down with someone who loves eggs. But don't worry, you'll be upgraded to the château in your second year. Oh, and see that building past the garden? That's the château library—"

"Home to all the classics," Ava said, her face lighting up. "King. Rowling. Salvatore. Sure, it's not as grand as the academy library, but it works in a pinch."

"You think Rowling is a classic?" I asked, unable to hide my amusement.

"Ava doesn't think," said Zach. "Wait until you see her in a flag fall match."

Flag fall . . . The name triggered something in my memory. "What is flag fall, exactly?"

Zach stopped in his tracks. "Only the best sport in this world! I'm a Raider—"

"Me, too," said Ava. "It's chaotic, and the stakes are pretty high. The aim is to capture flags and waypoints, all while trying to, you know, stay alive—"

"Michael's team made it to the grand final last year," said Zach. "It was the highlight of my life."

"That's not saying much," said Ava. "Anyway, it's truly an amazing sport . . ."

Her words faded into the background as two familiar figures caught my attention by the jacuzzi. Sophia was nestling against Aran on the steps, all signs of her earlier rage gone.

"Aran and Sophia," said Zach. "Astaroth's power couple. He's got to be the luckiest guy here—Sophia is fire."

Ava shook her head. "She's the lucky one. Aran is the only man who could steal the queer out of me. Can't understand half of what he says, though. Like he's talking through yesterday's oatmeal."

"He's captain of the flag fall team," Zach added. "Want to meet them?"

As if having heard our conversation, Sophia looked our way. Her lips pressed tightly together, and the anger in her eyes let me know that she would happily flay me alive given the chance.

"Maybe some other time," I said, my stomach knotting. "What's that building over there?" I pointed to a random circular structure.

"That's the sauna—it's a lifesaver during winter," Zach explained.

"And clothing," Ava added with a wink, "is optional."

"Let's check it out," I suggested, dragging them away from Sophia and Aran.

What was happening to me? First Nester, now Aran—even the sight of naked men jumping into the river had caused my pulse to race. It was as though the awakening of my powers had done more than just cause the lights to flicker. A dormant part of me was coming to life, sending shivers down my thighs.

I dived mouth first into my beer, and before I knew it, I was on my sixth drink. Watching Zach and Ava's playful banter brought a smile to my face, reminding me so much of Dustin and Georgie. It was a welcomed slice of familiarity that helped calm my tingling nerves. We explored a herb garden, peered through a telescope in the observatory, admired artwork in the studio, and even peeked in a meditation room—the château had it all.

After the tour, we joined a table of students playing drinking games with cards. Before long, my yawns outnumbered my sips of beer. Exhaustion had caught up to me. I couldn't remember the last time I'd slept.

I rose from my chair, legs wobbling slightly, and stretched. "I'm going to call it a night."

"So soon?" Morgan asked. "On your first evening? That's how bad reputations are built." He dropped his voice to a whisper. "I've got some candy that'll burn away any tiredness. It might even make you more . . . enjoyable."

It took little imagination to understand what Morgan was talking about. Party drugs were no small fixture in life in Lafayette, but it was one temptation I'd never given into. "Awfully kind of you, but I'll pass. Good night, everyone."

CJ, who sat on Morgan's lap, stood and stretched. "I'll come with you?"

I shook my head. She was in her element, and although Morgan wasn't my cup of tea, she seemed quite taken with him. "No, you stay and enjoy the party. Make all these folks suffer for me."

"You sure, babe? I don't mind."

"Positive."

I passed the booming speakers and made a beeline for the fledgling cabins. The dance floor near the woods was now crowded with pumping bodies, and several couples were making out on the log benches around the firepit. My exhaustion had dulled my senses to the point where I didn't recognize the person sitting closest to my path until he spoke.

"You look lost," said Aran, glancing up from the stick he was swirling in the coals.

I looked around, half expecting Sophia to materialize from the shadows with a knife. The coast was clear, so I stopped beside him. "Being lost is part of my personality."

He flashed a grin. “In that case, welcome to Astaroth. We’re all just wanderers here, trying to figure our own way through life.” He tossed the stick into the fire and stood. “Heading to bed?”

“Trying,” I said. “But I don’t have the faintest idea what cabin to bunk in. Do we just pick any?”

“Sleeping alone on your first night? How intrepid of you.”

I playfully slapped his shoulder. It was hard as stone. “I’ll have you know that I’m a respectable lady.”

“Not sure you belong here, then,” he said with a laugh. “Come on, I’ll help. You’re lucky I found you—there’s plenty of bad influences here who’d force you to drink till sunrise.”

“My hero. Where’s Sophia?”

He ran his fingers through his hair. “She had to make an appearance at her château’s party. It’s a rule that every Uriel student must attend.”

We walked in a silence for a few moments, but I needed to hear his Australian accent again.

“So, how did you end up here?” I asked. “Astaroth, I mean.”

“Kangaroos.”

“Huh?”

“Kangaroos. You know, hippity-hop? Giant bouncy rats? I was rounding a mob up on our farm back home—I needed some footy trip money—when *poof!* A bunch of weirdos rocked up and said I was a demon. Said the day before my powers had awoken and I had a place at Astaroth Academy if I wanted it.” He leaned in with a sly grin. “I told them to get off my land, or I’d sic my dog on them.”

I pictured it all in my head so clearly. Aran in tight jeans and a flannel, a knife strapped to his belt—no, a whip—and tall boots. It was an image I'd hold onto for a long time. "What did they do?"

"Well, first they showed me some stuff that I'll never forget. Made me think I'd had a few too many tinnies, you know. Flying around, making the ground bubble—all of it. When they came back the following day, they convinced me to check this place out at the start of term. That was three years ago now, and it's been incredibly profitable since."

I stared at him. "Profitable? You found out you're some kind of demon, and your first thought was to profit from it?"

"Well . . . maybe not first. But it was a close second. Money makes the worlds go round—you either have it, or you have a hard life. Given the choice, I'd rather have it."

We stopped in front of the first cabin and he turned to face me. "What's your story?"

How did I answer that? Tell him about my childhood spent family hopping? Never staying somewhere long enough to see two Christmases in a row? Leaving the foster care system to live with Georgie when I was sixteen? "There's not much to tell," I said eventually, my voice quiet. "I came from a small town in Louisiana—"

"Rubbish."

I stared at him. "No, really—"

"Who cares where you're from? Tell me who you are."

Was he drunk, or was it me? "What do you mean?"

"If you could only do one thing for the rest of your life, what would it be?"

I thought about it for a long moment, then shrugged. "Well, writing, I suppose."

"Columns? Diaries? Manuals?"

"Novels."

His eyebrows made a perfect arch. "Well, I wouldn't have guessed that."

"But you guessed manuals?"

"What sort of stories?"

I blushed. "Romance." When I first admitted that to Georgie and Dustin, they'd teased me mercilessly. "Fantasy romance."

"Well, if there's something that excites me, it's a steamy elf hookup story. Published?"

"Trying," I admitted.

"I expect a signed copy when you do."

"Might be waiting a while."

"I've got time. Providing this demon war doesn't kill us all first."

Not for the first time, hearing mention of this war put me on edge. "I still don't understand what it's all about."

"You're not special in that," Aran muttered. He buried his hands in the pockets of his shorts. "They tell us it's a battle between good and evil and expect us to believe them when they say we're on the good side."

"You don't?"

"No. Well, yes. Sort of. But how can we know for sure? I mean, those who control the information control the people, right? I saw it back home all the time. The news doesn't stand for facts anymore but the tailored narratives of the highest bidder. And the public? They swallow it without a second thought. It's absurd. But the same thing happens here. How can we know the truth when we only have access to one side's story?"

Good heavens, men and their conspiracies. But honestly, he could talk about cow hoof trimming, and I'd hang on to his every word just the same.

"Why would they lie to us?" I asked. "Surely someone would know something and let the word out."

He chuckled bitterly. "Spin a grand lie enough times, and it becomes truth to people." He opened his mouth but then closed it again, laughing helplessly. "What I'm saying is, don't blindly trust those who monopolize knowledge and stand to gain from your actions. Also, maybe I should go easy on tequila for a bit."

I was about to reply when a sharp pain shot through my stomach. I doubled over and clutched my belly, struggling to breathe as the searing sensation spread through me.

"Alina?" Aran sounded alarmed. "Are you okay?"

I gritted my teeth. "Just a . . . cramp. It'll pass."

He hesitated, hand touching my back lightly. "You don't look so good. I'll take you to the medical center."

I straightened slowly, taking a deep breath to steady myself, and looked at the nearby cabin. "I'm fine. This where I'm staying?"

"Yeah, but maybe you should—"

"I'm really alright," I said, smiling with effort. "I just need some rest. Good night."

I hurried into the cabin and shut the door behind me. My heart raced as I sank to the floor, forehead pressing against the cold wood. *Why now? In front of Aran, of all people? He'll think I'm crazy, just like everyone back in*

Breaux Bridge. Taking deep breaths, I felt the pain gradually recede. It was just a brief episode, but the timing couldn't have been worse.

I pulled myself together and looked around. Ten bunk beds were spaced across the room, and a large stone fireplace dominated the far wall. The floor was inlaid with flagstones, and the kitchen and bathroom looked pleasant enough for an academy dorm.

I chose the bottom bunk against the far wall, away from the bathroom, to minimize any unnecessary noise. A small greeting bag awaited me on the pillow containing essential toiletries. What was noticeably missing, though, was a change of clothes. The idea of spending another day in my bloodied Taco Express uniform was far from appealing.

I brushed my teeth and crawled into bed. I lay there for a moment, staring at the underside of the mattress above me, the noise from outside drifting in. My eyelids grew heavy, and sleep swept aside my fantasy of magically silencing Machina for good.

Chapter Nine

The abrupt jostling of my arm wrenched me out of my sleep. My heart hammered against my rib cage as my eyelids fluttered open, squinting against the harsh morning sunlight. I stared up at a boy, no older than sixteen, who hovered over me. His thick glasses made him look as surprised as I felt.

"Heck," I said, quickly pulling the sheet up to my neck. "What's the matter?"

He lowered his gaze and rocked from foot to foot. "I'm sorry, I'm sorry. I didn't mean to startle you." His hands bunched the hem of his shirt.

I took a calming breath and forced a smile. "Hey, it's okay, I'm fine now." I looked through the cabin—though the other beds had been slept in, it was deserted. "What's up? Do you need something?"

He didn't meet my eyes. There was something different about him, but I couldn't quite put my finger on it. "Almost everyone is gone, and class starts in forty minutes. You're going to be late. I don't want you to be late."

I scanned the room again. Suitcases, which hadn't been there when I'd gone to sleep, were strewn about, flopped open with their contents exploded everywhere. Had I really slept through it all? Then the boy's words registered. Class? On a Saturday? I'd been hoping for some time to get used to the idea that my life had completely, and inexplicably, changed forever.

I sat and brushed my hair from my face. My head was foggy from all the drinks. "Almost everyone? Who else is here? And what class?"

The boy hurried to the foot of the bed, where a beige Louis Vuitton suitcase sat, clothes in a pile around it. He crouched and read the label. "Christina Joyce."

Through the haze of my mind, I pieced it together and figured it must be CJ. I wrapped the sheet around me—unnecessary, as the boy was now preoccupied with running his finger over the glossy exterior of the suitcase—and climbed out of bed to look into the top bunk. CJ hugged her pillow, as pretty as a picture, sleeping soundlessly. I'd once seen a photo of me sleeping and had nightmares for the next year.

I gently shook her arm. "CJ? CJ, we have class soon . . ."

Her eyes drifted open, and she smiled briefly, then yawned. "Class? On the weekend?" She stretched out. "These people really are demons. What class?"

I shrugged and looked back at the boy.

"On your bedside table," he said without glancing up.

A large manila envelope sat unopened beneath the lamp. I broke the seal and emptied the contents into my hand. Sheets of paper stapled together held all the information I needed for Astaroth Academy. From bus routes to a campus map. Rules and regulations—which were entirely too long—to sports tryouts and student organizations. On the very first page was a class schedule.

I rubbed my bleary eyes and held the paper to my nose. Saturday at ten was Demon Sorting in building C-fourteen. I picked up my phone, but it was dead.

"What's the time?" I asked the boy.

"Nine twenty-two," he said without looking at his watch.

"Son of a biscuit! CJ, we've got half an hour to get to Demon Sorting!" I had a motto: if you weren't ten minutes early, you were ten minutes late. The thought of being late on my first day filled me with anxiety. This was not the way I wanted to start my time at the academy.

CJ sat with a groan, her Afro frizzing in a perfect circle, and raised an eyebrow as she noticed the boy by her suitcase. "Bit young for you, isn't he?"

"I would never!" I said, placing a hand on my heart.

"Just playing," she said. "I got my spice last night." She closed her eyes and smiled wistfully. "Oh, sweet Morgan."

"You must be hungry," said the boy, standing up scurrying over. "Are you hungry? We can get breakfast on the way. I memorized the map last night when I arrived. I know where everything is. I know where the Arcane Garden is, and the Elemental Sandpit, and the Loft, and the library—"

"Okay, now," I said, holding up my hands to stop his flow. "Give me a sec to freshen up." I grabbed my toiletries and hurried into the bathroom. After a few minutes, I came out wearing Aran's flannel and my dirty jeans, feeling just as grimy, but at least my teeth weren't fuzzy anymore.

"I'm going to skip breakfast, babe," CJ said as she pulled a top from her suitcase. "I'll meet you in class—I need to do some damage control with this face."

I didn't know what she was talking about. To me, she looked as pretty as a peach. "Don't be late," I said. "I need to hear what you and Morgan got up to."

She flashed me a cheeky grin. "I'm not sure you could handle the details."

I followed the boy out of the cabin. The grassy area around the campfire was a mess of empty beer cups and trash from the night before. A handful of people were passed out on the lawn. I smiled as I recognized a few of them from the drinking games. It looked like CJ got one up on them, after all. We hurried past and followed the river through the forest. A fog hovered over the rushing water, almost obscuring the other side.

"It was kind of you to wake us up," I said, panting to keep pace. "It would have been embarrassing to miss my first lesson. I'm Alina."

The boy didn't slow. "I enjoy helping people. It makes me feel good to help people. My name is Eben."

"Well, Eben, it's a pleasure to meet you. But I can't remember seeing you at the party."

"Parties aren't preferable to me," he said quickly. "They're typically loud, and people can behave differently under such conditions." He increased his pace. "I arrived later at the academy than the rest. I wasn't initially expected to attend this academy. This is my second one."

"Second? There's another academy?"

"Indeed. There's a multitude of academies. Last year, I attended one on Noverna. However, I had no desire to return there, so I chose this academy instead."

Noverna. The name sounded vaguely familiar. After a few moments, I realized I'd heard it during the Choosing. The student representative had mentioned it as a place to be wary of.

"Aren't we at war with them?"

"Indeed, that's the general state of affairs," Eben confirmed. "Usually, after enrolling in Sevit, I would be ineligible to attend Astaroth. But they have identified me as a unique case. I was top of every class."

We reached the bridge and turned left, hurrying out of the forest and stepping onto the expansive, hedge-bordered lawns. A tall building, shaped like a rose, emerged from the mist ahead. People wandered about the grass, and a group gathered around an oak tree at the center. As we neared them, I recognized a few faces, and instantly wished we'd taken a different route. Before I could alter our course, Aran waved us over.

I trudged toward him, shoulders sagging.

"Really getting your money's worth with that outfit, huh?" he asked.

"Sustainable fashion is in right now," I said lamely. "Who knew eco-chic could look so good?" This was not the morning I'd hoped for. How much did he remember about my episode last night? Did he think I was crazy? I would.

Morgan dropped from his perch in the tree, eying me with a look of disgust. "You're *still* wearing his shirt? What the hell has he done to you? Listen here, new girl. Aran is bad news. You're better off forgetting him and finding a cultured gentleman, such as myself." He offered me his hand, and I regarded it with the same enthusiasm one might have for a warty toad.

Aran rolled his eyes. "How are you feeling? I was worried about you."

My stomach fluttered. He was worried about me? "Like a reheated corpse, but I'll survive. You?"

"Dry as a dead dingo's donga," he said. "But we're off to Little Peak—the nearest village—for a bevvie. I'll be right after that."

Though I wasn't exactly sure what he'd said, I couldn't help but grin. Beside me, Eben had begun rocking again.

"We're late for class," I said. "We'd better run."

He leaned back. "You're not late."

"It starts at ten."

"No, it doesn't. The professors had their annual welcome-back-to-hell party last night. I doubt anyone will be on time this morning."

I closed my eyes, relishing the news. "Thank God. I don't think I could function without a coffee."

"Coffee is bad for your teeth," Eben blurted.

There was a moment of silence, then Aran broke it with a chuckle. "You're absolutely right." He looked at Eben as though seeing him for the first time. "But it does wonders for your soul."

Eben blinked. "I wasn't aware of that."

"It's our little secret, okay?" Aran said, leaning in conspiratorially.

Eben's eyes brightened. "I am rather excellent at keeping secrets." He looked at me. "Can we go now?"

"Of course. Let's get that coffee." We stepped off and I glanced back at Aran. "I'll return your shirt as soon as I wash it."

"Don't bother—it suits you better."

The cafeteria was something from a dream. Circular communal tables dotted the first floor, sparkling chandeliers above them. The second level had a cozy corner with plush armchairs and sofas that were perfect for a more intimate dining experience. But the third level was the most impressive—it had a sprawling outdoor terrace with breathtaking views of the surrounding forests and mountains. Umbrella-topped tables filled it, and there was even a small garden with fresh herbs and vegetables that could be added to your meals.

The food choice was equally wonderful. Besides the fried and baked foods, there were also healthy options, such as colorful salads, grilled vegetables, and freshly made smoothies. The pastries displayed in a glass case were miniature works of art, with delicate icing and intricate designs. The aroma of chai wafted through the air.

"Free?" I repeated when I asked one attendant how much the buffet cost. "Are you sure?"

"Of course, dear. Take as much as you want, and then some. This isn't like one of those costly Earth schools. We want our students to do well, and that means full stomachs."

I didn't argue but hurried to the warm sandwich station and grabbed two eggs Benedict rolls to go—one for me, one for CJ. Eben joined me with a tray full of coffees.

"Someone's thirsty," I teased.

"Who?" he said, looking around.

I'd only known the kid a minute, and already he had my heart. "Are you going to drink all those by yourself?"

He shook his head so hard that some coffee spilled out over the top of the take-out cups. "No. But your friend said it does wonders for the soul, and I want my soul to be wonderful, so I will drink two of them. I have one for you and one for Christina."

"That's awfully sweet of you," I said, taking one to help lighten his load.

He guided us through a circular garden of rosebushes and into a network of open-air corridors branching out from the cafeteria like rays of sunlight. Soon, we joined a group of students gathered around the entrance to a tall building. Everyone wore the same outfit of frazzled hair and bloodshot eyes, the smell of hangover thick in the air.

"Good to see they look how I feel," I said to Eben when we found an empty bench.

"Hungry?" he said as he delicately unwrapped a banana.

"Well . . . yes. And a little tired and terrified."

He paused with the banana halfway to his mouth. "I'm terrified of loud noises. They make me jump. What are you terrified of?"

I inhaled the smell of my roll, and my stomach growled. I took a bite and chewed. "So much. But right now, well, I guess I'm terrified at how lost I feel. I mean—magic? What happens if I don't have any?" I licked the hollandaise sauce from my fingers. "There's some part of me that thinks I might have lost my mind, and all of this is just some sort of delusion. And not even a good one. Demons? Where are the horns, Eben? Where's the cloven hoofs and pitchforks?"

He chewed his banana thoughtfully. "Maybe you're not frightened. Maybe you're just excited. My mother says it's hard to tell the difference sometimes. That the body and mind don't always agree, and things can get mistaken."

I opened my mouth to explain that I was thoroughly and undeniably terrified, but caught myself when I realized there may be a touch of truth to his words. Though I preferred to blend into the background and avoid attention, there was a part of me that wanted to stand out and be different. A part of me that wished my anxiety didn't hold me back from exploring new possibilities. Learning magic would open me up to a world I couldn't have imagined, but it also made me vulnerable to failure and ridicule. This thought made my stomach churn uncomfortably.

"Maybe you're right," I said. "I guess time will tell." A sudden thought made me face him. "What does it feel like when you use your powers?"

"I don't know."

I stared at him. "You don't have powers?"

"I do. It's just . . . it's like how you breathe. Or blink. It just happens. No thinking."

"So, it doesn't feel like a demon is trying to rip through your stomach and steal your mind?" If there was a way I could tie Machina into this magical world, then I'd be one step closer to finding a way to destroy her.

He shook his head, glasses slipping to the end of his nose. "No, no, no. That's not fun." His gaze drifted over my shoulder. "I don't feel like that anymore—"

"Oh, here's CJ," I said, noticing her approach, happy she'd made it on time. She walked with an elderly woman whose white hair was gathered in a messy bun. Dark sunglasses concealed the woman's eyes, and she wore a drab green coat. Although she smiled at something CJ said, she did not strike me as a cheerful person.

They reached the doorway, and the woman turned to face us. "Alright, quit the blabbering." Her voice was dry as the Sahara. A hush fell over the group as she took a final drag of her cigarette then flicked it to the pavement to crush beneath her boot. "Inside with you all. Let's get this over with."

The lecture hall was stadium style with grandstand seating. Unfortunately, the rows of seats in the middle and back—my preferred territory—were already claimed, meaning we were left to occupy the dreaded front row.

The professor, her eyes still hidden behind her sunglasses, set her briefcase down with a thud. She took a drink from a coffee cup, which I suspected held something stronger than a latte, before sparking another cigarette. Her lips pursed as she scrutinized the room. A click of the keyboard made her name appear on the screen behind her—*Maviir Shae.*

"That's my name. Not Mav. Not Viir. Maviir. I usually teach demons how to use Aeria Kinesis, but because of a last-minute loss at boozy balderdash last night, I have the privilege of sorting you into your demon types today." She took a long drag of her cigarette, then perched on the edge of the desk with smoke wafting around her. "Rules. They are important. The first rule for today is: do not speak loudly. My head will explode if anyone is above thirty decibels. Unlike you, who have the afternoon free to orientate yourself, I must attend a conference. Let me assure you, it would not do well for me to show up with an exploded head.

"Now, before we delve into your placements, let's touch on demon kinesis. What is it—?"

Eben's hand shot up.

She ignored him. “Without first establishing a clear understanding of what demons are, answering that question would be pointless. Allow me to clarify that demons are not the malevolent entities often depicted in tales and films. Fundamentally, we possess unique abilities and inhabit one of the four realms linked to Earth via the Shadowgates.”

I leaned in, hanging on to every word. This was what I wanted to know. Beneath the surface, beyond my problems with Machina, what made me feel so different from everyone else I’d ever known?

“We are currently on Cronix, the Cryore world. It bears a striking resemblance to Earth, though with variations in climate and biodiversity. There are three other realms: Fernyre, the Faezre world; Zephtura, the Aeria world; and Noverna, the Terre world.” She took a swig of her drink and another puff of her cigarette. “Where do you fit into all of this? Since you’re on Cronix, a world ruled by demons with the power to control ice, does that mean you’re all ice demons?” She paused again, allowing her words to resonate.

I glanced behind me and saw a mix of reactions from the students; some nodded, but others looked just as confused as me.

“No,” Maviir answered herself. “Remember when I said demons aren’t the malevolent entities depicted in tales? That’s largely true, but not absolute. Much like humans, we have our rotten apples, a significant proportion of which hail from Zephtura and Noverna. This isn’t a reflection of the realms themselves but the corruption that governs them. These demons in power aspire to monopolize all the Shadowgates, Earth’s included. They’ll resort to any means to achieve this, and that’s dire news for all of us.”

At her words, Eben's fingers twisted together, forming knots in his lap. He'd mentioned his time on Noverna earlier, and if I had to guess, I'd say this discussion was stirring up some unpleasant memories for him.

"But, I digress," Maviir continued. "The evil doings of some demons are a topic for another day. At this moment, what you need to understand is that each one of you is either an Aeria or Terre demon."

Silence followed.

"But you just said Aeria and Terre were evil," called a guy from behind me. "Now you're saying that we're one of them?"

Ash from Maviir's cigarette dropped onto her coat. "Not one for listening, are you? I pointed out that their ruling factions are evil, not that they themselves are inherently evil. The distinction is crucial. The conundrum you should be pondering is, why are you on Cronix if you're not a Cryore demon?" She arched her eyebrows.

The student stumbled through a response. "So, um . . . why are we?"

"Excellent question! It's because demons from Cronix do not rip souls."

A shiver ran down my spine. *Rip souls?* What kind of ominous crap was that? Chairs squeaked as people shifted uneasily.

"Moving on," said Maviir, snuffing out her cigarette on the desk. "Let's sort you into your demon types—"

"What does that mean?" CJ interrupted loudly. She rose to her feet. "Rip souls? You're not seriously going to leave it at that, are you—"

"Lower your decibels, CJ," Maviir said, tilting her head forward and kneading her temples. "Exploding head, remember?" After a long moment, she sagged on the desk, her elbows on her thighs, and removed her sunglasses. "I'd hoped to avoid this conversation today. It's considerably less pleasant with a hangover. But, seeing as you are not to be distracted . . ." Her hands sank into her lap. "Soul ripping is the most horrendous act demons have inflicted upon humans. The easiest way to understand this is if you look at Earth as a succulent cut of rib-eye steak. All demons want it, but Zephtura and Noverna are so desperate, they'd consume it in one sitting. For thousands of years, they've feasted on Earth, reducing it to a bare, gnawed-on bone. Eventually, Cronix and Fernyre had to step in, and during the mid-twentieth century they locked all Shadowgates to Earth for any demon. Assuming they had won the battle, they resumed their peaceful existence. But the enemy, the *Reavers*, did not sleep. They schemed, devising a way to dispatch their soldiers back to Earth once more."

Her expression turned grim. She stood and paced in front of the desk. "What I'm about to share with you is distressing, but it's a reality you will have to face sooner or later." She cleared her throat. "The Reavers discovered a way to substitute the souls of newborn human babies with the souls of newborn demon babies. In doing so, demons grow up inside these stolen bodies, living under the illusion that they are human. That is, until their powers manifest. The Reavers trapped on Earth when the Shadowgates were sealed then gather these hybrids and indoctrinate them into their army. The hybrids, in their human bodies, can traverse the Shadowgates freely, making them invaluable assets."

I stared at Maviir, struggling to process her words. Was she saying that this body wasn't mine? That I had stolen it? Was I . . . was I some sort of body snatcher? My gaze dropped to my hands. I opened and closed fingers that now felt strangely disconnected from me.

Chapter Ten

The room's silence stretched on in the wake of Maviir's revelation. An uncomfortable thought wormed into my mind. Say I was an imposter in this body, what were the chances it could develop a way to fight back? To repel me like white blood cells attacking a foreign substance? What if Machina was not a creation of my mind, but this body's protector? Was it possible she existed solely to destroy me?

Around the room, faces shifted between shock and disbelief. Some students covered their mouths with hands, others whispered urgently to the people beside them.

"That's not true," CJ said, her gaze locked on Maviir. "You're lying."

Maviir sparked a new cigarette, taking a long drag before answering. "It's common to feel guilt or anger about what's happened to you, and it will take time to come to terms with your past. It's vital to know that you are not responsible for the sins of the Reavers. You were an unwitting participant in a plan far bigger than yourself." She scanned the room, locking eyes with each of us. "This is a lot to process, but you are not alone. If anyone would like to speak to someone about this, please remain after class."

She scratched her hair with the fingers holding her cigarette, then ambled over to a table holding two glass boxes. "I've been sidetracked enough for one day. Let's get you sorted so you can enjoy your free afternoon." She picked up the first box, which was filled with sand, and placed it on her desk. "Some of you might have noticed how the air can respect your wishes, or how the earth can shape to your desire. These manifestations can be subtle, or more magnificent." She returned for the second box, which was filled with something that sparkled at the bottom, and placed it next to the first. With a click of the mouse, a list of student names appeared on the large screen. "Others will be clueless, which is why we must run you through a test. First up is Daniel Abbott. Come down, lad."

A guy my age descended the stairs stiffly. He reached Maviir, head high, but his eyes betrayed his fear.

"Place both hands on the box of glitter," she said, tugging him closer by his arm. "Excellent. Now close your eyes and feel for a connection to the air inside. Search for a hook . . . something drawing you in by your chest . . . Can you feel the solidity of currents? Can you twist them? Pull on them like a puppeteer? No? Fine, fine. Let's try the next box."

When Daniel placed his hands on the next box, they shook so badly that he was in danger of knocking it to the ground.

Maviir stood behind him, looking over his shoulder. "Again, close your eyes . . . feel for that tug . . . that hook . . . Pull on it, reel it in—yes . . . yes, exactly! Now, spin it like a ballerina!"

I leaned forward to get a better view. The sand in the box slithered around, slowly at first, but quickening with each moment. It wasn't as spectacular as the magic I'd seen Nester do, but it was magic all the same.

Daniel's eyes bulged. "I'm doing it!"

The room burst into applause, Maviir's unsettling origin story forgotten in the face of the magical display.

But as Maviir called down the next student, CJ's mood sunk lower. "She's joking, right? This whole ripping souls thing—it's some sort of twisted prank."

After everything I'd been through, I no longer felt I knew enough about anything to form any sort of opinion. I turned to Eben. "You were on Noverna, right? Do they rip souls—"

"You were?" CJ cut in. "Tell me Maviir's lost the plot. Or . . . or say it's not as bad as she made it out to be."

Eben's discomfort was immediate. He drummed his fingers against the side of his head and dropped his gaze to his feet. "Yes. They rip the souls from human babies. It is true. But it is not all the truth."

This surprised me. "What do you mean?"

His fingers moved faster. "Cronix and Fernyre are not innocent in all this. They are not victims."

CJ covered her mouth with her hand. "They rip souls too?"

He shook his head. "No, no, no. Not rip souls—"

"The next person who speaks out of turn"—Maviir's voice cut through the room like a whip—"will have the privilege of spending their afternoon cleaning the pigsty." Her gaze burned into us.

I sank lower in my chair, holding my tongue. It seemed every moment that I spent at the academy raised more questions that needed answering. But as the list of students yet to be sorted dwindled, I forgot about my need for an explanation as a prickle of fear gripped me. I would have to try to perform magic in front of everyone. What if I failed? The embarrassment would kill me. I might as well dig a hole and bury my head in it right now.

By the time my name was called, my mind had melted into a gunky pool of terror. I forced myself to stand and made my way to Maviir, focusing on not tripping over. The eyes of the class blasted holes in the back of my head.

"Hands on the box of glitter," Maviir directed, her voice dull from the repetitive instructions. "Now, close your eyes . . ."

I did as she said, searching for that elusive pull. Seconds dragged on, and I felt nothing—no magical energy coursing through my veins, just the heat of embarrassment burning my cheeks.

But then, as I was about to give up, a breeze danced across my skin, raising hairs. A sensation of weightlessness found me, making me feel as though I were a part of the air itself. My fingers splayed wide on the box on their own accord.

"Well done," droned Maviir, "you're an Aeria demon. Though, not a powerful one."

My eyes snapped open. "Oh, my," I whispered. The glitter moved. It wasn't smooth or graceful but flopped around like a fish out of water. I didn't care. I had magic. I had actually performed magic. *Harry Potter, eat your heart out.* A smile broke across my face as I heard CJ's cheer.

"Do you plan on standing there all day?" asked Maviir. "Or just until your fan club finishes?"

I pulled my hands away from the box, watching the glitter settle back into place, wishing I had a little longer to play with it. I turned to leave and grazed the box of sand with my hand.

"Wait!" cried Maviir.

But I'd already felt it.

Something, a feeling deep inside, had shot through me, anchoring my feet to the floor. My breathing slowed, and a heat rose in my chest.

Maviir was at my side in an instant, her cigarette tumbling from her lips as she grabbed my shoulders. "Do it again."

The joy I'd felt just moments ago washed away in a rising tide of apprehension. I turned to CJ for support, but she gave a helpless shrug. Until now, Maviir hadn't demanded anyone go again.

Seemingly frustrated with my hesitation, she grabbed my wrists and forced my hands onto the sandbox. I clenched my fists instinctively, knuckles pressing against the glass, and pushed outward. A collective gasp filled the room as the sand burst into an energetic swirl.

"I—I don't understand," I said, watching unblinkingly. "I can do both?"

It took a moment before she found her words. "My dear girl, you do not understand indeed!"

Chapter Eleven

The fine grains of sand swirled before me in response to my unspoken command. I stood hypnotized by the display. Just moments before, I'd believed I was powerless, about to embarrass myself in front of everyone. But now it seemed I had more to offer than I could have imagined. If I could make glitter and sand move with a thought, what else could I do? Was it possible that I had the strength needed to silence Machina once and for all? To end her reign of terror? It was an enticing thought.

As I lifted my gaze beyond the display, my stomach clenched as hundreds of awestruck eyes stared back. I let my arms drop to my sides and stepped back. No one cheered this time, but whispers tore through the room like a gust of wind.

Maviir cleared her throat. "That's all, girl. Return to your seat."

I hurried back, hunching low to avoid the stares, and sat with the others. Though CJ looked surprised, it was nothing compared to Eben. His jaw hung open, and his magnified eyes bore into mine.

"They were right," he whispered, fingers tapping frantically on the table.

"Who were?" I whispered.

"Two powers. They said it was so but didn't believe. It all makes sense."

I was glad something made sense, because his rambling didn't. "Just another way for me to be different," I said, feeling hundreds of eyes burning into the back of my head.

CJ squeezed my hand. "Babes, it makes you extraordinary."

"Lucky me," I said dryly, resting my chin on the bench and wishing class would end already so I could find a dark corner to hide in.

The class couldn't hold my interest after that. CJ had manipulated her glitter into a graceful swirl with ease, and Eben, already proficient, molded the sand into an animated figure of a running man. It dragged on until twelve thirty, by which time Maviir had exhausted her cigarette supply. After my sorting, she seemed even more detached, gluing herself to her phone. Intermittently, her gaze flitted up to me, lips pursing briefly before her fingers resumed their tapping.

Finally, the last student was sorted, and Maviir stood and stretched, arching backward with her hands in the air. "Thank God that's over." She dusted ash from her coat and moved in front of her desk. "Demon Kinesis classes will begin Monday, with me instructing the Aeria students. If you haven't done so already, I'd advise purchasing a SIM card for your phones—important updates often get posted on the academy website. Plus, it will let you stay in touch with your family and friends back home."

With a pang of guilt, I realized how worried Georgie and Dustin must be. It was unlike me to go off-grid for a whole day. I needed to let them know I was safe, even if it wasn't the truth.

"Buses to Little Peak leave from the library every half an hour," Maviir continued. "The village has shops to cater to all your needs, as well as some excellent bars. It also serves as a transit center to nearby regions with regular train services crisscrossing the mountains. I recommend you plan a weekend trip to Starhaven sometime; the night sky there is mesmerizing."

She powered down her computer, the screen flickering to black, and strode toward the exit. "Don't forget to pick up your student cards from the desk on your way out. They come preloaded with education funds, sufficient to cover your necessities while you're here." After a pause, she motioned toward a tray of envelopes on the desk. "Well? What are you all waiting for?"

When we stepped outside, the group buzzing with excitement, I became firmly lost in my dark thoughts. Two powers. How on earth was I going to learn two? The stress of it made me want to vomit.

CJ watched me, then flicked me on the ear.

"Ouch! What was that for?"

"Because I can't have you walking around looking like you've eaten a dodgy prawn," she said, cocking her finger again.

I jumped out of reach. "Easy for you to say. You're not the one that everyone's gossiping about." I'd already heard my name whispered more times than I could count.

She looped her arm around mine. "Alina—we've done *magic*. Magic! And you've done it twice. Most people dream of this stuff, but then go back to their nine-to-five."

"I know. It's just . . . heck, I feel like there's so much pressure now."

She rolled her eyes. "Pressure makes diamonds."

Eben perked up. "Do you know diamonds are apparently a girl's best friend?" He frowned. "But I don't understand how that would work."

There was a pause, and then the corners of my mouth turned up. I shook my head, unable to stop the spreading grin. He was so innocent it hurt. "Be careful—friends make strange bedfellows."

He furrowed his brow as though trying to understand astrophysics. "Strange bedfellows? I will ask Mother about that one."

"To be a fly on the wall for that conversation," CJ said with a grin. "Come on, let's check out the village."

"Christina, would you mind if I joined you?" Eben asked. "I require some garments, and I would appreciate a SIM."

"To call your girlfriend?" she asked playfully.

His eyes widened. "No. Definitely not. I am just calling . . . well, it is a private conversation, and I should not be telling you."

"I'm just teasing, hun. Of course you can come with us. Do you know where the library is?"

He brightened. "Certainly. I have researched every building in the academy. Do you know the library is shaped like a rose?"

We joined a line of students on the far side and, after a brief wait, a double-decker bus pulled up in front of us. We climbed to the open-air top deck and took seats at the front. The sun's warmth washed over my face, and for a moment, the chaos that surrounded my life seemed to fade.

We passed the lake, now filled with swimming students and paddleboats, and drove onto the forest road that led past the military compound I'd arrived at the day before.

Eben touched my shoulder, pulling me from my thoughts. "I just wanted to tell you how special you are," he said without lifting his gaze from his feet.

For a moment, I was too stunned to say a word. He didn't strike me as the type to openly share emotions. "That's sweet of you, Eben. Thank you."

"I know you are going to help many people."

There it was. Expectation. "I'm afraid you have too high an opinion of me."

"No, I don't. You are special. It shouldn't have happened. All those powers. I didn't believe it. But it makes sense."

CJ, who'd been listening with one eye open, sat straighter. "I still don't get how it works. Why does Alina have two powers when everyone else only has one?"

His fingers paused. "I have been told it means her soul is born of Terre and Aeria parents." He scrunched his face and shook his head, glasses slipping to the end of his nose. "I am sorry if that is too distasteful to discuss."

Her eyes lit up with amusement. "But there are so many fit lads here. Surely, hookups happen all the time?"

"All the time," Eben agreed. "People are always hooking up, even when I'm on the top bunk. But no babies are ever born. Their souls are not compatible. The magic battles each other, and no one wins." He glanced at me. "Except for Alina. She won, so she is special."

His words flung me back through the years to all the times doctors had diagnosed me with dissociative identity disorder and medicated me accordingly. I had believed them for the longest time. But now, a cold clarity settled over me. Machina wasn't a figment of my imagination or a symptom of some medical disorder. And my theory that she was my body's defense mechanism was already on shaky ground thanks to the discovery that I had two powers. Following Eben's reasoning, did that point to Machina being the other part of me? Aeria or Terre? What if, instead of our incompatible magic wiping us out before birth, we'd lived, caught in an unending battle for control? This thought plagued me until the forest parted, revealing a picturesque village snuggled into the mountainside. The charming stone cottages had window boxes filled with vibrant flowers, and the cobbled streets were alive with pedestrians and horseback riders. There wasn't a car in sight.

We came to a stop in a bustling town square, where a fountain took center stage. The smell of freshly brewed coffee filled the air, and shops painted in shades of blue, yellow, and red lined the perimeter. As I took it all in, a comforting feeling washed over me. It was as though I had been away for a long time and was finally coming home.

We disembarked and CJ wasted no time in leading me into a boutique clothing store with a variety of sundresses in the window. I'd never been one for dresses, lace, or heels, always preferring the comfort of jeans and T-shirts, but CJ was very persuasive, and I left the store with a paper bag filled with clothes.

We spent the next few hours wandering the winding lanes, adding to our growing list of purchases. Among my finds were toiletries, a SIM card and phone charger, and a well-loved copy of *A World of Difference—Exploring the Cultural and Social Divide Between Humans and Demons*, which I'd discovered in a charming bookstore crammed with exciting reads. To my relief, my student card seemed to have no spending limit.

After a long afternoon of shopping, we sank into the comfort of a bar with dark wood beams and well-worn chairs. It smelled of mulled wine, and classical piano music played in the background. Outside, the valleys were hidden beneath a sea of drifting clouds.

"I'm as knackered as a shagged-out whippet," CJ said, letting her bags fall beside her chair.

I collapsed into the seat by the window, feet throbbing. "You really have a way with words."

"Tell that to Mrs. Berthal, my old English teacher." She waved the server over. "Three tequilas and three lagers," she ordered before the man opened his mouth.

"CJ!" I said. "Eben's only sixteen."

"I'm a really good drinker," Eben said quickly. "I practiced a lot on Noverna. It helped me to make friends and fit in."

"We're already your friends," I said. "You don't need to drink to fit in with us."

He unwrapped a candy from his bag. "I know. But there are no drinking restrictions on Cronix. I would like a drink, please."

The beer was heaven on my feet, easing the ache from all the walking. I plugged my phone into the nearest outlet and sank deeper into the comfortable chair. As the evening wore on, the bar filled with familiar faces, many of them students I recognized from the Choosing. The setting sun cast a warm glow over the mountains, and a cool breeze blew in. The atmosphere turned lively.

I finished the last of what was perhaps my fifth beer, then collected my phone. "I'm off to the ladies'."

"Don't forget to wash your hands," CJ said, not looking up from her thumb wrestle with Eben.

I waved her away and pushed through the tight press to the bathroom. At the sink, I spent a minute adding my new SIM card to the slot in my phone. It buzzed to life as dozens of messages flooded in, all from Dustin and Georgie. Reading the first few, I knew they would all be the same:

Where are you?

Did you hook up?

Dustin's wrangled you a snake if you're interested.

Do you hate us? What did we do wrong?

I replied, assuring them I was fine. That I needed a break from everything for a while, and I'd be back in about a week. I wanted to call them and fill them in on everything, but who would believe it? I hardly did.

As I headed back to our table, I spotted Aran across the room and found myself filled with a rush of warmth He looked damn fine in a tight white tee—not that I'd seen him look anything other than perfect. I brushed a strand of hair behind my ear and glanced down at my new outfit—snug black jeans with a flowy white top, not a drop of blood to be seen. If there was ever a time I should talk to him, it was now. Not that anything romantic was in the cards—he was in a relationship, and my life was complicated enough—but harmless flirting never hurt anyone.

I took a deep breath to steady my nerves and made my way toward him, but then I noticed he wasn't alone. I stopped halfway across the room as I recognized Raphael's leader—a pretty blond with perfect heart-shaped lips. They were in the middle of what looked like a hushed yet intense argument, her eyes slits of anger as she jabbed at his chest. Aran glanced over his shoulder as though worried about being overheard.

I looked around, unsure of what to do. It didn't seem like a conversation I wanted to tangle myself up in, but a nagging curiosity prodded at my mind. Against my better judgment, I slipped behind a stone pillar and peered around its edge. Growing up with Georgie, I'd become all too familiar with the telltale signs of a cheating partner. Aran's behavior was suspicious, but could he really betray Sophia like that? He'd all but told me he loved her. The thought of him being the same as every other scumbag was too much to think about.

Aran leaned in and said something I couldn't catch over the bar noise, and she laughed bitterly. I did not need to see any more. I pivoted on my heel, planning on making a quick exit, but collided with something solid. The sound of glass shattering filled my ears as a tray of drinks tumbled to the floor.

I froze, wide-eyed, taking in the scene. The mess of spilled drinks and broken glass. The hushed silence that followed. The gazes snapping in my direction.

The server I had bumped into hissed and dropped to her knees to clean up. "You silly girl!" she fumed. "Mind where you're going!"

"Oh, heck—I'm so sorry!" I squatted to help. "I didn't see you there."

"It's hard to see something when you're busy spying."

My cheeks burned as I picked up a piece of glass. "It wasn't like that—"

"Alina?" came a voice behind me. I groaned as Aran knelt, gently taking my hand. "You're bleeding."

A bead of blood ran between my fingers. I hadn't felt the cut. "Just a scratch, nothing to worry about."

He glanced at the people surrounding us. "What happened? Did someone bump into you?"

The server huffed, straightening with the tray in hand. She cast a seething glance my way. "She was spying on you from behind the column and didn't bother to look when she took off."

I glowered at her, wishing I had bumped into her harder.

Aran released my hand, his expression shifting from concern to confusion. "You were snooping?"

"No, it wasn't like that," I stammered. "It was an accident. I mean, well, at first—"

His face tightened. "Is this how you go about things in Louisiana?"

"No, you don't understand . . ."

But the look he shot at me made me shrink back.

"Let me give you some advice," he said coldly as he stood. "If you want to survive here, in this academy, in this world, you better learn how to keep your nose out of other people's business." He turned to leave but stopped. "And for extra credit, I suggest you forget what you saw here today. Information is dangerous in the wrong hands." He stormed off.

Chapter Twelve

A wave of heat crashed over my cheeks as I picked myself up and weaved through the crowd back toward our table. How could Aran treat me like that? I wiped my hand across my eyes in a stupid attempt to hold back tears. I was right about him all along. He was just another player. Another stupid jerk who didn't care about anyone but himself.

I sank into my seat and pressed a napkin against my cut hand. Eben, with his nose buried in a pack of candy stickers, didn't look up.

"Where's CJ?" I asked, trying to keep my voice even but failing.

"She went to give him a piece of her mind, but I don't think it is going well."

"Give who a piece of her mind . . ." I trailed off as I spotted her and Morgan against a nearby wall. CJ had her finger tracing over his chest, while he, smirking, twirled her curly hair around his finger.

"Looks like she wants to give him more than her mind," I grumbled, slumping lower.

Eben glanced up briefly. "Is something bothering you, Alina?"

"Oh, no—I'm just being silly. It's nothing."

"I've seen my mother cry before. She does it for nothing sometimes, too." He shuffled through his pile of stickers and offered one to me. "Do you want my platinum Neron sticker? It is the best one I have. It makes me smile and may make you smile as well."

Oh, Eben. If more men had half the heart that he did, the world would be a better place. I took the sticker. "Thanks. You're too good to me. Do you think this Neron can help me with my problems?"

"Maybe," he said thoughtfully. "He is powerful. What problems are you facing?"

Where to start? In the end, I sighed and shook my head. "Heaven knows. Sometimes, I feel like I'm stuck in a staring contest with a statue, and the second I blink, I'll lose and my life will end."

"I wouldn't recommend engaging in such a game," he said seriously. "Statues are likely to win almost every time."

"You're telling me." I turned the sticker over in my hands. "It's not just about statues, honestly. Can I tell you a secret?"

"I am good at keeping secrets."

"I think I'm different from everyone else here. It's like I have some beast living inside me, constantly fighting to drag me down. Crazy, huh?"

He resumed his search through his collection of stickers almost franticly. "No. No one should experience what you're going through. It's not normal." He selected a round sticker of a figure named Raven Cross and placed it on his shirt. "And you're not."

"Not what?"

"Crazy. No one should feel like you. It's not nice. But I have."

His words took a moment to penetrate. "You've felt like me?" I asked, almost desperately.

He nodded. The noise in the bar seemed to dim.

My chest tightened. "How did you stop it?"

"I was like you," he said, stickers tumbling from his grip. "I was special. They told me I couldn't stay special because it wasn't safe for me. I wasn't strong enough to be special." He spoke faster with each word, and I found it hard to keep up. "I had two powers. I was a baby of Aeria and Terra, but they were fighting inside me, and it hurt. All the time, it hurt. They said I would die if I didn't remove a part of my soul. I did not want to die. That is my secret."

His confession floored me. I wasn't alone in this fight—Eben had faced the same struggle. And he had beaten his demons. That meant I could, too.

"How did you do it? How did you fix it?"

He rocked back and forth, drawing curious glances from the surrounding tables. "It is dangerous. Very dangerous. It almost killed me. I don't think you should do it."

"I have no other choice. Eben, look at me. I need to do this—I . . . I think I'm going insane."

"If they catch you doing it, they will expel you from the academy. Astaroth wants demons to have more powers. They don't understand. They don't understand the danger. And you may lose all your power."

All my power? I'd sacrifice it in a heartbeat to be rid of Machina. "I don't care. I don't need it. I want to be normal again. You said you would have died if you didn't remove one power, right? What happens if I do nothing?"

A look of fear fell over him. "You are stronger than me. You wouldn't die."

"What would happen, Eben?"

He grimaced and pulled away. "Your mind would shatter."

I stared, unmoving. "How do I remove part of my soul?"

"No, no, no. It's dangerous—"

"I don't care. Can you do it for me? Sweet Eben, will you help?"

He didn't answer.

"Eben?"

His gaze drifted to me. "Exorcisms are dangerous and illegal. We could both be killed." With trembling hands, he gathered his stickers and arranged them in a pile.

"Eben?"

"I will help because you are my best friend. But it will not be easy. I don't want you to die."

Chapter Thirteen

The bar, which only moments earlier felt lively and exciting, now pressed in on me in a suffocating squeeze. I needed space to process what Eben had said. If he could cure me, make me whole again and put an end to this nightmare, then I had to take that chance regardless of the risk.

Eben placed his stickers into his pocket. "This must be our secret, and no one else can know. Not even Christina."

"You mean I can't publicize my descent into madness?" I asked. "It will be tough, but I'm sure I'll manage."

The speakers blared a new song. I sighed, no longer in the mood to drink. "I'm going to leave. Will I see you tomorrow?"

He stood. "I will come. The tequila here makes my toes feel funny."

"You and me both," I said, grateful for his company. I still felt wildly out of place at the academy, and though Eben was new too, at least he knew where everything was and how things worked. As weird as it sounded, he had already become my safety blanket. A sixteen-year-old kid was my comfort.

We collected our belongings and my gaze fell on CJ. She was still on Morgan's lap, her laughter filling the air as she pinched his chin. Aran had joined their table, his gaze locked on his drink. The last thing I wanted was to go over there, but I needed to let CJ know I was leaving. I sucked it up and, keeping my eyes locked on CJ, made my way through the crowd.

"Babes!" she cried when she saw me. "You've got to see this—Hudson is proper mortal drunk and can't tell his toes from his tits!"

The guy named Hudson, the same idiot who told me at the Choosing to do Château Michael a favor and go back to Earth, was chewing fries like a cow put to pasture. "Ain't that a hoot," I said unenthusiastically. "We're going home for the night. It's been a long day."

"Already?" CJ said. "Stay for one more?"

"I'm beat. I'm going to grab some supper and hit the bed."

She disentangled herself from Morgan and stood. "Okay, just let me grab my bags—"

Everyone at the table groaned.

Morgan glared at me. "Come on, double demon. Stick with us. You're a hot commodity now, so start acting like it."

"Let her go," Aran said, and despite myself I looked his way. His expression was cold and hard. "It's already too crowded here."

I turned back to CJ, trying not to let my hurt show. How could someone who'd been so wonderful turn into such a jerk? Yeah, I get that I may have been trying to eavesdrop, but still . . .

"You stay," I told CJ. "Eben's taking me home."

"You sure?"

"Positive. I'll see you when you get back."

The night air outside was a welcome relief. We ambled to the main square, where couples strolled hand in hand beneath the golden glow of the lamplights. Eben buried his nose in his stickers once more as we waited for the bus. The line was significantly shorter, and when we climbed to the top level, only a few others joined us, most preferring the warmth inside.

We sat in silence for most of the trip, my mind spinning with excitement and dread at what we were about to do. How would it feel to purge myself of Machina? And if things didn't go as planned, who would show up to my funeral?

I edged closer to Eben. "When do we start?" I asked, glancing back at the group of guys behind us.

"Start what?"

"The exorcism." My throat tightened around the word. "When do we get rid of this thing inside me?"

He pulled out a round candy and read the wrapper. "It will take a long time to organize. I need to find the correct book, and the candles, and the location."

"But . . . Astaroth will have those things, right?"

He pushed his glasses up his nose. "Astaroth won't have everything we need. Exorcisms are illegal, and so these things will be hard to find."

"Son of a biscuit," I cursed, then took a breath to calm myself. "Okay, so you need to find these things. How long will it take?"

"It will take a week or two. Maybe longer."

"Heck!"

His feet tapped.

"Oh, Eben, I'm sorry. I'm just stressed out." I moved to grab his hand but caught myself, not wanting to make him uncomfortable. "It's just that everything feels so messed up right now."

"That's alright. My father used to lose his temper, too." He rifled through his bag and offered me a candy. "This one is caramel and ice cream and lasts an entire hour."

I took it, turning it between my fingers. "Thanks. I'll save this for after supper." I smiled, hoping to lighten the mood.

His feet stopped their tapping, and he looked at me with a serious expression that was rare for him. "Maybe it is a good thing the exorcism will take time to prepare. My mother says good things take time, and great things take longer. Maybe you will learn to control this other part of you. We might not need to do an exorcism at all."

"Machina is uncontrollable," I said firmly. "She'll destroy me if I don't do something. That's why I need you."

We reached the library, the bus hissing as it opened the door. Students dispersed in every direction.

"I'm going inside," Eben said, looking up at the rose-shaped building. "They may have a new copy of the *Underworld Gazette*, which is very good and sometimes funny. Will you be alright getting back to Michael by yourself?"

Under normal circumstances, I would've leaped at the opportunity to explore any library, let alone a library for demons. But the emotional roller coaster of the day was just too much. "I'll be just fine. Thanks, Eben. For everything. I'm glad we're friends."

His fingers twitched and his stickers slipped to the ground. He bent and picked them up. "I like you a lot, Alina. You are not what I expected. Keep fighting. I do not want you to get hurt. They are after you." He hurried into the brightly lit building.

I ambled to the cafeteria. *They are after us all, Eben. Even you.* It was funny how, even though I had no real idea who or what the Reavers were, each time I heard them mentioned, my fear grew deeper, and it was all I could do not to shudder.

I grabbed a take-out box of vegetable lasagna and a bag of chocolate éclairs, then wandered back to my cabin. The forest was beautiful at night, with the sound of crickets chirping and the rush of water from the nearby river. The smell of pine and wildflowers filled the air, soothing the aches of a long day from my bones. I arrived at my cabin and found it empty, which was perfect.

I ran a bath and lit a candle, enjoying the silence as I ate my supper and gazed out the window at the moonlit mountain ranges in the distance. The warm water leeched away some of my worries, the bubbles easing my stress.

It was a countdown now. Weeks was all that remained for Machina and me to coexist. There could be no compromise; it was a battle with only one survivor.

One way or another, the ongoing struggle within me would soon end. Our fates would be unlinked—forever.

The roar of a dragon jolted me awake the following morning. My heart pounded a frantic rhythm, eyes snapping open. As I emerged from the fog of sleep, I recognized the sound and slumped back down with a groan. Amber, a girl in the next bunk, urgently needed nasal surgery.

Despite the abrupt wake-up and the ungodly hour of six in the morning, a strange sense of rejuvenation coursed through me. It felt as though a weight had been lifted, leaving me free for the first time in memory.

I had explored the academy's website on my phone last night. My first Innate Abilities class was at nine. On a Sunday. What were these demons thinking? That wouldn't fly back home. Luckily, this was the only weekend when classes were scheduled.

I climbed out of bed. CJ looked like Sleeping Beauty again. If, of course, Sleeping Beauty smelled like she'd passed out from tequila. Careful not to wake her, I freshened up, placed a bottle of water next to her pillow and left the cabin.

The firepit smoldered in the mist that blanketed the grounds, and though the air was crisp, it was not uncomfortably cold. A stunning sunrise bathed the valley in golden light.

As I bounded along the river path, the world seemed to shine with a newfound brightness. The birdsong was sweeter, and the trees had painted themselves extra hues of green and orange. I soon passed the bridge and stopped at the pebbly edge of the lake. The mirrorlike surface sparkled with the sun's reflection. A timber bar was perched farther around the beach; it looked more like a charming shanty than anything. Its most unique feature was a winding water slide that started from the rooftop and ended in the water. This must be the so-called Shack everyone mentioned.

A breeze whisked away the lingering mist that hovered over the lake, unveiling a château isolated on an island in the middle. Squinting, I read a sign naming it *Château Uriel*. A fleeting curiosity about how students accessed the island crossed my mind, but my attention was soon returned to my path.

A tempting spread of international delicacies greeted me for breakfast in the cafeteria. From the classic cereal to the pho and huevos rancheros, there was something for everyone. I loaded my plate with waffles and strawberries and a dollop of whipped cream, then sat outside to soak up the morning sun and watch as the lawns slowly came alive with students.

I finished earlier than expected and decided to explore the academy's library. The prospect of discovering the mysteries of a demon world sent a thrilling pulse through me. If I banished Machina and was expelled, at least I would walk away armed with some valuable knowledge.

Nothing could have prepared me for the breathtaking sight that awaited me. The walls, made entirely of glass, were shaped like the petals of a blooming rose, creating the illusion that I walked into the heart of a flower. The high-vaulted ceiling curved in elegant bends, allowing natural light to flood the room and illuminate the rows upon rows of bookshelves that reached up to the sky. It was like stargazing from the depths of a well.

I twirled, absorbing it all in awed silence. The air was heavy with the smell of aged books, and there was a hint of sandalwood from candles burning nearby.

"I could get lost in here," I whispered.

"Unlikely," came a voice from behind me.

I spun to find an elderly lady watching me with a kindly smile. She wore a pink cardigan and had an ink smudge below her lip.

"There are plenty of exit signs," she said.

"Oh, I meant—"

Her smile deepened. "I know what you meant. I feel the same way every time I step foot in here. I'm Amelia, the librarian." She placed her bundle of books on a nearby bench. "I love watching new students experience this place for the first time. Seeing others find joy in it is deeply fulfilling."

"I can see why." My eyes drifted among the rows of bookcases. "We have nothing like this where I'm from. I don't even know where to start."

"A wonderful problem to have. May I suggest the section on demonology? It seems a topic of interest among our students, and I believe you'll find it quite enlightening." She gestured to a row of bookcases in the back corner. "Or, if you've a mind for fiction, you'll find both human and demon novels on floors five and six. I highly recommend exploring the books written by our talented demon authors, especially their take on romance. It adds a whole new dimension to the genre. If you're interested in ancient texts and grimoires, they can be found on the top floor."

I laughed helplessly, overwhelmed by the options. "Well, that doesn't simplify things."

Amelia's eyes shone with delight. "Finding your book is only half the battle; the other half is deciding where to read it. If you're after fresh air, we have outdoor terraces on every level, with views of the surrounding mountains. For those who prefer a quiet space, we have dedicated rooms on the second and third floors. And if you're looking for a cozy nook to curl up in, the lower levels have a range of chambers to cater to your every need. I must confess, basement levels one, two, and three are my personal favorites. They have fireplaces to warm you on chilly days and, of course, freshly brewed coffee to keep you alert during those late-night study sessions."

I pulled my gaze from the millions of books and shrugged. "I suppose I'll try them all."

"That's the spirit," she said. "Call if you need me. Just not too loud. Silence, remember." She gathered her books and disappeared into a narrow opening between towering shelves.

After reading a few signs and finding the stairwell that was hidden inside a large grandfather clock, I climbed to the second floor. I was in the history and lore section, about to pull out a book titled *The Great Divide—The Separation of Cronix and Earth*, when a conversation drifting through the aisles caught my attention.

"I'm telling you, she was really nice," a boy's voice insisted.

"I call bullturd," came a girl's reply. "Nobody who has that much power can be nice. Seriously! I bet it's gone straight to her head."

"You're wrong! She smiled at me during the Choosing, and, well . . . and I even think she winked."

I froze as I realized they were talking about me. In a slight panic, I glanced around for a place to hide, but there was no time. I grabbed the nearest book and lifted it to shield my face.

The girl snorted. "Winked? She probably had something in her eye—Oh."

Their footsteps stopped behind me. I cringed, wishing I could just disappear already.

"What's up? Why'd you stop?" the boy asked. There was a second's pause. *"Oh!"*

I put on my best casual smile and turned. The girl's purple pigtails framed a face that was caught in horror. She blinked, then readjusted the mound of books she carried, forcing a look of pleasant surprise.

"Hello," she said, cheeks reddening.

"Hello," said a boy I recognized from the Choosing. He had worn the yellow Pokémon shirt.

"Hey," I said awkwardly. "I didn't hear you coming."

"We're sneaky sometimes," she said with fake cheerfulness. "You're a fledgling, right?"

"As new as morning dew."

"That's cool," she said. "We're newbies, too. I'm Anya and this is Oliver."

"We've already met," I said to Oliver. "Congratulations on your selection."

He rubbed his neck. "Yeah, I was just glad to not be last, you know?" His mouth dropped open. "Not that being last is bad or anything!"

I shrugged. "No use crying over spilled gravy. What are you up to?"

"Exploring," said Anya. "Have you been to the farm yet? I mean, OMG, the animals here are ridiculously adorable. And the greenhouse? Some of the plants smoke like they're on fire, if you can believe it. Honestly, Astaroth is a wonder. There are *so* many places to see." Her words tumbled out rapidly as if she were racing against the clock to get it all out.

"We're heading to the terrace for a bit before class," Oliver said. "Want to join?"

I checked the time on my phone. I still had a good forty minutes. "Sure. I want to hear all about Gabriel."

The view from the terrace was spectacular; every nook of the sprawling grounds was in sight. Anya, however, seemed oblivious to the stunning view as she dumped her books onto a table, collapsing into a chair. "Six years to read all these?" she lamented. "It's like the academy expects me to sprout extra heads."

"Who said you'll last six years?" Oliver said. "You'll probably get kicked out way before then."

She rolled her eyes. "Keep dreaming."

Even though they were as different as night and day, they seemed like they would make an adorable couple.

"So," I said, leaning in. "How's Gabriel?"

"Incredible!" Oliver said, brushing his sandy hair from his face. "The château is seriously enormous and has these hidden rooms and secrets *everywhere*. And you won't believe it—they have a games room with every console you can imagine! It's a dream come true."

Anya couldn't contain her exasperation. "It will be the end of his social life. He spent the last two nights glued to the screen with his other nerdy friends. I saw one of them pop a pimple at the dinner table the other day. It was so *gross*. I told Oliver he needs to meet normal people, but he won't listen."

"My friends are normal. Just a different normal than you."

"Can't you hang out with the cool sort of normal people?"

"You mean the ones who party *all* night?" he asked. "Alina, it's so loud, I can't sleep. I think our château is full of alcoholics. No, seriously. I have to go for a walk through the caves just to find somewhere quiet—"

Anya clamped a hand over his mouth. "Zip it! You know we aren't allowed to talk about the château."

He pulled her hand away, a playful smirk tugging at the corners of his mouth. "Technically, the location of Château Gabriel is supposed to be a secret, but I bet there's a bunch of books in here that practically have arrows pointing to it."

"That's not the point," Anya said. "They're testing us and will string us up to the aqueducts if we fail."

Oliver's smile widened. "Now, who's giving away secrets?"

Anya slapped a hand over her own mouth. "Please don't repeat that to anyone."

"I won't tell a soul," I said, liking these two more and more.

"Anyway," Oliver said. "How's it going with being a double demon? Must be fun."

I sank a little in my chair, hardly wanting to talk about that. "*Fun*'s not exactly the term I'd have chosen. It's more nerve-racking than anything else. Everyone has such high expectations of me, like they want me to pull a rabbit out of a hat, but all I've got is a silly little visor."

Oliver's face turned a shade redder. "I think you'd look good in any hat."

Anya looked at him the same way one might look at a dog chasing his own tail. "He's got a crush the size of this library, and about as subtle, too."

"Anya!" he shot at her. "That's not true!"

A genuine smile broke through my worry at the amusing exchange. "Oh Oliver, I appreciate the compliment, really. Thank you." Hoping to set him at ease, I changed the topic by grabbing one of Anya's heavy books, called

The Gate Key. "A bit of light reading, huh?" I flicked through the pages that were scans of handwritten notes and sketches.

"Fascinating, isn't it?" she said. "Did you know that any demon who was born on a demon world can no longer travel to Earth?"

I nodded. "Yeah, we heard something about that yesterday. But what's this key thing about?" I examined the pages closer.

"It's the key to reopen the Shadowgates to Earth. It's terribly exciting—"

"More like terrifying," said Oliver with a shudder. "If those nutters on Noverna or Zephtura reach Earth, then it's over for everyone we know back home."

"They're not *all* bad," I said, thinking of Eben. "I know someone from Noverna, and he doesn't have a nasty bone in his body."

They stared at me.

"You mean he doesn't have any stabby-slashy vibes?" Anya asked, miming someone with a knife.

"No, he's just like us."

They exchanged a look.

"Guess I need to do more research, then," she said eventually. "I suppose it's possible they aren't all bloodthirsty monsters."

I flicked through a few more pages, trying to rationalize my response. I'd only known Eben for one day, and already I was rushing to his defense. "Where are they keeping this key?" I asked. "Surely, it's under maximum security?"

"No one knows," Anya said. "Some don't even know the gates can be reopened. Personally, I think it's for the best. Your friend might not be that bad, but from what I've read, the Reavers are a pack of savages who wear the bones of their victims as battle armor."

"Can't we talk about something else?" asked Oliver, shuddering. "This freaks me out."

I closed the book and set it back on the pile. "Agreed. What class do you have first?"

"Innate Abilities," said Anya. "I hope they teach invisibility—how cool would it be to sit in a library and read completely undisturbed?"

Oliver stared at her in disgust. "You'd waste invisibility on *reading*?"

"And what would you use it for? Sneaking into the games room at night?"

Oliver opened his mouth to argue but shut it again with a shrug. Anya rolled her eyes. "Boys. Anyway, what have you got?"

"Innate Abilities, too," I said.

"We must be doing it together!" cried Anya. "Sweet!"

Chapter Fourteen

After we left the library, Oliver, Anya, and I hurried through the open-air passageways and joined a group of students waiting outside classroom B-seven. Eben met us under a lemon tree, his shirt now covered in stickers. He looked me in the eye for the briefest moment and smiled before dropping his gaze.

"Good morning," I said cheerfully. "I love your stickers."

"And good morning to you, too, Alina. Yes, they are quite nice, aren't they?"

Arms hugged around my waist from behind. I spun out of the hold and found CJ beaming at me, looking all serene like she'd arrived straight from a meditation retreat.

"Good morning, babes," she said brightly. "Aren't you looking tasty in your new outfit?"

"Jeans and a shirt? I wouldn't exactly describe it as tasty."

"Taste is in the eye of the beholder." Her gaze landed on Anya. "I *love* your hair. What color is that?"

Anya, seeming surprised that someone like CJ was speaking to her, took a moment to answer. "L-lavender."

"It's wonderful on you. Keep rocking it." Her gaze wandered over my shoulder and her eyes widened. "Who's this tall drink of water?"

A middle-aged man strode through the crowd, a well-worn satchel in his grip. His spectacled face was ruggedly handsome, and his tweed jacket gave him a scholarly, yet adventurous look.

He reached the door and turned to us with a smile. "Good morning, ladies and gentlemen." His British accent was smooth and comforting. "Please, make your way inside."

Unlike the Sorting class, there was a notable scramble for the front seats, leaving us to fill the spots at the back. The professor entered last, placing his satchel on the desk. He clasped his hands together and waited for the chatter to die down. Most conversations dwindled, but a cluster of boys remained engrossed in their discussion.

"Quieten down, please," he said after a moment.

The group either didn't notice or didn't care.

Clearing his throat, he lifted one hand, palm upturned. With a pinching motion of his fingers to his thumb, the chatter ceased abruptly. Then, like something from a Pinocchio film, the group sprung to their feet and bounded down the stairs, arms swaying lifelessly and heads lolling.

"He's controlling them," breathed Oliver. "Wicked!"

When they reached the floor, they bowed deeply and, in pairs, glided around the room, performing one of the most hilarious waltzes I'd ever seen. Everyone burst into laughter as they spun and dipped, their faces void of comprehension.

The professor's eyes crinkled with amusement as one of his fingers tapped along to a rhythm only he could hear. After a minute, it concluded, and the four boys, snapping out of their trance, looked at each other in bewilderment. They hastily disentangled their hands, turning to face the rest of us, their cheeks reddening.

"Gentlemen, thank you for the exquisite demonstration of what might be my most cherished ballroom dance. Now, if you would be so kind as to return to your seats, we can begin our lesson."

They hurried up the stairs and slumped low in their spots.

When the professor spoke once more, the room was dead silent. "Welcome to your inaugural Innate Abilities class. I am Professor Harper Conrad, and while I'm delighted to instruct you in this fascinating subject, I must caution you: many may find this subject thrilling, but others will find it immensely challenging. Unlike Demon Kinesis, where particular abilities are determined by one's birthright, everyone here possesses the same innate skill set, though mastery will differ significantly, depending on your natural aptitude." His blue eyes swept across the classroom, briefly lingering on mine. "Would anyone like to venture a guess at some of the Innate Abilities?"

For a moment, no one volunteered. Then, unexpectedly, Oliver hesitantly raised his hand.

"Yes?" asked Harper.

"Making people dance?"

Laughter filled the room again, and Oliver sank into his seat.

"Precisely!" cried Harper. "Mind control is indeed an Innate Ability. What's your name?"

"O-Oliver."

"Well done, Oliver. Now, mind control is both the simplest and most complex of abilities for demons. Manipulating a human mind is relatively easy, but attempting to control a demon's mind demands a much higher level of expertise. Demons can resist, so success hinges on the skill of both parties involved." He leaned over the computer on his desk and tapped the keyboard. A projector screen unfurled from the ceiling as the lights dimmed, and a presentation slide glowed to life.

He skipped the first slides before resting on one with an extensive table, divided into three columns—beginner, intermediate, advanced.

"Heavens," I gasped, skimming it. Demons were capable of far more than flinging hurricanes from their fingers. The list had everything from specter sight, invisibility, gaseous flight, telepathy, healing, illusions, and much more.

"Don't be daunted by the magnitude of the abilities that lie within you," Harper said. "Many of these are advanced skills that won't be taught at the academy but will require specialized training and permits to wield. For now, all you need to concentrate on is the art of mind reading." He navigated to the next slide, displaying a breakdown of the class into groups of four. "This is a practical lesson, so please find an empty space and settle into your groups."

We did as we were told, and I was happy to see that I was in a group with Oliver.

"Thank God," he whispered as we watched Anya sit beside Eben across the room. "I thought I was going to be stuck with her."

"I thought you two were cute together," I said.

His face screwed up. "As if! We're just friends. She doesn't stop talking."

Kaitlyn from Gabriel and Kirra from my dorm joined us. Once everyone had settled, Harper called his instructions.

"Pair up within your group . . . One will be the reader, the other the book . . . Gaze into each other's eyes. Breathe in . . . and out. Do not look away, but search for more, for meaning. Breathe in . . . and out. Immerse yourself into their world, their depths, their soul. Breathe in . . . and out . . ."

I struggled not to laugh as Oliver's face contorted with concentration. I had a little brother at my second foster home. He had large ears and an easy smile. Oliver reminded me so much of him.

"Clear your mind of all thoughts . . . Thoughts are barriers. Breathe in . . . and out. Excellent. Now, maintaining eye contact, focus on your partner's aura . . . sense a connection, the delicate strands of shared energy . . ."

As I peered into Oliver's eyes, a small part of my mind quivered, like a fly caught in a web. It vibrated insistently, though it was somewhat subdued. A bead of sweat trickled down Oliver's brow, and with a start, I realized those vibrations were his attempts to gain access. I found it was easy to push back, to deny him, but he was trying so dang hard that it was difficult to watch. I relaxed and allowed the fly to buzz in. A voice echoed through my thoughts. It was Oliver's, but he was supposed to be reading my mind, not the other way around.

This is so embarrassing. Why can't I do it? She's going to think I'm so lame. Probably the only one in class who can't . . . huh?

Oliver's mouth dropped open, and he recoiled in surprise. The fly in my head vanished instantly.

"I did it!" he exclaimed, staring at me with wonder. "I was in your head!"

I grinned widely. "You're a lot stronger than you look. How many times have you done that before?"

"Never," he said, sitting straighter. "That was my first time, I swear!"

"Well, I'm impressed. But next time, you might want to close off your thoughts so I can't hear them."

When it was my turn to practice, I quickly established a connection with him. I followed the threads of energy and encountered the delicate barrier of his consciousness. I pressed against it and broke through. A torrent of disorienting thoughts, emotions, and images assailed my mind. However, once I anchored myself within him, I sifted through them. Amid the clutter, a voice, clearer than the rest, sounded.

She's so beautiful . . . If only I were her age, maybe I'd have a chance . . . Maybe she'd take me seriously . . . Is this love? Or have I just had too much sugar again? Note to self: ease up on the Pop-Tarts . . . Wait—Alina?

Oliver snapped his eyes closed and yanked away, severing the connection between us. I was catapulted from his thoughts and slung back into my body.

After I steadied myself, I was met with his wide, petrified eyes. "I—I didn't mean it," he stammered. "I was just messing around. I knew you were listening, so I thought it would be funny to make you think I, you know, liked you . . . in that way."

With a soft sigh, I leaned forwards, smiling gently as heat rose to my cheeks. "Oliver, it's okay," I assured him. "I already love you as a brother too."

It took a moment, but eventually, a hesitant smile crossed his face. "Oh, right. Yeah, that's exactly what I meant. You're like a sister to me. Yay for siblings."

A shadow loomed over us before it could get any more awkward.

"Alina Rose?" Harper said.

"That's me."

"Would you accompany me outside for a brief discussion?"

My lips parted. What could I have possibly done wrong now? Wasn't it bad enough that I had been singled out yesterday? "Sure."

I trailed him out of the classroom. After closing the door, his expression turned grave. "You, my dear, are in for a spot of hell."

Chapter Fifteen

Harper's penetrating eyes peered over the rim of his glasses, rooting me to the spot. All traces of his earlier cheer had vanished, replaced by an ominous expression.

"Pardon?" I asked. I was in for hell? What did that even mean?

"I would be lying if I said the next few months were going to be easy on you," he said, studying me closely. "It's hard enough discovering your whole life has been a lie, but to learn you have two powers must boggle your mind."

"Bit of an understatement," I admitted. "This isn't exactly how I imagined spending the week."

"How did you imagine it?"

I thought for a moment. "Work, sleep, repeat."

"Is that good or bad?"

I shrugged. "It just is."

His head tilted to the side. "So, you're saying Astaroth is an improvement?"

Could I say that? Sure, I had made some friends, been given a debit card with seemingly endless funds, and even read someone's mind. But the flip side? Well, it turned out my soul had stolen this body, I was involved in some magical war, and the guy I was crushing on not only had a girlfriend but now hated me.

"Yet to be determined," I said.

He gestured for us to stroll along the pathway. "There are some matters we need to address before you settle into academy life. Your situation at Astaroth is unique, and I'm afraid we're not entirely equipped to handle it. As a dual demon, you have an extra ability to master, yet your schedule is already full—"

"I don't mind dropping one of my powers," I said quickly. It was something I'd considered last night. If I only had one power, perhaps everyone would stop thinking I was something more than I was.

"I mind. It would be a terrible sin to allow you to neglect such a gift."

"But nobody else has two abilities—I'd rather be like them."

"You're not like them, Alina. You're much, much more." We reached a garden with a sundial in its center and took a seat on a bench nearby. Birds danced atop the glowing clockface. "How much do you know about the war between demons?"

His change of direction caught me off guard. "Not much. I mean, I know they—the Reavers, right?—want to take over Earth, but they can't because the gates are locked."

"Yes. And do you know how they were locked?"

"Maviir said something about them feasting on Earth until it was a carcass or something, so the gates were locked to stop them from destroying it. But it didn't make much sense to me."

Harper smiled, pulling off his glasses and cleaning them on his shirt. "Well, Professor Shae certainly has a way with words. Earth was once a hub for all demons, rich in the natural resources we all want. However, unlike those from Cronix and Fernyre, the demons from Noverna and Zephtura—the Reavers—indulged in excess, exploiting Earth for all it had without a care for the repercussions. They believed Earth to be theirs by right of power. The demons you heard mention of in the Bible? They are Reavers. In fact, I'd hazard a guess that any malevolent demon you've heard about was a Reaver."

He watched me closely as he spoke, but I struggled to see my part in all of this. "But now they're locked away in their own worlds, right? They can't hurt anyone anymore?"

"For the time being," he agreed. "And it's all thanks to the Radiant Alliance. Have you heard of them?"

I shook my head.

"They were a group of Cronix's and Fernyre's fiercest warriors, assembled to combat the Reavers in a war that spanned a millennium. It came to a head at the beginning of the last century when a strategy to seal the highways to Earth was developed. It was in the shadow of this chaos that the most horrific crimes in human history were hatched."

My chest tightened. "The ripping?"

"The ripping. A technique to bypass the gates and invade Earth once again."

The weight of all those lost souls pressed down on me. Life was hard enough without that sort of guilt feasting on my insides. "I understand this is all terrible, but I'm still not sure what any of it has to do with me."

He took out his pocket watch, opened it, and frowned. "Because the gates won't stay locked forever. The hunt for the key has begun, and armies are amassing. The time for action is upon us, and you, as a dual demon, hold great value to the side you choose. The power to wield two magics has not been seen in my lifetime, but history speaks of the destruction such a wielder can cause. You, Alina, will be a formidable ally to either army seeking the key."

My gaze wandered to the birds perched on the sundial. How could I be so pivotal in a war I barely understood? And why was Harper trying to convince me my powers were super rare? Eben had been a dual demon, so I couldn't be too special. Something didn't add up.

"So, you're unloading all this on me because you think it's going to . . . what? Scare me into joining your army?" I asked.

Laughter bubbled from deep within his chest. "Heavens no. I would never ask such a thing. At least, not yet. You have many years of schooling before you'd even be considered by the Frostfires. No, my dear, I tell you to warn you. Secrets are scarce in the demon world. News of your powers will already be with the Reavers, and it would be irresponsible of me to not prepare you. This is why I can't let you drop one of your abilities. You need to be able to defend yourself when the time comes. And, at risk of sounding a tad dramatic, they *will* come for you."

"I always knew I was destined for fame," I said, tired of hearing about the Reavers. "Good thing we've got a bunch of soldiers just down the road, right?"

"Don't put your trust in the academy's security." He stood and straightened his jacket. "They're not as polished as one might hope of a professional military outfit. Now, enough of all this doom and gloom. Since we've agreed you will not drop an ability, you will attend Aeria Demon Kinesis with Professor Shae, as scheduled, and on Friday evenings, I'll train you in Terre Demon Kinesis. Don't worry, I take pride in my skills, and I'm sure I can get you up to par in no time."

He started back to the classroom.

"Not much time for living, huh?" I said, hurrying to catch up.

"Curse of the gifted. I'll update your planner on the lesson details."

An idea struck me as we reached the door. "Professor Conrad, if there was a way for me to, well, to only have a single power, wouldn't that fix everything? The Reavers wouldn't want me anymore, and I could go back to being sort of normal."

He regarded me curiously. "Pondering impossibilities is less productive than sweeping leaves in a storm."

"But what if it's not? What if I removed part of my soul—say, the Terre part—wouldn't that mean I would no longer be hunted? The Reavers couldn't use me in their army if I were the same as everyone else. You wouldn't have to worry about the key being found."

"My dear, even if there were a way for you to remove half of your soul—which I can assure you, there is not—I would never recommend such a dreadful action. Doing so would be like cutting the eyes from a person because they could both see and sing. Now, Miss Rose, after you . . ." He opened the door for me to enter, ending any debate.

I stepped inside begrudgingly. He'd just lied. I knew there was a way to exorcise half of a soul. Eben had been through it. So, what would a professor gain from lying to me? None of it made sense.

Chapter Sixteen

Despite Harper's warning and the knowledge that the Reavers still had their sights set on me, my first week at Astaroth was enjoyable. Though the classes left me wanting to scream for either joy or frustration, I found myself smiling more than I had in the last few years. I put this down to a healthy mix of making new friends, exploring the perks of being a demon, and knowing that by the end of the month, Machina would be out of my life for good.

While I found my Innate Abilities class a breeze, mastering Aeria was considerably more difficult. The lessons were held at the Perch, a platform overhanging the waterfall higher up the mountain. The location offered a perfect view of the academy below, with mist and spray rising on the air currents. My classmates could manipulate the vapor, but my attempts felt more like a half-drowned rat playing hocus-pocus.

We conducted Demon History classes in the catacombs beneath the academy grounds. I absorbed the information quicker than most, but that was a double-edged sword. By the end of our first session, I could effortlessly recount many instances of demonic influence on twentieth-century politics, but this irritated my classmates who had to flip through the hefty volumes to answer questions.

The glares from my fellow students were nothing compared to the Aran situation. Somehow, in a place as enormous as the academy, Aran was everywhere I turned. If I dipped my toes into the lake for an evening swim, Aran was on the shore, skipping stones. If I curled up with a book in the campus café, there was Aran, nursing a coffee at the next table over. And even on Wednesday, when CJ, Eben, and I had gone to Little Peak to catch a movie, Aran showed up with his crew. Gone was that playful grin that could light up a room. Now, whenever we crossed paths, his smile was replaced by a hard line, like he was constantly biting back words.

A buzz of excitement filled me as Thursday afternoon rolled around, bringing with it Beastiary, the class I'd been looking forward to most. It was held in an outdoor classroom hidden in the woods on the way to the Perch. Benches lined a circular clearing above flowers waving in the breeze. Natural wood enclosures built from interwoven branches were tucked among the trees, and a plump man wearing a vivid orange-and-yellow overcoat greeted us as we arrived.

"Jeans and shirt, *again*?" came an obvious whisper from behind me. "Can't she afford anything nice?"

I didn't need to look to know it belonged to Trishelle. She was Uriel's latest gift to me—a mean-girl apprentice, courtesy of Sophia, intent on making my days at the academy a living nightmare. Her nasty tongue would have been brutal if it weren't so dull.

"Maybe she enjoys looking like a homeless tramp?" said Clara, fledgling enemy number two. Though she was smarter than Trishelle, her squeaky voice took the bite out of her insults. It was like being nipped at by Minnie Mouse.

I stared ahead, trying to ignore them. But, still wet and cold from the Perch, my emotional state wasn't near the fortress I'd hoped it would be. Fortunately, I had a CJ up my dripping sleeve.

"Or maybe"—she rounded on them—"she doesn't need clothing to compensate for a shit personality, unlike you two broke Bettys. Jog on, you wanky prats."

I glanced over my shoulder to see Trishelle and Clara looking like they'd been slapped. Trishelle, finally shutting her mouth, huffed and stormed away.

"Thanks," I muttered. "But you shouldn't have done that. They'll come after you next."

"Let them," CJ said indifferently. "It's been a minute since I've gotten into a good scrap. I'm worried I'm losing my claws." She brushed the hair away from my face. "But, babes, if you let people talk trash about you long enough, you'll start to believe it. You need to stand up for yourself."

Confrontation had never been my thing; I always thought of it like a street rat—best left alone if I didn't want to get bit. "I know, but . . ." I trailed off with a helpless shrug.

She studied me for a moment, then sighed. "Anyway, I didn't do that for you. Those Uriel snobs need to be taken down a peg. Always strutting around like they're better than everyone else, just because they cinched last year's championship."

She had a point. Every Uriel student I'd met had an attitude problem. While I'd hit it off with the Gabriel and Raphael crowds, it seemed like Uriel was a breeding ground for arrogance.

The plump man in the center of the circle cleared his throat, drawing silence over the gathering. "Welcome to your inaugural Beastiary class," he announced with a wide grin, his ginger hair ruffling in the gentle breeze. "I'm Professor Finn Cress, and I'll be guiding you through your fledgling year of Beastiary, which is, in my humble opinion, the most captivating subject Astaroth offers." He clapped his hefty hands together, rubbing them eagerly. "Alright, show of hands—who among you has spotted the elusive shadow faun lurking in these woods?"

His question was met with deafening silence; not a single hand was raised.

"I suppose that's to be expected," he said, somewhat disappointedly. "Let's change that, shall we?" With a gentle blow on his fingertips and a theatrical snap, he conjured a swirl of purple smoke. From within the mist, a tiny black puppy emerged with a pop, causing a ripple of surprised murmurs among the students.

I leaned closer and saw it wasn't a puppy at all. It had the head of an eagle, with sharp, twitching ears; the body of a lion; and delicate wings folded against its black fur. It watched us curiously, then let out a sound that was part cry, part chirp, and entirely adorable.

"Heavens," I whispered, fascinated by the creature.

"You can say that again," CJ said, clinging to my arm.

Even Eben, who'd been meticulously organizing his candy into rows on the bench, paused and pushed his glasses to the bridge of his nose, gaze now fixed on the shadow faun intently.

Finn smiled down at the creature. "This is Billy, a fine example of a young gryphon. Marvelous, isn't he? During your time at Astaroth, you may be presented with a chance to bond with such a magical creature. But allow me to manage your expectations. While all shadow faun bond with demons, not all demons will bond with shadow faun." He walked in a small circle, Billy bounding after him. "Bonding is a mutual choice, a sort of magical agreement, if you will, and shadow faun will only choose a companion they feel is worthy of such an honor. This bond is for life and offers unshakable friendship to the faun and grants the bonded demon a host of magical enhancements."

"When can we bond, then?" asked CJ, who looked ready to leap into the clearing and kidnap Billy.

"You may not attempt to bond until the end of the year," said Finn. "The process, as curious as you understandably are, cannot be rushed."

"Seriously? The whole year?" Clara asked. "So, what's the point? If we can't bond now, isn't this all just . . . I don't know, pointless?"

"Pointless?" Finn repeated, his smile faltering. "The point is to learn before you leap." He shot her a disdainful glance before shifting his attention back to the class. "I have the duration of the year to equip you for a potential bond. The château that triumphs in the championship will have the privilege of first selection. This results in a higher chance of finding a compatible companion." He cleared his throat and smiled again. "Now, perhaps a little show-and-tell will enliven the atmosphere."

The purple smoke billowing from Billy thickened, forming a swirling vortex around Finn's feet. Finn rocketed into the air with a thunderous crack, soaring a hundred feet high and leaving a cloudy trail in his wake.

For a moment, he hung suspended, dark against the blue sky, then, with another thunderclap, he was propelled in a different direction. I jumped to my feet, craning my neck for an unobstructed view through the forest canopy. He crisscrossed above us like a pinball, while Billy watched from the ground. After a minute, Finn landed back in the clearing to enormous applause. He bowed, grinning, his orange hair in disarray.

The only person who seemed less than amazed was Trishelle.

"So what?" she said. "I've seen Aeria demons do the same thing. Only, they don't smoke like a chimney when they do it."

Finn, looking slightly put off, tried to smooth his hair. "Indeed. Aeria demons can manipulate air currents for self-propulsion. But what about Terre? How do they fly without the bonding of a gryphon? Each shadow faun imparts a distinct set of magic enhancers." He snapped his fingers, summoning a black bear, no larger than a koala. As the bear's purple smoke enveloped Finn, he kicked off and slid around the clearing as though it was a frozen lake.

"Take Tess here, for example," he said while gracefully drifting past. "She can eliminate all friction on any surface." He executed a perfect pirouette, arms raising above his head like a ballerina, and finished back in the middle, where he snapped his fingers once again. This time, a chameleon the size of a cat manifested on his shoulder. Its smoke drifted over Finn, who shimmered for a moment before disappearing completely. "Chester can turn anyone, or anything, invisible," his voice echoed eerily from nowhere. "Quite a useful skill to have."

It took all of my self-control to stop me from bolting forward and taking Chester for my own. Having the power to disappear, to dodge all the scrutinizing gazes, the judgment of others—that was a most potent kind of magic.

A sheen of sweat glazed Finn's forehead when he reappeared. "Alright, before we hit the books, a little interaction with these faun should be a nice treat. Please form groups of five."

For the next while, we sat in our groups and waited for Finn to introduce his creatures to us. They were apprehensive and quickly shied away from most students. I didn't have high expectations that our group would be any different.

"Now, remain calm and avoid any sudden movements," Finn said when he reached us, his shadow faun hiding behind his legs. "If they find you likable, they will— *Oh, my!*"

Billy the gryphon darted out from hiding and pounced onto my lap, his tongue licking my nose. For a moment, I was too shocked to react but then I ran my fingers through his soft fur—a sensation like holding a hand out the window of a moving car.

"Extraordinary!" Finn exclaimed, eyes widening in wonder. "Billy is very fond of you—and what do we have here?"

Tess and Chester, following Billy's lead, bounded onto my lap, toppling me over. A burst of laughter bubbled out of me as the creatures' warm bodies pressed against mine.

"Professor Cress," I said, nestling Tess to my cheek. "I believe I'm in love—"

My sentiment was cut short by a seething tide of rage that surged within me. Machina's presence flared in my stomach, clawing its way toward the surface of my mind.

The force of it knocked me back onto my elbows. My muscles locked up as I fought against her, teeth gritting from the effort. It was the worst attack I'd experienced on Cronix.

I pushed back with everything I had, slowing her rise. It took moments that felt like a lifetime, but I eventually locked her back in her prison and secured it with a wall of hatred.

Chester, Tess, and Billy scampered off me as though I'd sprouted ten-inch fangs. They retreated a few steps, then held their ground apprehensively.

I steadied my nerves, drawing deep breaths, and extended a hand toward Billy. He jumped back, nose twitching, then vanished in a puff of purple smoke. Tess and Chester followed.

Finn spluttered, bewildered eyes darting from me to where the shadow faun had disappeared. "Extraordinary," he said. "What did you do?"

"I didn't do anything," I lied, dropping my gaze. Every time something good came into my life, Machina had to show up and ruin the party. The shadow faun had felt her darkness, and like me, despised it.

"Extraordinary," he said again. He clicked his fingers, but they did not return. "Seen nothing like it," he muttered, retreating to the center of the clearing. "Alright, everyone, gather around . . . yes, all of you. We'll be starting our theory work earlier than expected. You'll each find a copy of *From Shadow to Shine—Understanding Shadow Faun and their Powers* in the shed. Please read chapter one."

The class groaned—this time, not just Uriel.

"Good one, *Alina*," muttered a boy named Braxton. "Way to kill the mood."

His words stung, but I couldn't hold it against him. *Nice to meet you, Braxton, here's the real me, Alina Machina, the misfit.* I couldn't meet anyone's eyes as I trudged toward the shed.

CJ caught up with me. "You alright, babe?"

"I'm dandy," I said, kicking a stray pebble.

She watched me for a moment. "What happened back there?"

"Just got a headache, is all."

We spent the rest of the class studying the different shadow faun and their abilities. I tried my best to concentrate on the text, to ignore Uriel's whispered insults, but by the end of the class, my head throbbed, and my focus had frayed to nothing.

"That's all we have time for this afternoon," Finn eventually said, his voice having lost the cheerful quality he'd started with. "Our next lesson is Tuesday morning. Please study the entire first chapter—digital copies are available on the academy's website under *Resources*—and be prepared for a quiz."

As we lined up to return our books, someone jolted into me from behind, knocking my book to the ground.

"Watch where you're going, creep," said a girl who looked like she could bench press a cow. Her friends snickered behind her.

My emotional dam crumbled, and before I knew it, hot tears streamed down my cheeks. I ignored my fallen book and bolted down the woodland trail. I took the mossy steps in a leap and only slowed when I reached the stone bridge that arched over a stream. There, with my back against the cool wall, I let myself splinter.

I was tired of it all—the bullying, the pressure, and Machina. What did I do to deserve any of it? I'd never asked to have my soul ripped out by demons. I'd never ask for Machina. And now, not even shadow faun could bear the sight of me. My life was an instruction manual on failure.

"Alina?"

I wiped away my tears and turned to see Eben standing there, watching me timidly.

"Oh, hi, Eben," I said in a feigned cheerful tone. "Cool class today, wasn't it?"

"Please don't be sad," he said, edging closer. "It's not nice when friends are sad. It makes me sad, too." He rummaged through his pocket and pulled out a wing-shaped candy, offering it to me. "This might help."

I accepted it. "Thank you, Eben. Really, I'll be okay," I said, hoping I sounded more convincing to him than I did to myself.

"I know you will. You're the strongest person I know. Mom says time heals everything."

"She's a smart woman," I said, slumping back against the bridge. "But time is something I don't have. You saw what happened back there—that was Machina. She's getting stronger. I'm . . . I'm afraid I won't be able to hold her off much longer."

He walked past me and crossed the bridge, watching the flowing water.

"When can we do it?" I asked, following. "The exorcism. Have you found what you need?"

He shook his head. "No. It is a lot of stuff we need, and I have not found it all. I do not think I want you to do it. Exorcisms hurt. It could kill you."

I strode in front of him and blocked his path. "I don't have a choice. Please, when can we do it?"

He turned around and started walking back the other way. "Tomorrow night. After everyone is asleep. We can do it tomorrow night."

"No one sleeps on Fridays," I said. "Can't we do it tonight?"

"Professors sleep on Fridays. I need the professors to be asleep."

Chapter Seventeen

After waking up the following morning, it took less than a second for the Beastiary ordeal to replay in my mind.

My insides shriveled at the memory of the looks of terror on the shadow faun. I understood that look. It was the same one that reflected at me in almost every Breaux Bridge mirror.

But one way or another, things were about to change. That night would be a turning point in my life. The exorcism was my one true chance to destroy Machina, this unwanted part of my soul, a task the meds and booze had failed to accomplish. As I swung my legs out of bed, a flicker of nervous excitement tingled through me. I was finally going to be normal.

I paused.

Alternatively, I might die.

It was a grim thought, but I buried it deep down. I had to trust that Eben could do it.

Moody clouds rolled across the sky, blocking out the sun and drenching everything in their path. It wasn't a downpour, just constant, miserable drizzle.

Our umbrellas offered minimal protection against the swirling rain, but despite our soaked clothes, CJ's enthusiasm remained unshakable.

She chatted away, as happy as a songbird, while we walked to our first class—Signs, Symbols, and Wards—which was instructed by Audrey. I'd had nothing to do with Audrey since she'd dumped me in Aran's room, which didn't bother me. She wasn't exactly the warmest person, and if I was being honest, I thought she was terrifying.

As I watched CJ gleefully splashing through the muddy puddles in her ankle booties, a rush of affection filled me, and I realized how little I knew about her. Sure, I knew the basic stuff—she was from Newcastle, had the charm of a seasoned salesperson, and would choose the ideal outfit over punctuality almost every time.

Yet, the most crucial thing I knew was how much I would miss her if I lost my powers and was sent back to Earth. In the brief week we'd known each other, I had grown to love her like a sister. She would fit in perfectly with Georgie and Dustin, and the thought of life without her left me feeling like I was losing part of myself. The better part.

Signs, Symbols, and Wards proved to be fascinating, though demanding. Audrey held a different approach to teaching than the other professors, commanding the room through intimidation. From her ink-covered skin of various demonic sigils to her sharply cut hair, every part of her screamed *danger*. A single look from her could liquefy lungs and sizzle tongues. Unlike Harper, she never used her abilities to maintain discipline. Not once was any student dim enough to make her.

We spent the class immersed in the world of ancient demonic script, and their historical use as a means of protection against possession and influences. It was cool to see how, with just a few powerful symbols, someone could trap and control demons. On the flip side, we learned about the risk of incorrectly drawn symbols, which could lead to disastrous consequences worse than death.

Our day continued with a sleep-inducing Ethics and Morality class, which could be summed up in one sentence: don't be a jerk. Following the lunch break, we plunged into the mysteries of Precognition and Clairvoyance, and finished the day at the Perch for Innate Abilities with Maviir. Maviir, who delighted in the rain from the safety of a shelter, instructed us to stand on the ledge amid the downpour. Our task was to summon an air umbrella to block out the storm. Failure, which I experienced spectacularly, resulted in a thorough drenching.

"You're not focusing," Maviir cheerfully called over the weather. "Breathe and sense the connection."

"I am focusing," I snapped, arms held above my head in a vain attempt to make the wind behave. "The connection's just not there—"

A clap of thunder exploded around us, making me jump. The air crackled with electricity, and then a fork of lightning split the sky above.

"Oh, alright, come back in," Maviir conceded with a sigh. "Can't afford to electrocute another fledgling two years in a row."

"You'll get it next time," CJ comforted me as I joined her under the shelter. She was perfectly dry, her umbrella having been considerably more effective, and existent, than mine.

"Yeah, suppose I will," I said, wringing water from my hair, knowing it was a lie.

She conjured a breeze from her hands to help dry my face. "So, the Shack. You coming or what? A demon DJ from one of the valley cities is coming—she's huge on Cronix."

"I'll see how I feel after Harper's lesson," I said, knowing the chances I'd ever go to the Shack again were slim.

She closed her eyes and sighed at the mention of Harper. "What I'd give to have a one-on-one lesson with that worldy. He's proper lush, like a fresh pint of beer." She opened her eyes and leaned in. "Will you ask him about his stance on professor-student relations for me?"

"Reckon I could," I said with a grin.

When the class ended, we made our way down the muddy hill toward the cafeteria. The storm had escalated into a torrential downpour. Fortunately, CJ shared her magical umbrella, as the human one I had was utterly useless. When we passed the shops, I stepped under the supermarket awning.

"I'll meet you inside," I said. "I need to grab some things."

As she turned to leave, a wave of sadness washed over me. I wouldn't see her after Harper's class. I wanted to tell her how much her friendship meant to me, how I couldn't have survived Astaroth without her. But what could I say without raising suspicion?

"CJ," I called. Rushing forward, I wrapped my arms around her and squeezed. "Thanks. For everything."

She stiffened for a moment, before returning it. "Oh, babes, it was only an umbrella."

"For being kind to me at the Choosing. You didn't have to, and it made all the difference."

She pulled back and held me at arm's length. "Kind? Alina, I should thank you. I didn't have many friends in Newcastle. Well, true friends, that is. The lasses, they had their issues, and the lads saw me as some sort of trophy." She pulled me in for another hug. "Being nice to you is the easiest thing in the world." We stood there for a moment, boots sinking into the lawn as the sky fell around us. Eventually, we separated. "Anyway, enough of this soppy stuff, you'll make my mascara run. I'll see you laters, right?"

I nodded and watched as they hurried toward the cafeteria as a flash of lightning lit the brooding world above.

Passing the Grinning Gargoyle Café, I stepped into the liquor store and bought a flask of vodka and a bottle of soda. I took a few sips of soda, then poured in some vodka and took a long drink, grimacing as I swallowed. It had enough punch to make my liver quiver. I took another sip, knowing I'd need the liquid courage to survive the next few hours.

Before long, the cafeteria clock signaled a quarter to six, and I left for Harper's class on lead feet. As I neared the sundial park, a group of students approached from the other direction. They wore rigid black leather tops that were reinforced with shoulder and elbow pads. The bottoms were sleek, formfitting trousers that clung to their bodies like second skins and were tucked into sturdy boots with chunky soles. Each wore a red-and-green cape secured on their shoulders. I nearly tripped over my own feet at the sight of them. They looked like modern-day gladiators.

As they neared, one of them waved and hurried forward. "Hey, Alina! Where's your leathers? Come try out."

It was Zach, the guy who'd hit on me at the Choosing after-party. Ava was by his side, her eyes drifting down my damp clothes. And behind her . . .

Aran's frosty glare cut me to bits. Though he looked like he'd stepped out of a fairy tale, with his strong jaw and broad figure, I was not in the mood for his crap. I crossed my arms. This was supposed to be my last night—I didn't need some jerk making it worse.

"Alina?" Zach said.

"Oh, sorry." I tore my eyes away from Aran. "Try out? What for?"

"Michael's flag fall team," Ava said. "We're on the squad, remember? Or, at least, we were last year." She fixed Aran with a pointed look, but he didn't seem to notice.

I thought back to what I'd heard about flag fall. "Your sport, right? Like Quidditch?"

Zach snorted. "Not a comparison I'd have used."

"It's more like rugby, but with rhinoceroses," said Ava.

"And poachers," Zach added.

"And a whole lot of trying not to die," finished Ava.

Zach grinned, the large gap between his teeth obvious. "It's great fun! Come and try out—maybe you can take Ava's spot as a Raider."

Ava punched him in the arm.

"Ya'll are sweet for inviting me, but I've got a class," I said. "Maybe next time."

Aran pushed past the others and continued down the walkway. "Come on, we have a lot to get through. No doubt Alina will be there anyway, watching from a distance."

He was such. An. Idiot. For a wild moment, I considered the runes I'd learned earlier that day. But trapping him in a fiery pit would be too kind.

"Please tell me that wasn't sexual tension," said Ava, looking crestfallen. "I've got Zach beat, but who can compete with Aran?"

I glared at Aran as he walked away, cape fluttering behind him. "I'd have more sexual tension with a snapping turtle than with him."

Ava and Zach groaned. "Sexual tension," they said together.

Ava rubbed my back comfortingly. "When it ends in heartbreak and you need a shoulder to cry on, I've been told mine are soft as clouds."

Zach rolled his eyes. "Your shoulders are like cat teeth." He gripped my hand gently. "Anytime you need to talk things through, I'm here for you. Perhaps over a nice Italian dinner."

They trotted after the group, boots thumping heavily. I pulled out the bottle of mixed soda and downed it in one go. *Stupid Aran and his stupid, beautiful head.* Well, I wouldn't have to worry about him for much longer. He, and everything else, could be a distant memory.

I stormed to the classroom and found Harper leaning against the wall, reading a paper. He glanced up when I approached, then stood and folded it with a flick.

"Good evening. Ready to begin your journey into the realm of Terre?"

"Guess so," I muttered. "Not like I have anything else I'd rather be doing on a Friday night."

He wrinkled his nose. "Tough first week?"

It took me a moment to realize I must reek of booze. I nodded.

"I wish I could assure you that things will get easier. Unfortunately, the challenge you face is quite significant. What I will say is, there will come a time when you reflect on these days fondly." He removed his glasses and gazed at me intensely. "However, Alina, I must beg you to eat your troubles rather than drink them in the future. Teaching power to someone who is bloated is far simpler than teaching it to someone who is drunk." With that, he opened the door and stepped inside, leaving me to stare after him.

That tone set the precedence for the entire class. It was difficult to become motivated when I knew anything I learned would likely vanish before dawn. Harper, pacing in frustration, knew my efforts were not up to scratch. As soon as the effects of the vodka took hold, I became even more hopeless at manipulating the sandbox, to where even the smallest grain of sand defied my efforts.

"I find it incredible," Harper said as he shoved away the box, "that you would broach this topic with such careless disregard after the warning I gave you earlier this week. If I were being pursued by the Reavers, I'd do everything possible to safeguard myself. One could be forgiven for thinking you hardly care for your safety at all!" He straightened his jacket, then walked to the door. "We will meet at the same time and location next week. Do try to demonstrate more restraint." Without a farewell, he briskly left the room.

Chapter Eighteen

I sat on the edge of my bed and watched the storm rage outside the window. Rain drummed on the roof, and the wind howled through the surrounding trees. Crashes of thunder boomed in the distance, and blinding lightning lit the glass.

Eben had said he'd text me when he was ready, but my phone had remained lifeless for hours. To keep from completely freaking out, I messaged Dustin and Georgie to see what they were up to. Though initially offended at my "off-grid" time, I had convinced them it was best for my own sanity.

Despite the distraction, my mind kept circling back to the task at hand. Would it be painful to tear away half my soul? After we finished, would I still be the same person, or would it forever change me? And what, exactly, was the chance of survival? It wasn't something I could simply Google.

At eleven thirty, as I spiraled deeper into a whirlpool of anxiety, the sudden buzz of my phone jolted me. It was Eben.

Please meet me outside your cabin now.

I leaped to my feet and rushed outside to find him standing in the pouring rain. He wore a long yellow raincoat dotted with stickers, and rubber boots. His eyes, far from their usual bright and cheerful selves, now held a worried edge. He wore a backpack and carried a small cardboard box.

"It is time for us to go," he shouted over the downpour. "We must go now. Are you ready?"

I didn't bother with an umbrella. "As ready as I'll ever be. Thank you for doing this—"

He turned without waiting for me to finish and hurried along the river path.

I chased after him, wet to the bone.

"What's in the box?" I shouted after a while, needing to talk so I could get out of my head.

He cracked the lid without slowing. A large lizard with a frilled neck sat on a mound of tissues.

"Her name is Christina," he said.

My first thought was not how weird it was for Eben to bring a lizard to my exorcism, but that it was named after CJ. "You really like CJ, huh?"

"My mother's name is Christina, too. She makes the best apple pie for my birthday."

"It's a beautiful name," I said, keeping the conversation going. If I was to make it through the night without giving in to fear, I needed to keep my tongue moving. "What's your dad's name?"

"Andrew. But Mom gets upset when I talk about him. They don't speak anymore, and I don't see him as often as I used to. The kids at school said it's because I'm difficult, and that's why he left."

The way he said this, as though it was perfectly normal for a father to abandon his son, broke my heart.

"Oh, Eben, I'm sorry. Your dad is making a terrible mistake by missing out on you. You're the sweetest boy I know."

"Yes, that is what Mother says."

A loud clap of thunder echoed overhead, causing me to jump. The downpour intensified. Eben trudged ahead, seemingly unaffected.

"I wonder if Christina will mind sharing her body with you," he said.

I almost tripped over. "What do you mean?"

"When I remove the part of your soul, I'll need to put it somewhere. If I release it, it could find another body to possess, and that could be very dangerous."

"You want to throw my soul into a lizard?" Machina was a nightmare, but a lizard? Did she deserve that? Did anyone? I bit my lip, and for the first time, as the reality of the situation hit home, I questioned whether I was capable of such cruelty.

We emerged from the forest and followed the path that cut across the lawn and led to the nearby shops. I couldn't tell if my teeth chattered from the cold or from the fear that had settled within me. Up ahead, two figures rushed toward the library, barely visible through the sheets of water. Faint music drifted from the Shack, drowned out by the roar of the storm.

Once we passed Alfio's Pizzeria, we took the winding road up the mountain toward the small neighborhood where the professors' accommodations were located. Finally, wet, muddy, and miserable, we stopped in front of a cold and sterile cabin. Where the other cabins had gardens and deck furniture, this one was void of any sign of inhabitance, as though it were an abandoned hospital.

"This is Audrey's office," Eben said, stepping onto the porch. "We need to break in."

"Are you crazy?" I asked, looking around wildly. "Audrey will kill us!"

He gently placed his box down. "I know. I heard rumors about her on Noverna. They made me too scared to sleep. But we must get inside. Are you sure you want to do this?"

I rubbed my arms. Six years was a long time to be a prisoner in my body. "I have to."

He nodded and turned toward the window. "I am required to break the glass, which is very dangerous. Please step away. It could shatter, and I don't want you to get hurt."

I retreated a dozen steps, then watched as he grabbed a rock and smashed a hole in the window. Shards of glass rained around him, the downpour drowning out the noise. He reached in and unlatched the lock, lifting the window high enough for us to climb through.

The interior was as unwelcoming as the front. The plain and featureless metal walls lacked any color, and the absence of paintings, rugs, or any other decor added to the chilly ambiance. At the end of the room, a small desk pressed against the wall, with a collection of liquor bottles displayed on the shelf above it. The bookshelves spanned two walls and hosted hundreds of aged, delicate tomes. Their chaotic arrangement, with them thrown cruelly on top of each other, was devastating.

Eben set his box on the floor and fished a flashlight from his bag. He used it to search through the books. Minutes passed, but it felt like hours. I shifted my weight from foot to foot, half expecting the door to burst open and Audrey to blast us to dust. I distracted myself by browsing the liquor shelf. There was only one full bottle of gin left. I took a swig for old time's sake, and as I put it back, a framed photo caught my attention. It sat atop a pile of papers, the only evidence of a human touch in the room.

I picked it up and saw that it was a picture of a very young Audrey holding a child in her arms. Gone were the tattoos, and her hair was much longer. A maternal love radiated from her, surprising me. I'd never imagined she could possess such an emotion. What had happened to her to make her the nasty woman she was now?

As my gaze lingered on the child, I drew in a sharp breath. He looked exactly like Aran. I lifted the picture closer. No, not Aran, but someone I knew. Someone special—

"I've found it, Alina," Eben's voice echoed hauntingly.

With a last look at the photo, I placed it down, turning to Eben, who'd retrieved a bulky leather-bound book from the shelf. He made himself comfortable on the floor, cross-legged, flipping through the yellowing pages. I knelt beside him as he stopped near the center, his eyes studying the text. He rocked side to side.

"What's wrong?" I asked.

A soft keening sound came from his throat, then, with a sharp shake of his head, he continued flipping the pages. He landed on a new section and placed the book on the floor. From his bag, he pulled nine black candles, setting them in a circular pattern and lighting each one. His eyes were wider than usual, and he moved frantically.

"You sure everything's okay, honey?" I asked, butterflies growing in my stomach.

"Yes, everything is okay." He placed Christina inside the circle, then sprinkled a ring of white powder to encircle the candles. He pulled something small from his pocket and handed it to me. "Swallow this."

It was a purple pill. "What is it?"

"It will focus your essence. You will notice things you have never noticed. You will find the part of your soul that does not belong, and we will remove it."

I rolled the pill between my fingers, eying it skeptically. "But . . . what, exactly, does it do?" I'd never been in the habit of taking unprescribed drugs, and the thought of it didn't thrill me.

"I don't know. I've never taken one, but I know it is needed. Morgan sold me this one."

"Great," I muttered. If Morgan sold them, I couldn't imagine they were for high blood pressure. "And it's necessary?"

"Yes."

I stared at the pill for a long minute, wrestling with my apprehension. In the end, I placed it on my tongue and swallowed it. What choice did I have?

"You should sit in the middle of the circle now," Eben said. "It will not take long."

No sooner had the words left his mouth than an immediate disorientation swept over me. I stumbled into the circle and dropped to my backside, and the effects glued me to the spot. A few moments later, an odd sensation bloomed inside me. It was as though I were floating, my veins humming with a numbing energy. The candles now glowed with an intensity and beauty that I'd never experienced. Power pulsed around my fingertips, vibrating the air, filling me with a sense of awe and wonderment. I grinned, looking at Eben, who now had a halo of light around his head.

"Thank you," I said, my voice distant and dreamy. "You've been a real friend."

His cheeks glistened with streams of tears, each one glowing a unique shade of green. "Goodbye, Alina," he said, his voice trembling.

But as our heartfelt moment lingered, a terrible force intervened. Without warning, Machina attacked. It was like she'd sensed her time was ending, and she wasn't going down without a fight. Her tendrils tore through my insides, trying to steal my grip on reality. I fell to my back, staring at the ceiling, horrified at her strength.

Don't do this! a scratchy voice cried out in my mind. *Wait, Alina!*

Through the drug-induced fog, I realized who that voice belonged to. She'd never spoken before, not with words. But there was no mistaking it. Machina had found her voice.

Salty tears reached my lips as I shook my head in despair. "I must! Don't you see? We can't go on like this."

There's another way! she pleaded. *There has to be another way!*

"There's not."

She roared in defiance, a primal shout of fear as she thrashed with everything she had. My vision filled with pops of color, my chest arching toward the ceiling.

"Alina!" Eben cried, but he might as well have been shouting from Little Peak. "What's happening—"

We can share the body, Machina begged. *We can sort through this . . .*

I shook my head as books tore off the shelves and swirled above me, suspended by some magical force. Memories flashed through my mind. All the times I'd cried in school bathrooms because no one wanted to be my friend, all the hurtful words whispered behind my back, the name-calling, the missed birthday invitations. All of it crashed through me.

I turned my head toward Eben, who was now just a dancing shadow of black mist. "Please . . ."

For a long moment, the shadow did not respond. Then it brightened, and colors filled the darkness, painting Eben back into existence. His eyes streamed, and he trembled all over.

"I can't do this," he sobbed, his voice garbled in my messed-up mind. "I'm sorry, Alina. I can't. Not for you and not for them."

His words punctured the pain, the confusion, the chaos, and left me with a fresh fear, one even greater than before. He was backing out. "You must! Eben, you're my last hope!"

He fell to his knees and frantically flipped through the book to a new page.

I jolted as Machina gripped hold of my mind. I fought the urge to regain my feet with a growl, knowing it was not me commanding my body. Time was running out.

Eben raised one hand toward me, the other tracing a line of text. *"Daemonium intra hominem superandum est per potentiam incantationum!"*

A wave of agony shredded me apart. My skin was an inferno and my breath a burning furnace. My eyes rolled back in my head, and I flopped about uncontrollably.

Wait! Machina shrieked.

Eben's voice filled the room: *"Et sic, in pace perpetua, daemonium conquiescet!"*

A powerful force, like a ship anchor, seized me at the core of my existence and dragged me down into the darkness of my soul.

Something was wrong.

I was sinking, engulfed in shadows, a void that seemed intent on devouring me whole.

My instincts screamed to fight back, to resist this force. I wanted to shriek, to beg Eben to stop the incantation, to end it all. But my body refused my call, instead paralyzing me, rendering me mute.

"Et sic, in pace perpetua, daemonium conquiescet!" roared Eben, stronger and fiercer.

The world folded into pain as an irresistible force surged through my chest. It swelled, pulsating and expanding until it threatened to consume my very being. Blind terror took over then, and my mind shattered. A piercing scream split the night as the building energy exploded outward like an atomic blast.

Chapter Nineteen

A stabbing pain split my body in two.

I blinked, opening my bleary eyes, and my senses slowly stirred.

The world . . . was it spinning, or was I? Blurred colors and distorted shapes hovered around me.

Where was I?

What happened?

The questions came, but the answers remained hidden.

My body felt like it'd been smashed upon the rocks and left to die.

Someone poured water on my face. I turned my head to the side, scrunching my eyes closed again. "Stop . . . please stop."

I lay still for a long while, panting, then opened my eyes.

The shapes around me pulled into themselves until their edges became more defined. I stared up into dark, heavy clouds. Bursts of lightning arced across the sky.

I lay outside in a storm.

Machina.

She came unbidden to my mind. There had been a battle with her.

And . . . and . . .

I groaned in frustration. The memory evaded me like a fading dream. I sat, gritting my teeth with effort, my muscles heavy with fatigue.

Lord have mercy.

I was inside a crater, twice as wide as I was tall.

The ground steamed and hissed as raindrops hit it.

Nothing made sense. There was a faint voice in the back of my mind . . . a voice that said things I didn't think . . .

A sound in the darkness.

A whimper.

It took three attempts to struggle to my feet, and just as many to climb out of the smoking hole. The area was scattered with debris, and nearby the skeletal frames of trees blazed like torches, casting writhing shadows.

"Alina . . ." The groan of my name reached me over the howling winds.

A jolt of adrenaline spurred me into action. It took all my remaining strength to drag one foot in front of the other, straining to find the source of the voice. Movement ahead caught my attention.

As I drew nearer, a horrifying scene played out before me. Ice ran through my veins. A young boy lay splayed in the thick, sodden mud, one hand raised in the air. Tendrils of smoke curled around his scorched skin. Crimson gashes crossed his exposed chest like dried mud. His bright-yellow raincoat had melted into his arms, and his glasses were blackened and twisted. Charred circles dotted his coat where stickers had once been.

"Eben!" The name tore from my lips. I stumbled and dropped to my knees beside him. "No, no, Eben." Every part of him looked in agony. I squeezed my eyes shut, willing myself to wake up. This had to be a cruel dream. Eben was fine, happy, eating candy in bed. But when I opened my eyes again, my prayers had been ignored.

"Help!" I screamed into the emptiness around me. "Someone help, *please*!"

"Alina," Eben's voice was a ghost of a whisper. "I'm sorry . . ."

A strangled sob escaped me. I leaned over him, trembling. "Hush and save your strength."

"I didn't want to . . . They made me . . . But they were wrong—"

"I know, Eben, it's okay," I blurted. "Just rest now. I need to get help . . . Oh, Eben, I don't know what to do. Just . . . just wait here."

His twitching hand found mine. "Urgent." The word was scratchy and raw. "They think they know . . . They wanted me to . . ." His eyes bulged, and he inhaled sharply. "To bring you back . . . but they don't know. You have two. Two . . ." He coughed and his body seized. "I couldn't do it . . . But they are coming. They are already here." His words spluttered as he gasped for air. "I'm sorry . . . tell Mom I—I miss her apple pie . . ."

A final, shuddering breath rushed from his lips. His back arched, then he slumped down, sinking into the mud.

I stared, unmoving. Then it hit me. *"Eben,"* I screamed. I shook his shoulders. "You wake up right now!"

He didn't answer. He didn't move. His eyes, which once held a beautiful light, dimmed until they seemed no more special than a stone in the woods. It was wrong. It was all wrong.

"It's okay," I sobbed, stroking his cheek. "I'll get you fixed right up—"

A hand rested on my shoulders, but I hardly noticed.

"It's just a bad dream," I said, leaning closer, "you'll be alright."

"Alina," a voice whispered behind me. "Alina, he's gone."

"No." I jerked away from the touch. "He's just tired—"

I was lifted from the ground. I thrashed, trying to break free, but all my strength had burned away. "No, please! I need to be here when he wakes up."

Through my tear-blurred vision, a figure emerged from the storm. Maviir. More people plummeted from the heavens to crash into the mud like comets.

"Jesus . . ." said Maviir. "What could have done this? Do you think . . . do you think the Reavers?"

"No," said the person carrying me, and a hush fell over the group. "It doesn't make sense for them to do this."

Why were they just standing there? Eben needed to go to the hospital. "Help him! Do something! He needs a doctor!"

No one moved. They stood frozen like stupid statues.

Harper stepped forward, face illuminated by the burning trees. "I'll take her to the medical center—"

"No," came the reply from the person supporting me. "She's not injured, and I have questions."

"Preposterous," Harper said. "Audrey, the girl needs attention!"

"And she'll get it," she said. "But something unprecedented happened here tonight. Something we don't understand. Would you have her pop off at the medical wing? How many lives can your conscience hold?"

Harper remained silent.

"Exactly," said Audrey. She turned and carried me up the slope.

Harper followed and gave my hand a squeeze. “It’s alright. Don’t worry, we’ll sort it all out.”

“Please,” I begged, losing strength. “Help Eben.”

But a chilling truth settled in the pit of my stomach. There was no help for Eben. There was no helping that sweet boy ever again.

Chapter Twenty

"Sit her on the couch," Audrey's voice echoed minutes . . . hours later. We'd climbed the pathway leading to her cabin. Harper, who'd carried me the last while, lowered me onto the stiff, unyielding sofa. He looked like he'd swam a lap around the lake.

He hovered nearby, studying me with a concerned look. "I'll make a warm drink," he said, as if speaking to a kid who'd just skinned their knee. "It may help with those chattering teeth."

"I'll take tea," said Audrey. "Unsweetened."

I wrapped my arms around myself. Her lounge room was just as cold and sterile as her office. No paintings. No carpet. No love.

No Eben.

"He's dead?" My voice was weak.

"Yes."

Tears splashed onto my lap. "And I k-killed him?"

She took a moment. "We don't know what happened."

My heart pounded against my rib cage, seeking an escape from those words. I'd killed someone. I was a murderer. Images of Eben's smiling face flashed through my mind, and my breathing turned frantic. He was only a child. He had a mom who loved him. He didn't want to be there tonight—he'd warned me against it, but I'd insisted. What had I done?

Audrey sat on a dining chair opposite me. "What were you doing in my office?" Her words were tight.

"I killed him," I whispered numbly.

"Snap out of it. What were you and the boy doing in my office?"

I met her stare. "Eben. His name is Eben."

"What were you and Eben doing in my office?"

I looked down at my ash-clogged fingernails. "We tried to fix me."

Rain lashed the windowpane.

"What was broken?"

A cough at the doorway. Harper had returned. "I found this near the body." He extended part of a book cover toward Audrey.

She accepted it, her lips moving soundlessly as she read the title. Her mouth dropped open. She whipped her gaze back to me. "*Daemonum Imperii Scriptura*?" She leaped to her feet and brandished the charred cover at me. "*The Scripture of Demons' Dominion*? Why this book? What would you burn down my office to learn?"

"Audrey!" said Harper. "You're terrifying the girl."

Her nostrils flared, eyes darting between Harper and me. She settled back into her seat stiffly. "This is no ordinary book. It is potent. Dangerous. A fledgling has no business with it whatsoever. What were you looking for?"

I huddled into myself, tucking my trembling hands under my armpits. How much could I tell them? Would they throw me in demon jail? Had the exorcism even worked? Eben's face flashed through my mind, the unseeing eyes. I deserved to be punished, to be locked in a cell. His death was my fault. "I persuaded Eben to exorcise my demon—"

The room erupted. Audrey sprang to her feet, while Harper darted forward, his expression horrified.

"Have you lost your mind?" Audrey said.

Before I could confirm her question, Harper crouched in front of me, his wet hair streaming into his eyes. "Alina, you can't expel your demon—you are the demon." He squeezed my wrists. "Should Eben have succeeded, you wouldn't be sitting here. Your body would be a shell and your soul gone, lost forever."

"The boy must have deceived her," Audrey said. "But why?"

I glared at her. "His name is Eben. He didn't trick me—he knew I wasn't like other demons. He knew he could remove a part of my soul, and then I would be normal. I'd be able to live in peace."

Harper leaned back with the same sad smile I'd gotten from people for years. He thought I was delusional. "You can't remove a part of your soul—it's an all-or-nothing deal."

I turned away from him and found Audrey frozen, staring at me intently. "Tell me exactly what Eben did," she said. Harper gave her a sideways look.

It took a moment to push past the pain of reliving the events, but then it all tumbled out in a rushed, uncontrollable mess. The ring of black candles. Christina, the lizard. And, after hesitating, the pill. I tried to explain the chaotic whirlwind of emotions, the overwhelming surge of Machina—though I avoided her name—fighting for her survival. I described how Eben had flipped back through the book to another page to complete the exorcism.

"He did what?" Audrey gasped.

"Changed to a new page."

An uneasy look passed between Audrey and Harper.

"What incantation did he recite?" she asked.

I sent my muddled mind back through the nightmare. "I . . . I can't remember. He said something odd, like he couldn't do it for me, or for them, and I thought he was going to stop. But he spoke in a strange language, Latin, maybe."

Audrey paced back and forth, and Harper collapsed into her chair, rubbing his forehead.

"Not for them . . ." he repeated. "You don't suppose—"

"I do suppose," said Audrey. "It confirms what we believed. They already wanted her for their army after she revealed her power on Earth. Word has reached them about her dual Aeria and Terre abilities. It was a dangled carrot, and they were starving. Now one of their own is dead. The boy, bless the poor fool, couldn't go through with it."

"It happened sooner than I expected," Harper admitted. "Though we knew the time would come."

I looked between them, catching on to what they were implying. "You've got it wrong—Eben isn't a Reaver, I know he's not."

"No, he wasn't a Reaver," agreed Audrey. "But it wouldn't be the first time the Reavers took advantage of the weak."

"I assume Eben reached out to Astaroth *after* Nester failed to recruit Alina?" Harper asked.

Audrey gave a curt nod, and he blew a long whistle. "My, we have been rather foolish, haven't we?"

Something screeched in the kitchen, making me jump.

"That will be the tea," said Harper. He hurried out of sight.

We sat in silence, my mind reeling. They were wrong. They didn't know Eben like I did. He'd never do anything to hurt me. To hurt anyone. He was as timid as a mouse, but smart. He would know if he was being played.

Harper returned with two steaming mugs—one for me, one for Audrey.

Audrey's tight-lipped frown deepened the wrinkles around her eyes. "I need you to remember everything. This is crucial. Think back. Can you recall anything Eben read from the book?"

I shook my head. "No, it was all gibberish."

"Focus. Cast your mind back—"

"I can't remember!" I snapped, overwhelmed and exhausted. "I can't remember a damn thing, okay? Listen, I'm done with this. I want to go home now. To Breaux Bridge. This place can't fix me no more than the doctors could."

Harper sat beside me. "I know it's a lot. But what those people did to Eben, it's not okay. We need to stop it from happening to anyone else. Eben was a good kid."

I nodded, tears splashing into my mug. "He is a good kid. I know he is."

"Then help us," Harper said. "Will you let me look inside your mind?"

The idea of someone else inside my head at that moment made me shudder. It was already too crowded in there. But if I could do anything to stop the Reavers, then I had to try. I swallowed and nodded.

Harper squeezed my shoulder. "Thank you."

A presence filled my consciousness. It wasn't a hesitant probing, like Oliver's attempts at mind reading, but a sharp arrow. I instinctively erected a mental barrier to block the intrusion, but Harper swept it aside as if it were vapor.

My memories came alive like a film reel spinning in reverse. The rigid sofa in Audrey's cabin, Eben's rasping breathing, the gaping crater, the burning trees, the cursed book—

Harper gasped and recoiled as if something had stung him. His presence tore away from my mind with jarring abruptness. "I—I don't understand . . ."

Audrey leaned in. "What is it?"

"Daemonium intra hominem superandum est per potentiam incantationum."

Audrey's mug of tea crashed to the floor and shattered. "No?"

He nodded, and she turned to me as though seeing me for the first time.

"What is it?" I asked.

"Eben's incantation was one to silence your soul," she said "But . . . why would he do that? What would it serve?"

Harper stared at me for a long moment. "She has two souls."

A chill raced through the room.

"Is that even possible?" Audrey asked.

"One other case has been documented," Harper said. "Though its authenticity is questionable. What if Eben believed, for whatever reason, that it was true for Alina?"

Audrey shook her head slowly. "I'm lost—we already knew she had two powers—"

"We knew nothing," said Harper, "because she does not have two powers. She has three."

As shocked as I was at hearing this, I doubted it matched Audrey's level. Her eyes bulged out of her head. "Impossible."

"The crater," Harper explained, "the fire—that's not the doing of Aeria or Terre. It was a blast of Faezre. It all makes sense."

"Sense? None of tonight makes any damn sense! Why hasn't she noticed this power before?"

Harper didn't answer immediately. "Because . . . because her second soul only awakened tonight . . ." he said, pacing again. "Her first soul, the soul of Aeria and Terre, awoke on Earth. Her Faezre soul awoke tonight in that blast."

A small smile tugged on my lips, and I almost laughed. *Three powers?* I didn't want two, but three? *Come look at me, Alina, the freak show.* And two souls . . . What were they implying? Machina wasn't a part of me, as I'd thought, but a separate living being?

My smile widened.

Absurd.

Audrey watched me with her head tilted to one side. "Maybe . . . if a ripping occurred to a body already powerfully occupied . . ." She nodded as if deciding something. "What's your birth date?"

"March twelfth, 2005—"

She strode to the mantelpiece and snatched up a tablet. Her fingers flew across the screen, her eyes narrowing as she read.

Harper's tight smile was crooked. "It seems we may have been too quick in our estimation of you. Based on this recent evidence, it appears likely you are more special than we ever could have imagined. For a body to host two souls, the Reavers must have accidentally tried to rip the soul from a demon baby and replace it with their own. Both souls cling to the body, fighting for control. Given the scarcity of full-blooded demons on Earth, such incidents should never happen."

I listened to his words, trying to make sense of them, but it was like he was speaking in reverse. "Which soul am I?"

"What do you mean?"

"Am I the original soul born on Earth, or the intruder?"

His gaze didn't quite meet mine. "Does it matter? You are who you are, and that is a good person."

"It matters," I insisted. I needed him to say it, to make it official.

He adjusted his wet coat. "Considering your primary abilities are Terre and Aeria, it's reasonable to assume that you are the guest."

"The guest," I repeated slowly, wishing it were that simple. It wasn't as though Machina had welcomed me into her body, offering me tea and biscuits.

"It does not make you evil," Harper said. "You had no control over what happened. Remember, they did this to you, as much as it was done to this other soul."

For years, I'd held Machina prisoner in her own body. Every time she tried to take back what was rightfully hers, I locked her away into the darkest pit of her stomach. The room spun, and nausea threatened to overwhelm me. I lowered my gaze and focused on my wringing hands.

Audrey drew in a sharp breath. "I've found them!" She passed the tablet to Harper.

The shock on his face echoed Audrey's. "Balder and Celia?"

"You know them?" Audrey asked.

"Every demon does," he said. He looked at the screen for a while longer, then passed it to me.

It displayed a photo of a powerfully built man with short, greying hair. Medals decorated his military uniform, and though he had a tough exterior, there was something in his eyes, perhaps a sparkle, which softened him. Beside the picture was the name *Balder Ryzon*, followed by a brief bio:

Balder Ryzon led a life of courage and devotion, committing himself to sealing the Shadowgates to Earth and helping to protect the billions of people inhabiting the hub world. Tragically, he and his wife, Celia, were assassinated after the gates were closed, leaving behind their daughter, Kali, to continue their legacy.

I scrolled. A photo of a beautiful woman with cascading auburn hair, wearing the same military uniform as Balder, smiled back at me. Her name was *Celia Ryzon*.

"Are they . . . are they my . . ." I couldn't finish the thought.

"Yes," said Harper gently. "In a way."

My hands trembled as a storm of emotions swirled within me. For as long as I could remember, questions about my parents had haunted me. Growing up in the foster care system, I'd always wanted to know who they were, what they looked like, and why they'd abandoned me. I'd spent countless nights silently crying, wondering if they ever thought about me or if they would be disappointed by the person I'd become. I'd imagined being reunited with them more times than I could count, that they'd randomly show up at one of my birthdays and we'd be one happy family again. That dream was now forever out of reach. They were dead. Murdered.

I handed the tablet back to Audrey, having no tears left to cry. I knew they were not technically my real parents, but that did not change the answers I now had. They had birthed the body I had stolen, so their blood was my blood, and for the time being, that was enough. I wasn't in a place to process everything I felt at that moment, but I knew the time would come when I would be forced to deal with it all.

The room was silent for a long moment.

Harper cleared his throat. "This night has weighed heavily on us all. We have much to contemplate, and the weariness of our minds doesn't help our understanding. A good night's rest is in order for us to see things clearly in the morning—"

"I have more questions," Audrey cut in.

"They can wait. I must insist."

She seemed ready to argue, but upon seeing his determined expression, she held her tongue.

"I'll escort you back to Michael," he said. "Unless you'd wish to visit the medical center?"

I shook my head, struggling to rise to my feet as a wave of dizziness washed over me. "To Michael." I started toward the door but stopped to ask the question that had been unanswered. "The explosion. Eben. That was me?"

"No," Harper said. "It was the other soul, though I do not believe it to be intentional. Eben had tried to confine it within a psychic prison with no hope of escape. I suspect the blast was a reflex—the soul's unconscious way of trying to survive."

I nodded, having come to the same conclusion. "Eben warned me that the Reavers were coming for me, that they were already here."

Audrey's eyes darted to Harper's, then she shook her head. "Put it from your mind and let us handle things."

I left the room. The last thing I wanted was another worry crowding my already overwhelmed head.

Chapter Twenty-One

Harper and I left Audrey's cabin and paused on the porch, the storm whipping around us in a frenzy.

"Would you mind if we take a drier route to Michael?" Harper asked.

"Kinda had my hopes set on swimming there," I muttered, too mentally and physically drained to guess at what route he talked about.

He raised his arms and made small circular motions with his fists. With a rumble, the ground in front of the cabin bulged, then split open like a mouth. A staircase carved into the earth led into darkness. Normally, I would have been astounded by such a display, but at that moment I was too exhausted to give it a second thought.

We descended into a tunnel supported by timber beams and lit by gold festoon lights along the walls. Harper waved his fists once more, and the staircase filled with dirt.

We navigated the underground network in silence. To distract myself from the image of Eben dying, I tried memorizing the path we took but soon grew lost. We passed a chamber filled with humming crystals and skirted a small lake that glowed with bioluminescent plants. After we crossed a set of cart tracks, we stopped at a staircase leading up into solid stone.

"This is us," Harper said, turning to face me. He removed his glasses and cleaned them on his shirt. "Word of the incident may have spread throughout the academy by now. No one knows the Reavers are searching for you, but students had arrived at the blast site before I did, so they could have pieced together some of what went down. They will have questions. It would be wise to consider your answers and only share as much as you are comfortable with." He paused for my reply, but what was there to say? He sighed. "Just know that I'm here if you need anything." He motioned, and the stone at the top of the staircase split open, revealing the rain-soaked world above.

I climbed into the forest where the lights of Château Michael glowed through the trees. The ground trembled as Harper sealed the tunnel entrance, erasing any evidence of the stairwell's existence.

Wanting only to reach my bed and fall into a deep, thoughtless sleep, I trudged toward my cabin and stepped into the clearing. The sight that greeted me made me freeze. I'd expected everyone to either be at the Shack or passed out, but it seemed that most of Michael had gathered around the fire, an enormous air umbrella protecting them from the downpour.

"There she is!" someone shouted.

The crowd surged toward me.

I backed into the woods, my breath hitching, but was soon surrounded by the throng, their shouted questions drowning out the storm.

"We heard the explosion over the DJ!"

"Is it true you're actually from Fernyre?"

"Did someone really die?"

"Tell us everything!"

I fought against the onslaught, but they pressed in until I struggled to breathe. "Please . . . give me some space . . ."

Hands clawed at my clothes, feet trampled mine into the mud, and someone yanked my jacket without care. The air around me turned thin. I was trapped, suffocating. I couldn't escape.

"Please," I pleaded, trying to inch my way toward my cabin. "You're hurting me."

A sharp voice filled my head: *I'm coming.*

I hadn't even felt the mental intrusion. When Oliver and Harper had done it, it had been obvious someone was there. This person had slipped in without a trace.

I didn't have time to think about it, because at that moment, Machina broke free. My fear transformed into a seething rage. I struck out wildly with my fist, crunching the jaw of a guy who'd wrenched my arm. He crumpled backward.

"Give me fucking space!" I roared.

The guy snarled, opening and closing his jaw. "You bitch!" he spat, stepping back in.

A voice boomed over the noise. "Out of the way!"

A figure battled through the crowd, shoving people aside until he reached me. "Leave her, Hudson, or I'll bury you!"

"She punched me!" Hudson said, blood trickling from his mouth as he made a grab for me.

Aran's fist connected with his nose first, snapping his head back in a spray of blood. Hudson fell into the people behind him, and Aran stepped in front of me like a shield.

"Anyone who lays a hand on Alina won't talk for a week," he shouted, glaring at the crowd. "Any volunteers?" A hush settled over everyone. "Didn't think so." He grabbed my hand and pulled me through the press toward the main château. We climbed the stairs to his room and he locked the door behind us.

He faced me, breathing like a bull. "Are you hurt?"

I shook my head. "No, just . . . tired." Blood seeped from a gash on his knuckles. "Oh, Aran, you're bleeding!" I pressed his hand against my damp shirt. "Does it hurt?"

He watched me with a raised eyebrow. "You've just been attacked by a mob of loonies, and you're worried about me? Alina . . . I think you've got a few roos loose in the top paddock."

Was it the lack of anger in his voice that made his words sound lyrical? Why did he suddenly care about my safety? He'd been a jerk the whole week. My head was too scrambled to work through it.

He withdrew his hand, awkwardly clearing his throat. A red stain remained on my jacket.

"Fancy that," he said. "You in my room, blood on your clothes. Just like old times. Well, you know where the shower is." He tossed me a towel from his cupboard. "I might have to start charging. Could make enough money to open my own menagerie in Little Peak."

I glanced at his animal cages, most of which were now empty. "I thought you already had one?"

"All gone to good homes."

Though the steaming water didn't entirely ease the aches and pains from the explosion, it removed the biting edge. I closed my eyes for a long while and let the water soothe my face.

A knock on the door interrupted me.

I snapped out of my trance and wrapped my arms around myself to cover my body. I was not prepared for another Sophia tirade. But it was only Aran entering the room backward, holding a bundle in his hands.

"I've misplaced my favorite flannel," he said, "but I've got a singlet and some footy shorts for you. It's the best PJs money can buy."

He placed the clothes on the vanity, and a sudden, despicable impulse gripped me. I wanted him to turn around, to run those eyes over me again. To take me in, naked. I was so lost in myself, so desperate to be held, that I no longer cared he had a girlfriend. I no longer cared I had Machina. I no longer cared.

I let my arms fall to my sides, my heart racing. A tingling sensation trickled down my stomach and to my thighs. *Turn. Look at me. Take me.*

But unlike the first time, he didn't glance my way. Not even a peek in the mirror. He patted the top of the clothes, then walked out of the bathroom, leaving me standing there in my shame.

Disappointment dragged me down. I wanted to turn this into a night of poor choices. To let his touch distract me from everything that'd happened and let me breathe without feeling like I was drowning. Sophia had made my life hell for the last week, and in that moment, though wrong, I didn't give a rat's ass about her relationship.

I found Aran pacing in front of the cages when I left the shower some time later. We locked eyes for a moment.

"It's getting late," he said, rubbing the back of his neck. "I've put fresh sheets on the bed for you."

"No, I couldn't possibly—"

"Course you could—it's too comfy for me. I'll take the sofa. Besides, Skippy here is sick, so I want to stay close to her tonight." He tapped a large cage holding a baby kangaroo, which seemed perfectly healthy.

"But—"

"No buts."

He steered me to the foot of the bed.

"Are you sure? It can fit us both."

He looked from the bed to the sofa, then settled on my lips.

I clasped his hands in mine. *Please. Please, just grant me this one thing. One tiny light in the darkness. One moment of bliss in a world of pain. One beautiful mistake.*

"No, I shouldn't," he said at last.

I swallowed hard, trying to hide my disappointment. "Yes, of course. I just thought . . . well, I guess I just thought." I climbed into bed and settled in the center, feeling as though I were alone in an endless ocean.

He switched off the light. "Good night, Alina."

"Night."

After a moment, he moved to the sofa. It groaned as he lay down. The room fell into an all-consuming silence. In that quiet, the emotional bomb within me detonated, and the events of the night exploded out. My throat burned as hot tears ran down my cheeks. I pressed a pillow over my face, trying to muffle the sobs that I couldn't stop any more than I could stop the storm outside. My stomach clenched as I held everything in. Who was I? A demon? A murderer? I had no idea. All I knew was I was not in Louisiana anymore, and no tapping of red shoes would ever take me back.

A hand touched my shoulder. "It's alright, missy," Aran said as he lay on top of the comforter. "Things won't seem so dark in the morning."

The smell of his cologne eased the tightness in my throat. His hand gently stroked my hair.

"It was my fault," I whispered. "I shouldn't have dragged him into it."

Aran's hand paused for a moment, then continued as he cooed softly.

"Eben's dead," I gulped out. "Oh, Eben's dead! What have I done?" And then I broke down into an uncontrollable sobbing mess.

He pulled my head onto his chest, and for a long moment, we lay like that—him comforting me as my tears splashed onto him. When I ran out of tears, I lay trembling against him.

"I'm just a simple country kid," he said, "so I don't pretend to know a lot. But what I do know is there's not a bad bone in your body. Whatever happened wasn't your fault. Sometimes life throws curveballs at us. Hurls them until all we can do is give up dodging and brace for the impact. It's how you take each hit that matters. You're a good person, Alina. Don't tell yourself otherwise."

I wanted to believe him. I wanted to think I was a good person, but how could I after everything that'd happened?

"I'm sorry," I whispered. "About last week at the bar. I shouldn't have been spying. I didn't mean to. I just got caught up."

"There's nothing to be sorry about. I'm the one who was a dick. Truth is, you caught me doing something I'm not proud of. I never wanted you to see me like that, so I guess I kinda lashed out at you because I was disappointed in myself, and that was not fair. I'm sorry."

His confession surprised me. Was he admitting to cheating on Sophia? I wanted to deny it, to make an argument for him, but there he was, lying in bed with me . . .

No. He'd been a perfect gentleman. He wasn't like the men Georgie had dated. He was different. I knew he was.

A part of me was relieved by the realization that he would never cheat on her.

A part of me was devastated.

Chapter Twenty-Two

Someone screamed.

The comfort of sleep was shattered like a glass breaking on the floor. My eyes snapped open as I jolted upright, dazed.

"Alina!"

"CJ?" I mumbled, squinted against the morning sunlight spilling in through the tall windows.

She ran through the open door and flung herself onto Aran's bed, making me bounce. "Oh, babes!" she cried, pulling me into a hug. "I've just heard! Don't you ever do that to me again. You've got my stomach all churning like a washing machine." She drew back and held me at arm's length. "Are you alright? Are you hurt?"

"Dandy," I said through a yawn.

But that couldn't be right. After everything that'd happened, I should be as far from dandy as possible. I did a mental check to see how I truly felt, to see if I was going to burst into tears or sink into despair. To my surprise, I actually felt stable, though dead tired. I didn't trust it. I forced myself to think of Eben, and though my heart ached, it somehow felt distant, almost as though the memory belonged to someone else. Perhaps I'd cried all my grief out and was now too numb to feel anything. But for whatever reason, I just felt . . . dandy.

Aran sat and stretched, his hair a mess. "Good morning to you, too."

CJ ignored him. "Are you sure you're alright? People are saying you blew Audrey's office sky high."

I was about to reply when I noticed the leaves and mud tangled in her hair. "Where have you been?" I asked, pulling out a purple petal.

She closed her eyes dreamily. "Heaven. Over and over."

A figure appeared in the doorway. Morgan, in all his smugness.

"Well, well, well," he said, arching an eyebrow at Aran. "I didn't think you had it in you."

"I don't," said Aran, rubbing the sleep from his eyes. "It's not what it looks like."

"It never is," said Morgan. He strolled to the fridge and grabbed a beer. "Thirsty?"

Aran shook his head and climbed out of bed wearing only his boxer shorts. Golden sunlight washed across his toned body. CJ gasped and gripped my arm as he stretched, his abs having no right to look as perfect as they did. He pulled on his jeans.

"What are you doing?" Morgan asked.

"Getting dressed."

"When did the uniform change?"

Aran didn't answer immediately. "I'm not going today." His gaze darted to me. "I need to sort out some things."

"Quite irresponsible for the captain to skip practice, wouldn't you say?" Morgan said. He opened the beer and tossed the cap onto the sofa.

"The team will understand."

"I didn't make you captain so you could decide when to attend practice. I made you captain so you would win. You won't jeopardize my last chance at taking home the château championship." He took a long drink. "Now, into your leathers. And take the girl."

Aran looked as though he wanted to punch Morgan. "Why would she come to training?"

A bemused smile crossed Morgan's face. "Since when are you so sloppy in the morning? Rumor has it she's a *Faezre* demon, the only one at Astaroth. If she's on our side, the other châteaux will have to revamp their teams to accommodate the new threat."

I slumped lower into the bed. How had word spread so quickly? "I don't want to join the team."

"It's not an offer," said Morgan. "There are no free passes at Michael. You are part of the machine, whether you like it or not. You're joining the team." He stood in front of the full-length mirror and pulled some grass from his hair. "Besides, it might do you some good. I had a childhood friend in Newark. He had the backbone of a wet noodle. But when I convinced him to join our . . . group, let's say, he transformed into one of the grittiest guys I knew. May he rest in peace."

I looked to Aran pleadingly.

"Where's she going to go?" Aran said. "We have a full roster."

"That sounds like a captain's problem to solve."

CJ gripped my hand. "Don't worry, you'll be amazing, I know you will. And it might be a good distraction from, well, whatever happened last night."

Her confidence was sorely misguided. "Yeah, amazing," I muttered, already feeling anxiety squeezing my chest. All those people watching me fail. *Fantastic.*

Morgan finished his beer and tossed the bottle into the bin. "Well, I'm beat. Off to bed for me." He looked at Aran. "Make it work, or I'll find someone who can." Then, with a wink at CJ, he bounded out of the room.

Aran sighed and removed his pants again. "Welcome to the team, I guess." He searched through his closet and retrieved a clean flag fall suit.

"I really don't want to join."

"Yeah, well, good luck convincing Morgan to change his mind."

I looked helplessly at CJ. "Please come?"

Her bloodshot eyes were on the brink of closing. "Course, babes. But I'm going to need coffee. I don't know what's worse—my hangover or my hair."

Before long, the three of us strolled down the cliff path toward the stadium. Unlike the previous day, the sun shone brilliantly, and the ground's moisture had nearly disappeared. Birds sang in the forests below, and a red fox watched us pass before slinking away.

Aran had given me some spare leathers from Michael's storeroom. They were well-worn, which he'd explained was better because they were suppler. Despite their rigid appearance, they actually allowed for a lot of movement. The added bulk and gave me a presence I couldn't have wished for. I felt powerful.

Unexpectedly, a tiny part of me flickered excitedly. Maybe it was because I'd never been on a real team before, or perhaps I just wanted to keep my mind too busy to think about what happened last night. Either way, the excitement surprised me, and made what I was about to do a little less daunting.

The field was shaped differently than it had been at the Choosing. It looked like a heavily bombarded war zone. Deep, muddy trenches criss-crossed from one side to the other, and ridges ran along the ground like rows of teeth.

"What happened?" I asked.

"It's been terraformed," Aran explained as we neared a group gathered by the Michael stand. "It changes for every match to keep it interesting."

A figure detached from the others and stormed toward us. I quickly recognized him. Hudson glared at us from behind two black eyes and a swollen nose, looking ready for round two—with me or Aran, I couldn't say.

He stopped a short distance from us, crossing his arms. "We need to talk," he said to Aran.

"No, we don't," said Aran, walking past him. "You're off the team."

Hudson's mouth dropped. "You're joking!"

"Nope."

He scrambled after Aran, yipping at his heels like a chihuahua. "You're kicking me off the team because of *her*?"

"No. I'm kicking you off the team because you're a wanker."

Hudson stopped in his tracks, spluttering. "Yeah, well, good luck winning a game without me. I'm the best Raider Michael has, and you know it!"

Everyone stared at me curiously as we joined the group. Ava looked like Christmas had come early, but Zach's eyes darted between me and CJ as if unable to decide where to let them rest.

"Everyone, meet our newest team member," Aran said, clapping my shoulder, "Alina Rose."

"No way!" Zach cried. "Raider?"

"Course, she's a Raider," said Ava, letting her eyes drift down my body. "Look at her. She has the figure for it."

Aran dropped his sports bag and rested his hands on his hips. "Our first game is only two weeks away, and we have a Raider who is not only a fledgling but has never seen a game. It's going to be tough to bring her up to scratch, so I need everyone to chip in and help."

A burly guy with a shaved head and a small tattoo below his eye raised his hand.

Aran looked at him. "There's no need to hold your arm up, Stanley. What's up?"

"I was just thinking," he said in a high-pitched British accent that was at odds with his build, "why have we got a new team member? Hudson wasn't so bad, was he?"

The woman beside him scoffed. She had jet-black hair and a powerful figure. "Good God, Stanley. Why have a brain if you don't use it?"

Stanley rubbed his chin. "Not really sure."

"She's Faezre. Surely, you've heard that by now?"

"So, it's true?" Ava breathed. "You have fire power?"

Everyone watched me. I shook my head. "No. Well, maybe. I don't really know." I sighed. "I've never used my power yet, not on purpose. So I'm not sure what use I'll be."

"Doesn't matter," said Zach. "Just having you on the team will screw everyone's strategies! They won't have a clue how to prepare for you."

"I wouldn't be surprised if they try to take you down outside the game," said Ava gleefully. "We've struck gold."

"I like fire," said Stanley. "Welcome aboard." He stepped forward and was the first to shake my hand with a powerful grip.

"Alright, alright, quick introductions," Aran said. "Alina, you know Ava and Zach, right? This is Stanley, a Shielder, as well as Trix"—he nodded to the broad woman with jet-black hair—"and Isabelle." Unlike the other two, Isabelle was tiny as a mouse and couldn't be older than seventeen. "Last, we have our Sentry, Elias." Elias looked every part an athlete, having both good looks and, judging by the way he held himself, a heavy dose of arrogance.

I smiled nervously at them but couldn't help feeling I was a splinter sticking out in their polished porch.

"So, flag fall," Aran said when Elias didn't bother looking up from his phone. "Essentially, it's capture the flag but on steroids. The aim is to score as many points as possible. Each waypoint is five, and the flag is fifty. The game lasts an hour, broken into twenty-minute thirds." His lips shifted to one side. "That's about it. Got everything?"

I stared at him. "You're missing some information. Like, all of it."

Ava laughed. "For an Architect, Aran is terrible at getting his point across. Teams are broken into role-based sections. The Architect directs the battle from that floating island, kind of like a general. Boots on the ground are the Raiders and the Shielders. Raiders get the glory, since we capture the flag and reach the waypoints."

Trix scoffed. "Shielders take pride in crushing the opposing Raiders. A point saved is a point earned."

"Try telling that to the fans," Zach said under his breath.

"Aran tries to tell me what to do," said Elias in a bored voice. "But half the time, I can't understand his ridiculous accent."

"Elias thinks he's the hottest Sentry around," said Isabelle. "But he's only good because us Shielders prevent anyone from embarrassing him."

Elias glared at her over the top of his phone. "Isn't it past your bedtime?"

I looked around the circle. "Architect, Raiders, Shielders, and a Sentry. Doesn't sound too complicated."

"It's not," agreed Aran, bending over and rummaging through his bag. "But it can turn into a dog's breakfast pretty quick." He straightened and handed me a small piece of wood adorned with runes and a length of cord looped through one end. "This should help keep you alive. Flag fall's not a game of badminton. There are real dangers on the field."

"So many dangers," said Zach excitedly. "Golems, earthquakes, lightning, tunnel collapses—" He listed them on his fingers.

"Not to mention the other team carefully trying to remove your head," said Trix.

"The talisman protects you from bad attacks, but you can still get ouchies," said Stanley.

I suddenly felt a lot more nervous. "So, let me get this straight. Flag fall is a lot more like magical MMA than capture the flag?"

Zach grinned proudly. "I think she's catching on."

"Couldn't have said it better myself," said Trix.

I tossed the talisman back into the bag. "I'm out. Dying in front of the entire academy is not on my bucket list."

Aran scowled at Zach and Trix. "Good work." He turned to me, his expression softening. "Listen, it's not that bad. Sure, it can be dangerous, but we take precautions against that, and serious injuries are as rare as hens' teeth. Besides, Morgan won't let you back out." He looked at the others. "Now, what have I missed?"

"A lot," said Isabella. "How about time stretch?"

"Oh, right," Aran said. "Teams can spend fifty points to add an extra five minutes in each third, but it must be called before the fifteen-minute mark of that third."

"And the Easter eggs," said Stanley.

Aran looked puzzled. "Easter eggs—Oh. You mean the hidden talismans? Yes, there are talismans of power hidden throughout the course. Find one, and your team can use it to gain an advantage."

"I'm confused," I said. "I thought we already had talismans?"

"We do. But these talismans have unique abilities, like boosting essence, enabling teleportation, or causing limb lock."

A small whimper escaped my throat. Why couldn't demons enjoy football like everyone else?

CJ squeezed an arm around my shoulder. "If you don't want to go through with this, we can back out. I don't give a damn how much of a hero Morgan thinks he is. If you want out, I dare him to say no to me."

I looked at their expectant faces. Was I truly willing to risk my life in front of everyone? Searching deep inside, I found I wasn't as worried as I should be. It was as if a transformation had occurred within me overnight. The anxiety that had weighed on my chest since childhood had subsided, giving way to a newfound adventurous—or perhaps careless—spirit. I wasn't sure what was going on, but I didn't care to question it.

"No," I said. "I'll do it."

The group burst into cheers and rushed forward to clap me on the back. Everyone, except Elias, who took a selfie with me in the background.

We spent the afternoon practicing. It was a lot to take in, but by the end of the day, I had a solid grasp of my role. It felt more like a game of magical chess than anything else, demanding strategy and forethought. I soon came to conclusions about the best course of action quicker than Aran did. Chess had always been a strength of mine, as it needed minimal social interaction.

When we eventually called it quits and headed to the bleachers where CJ slept, I was flushed with excitement. I'd discovered a sport that captivated me entirely. I was obsessed.

"I don't understand that last rush," I said to Aran as I replayed the final moments in my head. "Why did we burrow to the waypoint instead of capturing the flag?"

"Because the Shielders had the flag surrounded," said Aran.

"Yes, but if our Shielders and Raiders joined forces, we could have overwhelmed them."

"If our Shielders joined the flag grab, it would have left our flag vulnerable to their Raiders."

I shook my head. "No, it wouldn't have, because their Raiders wouldn't have reached our end in time. They were busy with the waypoints. We could have called in our Shielders for a last push and scored fifty points instead of five."

Aran opened his mouth, hesitated, then closed it. He opened it again and laughed. "You're right. I didn't consider that."

"Looks like Hudson's job isn't the only one Alina is going after," joked Ava.

He flicked his sweaty glove at her. "First she needs to master her Faezre." He turned to me. "I know you won't have lessons for it, but you need to put in the effort if we are to have any chance. I hate to say it, but your Terre and Aeria power is not enough to help our team now. We need fire."

I winced, realizing how much I'd neglected my studies since arriving. Once I'd concluded that I'd be returning home after my exorcism, I put little energy into improving. However, today changed things. I now had a newfound hunger for power. During those hours on the field, I wasn't the timid, self-conscious Alina I knew. I was alive.

"I will," I promised. "I'm going to the library after dinner to see if I can find some books that may help."

"No you're not," Zach said. "You're coming to the Shack for homework."

"Homework?" I asked, my spirits sinking. I'd had my heart set on a cozy nook by a fireplace.

"Don't worry, you'll love it," said Ava.

Chapter Twenty-Three

We hadn't reached far beyond the cafeteria's manicured lawns when the thundering sound of partygoers reached us. The Shack was packed, transforming the beach into something more of a nightclub. Outdoor tables were crammed full, volleyball games midmatch, and a flotilla of people bobbed on the lake, drinks in hand. On the rooftop terrace, the dance floor buzzed to nineties rock. CJ, who had been on the verge of dozing off moments earlier, sprang to life.

"Now, *this* is what Saturdays are for!" She hastily tried to tame her curly hair.

"I'll get the table," Isabella said. Despite looking too young to be allowed, her sharp tongue—which she'd lashed Stanley and Elias with relentlessly—made me feel she deserved a beer if anyone did.

"We'll help," said Ava, and the rest of the team, including CJ, squeezed through the crowd. Trix shot me a wink as she retreated.

"I see what you're doing," Aran called out to them as they left. "And it's not going to work."

I deflated at his words. After last night, how caring he had been . . . I guess, for a moment, I'd imagined what it would be like between us, and part of me was still lost in that fantasy. I shook my head to clear it. Aran

May was not for me, not when he had a girlfriend. Not when I was figuring out this whole Machina mess.

He led the push to the bar. "Why's everyone dressed weird?" I asked, noticing a color pattern—either red and yellow or red and black. Some even wore face paint.

"The league starts today," Aran said. "Ravenmoor Heights versus Thorn Cove. They were finalist last year, so it should be a good match—"

"Aran!" a bartender cried as we neared. She had edgy hair—one side shaved, the other braided—and heavily mascaraed eyes. She was pretty. Leaning across the bar, she swept people aside to clear a path for us. "Make some room, folks, make some room. Now"—she motioned for Aran to go to the front of the line—"how was your vacation?"

"A doozy," he said with a grin. "Shit hit the fan when I found a poacher on the property stealing sheep. I rocked up, ready to turn him inside out, but then remembered I wasn't allowed to 'demon' on Earth. The brute's dogs had me up a tree for hours." He laughed as though nearly being mauled was the funniest thing ever.

The girl snorted. "Got me beat. I had to put up with Mom's nagging about me finding a 'nice man.'" With the way she batted her eyelashes, it was obvious which man she wanted. "And Sophia?"

"She loved it in Aus," he said. "Met the folks, even tried her hand at mustering." His face fell slightly. "But, well . . . she had to come home earlier than expected for a friend's birthday. How about you? How's Mowgli?"

"He's the cutest little thing! Look—" She disappeared behind the bar and lifted a strange animal that I'd only seen on TV. It was a cross between a mouse and a rabbit, with a long snout and shiny black eyes. "I can't ever thank you enough," she said, cuddling it. "It was exactly what I needed. I've been feeling much better these days."

"Happy to help," said Aran, scratching the thing behind the ears. "As far as I know, you're still the only person on Cronix who has a bandicoot. They're bloody tough to find back home."

She hugged Mowgli one more time before setting him down below the bar. "I'll repay you one day, I promise. Anyway, what can I get you?"

"Nine lagers, thanks, two to go. The rest to the lounge."

"Done and done," said the girl, already pouring from the tap. She looked at me and raised her eyebrows. "Who's the shy one?"

"This is Alina," Aran said. "She just joined the team."

Her eyebrows shot up. "Really? Who'd she replace?"

"Hudson."

"Well, isn't that a fine thing to hear on a Saturday? I've never seen such an ego on a weasel before. Nice to meet you, Alina. I'm Kenna. Drinks are on the house for team members."

"I guess having demons try to kill you in the name of sport really has its perks," I said, taking the first glass.

We headed back outside and approached the end of the building. An enormous screen covered the wall. Footage of a flag fall stadium played on it.

"You two are so *cute* together," said CJ when we reached our seats. The team occupied a large U-shaped lounge in the middle of everyone standing, kind of like a VIP section. CJ draped her legs over Morgan, who wore a black-and-red cap backward.

He slapped the empty seat beside him, and with no other options available, I reluctantly sat down.

"How did it go, my little fire starter?" he asked, the smell of beer thick on his breath.

"Alright, I think," I said.

Aran sat on my other side. "She's being modest. Alina did great."

Morgan's eyes glinted. "I knew you would. And the Faezre? Tell me you made Swiss cheese of the stadium like you did Audrey's office."

There was an awkward silence. The only thing I'd produced was a gust of hot air, but I couldn't be certain if that was me or Stanley. "I, er . . ."

"Alina's game strategy is second only to mine," Aran said. "She hasn't had any training in Faezre yet, but it will come with time."

"Was I right, or was I right?" Morgan asked. He chinked my glass, spilling beer on my leathers. "What did you think of the sport?"

"I loved it," I said without hesitation.

"Pretty sure that's illegal in some countries," Morgan said.

"You think love should be outlawed everywhere," Aran said.

Morgan shrugged. "Look how happy I am without it."

This did not seem to impress CJ. "You never want to be in love?"

"Not intentionally."

"That's sad."

"Perhaps. But I'm not."

"So, you don't care about getting old and lonely?"

"Of course, I do," said Morgan, aghast. "Who wants to get old?"

The rest of the night was a whirlwind of drinks and laughter. I sat at the edge of my seat, captivated by the professional flag fall match. The teams' seamless coordination, strategic decoys, and cunning traps were nothing less than exhilarating.

The events of the previous night seemed like a far-off memory. It was as if an emotional barrier had formed in my mind, shielding me from any pain. I should have been shocked that my thoughts weren't consumed by Eben, but once the game began, I thought of little other than flag fall.

Thankfully, regardless of how intoxicated I became, I kept details of the prior night's events a secret. The last thing I wanted was for people to think I was insane for attempting an exorcism on myself, or to know that I topped the Reavers' hit list.

However, deep within me, something unexpected emerged—a desire to be liked—a need for it. I'd always aimed to blend in and remain inconspicuous, but as I danced on the table past midnight, I recognized that something had shifted, and I was all for it.

Chapter Twenty-Four

The next two weeks were a chaotic blur. When I wasn't in class mastering my abilities, I was consumed with either homework assignments, my Terre lessons with Harper—thankfully, I was doing much better than my first week—or flag fall practice. In the rare moments when I wasn't pushed to my limits, I pored over stacks of books in search of any information about dual demons.

Since the unsuccessful exorcism, my dreams had been plagued each night. Not by images of Eben or the explosion, which would have been more logical. Instead, they were haunted by the voice I'd heard in my head. The pleading voice, begging me to find a way. That voice had terrified me. Not because it was dark and twisted or anything like that, but because it had sounded rational. But Machina had killed Eben. It was her who'd ruined my life since she woke six years earlier. She needed to go. And if I became strong enough, then that's exactly what would happen. There would be no more deaths by our hands.

All of this left zero time for a social life, which I wasn't too upset by. The initial thrill of being noticed had turned stale. As the newest shiny thing at Astaroth, everyone wanted to hang out, inviting me to parties, dinners in Little Peak, and even a moonlight solstice soiree, whatever the heck that was. I'd become popular simply because I was the only Faezre demon at the academy. It was absurd and somewhat disheartening to see how people changed their attitude based on something so trivial. I mean, I couldn't even use the dang power.

I finally allowed myself some downtime on a sunny Sunday. CJ, Oliver, and I sat beside a stream deep in the woods, fishing rods in hand. I'd discovered the spot when I got lost attempting a shortcut to my Summoning and Conjuring class. The fish weren't biting—possibly because of CJ's impatient whipping of her line every few seconds. Then again, it could have something to do with our constant laughter at her stories of growing up in England.

"I've been meaning to ask," CJ said after an hour of catching water. "What's with the eyeliner? Trying to impress someone special?"

"Course not," I said, though I couldn't stop my cheeks from burning. Oliver glanced up. I focused on my fishing line to avoid making eye contact with either of them. "Kate and Tiffany gave it to me." Out of the corner of my eye, I saw Oliver relax. He'd grown fonder of me since our first mind-reading class. While flattered, he was far too young. Besides, he and Anya would make the most adorable couple.

"Kate and Tiffany?" CJ asked, mock vomiting. "Please tell me you don't actually *like* them? All they do is bitch about people."

"Like you're doing now?" I said, laughing as CJ threw a worm at me. "They're not so bad once you get to know them. Why don't you come to girls' night on Tuesday?"

"I'd love to, but that's the day Oliver has agreed to harvest my organs. I hate to miss appointments."

"Since when? You were an hour late to Innate Abilities on Friday."

"Yes, because I had a hair *appointment*."

Oliver and I looked at each other and then burst into laughter.

"I can leave you enough organs to go to girls' night, if you like?" he offered. "But I'll take your ears, so you don't have to listen to them."

"Sounds good, hun," she said. She tilted her head and watched him for a moment. "You know, you're really coming out of your shell lately."

His ears reddened. I hadn't noticed it before, but she was right. He was no longer the shy, awkward boy, but seemed surer of himself. Confident, even.

"You truly are," I said. "What's with this fresh shirt? Where's your yellow Pokémon one?"

"In the wash," he said, avoiding eye contact. "Can't wear it every day."

"And was that you pressing all those weights at the gym?" CJ asked.

"Oliver!" I cried. "I thought those arms were thicker!"

"It's good for my posture," he protested.

"And for the girls, I bet," said CJ.

He spluttered, and CJ and I laughed.

"Oh, leave the poor boy alone," I said. "He'll never hang out with us again if we tease him all the time."

"Fine, fine," said CJ. "So, let's get serious. Have you decided what you're doing for my birthday?"

"It's your birthday?" I said with feigned surprise. "Why haven't you mentioned it before?" CJ had gone on about it for the past week, even though it was still ages away. It was funny to watch someone older than nine get so worked up about their own birthday celebration.

"Quit joking," CJ said. "Birthdays are important to me. Mom threw the *best* parties. Angels, fairies, vampires—"

"Vampires?" Oliver said, looking up. "For a girl's birthday?"

"No," said CJ. "Vampires for a *woman's* birthday. It was for my sweet sixteen—a Halloween theme."

"I can't top that," I said. "But I have something special in mind."

"Special? Tell me!"

"Nope."

She leaped onto me and tickled me in the ribs. "Tell me or I won't stop."

I tried to fight her off, and we both rolled around the bank, knocking over the tackle box. Eventually, we gave up and flopped down, breathless. The grin on Oliver's face said he'd enjoyed it entirely too much.

"So, Oliver," CJ said. "I need a dapper gym junkie to be my date. Busy?"

"Work is murder at the moment—I have a few organs to pluck that day—but I may make it—"

"There you are," a voice interrupted from behind us.

I turned to see Aran, Morgan, Zach, and Ava approaching along the riverbank. I straightened and pulled a leaf from my hair. "Hey. How did you find us?"

Morgan plopped down between me and CJ. "It's my job to know where my number-one asset is." His attitude toward me had changed over the last couple weeks. He was no longer a bully but spoke to me as though I was a person worthy of his time.

Zach settled on my other side, smiled at CJ, then winked at me. "Fishing? You really are a catch."

Ava groaned. "He's been thinking about that line the whole way here." She turned to him. "She is not interested in you," she said slowly.

"And you think she wants you?"

"Obviously."

Zach laughed but cut it short. He looked to me uncertainly. "You don't, do you? Want her?"

I shook my head, and relief spread across his face.

"Not yet, she means," said Ava, grabbing CJ's forgotten fishing rod and casting the line into the water. "But she'll come around."

For a moment, the only sound was the rushing stream.

Morgan ruffled my hair. "So, how's my favorite girl? Ready to win us the season's first flag fall game?"

"Favorite?" CJ said. "Should I be jealous?"

"What's there to be jealous of? You ended it with me."

"You broke up?" I asked, surprised. She'd kept that news quiet. Not that we'd had much time together with everything going on.

"If we were ever together," said CJ.

"Of course we were together," said Morgan. "Don't downplay what we had."

She snorted. "Yeah, together. You, me, and every other girl in Michael."

"Didn't make it any less special," he said, picking up a worm from the tub and examining it.

I watched CJ to see if she was only pretending not to care, but I was happy to see Morgan's antics barely seemed to bother her. I guess they hadn't been together long enough to develop strong feelings.

"Ah, the classic unfulfilled love saga," said Zach. "Seems to be a trend lately." He looked pointedly at Aran.

Aran glared at him. "Drop it."

"Drop what?" I asked, curiously.

"Breakups," Ava explained. "Sophia and Aran split."

It took a moment for Ava's words to sink in. They'd broken up. Aran was single. Aran was available. My breath quickened. Did that mean . . . Was there a chance? I caught myself midthought. *Damn it, Alina! Get a grip. He is off-limits.* All men were for as long as Machina still raged inside me.

But as my mind wandered back to the night we spent together, I couldn't stop a small smile from playing on my lips. Even though nothing physical had happened, emotionally, it felt like we'd shared more than just a cuddle. It took all my restraint to stop myself from jumping up and down for joy.

"Oh?" I said, forcing concern into my voice. "Are you okay?"

"Fine," said Aran. He skimmed a rock across the water's surface, then searched for another and said nothing else.

"She might come to her senses," I said, praying it wasn't true.

"I don't see it happening that way," said Morgan. "Seeing as Aran broke up with her."

Sweet Jesus! Aran was single, and it was his own choosing. The sun's warmth caressed my face, and my hair danced on the breeze. It was a good day.

Morgan leaned toward me. "Look happier, why don't you," he whispered. I quickly dropped the smile that had crept onto my lips.

"Women," Aran muttered, skimming another rock. "More trouble than they're worth. I'm going solo from here on out."

"We're trying to distract him from girls for a while," Morgan explained. "You steer clear of him with your humps and bumps. He needs to focus on winning flag fall. On that note, so do you."

That night, as I lay in bed clutching my pillow to my chest, a warmth filled me at the thought of Aran. Of his lingering gaze while I'd showered, of the hours he'd comforted me in his bed . . .

I felt the sensation of his arms holding me, smelled his cologne—earthy and rich—and the electrifying touch of his fingers through my hair.

An urge ignited within me, cascading through my veins like wildfire. My body tingled with energy. Carefully, I traced my fingers down my chest and over my stomach.

I moved my hand lower and a flush burned through me. My breathing deepened as I touched myself. My movements were minimal, cautious not to wake anyone, and as I imagined Aran's touch, I gasped, and all my senses blurred.

That night, I slept in peace.

Chapter Twenty-Five

At long last, my efforts in enhancing my Aeria and Terre powers were paying off. Although I couldn't compete with the top students, at least I wasn't at the bottom. This was a win. Faezre, on the other hand, was a completely different story. It was more Russian roulette than anything. An occasional flame would come to hand when summoned, but it brought about a disorienting sense of vertigo. My mind would spin and my vision blur, prompting Oliver, who accompanied me during practice sessions near the sandpit, to stop my training for fear of my safety.

As a bonus slice of cherry pie, Machina had been silent since the exorcism. She'd not attempted to seize control once. It was as though she knew I was doing everything in my power to banish her, and she'd chosen silence to persuade me she wasn't worth my attention.

On the morning of my first flag fall game, a Saturday, I was both surprised and concerned about feeling perfectly fine. There was no consuming fear tearing at my chest or the breathlessness of an anxiety attack. My life didn't flash before my eyes, and not once did I entertain the thought of running back to Earth. Instead, a hint of excitement stirred within me—not butterflies but an eagerness to discover what I was capable of. I'd watched many professional games over the previous weeks, learning lots about strategy and flow. However, those experiences couldn't provide me with the thrill of being a participant, which, for me, was the most exhilarating part.

While fixing my hair into a tight bun in the bathroom, I saw that my reflection had further transformed since I'd arrived at the academy. The dark rings below my eyes had vanished, and my once dull skin now had a hint of color. I stood taller with my shoulders pulled back, and as crazy as it sounded, my hair appeared to glow. Maybe Georgie was right about Taco Express grease ruining it. I smiled and twirled, my red sports bra catching the window light. I was having a sexy day.

The game wasn't scheduled until three in the afternoon, which meant I had to spend most of the day pretending I wasn't itching to step onto the field. The cafeteria was decorated in the silver and yellow colors of Michael, as well as the blue and rose of Uriel, our opponent. When I entered with CJ and Aran, cheers erupted, not only from Michael but also from Raphael and Gabriel. I grinned as I walked through the crowd. People patted me on the back and wished me luck. I knew better than to think they all liked me; most were simply excited to see Faezre in action. And, naturally, they wanted to see Uriel defeated.

I grabbed a tray and joined the bakery line, but everyone stepped aside and ushered me to the front.

"Thanks, but I couldn't," I said.

"Course you could," said Morgan, taking advantage of the express line to the donuts and loading his plate. "You're on the flag fall team."

A professor who appeared to be in his forties nudged me forward. "Crush them for us."

"Ya'll are too kind," I said, placing an egg bagel on my plate. I grabbed a freshly squeezed orange juice and headed for the patio when someone collided with me, knocking my tray to the floor. The glass broke and juice splattered everywhere.

"Heck! I'm sorry—" I said, even though it wasn't my fault. I stopped when I saw Sophia, accompanied by her cheer squad: Trishelle and Clara.

"I guess you were too busy playing homewrecker to watch where you were going," she said loudly, silencing the cafeteria.

I knelt to pick up the broken glass, my cheeks flushing. "I had nothing to do with you and Aran—"

"Save it," said Trishelle. "We've seen the way you look at him."

Clara nodded. "Like a fat kid looks at a muffin."

"Clara!" Sophia scolded quietly. "You can't say *fat kid* anymore. It's disrespectful." She cleared her throat. "What she meant to say was, like a *starving adult*, from, like, Utah or somewhere."

I sliced my finger on a shard of glass. Blood beaded out as I yanked my hand back and sucked the cut. *Again? Really?* I stood and met Sophia's eyes. What had I ever done to them? I thought mean girls were a thing of the past, but it seemed some people never grew out of being cows. I turned to find a broom to clean up the mess and noticed a ring of people had gathered, looking on with anticipation.

"That's right, walk away," said Sophia. "Like the trash you are."

Something snapped inside me. I spun around and strode back. "Walk away?" I said, enjoying the moment her smirk fell. "I can't imagine how hard it must be for you to realize that, despite all this"—I gestured from her head to her feet—"you couldn't keep Aran from walking away. Do you ever wonder how hot you'd have to be to hide a shit personality?" Audible gasps rose from the audience. "The answer is, a hell of a lot hotter than you."

She bristled as though I'd flicked her on the nose. Her gaze flitted to the grinning faces of people she'd bullied in the past and she firmed her jaw. "Yeah, well, you're . . . you're a freak. Nobody really likes you."

I yawned loudly. "That's the best you've got? Go on, try again."

Sophia opened her mouth to say more, but Trishelle and Clara quickly stepped in and guided her away toward the restrooms. Her face was flushed as she glared back at me. The cafeteria filled with applause, and I couldn't help but grin.

Some guy created a vacuum of air to gather the glass shards, whisking them into a pile. "Good luck today."

"Thanks, honey," I said, then headed outside to where Aran and CJ stood, watching me.

"Brutal!" CJ exclaimed. "I didn't know you could go full radge. She won't recover from that in a hurry."

I sat at their table, blood pounding in my ears. "Neither did I," I said. And then, as if a switch had been flipped, the fury I'd felt vanished, leaving me feeling sick to my stomach. "Did I go too far?"

Aran wore a strange expression. His lips were tight as he looked at me. He gave a small shake of his head. "It was unnecessary."

"Unnecessary?" said CJ. "Sophia needed to be put in her place. She's a vile bitch who won't stop until someone makes her."

His gaze hardened. "That doesn't mean Alina should pull her threads until she completely unravels. Alina's supposed to be the reasonable one."

I couldn't believe what he was saying. I'd just been attacked by Sophia because he'd broken up with her, and now he was having a go at me? "She started it. I didn't ask for any of that. You think I enjoy being laughed at?"

"You could've ended it by walking away," he said. "I guess I didn't realize you had that in you." He stood with a slice of vegemite toast. "I've got things to do. I'll meet you in the locker rooms at one thirty."

I stared after him as he left.

"Don't worry about it," CJ said. "He probably has some demented residual feelings for her. They'll go away in time."

"I'm not worried," I lied. "Maybe now Sophia will stop giving me grief every chance she gets."

"Exactly! Anyway, let's forget about it. How do you want to spend the morning? We can do anything. Except the library. Please don't say you want to go to the library."

"I want to go to the library."

She groaned. "Why do you hate me?"

"I need a distraction for a while."

"You're lucky I'm a good friend," she said. "Otherwise, I'd be going to the artesian market in Little Peak with everyone else. Will that hot librarian work today?"

"I assume you mean Jason, not Amelia. Yes, he works weekends."

"Then what are we waiting for?"

Chapter Twenty-Six

While the preparation chambers for flag fall were impressively equipped, having everything from ice baths and saunas to fridges packed with sports drinks, and even float tanks, it was clear the facilities were designed with the high-risk nature of the sport in mind. A section was dedicated to rehabilitation equipment, an *Unwell Room* was filled with medical supplies, and there was a strangely large number of defibrillators attached to the walls.

As the sound of the crowd above grew to a roar, Isabella and Trix warmed up on the treadmills, Stanley practiced his Aeria attacks on a wooden target at a three-lane range, Zach got a deep-tissue massage, and Elias, with his headphones on, danced in front of the mirror.

I glanced at my watch for the twentieth time in thirty minutes. It was 2:50, yet I was still surprisingly calm. A month ago, the thought of giving a speech would have robbed me of sleep. Now I was about to play one of the most dangerous sports on Cronix, with a roaring audience filling the stadium, and I felt . . . nothing.

"Bring it in," Aran called, cutting my lack of concern short. We gathered around him in a tight circle, and I was startled by the blazing determination in his eyes. "Do you hear that crowd out there? They are here to watch us grind Uriel into the dirt, to settle the score after the grand final last year. This is our chance to show Astaroth we're not just a bunch of carrots in leather. We know their strengths and their weaknesses but make no mistake—they've been watching us too." He revolved slowly on the spot. "They have a plan, so expect the unexpected, but know that a thousand plans won't stop us if we put in the effort. That's all I want from you—effort, all the time, in all ways."

"I'm going to send them to the Unwell Room," Stanley said, mashing a fist into his palm.

I would have laughed if it wasn't for the serious expressions on everyone's faces.

"Then let's do it," Aran said, his voice ringing with confidence. "Let's give the academy something to talk about!"

I followed Aran out of the change room and into the tunnel, my pulse racing as the first inklings of adrenaline surged through me. We stopped at a bench that held eight talismans, and Aran tied one around each of our necks as we filed past.

"Remember, this will protect you from the worst attacks," he said as he secured mine, "but it won't stop you from getting hurt if the force is strong enough. Don't think you're invincible." He held me at arm's length. "You good?"

I nodded, still off-balance by how confident I felt.

He clapped my shoulders, then turned and started onto the field, the roaring crowd deafening. "I literally shit my leathers in my first flag fall match. I can't believe you look like you're about to go for a stroll in the park."

"Was there a talisman out there for loose bowels?"

"No, but I found one for invisibility. That helped a lot."

We reached the middle of the field and I spun in awe. The bleachers were packed with people on their feet, waving flags and cheering. A grin spread across my lips as I took it in, savoring the moment. No wonder professional athletes put themselves through hell for this.

The Uriel team stood on their flag mound, surveying the vast terrain that had been terraformed into a battlefield. The ground was scarred with zigzagging ridges, and craters pockmarked the area. There were spires, cracks, and a fog separating the two flags. Above them were floating Architect islands and smaller pieces of land.

Uriel's team captain, Zane Kissinger, stood alongside the referee. Aran jogged to join them while the rest of us hurried to our flag, breaking into our Raider and Shielder groups.

"Pretty similar to what we trained on," said Zach. "See the waypoints on the aerial boulders? They'll be easiest to reach earlier on."

I nodded, but only half listened. I took in the lay of the land, memorizing each feature. Who knew when that information would be useful? In strategy, knowledge was power, and I needed all the power I could get to survive unscathed.

No. Not unscathed—to win. I didn't care if I got hurt. I wanted to rub Uriel's nose in the dirt.

Heads, I heard Aran's voice in my mind. I looked back to see the referee flipping a coin. All three bent down to see the result. Aran gave us a thumbs-down.

It's tails. Don't worry, we don't need to choose to win.

Having studied professional matches, I knew the significance of winning the toss and selecting the talismans. Choosing the three talismans to be hidden in the arena allowed you to shape the battle to your advantage, either by amplifying your strengths or exploiting the enemy's weaknesses. Though not vital to win, it sure helped a lot.

A stone pillar erupted beneath Aran's feet, lifting him onto his island.

Teams ready, announced an unfamiliar voice, presumably the ref's. *In three . . . two . . . one . . . capture the flag!*

We sprang into action, scrambling down the scree slope. The audience's roar vanished, leaving only the sound of my heartbeat. Ava led the charge, reaching the base first and not slowing at the nine-foot-wide chasm. She gestured with her hand and ran across the gap as if on an invisible bridge. It was a move we'd practiced often, involving the creation of a highly pressurized air floor. Zach went next and I followed, not looking into the black abyss.

"First aerial boulder on the right," Zach said, climbing up the next hill.

"Taking the easy one first?" Ava asked.

I stared at the floating boulder surrounded by a racing asteroid field. "That's the easy one?"

"Piece of cake."

Aran's voice echoed in our minds: *Their Raiders and Shielders have bunkered down near their flag . . . I think they're constructing a golem*—Ava cursed—*so make the most of the open field while you can. Raiders, you'll have this initial period to hit as many waypoints as possible, but steer clear of their flag; it's too risky with their entire team there. Shielders, give them hell—our Raiders won't need you for the moment. Drag it out as long as you can.*

"Interesting strategy," Zach said. "Seems like this is their plan to counter our fiery friend here."

The destruction golems caused on the battlefield was astonishing. They were monstrous beasts with immeasurable strength that could change the tide of a game in an instant. I wiped the sweat from my brow, ignoring the way my stomach flipped on itself.

Zach reached the top of the ridge and leaped high. Ava thrust her hands forward, catching him in a pocket of air and propelling him toward the asteroids. It looked like the stones would tear him apart, but as he neared, he extended his hands and the rocks ricocheted off each other to fly wide in response to his Terre power. He landed in one piece.

Raiders, watch out! Aran's frantic voice filled my head.

I turned to find Uriel's Sentry had launched a rock at Ava. Without thinking, I threw my arms forward, fingers spread wide, and caught the stone's trajectory. I created a ramp in its path, but its speed carried it right through it. I latched onto it desperately and pulled with all my might, trying to knock it off course, but it wasn't budging. As it neared Ava, I squeezed one eye shut and waited for the impact—

The rock gave in and swerved at the last instant, narrowly missing Ava and crashing into the hill beyond.

"Nice one," Ava said with a wink before turning back to Zach. "I'd like to see what else you can do with those hands."

Five points to Michael! the ref announced.

Zach had reached the waypoint. We scored the first points!

"Piece of cake," I said, feeling lightheaded.

Zach landed beside us. "Turns out Zane trained over break. This just got a lot more difficult."

When you're done chatting, Aran said, *follow the crevice to your eleven o'clock and take the left fork; there's a waypoint in the pit.*

The following points came with little trouble, and by the time we reached the third, I wondered if the whole game would pose any challenge at all. I mentioned this to Ava as we dashed through a tunnel system toward the center of the field.

"Sweet Alina," she panted between breaths, "nothing is easy when you fight a golem. Once it's built, we'll be lucky to get another point."

By the end of the first twenty-minute period, Trix, Isabella, and Stanley had hindered Uriel's team so effectively that they still hadn't completed their golem. We led forty-five to nil. As we entered the locker room, sweat dripping from me, my one thought was the need to hit the gym with CJ and Oliver. My legs trembled from exertion, and my lungs ached. I hadn't done cardio in a long while.

"Everyone, good work out there," Aran said, handing out red Gatorade. "Shielders, outstanding! They weren't prepared for such a brutal onslaught. Isabella, top notch improvisation—that sandstorm left them confused as hell. Zane would have wanted the golem built already, so he's probably in the middle of a hissy fit right now." He looked at Ava, Zach, and me. "Raiders, bloody impressive start. Alina, that deflection was the duck's guts—truly great." He took a long drink. "But this isn't over. Everything will change once they finish their golem. This is where the game is decided. Everyone, effort, all the time, in all ways. Leave nothing on the field. And keep an eye out for those damned talismans."

"When do we unleash our secret weapon?" Isabella said, eying me over her drink. "No point having her if we can't use her."

"When the time's right," he said.

We returned to our flag mound in high spirits.

Whatever the Shielders were doing, it must have been hell for Uriel. The first fifteen minutes of the second third went just as smoothly as the first. The angry shouts from Uriel's team echoed across the field as we continued scoring points. Before I knew it, we were up ninety-five to nil.

But then it happened.

A bone-chilling scream tore through the arena, silencing the crowd and stealing my breath away. Ava slowed in front of me and looked up. We were deep in a ravine and couldn't see the source of the cry. We didn't need to.

Shit! Aran said. *They've finished. The golem is live and on the move. I say again: the golem is live. Shielders, get back to help Elias. Elias . . . Damn it, Elias, stop posing for photos and get your mind on the game! Raiders . . . good luck. Take your opportunities for waypoints, but don't take risks.*

We hurried up a narrow ledge, and I saw the beast in all its terrifying glory. A knot formed in my stomach. It was a humanoid monster, at least twice my height and as wide as a truck. It was made up of swirling winds and clouds, its body constantly shifting shape. Flashes of lightning sparked within its chest as it took lumbering steps toward our flag.

"Sweet Lord," I gasped. "We have to fight that?"

Zach stared beside me. "There is no fighting that. All we can do is keep out of its way."

A whistling sound pierced the arena. Air rushed past us, drawn toward the creature, its gapping mouth sucking in as its chest expanded. My hair ruffled on the current, and an uneasiness settled in my chest.

"We should move," I said numbly. Why was it sucking in its breath? Shouldn't it be attacking us with lightning or something? The whistling grew louder before coming to an abrupt stop. Eerie silence surrounded us. Its head swiveled to our direction. *Shit!* "It's going to attack!" I grabbed Ava's and Zach's collars and yanked them off the cliff. We plummeted toward the ground, tumbling end over end. I thrust my hands forward, praying my power would hold, and a bubble of air formed to cushion us and stop us from splatting into pancakes.

A roar of wind tore through the canyon followed by a jet of electrified air slamming into the cliff top where we'd just stood. The entire ridgeline exploded, raining debris down toward us.

"Crap!" Zach said, sweeping his arm in an arc. Rocks on the ravine floor shot up to form a shield above us. The resounding collision as the rubble crashed into it made my ears ring.

After the rock storm subsided, Zach waved aside his shield and stood. "Now that's what they call a real cliffhanger." He cracked a smile as he dusted himself off.

Ava and I glared at him.

"Too soon?" he asked.

Ava looked to me. "Come on, let's finish this before he tries another joke."

The rest of that middle third was as fun as a slap in the face. The ref's voice, which I'd previously liked, now grated on me. Every time he spoke, it was to award Uriel points. In just a few minutes, they'd made significant progress in closing the gap. Far from us scoring points, it was all we could do to stay alive.

By the time the second break arrived, I was exhausted and raging.

"Why didn't we build a golem?" I asked as I tore off my gloves. "It seems like that's all you need to win."

"It's not over yet," said Aran, his leathers still pristine. It must be nice, standing above it all, watching everyone else put in effort. "We're still ahead. Elias, it was kind of you stop trying to get that girl's attention long enough to stop that raid. Well done—"

"Unleash the fire," Isabella cut him off, folding her arms.

"When the time's right," said Aran.

"Which is when?"

"The last five."

"Crap, Aran!" Trix said. "You mean we're going through another fifteen minutes of that?"

"I don't want to play our hand unless we have to," Aran said. "It'll stand us in a stronger position going into our next matches."

"I think we have to," said Stanley, whose talisman now wafted smoke. "We haven't got long in us."

Aran looked from one face to the next, then sighed. His eyes settled on me. "Ready?"

I nodded. "As ready as I'll ever be." They were right. If we didn't act soon, it was game over. I did not want to lose my first ever game of flag fall.

"Then do it," Aran said. "But wait for my order."

When we stood on our mound again, waiting to begin the final third, my hands shook like crazy. It could have been fear. It could have been excitement. It could have been exhaustion. I didn't know. What I did know was, if we got it right—no, if *I* got it right—then victory was ours.

The whistle sounded, and we sprang down the slope, navigating the obstacles until we arrived at the highest point in the field. It was the ridgeline that now had a ten-foot cavity from the earlier golem assault. We huddled beneath it, unseen.

Zach clapped me on the back. "You're going to nail it."

"But bail if it gets too dangerous," said Ava. "Don't hurt yourself for a game."

I nodded and hugged them before they raced away to the left, heading to a concealed position Aran had scouted nearer to Uriel's flag. I stayed low, hoping Uriel's Architect hadn't noticed we'd separated. Our entire strategy hinged on me. If they caught on, our game was over, and I'd have to face the smug faces of Uriel students for the rest of the year.

Time crawled by, and each heartbeat added more nerves to my stomach. Zach and Ava were out of sight. The ref announced Uriel's score was now sixty-five to our ninety-five. *Come on.* It was time for us to fight to keep our lead again. I flexed my fingers, eager to start.

Get ready, Alina, Aran's voice rang in my head.

I tensed, waiting for my chance. It was my moment to show everyone what I was capable of.

Now, Alina! Unleash the beast!

I jumped to my feet and found the advancing golem instantly, its unseeing eyes scanning the field. I raised my arms, feeling the weight of the team on my shoulders. If we won from here, it would be because of me.

But if we lost . . .

My arms dropped slightly.

No. We couldn't lose. I'd practiced my ass off for this match. I had to prove to myself that I had grown in my time at Astaroth, that I wasn't the same old Alina.

But a seed of doubt found my throat.

I clenched my jaw and straightened my arms.

The crowd's roar surged. Their gazes burned into me—watching, judging.

Sweat trickled into my eyes.

Alina? It was Aran.

I swallowed again and, with trembling hands, searched for the power deep within. I reached for the inferno.

But it wasn't there. The force I'd always felt during my training was gone.

Alina! The fire wall! Aran's voice was urgent. *Ava and Zach need the fire wall to get the flag!*

What was happening? Why had my power vanished? I looked around, the faces in the crowd sharpening into focus.

An angry bellow shook the ground. My gaze snapped back to the golem. Its head was locked on me. It inhaled deeply, its chest expanding as the surrounding air was drawn toward it.

Alina! It's going to attack!

My cloak whipped around my legs. I had one last desperate look for my Faezre, my pulse racing, but it was nowhere to be found. I was as void of power as a slug. With my heart pounding, I turned and leaped off the cliff and into the chasm.

My Aeria was weaker this time, and although it cushioned my fall, I still collided with the ground and pain fired through my ribs. My head spun as I rolled and pressed against the rocky wall, the ridge blasting apart for a second time. Stone and earth showered down, and a rock struck my shoulder. I cried out as smoke drifted from my talisman.

Shielders, get to Alina! Aran's voice was frantic. *Uriel knows where she is—they'll try to incapacitate her—*

Isabella's voice joined Aran's: *But their Raiders are near our flag. We'll leave Elias vulnerable if we go—*

Just get there!

I sat, shaking, terrified of the next voice I'd hear in my head. But no matter how much I willed it not to happen, the ref's voice soon echoed in my mind.

One hundred-and-twenty-five to ninety-five.

Uriel had captured our flag.

Guilt and shame paralyzed me. I hid against the cliff, wishing I'd never been born. So many eyes watched me, and though I couldn't hear laughter over the ringing in my ears, I knew how foolish I must look. By the time Stanley, Trix, and Isabella found me, I couldn't look them in the face.

"Pull yourself together!" Isabella snapped. "You still have a chance to fix this. Just stop crying—it's embarrassing."

Aran coordinated my return to the Raiders, but Uriel's score had blown out to one hundred and thirty-five. Zach and Ava had found a few easy waypoints, bringing us up to one hundred and ten. Upon seeing me, their usual warmth vanished, replaced with a coldness I'd never seen from them. It hurt more than my injured ribs.

"Quit apologizing," Ava said as we sprinted through a canyon's horseshoe bend. "Let's focus on stopping them from destroying us by a record lead."

"I thought I could do it," I said. How could I make them understand? I should have been able to use my Faezre. It had always worked at practice. But now, something was off. Something had broken inside me. I was about to apologize again, but something shiny caught my eye. I slowed. It was a glint of gold in the shadows.

"What's that?" I asked.

"Come on, Alina," Zach said, doubling back. "We don't have time . . ." His voice trailed off as he followed my gaze. "No way!" He rushed over and pried the item from the wall. "Alina, I could kiss you!"

It was a golden talisman.

Ava snatched it from his grip and read the runes.

"Is it enough?" I asked. "To fix things?"

Zach grinned, displaying the large gap between his teeth. "It just might be!" His voice cut through my mind: *Aran, Alina has a talisman.*

What type?

Eye of Darkness.

My head burst with the excited thoughts of our entire team.

Alright, settle down, Aran said. *We've only enough time for one final push, but it must be for their flag. This is our last-ditch effort. Everyone needs to contribute. Everyone. Team leads, take charge and act as you see fit. I'll help when necessary, but we need your instincts to win. Only use the talisman when I say. Go get it!*

Ava's eyes sparkled with excitement. "Less than five minutes to snatch the flag," she said. "I like those odds. We'll make a dash for it—they won't expect that, not with their pet prowling about." She placed her hand on Zach's, and they looked at me.

My stomach dropped. What if I messed up again? In front of everyone? Once was bad enough, but twice? It would destroy me. Zach raised his eyebrows. I placed my hand on top of theirs reluctantly.

"For Michael!" Zach said, and we shot our hands into the air.

I didn't have a choice but to follow them out of the canyon and up the first hill, which offered a view of Uriel's mound. As we crested the ridge, a gust of wind shot overhead, forcing us back down a few feet.

Ava cursed. "They've fallen back to defend their flag. They know we don't have enough time to beat them by waypoints alone."

Zach checked his watch. "Less than two minutes . . ."

Ava scanned the area. "We could attempt crossing the north saddle—"

"It's in the golem's line of sight. We'd be obliterated."

The weight of our predicament pressed down on me. We were only there because of me. The team had trusted my abilities, and I was on the verge of rewarding them with defeat. I couldn't allow that. I had to find a way to use the talisman. And if I messed up again . . . well, it was no more than I deserved.

"Wait here," I said, scrambling to the peak and lifting my head just enough to glance over. A Shielder stood directly opposite us, her eyes scanning constantly. To the left, on a small outcrop, was a second Shielder. If we could crest this hill without being hit, we could safely follow the next chasm toward their flag. I waved the others up, then reached out to Aran. *If we use the talisman on the Shielder to our front, we'll have a clear path to the flag.*

You sure? he asked hesitantly. *We only have one shot at this.*

Positive. My power may have let me down, but I'd be damned if my strategy did.

Then win the game for us.

Zach pulled out the talisman and recited the runes. It glowed with power.

The Shielder to our front shouted, then fell to her knees, rubbing her eyes. "They've found a talisman!" she screamed.

"Go!" I cried, helping Ava and Zach over the lip. They sprinted down the slope before I'd even crested.

The ground rumbled.

Ava and Zach stopped in their tracks. My breath hitched. They turned back to me with wide eyes, then the sand beneath them opened like a monstrous mouth and swallowed them whole. When it closed again, there was no trace they'd ever been there.

I stared at the spot. *What? How?* Then, with a crashing realization, I understood. It had been a trap. Their Raiders knew we would make a final push and had helped their Shielders. My knees buckled beneath me, and I slipped a little way down the slope. What had I done? I was still the same, weak Alina from Breaux Bridge. I was pathetic. My breaths came in rapid, shallow gasps.

Always so dramatic, a voice echoed in my head.

I jolted. That voice . . . I'd heard it before. The night of my exorcism—

We go back much further than that dreadful night, my dear, she said. *I mean, sure, I mightn't have been as articulate back then, but we've communicated, if only through emotions.*

A trickle of cold fear entered my bloodstream. *Leave me alone,* I begged, rolling onto my back. *Why can't you leave me alone?*

Because you couldn't live without me. You're weak, Alina, you said it yourself. Soft as butter.

No, I said, trying to deny it. But she was right. I hadn't changed at all since arriving at Astaroth. All the learning and magic in the world couldn't fix what I had going on inside. The realization dragged me deeper within my body.

Just leave me be, I whispered. *Please, leave me alone.*

You don't mean that, she said. *You don't want to deal with all this pain. Do you want me to take it away?*

Somewhere in the distance, Aran's voice echoed in my head, but it was abruptly silenced.

He can't help you, Machina said. *All you have is me. Once again, I'm here to save your ass.*

Tears spilled onto my cheeks as I shook my head. It was too much. I didn't want to deal with it anymore. My thoughts blurred until I couldn't think, and a peace found me, a solace in the dark as I surrendered to her.

Chapter Twenty-Seven

As I lay on my back on the slope, staring into the open sky above as a thousand eyes watched me from the stands, I vaguely registered that I was no longer anxious.

I was no longer anything.

Guilt at surrendering to Machina should have torn me to bits. It'd been years since I'd given in to the temptation to shelter from the world, to give up control of my life. But I felt nothing.

Laughter echoed from the bleachers, fading in and out like an old radio.

The earthy smell of damp soil was thick and heavy.

Somewhere, I wondered what Machina would do now that she had control. What she wanted from me.

No, dear Alina, she said. Her voice didn't have the pitch of a woman's, or the bass of a man's, but hovered in between. *What do you want? You've imprisoned me in our body, you survive on a diet of booze and pills to keep me zombified, and you've even tried locking me up in a lizard. A lizard! Hardly what I'd call a friendship, is it? And yet, you want to use my Faezre?*

Reasonable. I'd not been a gracious host. How could I expect to use her power after all I'd done?

Admit you need me, she said. *Tell me you want me to win this game.* Her amusement was obvious.

From far off, the ref's voice joined hers. One minute remaining.

Ticktock, Alina . . .

The game was almost over. We were going to lose. I thought of Aran, of how upset he'd be. I didn't want that. *Win the game,* I said. *Please . . . I can't do it without you.*

Ugh, talk about needy, she said.

We rolled to our feet and scrambled back to the ridge. Our hands swept in a wide arc, fingers splayed as though dragging flames up from the earth. Heat radiated within us as a power, stronger than anything I'd felt before, welled inside. It twirled in the pit of our stomach, blistering hot, and I shrank away from it, terrified of its strength but awed by the potential.

A laugh escaped us as we stepped over the lip and shot our hands forward. A jet of fire erupted from them and soared through the air to smash into Uriel's flag mound, detonating in a blinding explosion.

When our eyes adjusted to the sudden brightness, a tunnel of flames cut across the stadium directly to their flag. But time was not on our side. It seemed impossible to reach the flag before the game ended.

Hurry! I pleaded.

Something inside shifted. It was as though our core had been realigned, redirecting the Faezre to course through our feet. We rocketed from the hill, propelling ourselves through the flaming tunnel at breakneck speeds.

The flag fluttered in the swirling wind as we closed the distance, arm outstretched. In a moment of desperation, our fingers wrapped around the heated pole, yanking it from the ground as we skidded to a stop, almost toppling from the hill. The tube of flames dissipated, letting the roars from the crowd filter down. It was louder and crazier than ever.

Michael has captured the flag, the ref announced. *Michael wins, one-hundred-and-sixty to one-hundred-and-thirty-five.*

An overwhelming thrill raced through us. I'd won the game for Michael—

No, said Machina. *I won for Michael. Never forget what I do for you.*

The team rushed forward, some soaring through the sky while others surfed ground waves. They tossed me into the air, shouting wildly. I emerged from the pit within, and raw emotion crashed over me. To go from despair to victory left me shaking and needing the support of Stanley when I was placed back on my feet.

"I've never seen anything like it!" Ava said, hugging me tightly.

"It was so hot!" cried Zach. "Literally."

But I only had eyes for one person. Aran gazed down at me, a sheepish smile on his perfect lips. "I think it's safe to say you've cemented your position on our team."

As his smile transformed into a full-fledged grin, I realized that no other man could come close to being as beautiful as him. He leaned in for a hug, and my heart fluttered.

Then something strange happened. Machina, who'd remained silent during the celebration, took over once more. She reached out, grasping Aran's leathers, and yanked him in. Our lips met forcefully.

What are you doing? I screamed, fighting against her. *He is off-limits!*

Aran, clearly as surprised as I was, froze, and I knew this moment would kill my social life. Rejection in front of the academy was guaranteed to haunt me forever. But miraculously, he relaxed into it and his mouth pressed hungrily into mine as his hand slid up the back of my neck, drawing me in tighter.

Aran was kissing me. Aran May was kissing me. As his lips opened, I felt his warmth, tasted him, and wanted more. I wanted all of him.

Take what you want, Machina's voice whispered in my head. *Don't let anyone stand in your way.*

Then, as abruptly as she'd arrived, Machina retreated, sinking back down into her resting place, leaving me in control once more.

Aran broke off the kiss, pulling back just a touch as his hazel eyes searched mine. His dimples appeared as his grin reached his ears. "That was everything I'd hoped it would be."

"You hoped we would kiss?"

"Didn't you—"

"Medic!" a voice shouted.

Startled, I spun to see one of the Uriel Raiders kneeling beside what appeared to be a smoldering rock. No, it wasn't a rock, I realized with horror. It was Zane, his leathers billowing like a chimney. He must have been caught in Machina's explosion. In *my* explosion. The crowd fell into stunned silence. Was he . . . was he dead?

I turned to Aran, hoping to find some reassurance that smoking players was a regular occurrence at the academy, that the talisman would've protected Zane, but the shock on his face was all I needed to know that I had crossed a line.

Two men carrying a medic bag dashed onto the field. They skidded to their knees beside Zane, one holding his hand, the other rummaging through his equipment. Slowly, Zane raised one knee and a flash of relief quelled the guilt inside me. But just because he was alive did not mean he was unharmed.

I took a step back. I'd almost killed someone. Machina had almost killed someone. If the blast had been just a little stronger . . . If he had been a little closer, he'd be dead. The stadium's press squeezed me until it was all I could do to breathe.

I had to get out of there.

I pushed past Aran and sprinted down the mound. Tears blurred my vision as I dashed out of the stadium and past the sandpit, the hum of a thousand gossiping voices trailing me. A stitch burned in my side and my breathing was ragged, but I didn't slow. I abandoned the forest track, pushing through the dense foliage deeper into the woods than I'd ever been before. It was only after I'd completely exhausted myself that I collapsed in a heap under the wispy branches of a willow tree. I curled in on myself like a newborn baby—or an old dying woman—and sobbed.

Why couldn't I live a normal life? Friday-night football games and human friends? Why did every moment have to be a struggle?

From the shadows of my mind, a voice chimed in, *Where's the fun in that?*

A fit of anger drowned out my self-pity. It was her. She'd done this to me. All of it. I sat up, fists bunched. "Who do you think you are?"

She gave a mental shrug. *Usually, I'm your protector. Though I have a nagging feeling that today I'll play the part of a comforting friend. Or—heaven forbid—a therapist.*

The way she spoke, like this was all some kind of joke, stoked the fire. "You're nothing but a cancerous growth, just here to destroy me."

Pot, meet kettle. We're demons, Alina. What did you expect, tea parties? And just for the record, the kid is fine. A bit charred, perhaps, but he will live.

"You could've killed him."

Easily. I could've left him as ash on the wind. But I didn't. I held back so I could help you win the game.

My throat tightened as her words sunk in. I had begged her to take over. Zane's injuries are on me as much as they are on her. "I don't want your help."

You need all the help you can get—

"Fuck off!" I screamed, startling some birds from the branches above. "Get out of my head. Get out of my life!"

Ah, anger. My old friend. It used to consume me, too. I was forced to live each day as a prisoner inside a body I had no control over. I hated you, Alina, more than I can ever express.

I opened my mouth to reply, but the words got stuck in my throat. She . . . hated me?

An understatement, if I'm being honest. I despised you. But as time passed, I grew. I realized that despite our differences, we are the same. So, given that I hold myself in high esteem, I suppose that means I have a certain . . . affection for you, too. Even if it is by proxy.

Her words left me reeling. This thing, who until recently had been diagnosed as a mental condition, was now telling me she liked me? I wasn't buying it. *If that's true, then leave me alone. Life is hard enough without having you kill everyone.*

Leave? You must be confused. This is my body. You are the intruder, not me. If you want to vacate the premises, I know a perfect lizard you could inhabit.

That wasn't my fault!

She sighed. *I don't blame you. Not anymore. But you've worked hard to imprison me over the last few years, and that shit leaves a mark.*

That's because you cause trouble when you're in control.

Trouble? Right, I'm the villain who protected us from Eben. I'm the villain who won flag fall, after you asked me to do it. I'm the villain who helped you make friends back home—

You made out with three cheerleaders!

They were hot. What did you expect me to do?

A breeze rustled the branches of the willow. *Hot? So, what, you're . . . gay?*

Gayer than a glitter-shitting unicorn.

But you kissed Aran!

A shudder rolled through our body. *Don't remind me*, she said. *I did that for you.*

It felt like a ton of bricks had been dropped on me. I already had enough to deal with, and this new revelation wasn't helping.

Machina's voice softened. *It's a lot to digest, I get it. I'll give you some space. But first, I need you to do two things for me. Stop calling me Machina. It's stupid, and I can't believe you called me that for so long. My name's Kali. Second, Ava is hot as hell. Let me hook up with her—*

Are you serious?

Dead serious. She's gorgeous. You owe me one for Aran. Think it over. Adios.

Chapter Twenty-Eight

I hid beneath those whispering boughs until the sky fell to the pastel pinks of sunset. My mind was a tangled web, and each strand I pulled only tightened the knot. Kali was a jerk, that was obvious, but the logic she had spoken with made it hard to dismiss her as evil. That one fact alone shattered the foundation I had built my justification on for keeping her buried inside. If Kali belonged to this body by birthright, where did that put me? Should I not be the one held prisoner?

As the shadows grew, I was still none the wiser about what to do. I couldn't imprison her indefinitely. Sure, she'd done some terrible things, but her justification for them . . . I mean, was the punishment worth the crime? As much as Eben's death had hurt me, it was an act of self-defense. And if Zane was really alright, like she believed, then was there any harm in her act? Flag fall was a contact sport, after all.

The hardest part to swallow was the idea that Kali had my best interests at heart. It wasn't until I thought about it logically that it made sense. If I died, she died. I got the impression an untimely death was not on her bucket list.

The problem was thinking of a way to stop her from stealing control whenever she felt like it. One option was to give her control. To share our body from time to time. I couldn't begin to imagine what that would mean for dating. For friends and classes. It could work with some rules and restrictions in place, such as no hookups. No murdering. No returning control for me to suffer through hangovers. But it would take some figuring out.

I leaned back against the trunk, head throbbing, more lost than ever. Maybe I'd have more answers after a shower and a good night's sleep.

A rustling from nearby had my head whipping around in that direction. My heart leapt to my throat as I spotted a pair of eyes watching me through the leaves. I kicked back against the trunk, a cry of surprise bursting from my lips.

The eyes belonged to a creature resembling a puppy with midnight fur and oversized ears. Her wings were folded neatly at her sides, and a purple mist drifted from her feet. As she pushed through the leaves, nose twitching, I noticed tiny horn stubs growing from her forehead.

My fear melted away in an instant to be replaced by a fluttering feeling in my stomach. She was the most adorable shadow faun I'd seen.

"Aren't you pretty as a peach?" I said, crawling forward on hands and knees. I wanted to reach out and pet her, to pull her to my chest in a snuggle, but I was terrified of frightening her away.

She was unlike any shadow faun I'd encountered in Beastiary class, but I had seen her type in the textbook. She was a wogle.

She lowered on her front legs, tail wagging, and launched at me. I caught her midair and fell over backward as her tongue went to work in licking every inch of my face. The dark clouds that'd hovered in my mind were brushed aside in a storm of saliva. Her breath even had the same adorable smell that puppies had.

It took a moment for the wogle to calm enough for me to sit and scratch her behind the ears. She closed her eyes, tilting her head into my touch. "Why aren't you afraid of me like the others?" I asked. Ever since my first Beastiary class, I'd been unable to come within five feet of shadow faun without them vanishing in terror. Finn had prohibited me from attempting to interact with them, insisting that whatever they saw in me was unsettling, and perhaps I'd be happier with a cat.

"I guess you're just brave," I said, stroking her silky fur. "What should I call you?" She rolled onto her back for me to scratch her belly, all four legs in the air. My mind wandered to a sticker I'd stuck on the back of my phone case. It was of a gallant looking man in glowing orange armor, with the name Raven Cross along the bottom. Eben had given me the sticker to cheer me up in Little Peak, and now every time I got overwhelmed or sad, I looked at it and remembered that beautiful moment.

"How about Raven? Would you like that?"

She flared her wings and her tongue lolled out of her open mouth.

I grinned. "Raven, it is." I racked my brain, trying to recall what a wogle's powers were, but all I could remember was the name. I'd look into it when I got back to the cabin.

As we played inside our tree cave, the golden sunset gave way to the deep blue of nightfall. When the stars twinkled into existence, Raven fell asleep on my lap, purring softly with an occasional leg twitch like she chased something in her dream. I marveled at how such a simple encounter could quieten the trouble in my mind. If I wasn't worried about CJ, who was likely losing it over my disappearing act, I would have spent the night right there, under the tree.

When I could hold out no longer, I gently nudged Raven awake. She yawned and gazed up at me with those large eyes.

"I have to go now, honey. But I'll come back tomorrow, if that's alright?"

She stepped off my lap and watched me with her head tilted to the side like she waited for me to say something more. I smiled, watching her strange behavior, but nearly choked when her eyes began to glow purple. Her purring grew louder, and she unfurled her wings as a swirling mist gathered around her paws.

"Dear, are you okay?" I said, but gasped as the pooling mist touched my hand. A flood of energy flew through my veins with an electrifying warmth. I pulled away, but what felt like invisible threads weaved part of my being with hers like strands of silk mending a hole. My pulse raced as the mist surrounded me, goosebumps springing where it touched. All I could do was sit and watch, mesmerized, until it slowly retreated back to her.

It wasn't until the mist dissipated entirely that Raven retracted her wings and sat with her mouth open in an unmistakable smile.

I raised my hands to my face to examine my fingers. The strange sensation had vanished, but something had changed inside me. I felt more grounded and at ease than I ever had in all my life. A hundred valiums couldn't give me this level of calm, this sense of belonging.

"Did you . . . Did we . . ." I hesitated, struggling to understand the question that lingered on my lips. Had I just bonded with a shadow faun?

Raven spun around gleefully, her tail wagging in delight.

All the Kali drama, the flag fall game, fell away. It was nothing; pale and insignificant compared to the love I now felt. I scooped Raven up and hugged her to my cheek. Now more than ever I wanted to spend the night with her, but I couldn't do that to CJ. It took all my will power to place her back on the ground and stand.

"I really have to go now, but I'll see you soon. Promise."

She gave a little yap as I stepped through the willow boughs. When I turned back around, she'd already vanished.

Finding Astaroth again proved to be a challenge. The forest had grown dark and eerie, making the path difficult to follow. I emerged near the shops, scratched from branches and caked in mud after stumbling into a bog. The tempting aroma of Alfio's Pizzeria nearly lured me in, but I couldn't wait to tell CJ everything that'd happened. I hurried across the dark lawn toward Michael.

As I passed the rose hedgerows, a force smashed into my back, knocking me to the ground. I cried out in surprise and spun to find three advancing figures. For one wild moment, I imagined them to be Reavers, but then their features came into focus and a new fear gripped me. Sophia, Trishelle, and Clara. An air vortex swirled within Sophia's outstretched hand. She had attacked me.

I scrambled to my feet and backed away, a sickening feeling filling my stomach. These girls weren't interested in talking about shoes.

"Hello, Alina," Sophia said, her voice falsely bright. "What a wonderful surprise to find you out here. Alone. It's the perfect opportunity to finish our earlier conversation from the cafeteria."

I glanced at Trishelle and Clara. Beating them in a fight was almost guaranteed, but how could I handle all three?

Piece of cake, Kali said, popping back into my mind.

No! I don't want you smoking anyone else.

So . . . you enjoy hospital food?

Maybe I can talk my way out of it—

You are seeing the way she is looking at us, right? Like we smuggled dairy into her soy-milk latte?

Sophia stopped a few paces away, her eyes flashing with something close to insanity. "Nothing to say?" she said. "Funny, you were quite chatty this morning."

"And stupid," Clara chimed in.

I hated Clara.

"So stupid," Sophia agreed.

I noticed something about Sophia then. Her hair was less than perfect, and . . . I squinted. Yes, her mascara was smudged. She'd been crying. I'd never imagined her to be vulnerable before, to be the same as everyone else, and it floored me. But if angry bathroom Sophia was scary, it was nothing compared to emotional, unstable Sophia. I needed to buy time until I figured out how to reach Michael alive.

"You're overly qualified in teaching stupid," I said, opting for the path of confusion while my mind scrambled for a plan.

"Look at her play the flattery card now that she's in the crosshairs," Trishelle said, mouth skewed in a twisted smile. "Well, it's too late for that."

I celebrated inwardly at how dumb these girls were. Only Trishelle could think that was a compliment.

"Why aren't you out enjoying your win?" Sophia asked, flicking Trishelle an irritated look.

It took a moment to realize she was talking about flag fall. It felt like the match had happened weeks ago. Was she seriously going to fight me because we beat Uriel? "It was only a game—"

"A game?" she echoed, voice rising. The air currents in her hand intensified, whipping back her hair. "You destroyed him, and you call it a game?"

I raised my eyebrows. Okay, so it wasn't about the game. "Zane was an accident. I never meant to hurt him."

"Zane? What do I care if you gave him a few blisters?"

"So . . . what's this all about?"

Clara groaned. "You are so dumb."

"Comprehensibly dumb," added Trishelle.

"She's talking about Aran," Clara said. "You know, the guy you stole."

It took a moment for the memory of our kiss to surface. So much had happened since then that it'd been lost in the chaos. Of course! Sophia would be upset about that. "That was nothing—"

"Hooking up with him in front of the whole academy means nothing to you?" Sophia said, stepping in with nostrils flaring. "I could've got him back. We could have fixed things. But you've ruined that now. You've ruined him." The strength of her Aeria flapped my cape behind me.

"I didn't plan it, it just happened," I said. Having seen Georgie go through countless breakups, I understood the pain it caused. "I'm sorry it went this way."

"It just happened," she repeated slowly. "Interesting. What would happen if you *just* vanished? Could I apologize and everything would be okay?"

I stepped back and bumped into the rosebush, thorns scratching my leather. I was trapped. I couldn't outrun magic, and I couldn't take them all on by myself.

"Why don't we talk about this over a cold beer?" I asked, mind racing for a way out.

Her face darkened. "Tempting. But no." She shot her hands forward, firing a jet of air at me.

I cocked my left fist, lifting soil into a shield. Her attack crashed against it with a muted thud. I jabbed my right palm forward, hitting the barrier with Aeria, sending dirt raining over them.

"I just washed my hair!" Trishelle screamed, her face caked in soil. She slammed her hands together, sending a shock wave soaring through the grass.

I leaped into the air, propelled by my own conjured wind, narrowly evading the attack. But I wasn't good at flying yet. The air shifted beneath me, and, unable to regain my balance, I spiraled out of control and plummeted back to earth. I crashed on my right foot, and pain radiated through my ankle.

A blast barreled into my stomach, hurling me away and knocking the breath out of me. I landed on my back and skidded along the grass.

Want help yet? Kali asked, amused.

No! I said, struggling to breathe. I couldn't trust her not to turn them into charcoal.

Suit yourself, she said as I got to my knees. *But try not to get too disfigured—I don't want Ava losing interest.*

A boot kicked me from behind, forcing me back to the ground.

"All you had to do was stay out of my way," Sophia said as I rolled over, groaning. She raised her hand, the swirling currents so close to my face that they stung my eyes. "It could have been so easy for you here. But now it's too late. Do you have any last words?"

In that moment, looking into the eyes of a psycho, all my fear vanished to be replaced by anger. I hadn't done anything to her; she had no right to treat me like yesterday's trash. If she thought I was going to be a doormat any longer, she was mistaken. "You know what amazes me," I said through gritted teeth. "How he ever liked you in the first place. It took him a while, but he eventually saw you for the pathetic creature you are. And now the whole academy is catching on. Soon, you'll have no one and will be forced to watch him move on while you wallow in self-pity."

Pain flashed behind her eyes and her jaw tightened. She nodded slowly. "You may be right. But you won't be around to find out. Goodbye, Alina." Air raced between her fingers, creating a high-pitched whistle.

"Sophia," said Trishelle, "I . . . I think she's had enough. Let's go before we do something we regret. She's not worth it."

Sophia's eyes never left mine. "No, she's not worth killing. But no one needs all their limbs, right? What's a hand between friends?"

A chill raced down my neck. She wouldn't. Even she couldn't be that crazy. But as I stared into her unblinking gaze, I knew I was looking into the barrel of a gun waiting to go off.

Kali! I cried. *I need you.*

Hair streamed back from my face as the whistling grew louder.

Kali?

Clara's gaze darted between Sophia and me. "Sophia . . . this is crazy. They'll throw you in a cell if you do this."

Sophia ignored her and leaned in closer.

"You're on your own," said Clara. She spun on her heels and ran into the darkness.

Trishelle, looking after her, swung her gaze to me. "I'm sorry, Alina. This wasn't the plan." She ran away, too.

Irritation burst upon Sophia's face as she glared at them. "I don't need you!" she screamed. "She's only a fledgling!"

Her distraction was all I needed. I flicked my fists apart explosively, splitting the ground beneath her. She fell screaming and I jumped to my feet and sealed the hole before she could fly out.

I stood there for a long moment, struggling to catch my breath, shock taking hold as my hands shook. Had she just tried to rip off my arms? Over a guy? What was wrong with people? My stomach flipped as an urge to vomit filled me, but I clamped my mouth closed and hurried to the forest surrounding Michael.

Chapter Twenty-Nine

I loved running when I was fourteen. I'd pack a book and some snacks, then set off through the countryside, not slowing until I found the perfect spot to read. No troubles could reach me out there. No foster care dramas. No bullies. No tears. After I'd spent hours lost in the pages, I'd run all the way home, sometimes arriving so exhausted that I'd collapse onto my bed, my legs trembling.

It was that same exhaustion that found me in the forest after Sophia's attack. A sense of horror at what had happened seeped in. She'd tried to dismember me. Pluck me apart with her power. Was that really what I was up against at the academy? That level of crazy? There obviously wasn't any sort of screening process to be admitted. *Oh, you're a demon? Here, let us teach you a thousand ways to kill someone with your mind.* It was ridiculous. Dangerous. And I was . . . I was exhausted.

I heard the Michael party before I saw it. Having zero desire to speak to anyone, I cut through the woods, making a beeline for my cabin in the hopes that no one would recognize me. Fat chance, considering I was still in my leathers, swishing cape acting like a beacon.

"There you are!" a voice called out before I'd even made the clearing.

My heart sank. Morgan and Hudson hurried toward me from a forest path to the right, dressed in togas. From the sour look on Hudson's face, it seemed they'd been arguing.

"Here I am," I said with a longing glance at my cabin.

Morgan, brows pulled together in a look of concern, gripped my hands. "Damn it, Alina—we were so worried after you took off like that. We thought maybe . . . maybe Reavers had gotten to you."

Hudson snorted at this, and I didn't need to be a mind reader to know how thrilled he'd be if that were true. I couldn't tell whether he hated me more for punching him or stealing his flag fall position.

I looked at Morgan, confused. Since when was he worried about anything other than himself? And how the heck did he find out about the Reavers? As far as I knew, that information was a secret known only by me and select professors. Obviously, student privacy meant nothing to them. "I'm fine. No Reavers, just psycho girls."

Morgan's frown lasted a second longer before turning into a grin. "Show me a girl who isn't a psycho, and I'll show you a good actor." He pulled me in for an awkward hug. "Come on, CJ has been frantic. It's driving us nuts."

He dragged me past my cabin—my sanctuary—to the party. It was a typical Michael celebration: booze, music, laughter, and shouting. People patted my back as we passed, congratulating me on the victory that seemed years ago. I spotted CJ illuminated by the dancing flames as she spoke with Aran, her hand on his arm. They were the only ones not wearing white bedsheets as togas. Aran, like me, was still dressed in his leathers.

Catching sight of me, CJ dropped her hand from Aran's arm—though a little too late for my liking—and rushed over, wrapping me in an embrace.

"Don't you ever do that to me again!" she said, squeezing tightly. "You scared me half to death." She pulled away, looking uncertain when I didn't return the hug. "Alina? What's wrong?"

Your arm on Aran. You, always looking so perfect, able to get any guy, yet always hanging around the one I like. I sighed, knowing I was overreacting. I was just bitter and sore and exhausted. That knowledge didn't make my irritation any less real.

"Nothing," I said eventually, and tried to smile. I'd planned on telling her about Raven, but now I wasn't sure I would. "Just tired."

"But it looks like you've been crying," said CJ.

Aran studied me, biting his lip.

"I'm dandy," I said before he could ask. "Just exhausted."

"You really put me through the ringer," he said. "We combed the forest but couldn't find a trace of you."

Morgan feigned vomiting. "Can we stop being so soppy? This isn't an Ed Sheeran concert. Let's grab a drink and celebrate! Alina, this is all about you."

I glanced at my cabin. "I'm not really in the mood, if I'm honest."

CJ took my hands and placed them in Aran's. "I'll babysit Morgan. You two lovebirds have unfinished business." She seized Morgan's wrist, hauling him away, despite his complaints about wanting to drink with the team.

Aran and I exchanged awkward looks. "So . . . the game," I said lamely.

He chuckled. "Not where I'd have started this conversation, but it will do. The game. I've never had a teammate run away after a win."

As I watched his lips move, all my weariness, my pain, seeped into the background. "I just went for a victory lap. A very long victory lap."

The memory of our kiss resurfaced, the touch of his lips, his tongue, and suddenly I found it hard to breathe.

He moved in, mouth twisted into that mocking smile. His breath was hot on my face. "You didn't do enough running in the game?"

"I had energy to burn."

"I can't have you burning out." His fingers grazed my hips, tracing around to my lower back where his hand settled. It took all my self-control not to arch into his touch. "You're too important to me."

My heart pounded. I was tired of fighting the chemistry between us. I wanted to kiss him again. I needed it. "I am? Tell me more. What do I mean to you?"

He tucked a strand of hair behind my ear. Then, as though he had all the time in the world, he leaned in, cheek against mine, and whispered into my ear. "Alina . . . you mean—"

Yes! Just say it! Tell me you want me. Tell me you need me. Tell me what you're going to do to me when we're alone.

"—that I will forever be in need of a new flannel shirt." He pulled away.

I stared at him for a full second. "You jerk!" I said, picking myself up off the floor. I slapped his chest, but he quick-stepped out of the way and caught my wrist, laughing.

"Come on—did you really think I had a serious side?" he said.

"No, but I assumed you had a heart."

His dimples deepened. "You know what they say about assumptions, right?" He let go of my arm and watched me with irritating smugness.

"Yeah, something about you being an asshole."

"Close enough." He looked over at the keg stands, where a wrestling match had erupted between two guys. "You know, for the first time in my life I'm not in any mood to party."

"Are you sick?"

"Maybe." He studied me for a moment, then, as though coming to a decision, gave a small nod. "Have I told you how hot you look in leathers?"

It took a second to gather myself. I would go through the whole Sophia ordeal all over again just to hear him say those words one more time. "I have eyes."

"Come on, I know exactly what we need." He gripped my hand and led me past my cabin and into the forest.

"Please tell me that's not a line you use on all the girls," I said.

"I've never shown anyone this—"

"Or that line—"

"—not even Soph . . . er, well, I've shown no one."

We left the narrow path, climbing over fallen trees and passing clearings blanketed with wildflowers. We eventually arrived at a mound of rocks that was half the size of a football field and reached into the sky. They were covered in lichen, with some trees growing out of the cracks. He turned back to me, one hand touching the stone as though it were an old friend.

"I need you to promise never to tell a soul about this."

"About what, exactly?" I said, looking around, trying to understand what *this* was.

"Promise."

Hearing the gravity in his tone, my smile wavered and I nodded. "I promise."

He watched me for a moment longer, then, satisfied, turned and squeezed through a narrow opening in the rocks that had been hidden behind a protrusion in the stone.

I stared, surprised that I hadn't noticed it, then hurried after him, having to shuffle sideways to fit into the passage. I rounded a bend and the press of cold rock eased. Aran helped me into a clearing.

My mouth fell open into a silent O.

I'd stepped into a secret glade completely ringed by stones. A sparkling stream ran through the center, its waters bubbling while stars twinkled in the open sky above. Aran released my hand, watching me as I absorbed the beauty of the place. Blue bellflowers dotted the grassy banks, and millions of fireflies danced on the breeze. A small pine forest stood at the far end. A feeling of magic buzzed in the air.

"Shall we?" Aran said, holding out the crook of his arm.

I took it, breathless. "Oh, Aran—this is a dream. How did you find it?"

We strolled down the slight hill toward the stream. "I'm a country kid at heart. I love being in nature, away from all the distractions." He swept down and plucked a flower. "The moment I stepped foot in here, all my worries disappeared, like I was back home." He handed it to me, and I could have died from the beauty of the moment.

"It's hard to believe you have any worries at all."

He gave a short laugh. "Normally, I don't. But it's also great for hangovers, and I get plenty of those." We stopped, and he turned to me, a serious expression on his face. "If other people knew of this, they'd ruin it. It'd become crowded and noisy and not the same. It has to stay our secret." He held up his little finger. "Pinky promise?"

God, he was beautiful. I shook his finger with mine. "Pinky promise."

We continued our slow pace. "Why?" I asked.

"What do you mean?"

"Why are you showing me?"

"Isn't it obvious?"

"No."

"Because I have to keep my top Raider happy."

I groaned, pushing away from him. "Your games will be the end of me—"

His arms caught me around the waist and drew me back in. His lips pressed against mine urgently, as though he'd been waiting for this moment as long as I had. They were soft and perfect. He stole not just my words but my very breath. As his mouth opened and his tongue explored me, a shiver of delight raced down my chest.

My thoughts melted away, leaving me lost in the moment. I leaned into him, needing more, desire burning through my veins. I wanted him, all of him, in every way possible. *Any* way possible.

I sucked his lower lip into my mouth, and a growl rumbled deep in his chest. His hands snaked through my hair, pulling me in deeper. His movements grew frantic as he gripped my ass, squeezing me in. It was happening at last.

However, with the knowledge came fear. What if I disappointed him? What if I couldn't match up to what he and Sophia had? Before I could continue that nasty stream of thoughts, he groaned and pulled away, his eyes burning into me. All trace of laughter was gone. Instead, he looked wild and hungry. Dangerous in the best way possible.

"You look hot," he breathed.

"You already said that."

"Let's cool down." He turned and started toward the stream, unbuckling his leather top and letting it fall to the ground, exposing his broad back. "I don't want you fainting."

The sight of his bare torso sent my desire into overdrive. I watched his ass as he walked. *Please, take those off. Show me who you are.*

He reached the stream and paused long enough to unhook his belt and step out of his pants.

A gasp escaped my lips. His body, the legs, those shoulders, all of it . . . I swallowed, drinking him in, wanting only to feel him pressed against me. Feel him inside me. The flames within me roared into an inferno, every nerve tingling with the need to be touched. Never in my wildest dreams had I imagined finding myself in a situation like this. The shudder that rolled through me fought to shake free my fear.

He walked into the stream, wading to the middle where water lapped at his chest. He turned to face me. "Your turn."

Every part of me wanted to run to him. To beg him to make me his own. But I couldn't so easily step out of my timid shell. I looked from him to his pile of leathers, then over my shoulder to make sure no one had followed us. It was one thing to fantasize about being with Aran but quite another to bare myself—body and soul—to the man I'd craved for.

My heartbeat quickened as I weighed desire against fear. "Turn around."

He gave a devilish grin, then spun.

I hesitated for one last second, then shed my armor, letting it fall onto the waving grass. My skin burned as a thrill soared through me. I took a step forward, then another, the sound of my racing pulse filling my ears. I stopped at the water's edge and, with trembling hands, hooked my thumbs under the fabric of my panties and slid them down. My bra followed.

"Alina," Aran's low murmur reached me. "You . . . Wow."

I jerked my head up. His gaze raked over every inch of my body, mouth hanging open. "Aran! No peeking!"

Though his inability to follow my directions only made me burn hotter.

"I'm sorry, but damn!"

"Aran!"

"Fine, fine." He spun back around. "But you're absolutely gorgeous."

I hurried into the stream before he had a chance to turn back, the cool water raising goosebumps on my skin. I waded to the middle and crouched, letting the water reach my neck, hiding my breasts from view.

My breath hitched in anticipation as I slid my hand up his muscled arm. He turned, ever so slowly, savoring the moment like a child unwrapping a present.

"Hi," he said in a throaty voice.

"Hi," I breathed, staring up into that face. That powerful jaw, the intense eyes searching mine. Those lips, begging to be kissed. The distance between us was torture. I needed him against me right now. I offered a timid smile as I stepped closer. His arm snaked out, hand cupping my cheek to guide my face to his. I let the water's veil fall away as I straightened.

Our lips met in blazing passion, our tongues stroking wildly. I arched back, pressing my chest against his, nipples hardening.

He growled again, sliding his hands under my ass and picking me up. I wrapped my legs around his waist, hooking my ankles.

He was already hard.

I felt every inch of him wedged between us, sending sparks through me. "Aran," I moaned, squeezing tighter against him.

He gasped, his body stiffening, his erection pulsing with need. "You don't know how many times I've thought about our first moment," he breathed, pulling my hair back and kissing a line down my neck.

I leaned away from him, opening my chest up to his roaming lips. "Did you imagine it would be like this?" I shuddered as he caught my nipple between his teeth and nibbled softly. Warmth bloomed between my legs as I melted into his touch.

"Never," he said, working his way to my other nipple. "Now I'll never stop."

He glided me up and then down the length of him, rubbing against my sensitive spot with each pass. My thoughts fell away. This was everything I needed. All I would ever need again. I grabbed his hair and yanked his head back, allowing my tongue to further explore. I wanted to taste him.

His grip on me tightened as he grew more urgent.

Then I couldn't hold back any longer. I reached between us, caressing him as I guided him to my entrance. He shook beneath me. Dragging my lips away, I locked my eyes on his, then slowly lowered onto him. I gasped as he entered, fingers bunching his hair.

"Oh, Alina," he moaned, eyes burning. He buried himself deeper, and I cried out as a wave of pleasure coursed through me.

With a hand possessively grabbing each ass cheek, he guided me up and down slowly.

"Yes," I breathed, arching my back, gazing at the star-studded heavens. "Oh, yes, don't stop."

He grunted, fingers digging into me as he skillfully managed our tempo. "We should have . . . done this . . . sooner."

Water rippled against our bodies, the cool breeze heightening my senses.

A storm of pleasure built inside me, growing with each thrust. We rose and fell together, our bodies melding into a single rhythm. "Aran . . . fuck me . . . yes, yes . . ." As the waves of ecstasy crescendoed, I dug my nails into the nape of his neck. "Harder!" I begged, placing a hand against his chest for leverage as my legs squirmed around him.

His hands spread me apart as he pounded with intent. Sweat beaded on his face. "Fuck, you feel so good!"

It was all too much. The pleasure consumed me, growing with every thrust, every gasp, every touch. I teetered on the edge. I knew there was no turning back.

"Aran!" I cried out as the climax hit like a tidal wave. I writhed on top of him, legs squeezing and contracting as the waves of my orgasm washed over me. He pushed himself deeper and held me firmly against him, his teeth grazing my neck. The world became a steamy mess.

When I drifted back down to reality, my breathing ragged, I crumpled into his embrace as my tremors subsided. His sweat mingled with mine, our hearts beating as one. I clung to him, never wanting to let go. He kissed me tenderly, then nuzzled into the crook of my neck. It was a moment of bliss that I never wanted to end.

"That was incredible," he whispered into my ear.

"I know."

Eventually, we made our way to the grassy bank, my legs quivering as though I'd run a marathon. We lay curled against each other, our eyes turned skyward to watch the stars. His fingers absently twirled strands of my hair. To say I was happy was an understatement. It was much more than that. For perhaps the first time in my life, I was at peace, both with myself and the challenges fate had given me. I was in bliss.

Chapter Thirty

The first light of morning peeked above the stone wall on the eastern side of the glade, filling it with a fiery golden glow, but it was birdsong that gradually stirred my consciousness. I blinked groggily, taking in my surroundings, my memory of the night's events still hazy. Slowly, an image of Aran formed in my mind, and I sat bolt upright.

"Hi there, Sleeping Beauty."

My breath caught in my throat. Aran lay beside me, his eyes filled with amusement. He was completely naked, the morning rays lighting him up like a Greek statue.

"Morning," I said, not knowing where to look. Then my eyes popped as he rolled onto his side, bending an arm and resting his cheek on his hand. His . . . his thing was hanging down to brush the grass!

I stared for far too long before I realized what I was doing. I looked away, and saw with horror that I was naked, too. *Heck!* I turned my back to him and covered myself by pulling my knees to my chest. A sharp pain erupted in my shoulder, and looking down, I saw a purple bruise ran down my arm. Either flag fall or Sophia had gotten me good. But I had more pressing issues.

"Don't peek until I dress," I said, scanning the area for my leathers. They weren't near the stream where I'd left them.

He snorted. "Really? After last night, you're shy?"

My mind drifted back to our moment in the stream. His touch. The passion. The fireworks. A smile crept to my face. After so long, I finally had him. I had the moment I'd hungered for since he'd first invited me into his room. It'd been everything I'd hoped it would be, and more. A tingling sensation prickled my skin.

"It was a good night," I said, glancing over my shoulder to see him grinning. Was he remembering the details like I was? Every breathtaking moment of it? Chewing my lip, I allowed my gaze to wander down his chest, over his abs, to his . . .

Yes, he remembered last night. Every inch of him remembered.

"Want a picture?"

I dragged my eyes back to his, closing my mouth. Where on earth did we go from there? "So, er . . . it looks like it'll be a nice day—"

"Nope. None of that small talk, thanks." He fell to his back, hands behind his head. "You can't be shy Alina anymore, not after what you did last night. Not after showing who you truly are."

I blushed furiously. "Stop teasing. I'm not normally like that."

"I hope you'll consider being not normally like that again."

My pulse quickened as I thought of the possibilities. Morning sex . . . in broad daylight? Where he could see everything? A spark of apprehension filled me, but the flames of desire burned it away.

"How soon is too soon?" I asked, not believing my nerve.

"Does right now suit your schedule?" He was fully hard now, towering proudly in the morning breeze.

I was mesmerized. "Let me check my calendar." Tentatively, I turned my body back to face him. One question lingered in my mind. "Last night, when we were, um—"

"Having sex?"

"Yes, doing that. Did you . . . you know"—I made a bursting motion with my hand—"finish?"

His teeth shone brightly as his grin widened. "Not so much. But last night was about you."

I groaned internally. Our first time together, and I hadn't bothered to see if he'd come? I'd been so caught up in it all that my mind had malfunctioned. That needed fixing. I leaned forward onto my hands and knees and crept a little closer. "Then this morning is all about you."

His eyes sparkled. Slowly, he snaked his hand down his body to grab his shaft. "Ready when you are."

In the aftermath, we lay panting on the soft grass, exhausted. He'd definitely finished that time. There was no confusion about it. I'd never had it in my mouth before, but having him climax in that way, feeling it so intimately, was a thrill I would never forget.

We lay like that for hours, wrapped around each other. When we mustered the energy to rise, it was to cool off in the stream. There was no post-hookup awkwardness. We chatted without pause. He shared stories of growing up on a farm in , while I opened up about my childhood in foster care—something I usually kept well-guarded. We discussed everything, from the flag fall match to the party I planned for CJ's birthday. He was even impressed when I told him about how Professor Conrad thought I was on track to becoming one of the strongest fledgling Terre demons.

Feeling in a safe place, I was tempted to confide in him about Kali. The other me was such a huge part of my life, after all, and I wanted to be transparent with Aran. However, memories of the judgmental looks I received in Breaux Bridge resurfaced, and I couldn't bear the thought of Aran looking at me in the same way. Not after how far we'd come.

As we lay in the grass beneath a pine tree, Aran suddenly sat upright. "Bloody hell, look at that!"

I turned to where he stared, and my heart filled with joy.

"Raven!" I cried, a grin spreading across my face. She bounded along the shoreline, chasing a butterfly. Her large wings flapped clumsily, causing her to stumble every few steps.

"You know it?" Aran asked incredulously.

"She found me in the forest after the match," I said, standing. Raven spotted me and raced up the slope. I caught her as she sprang into my arms, and we sat back in the blossoms, her face nuzzling mine with a puppy's enthusiasm.

"You understand how rare they are, right?" Aran said. "Wogles? I mean, even old Finn Cress hasn't bonded with one, and he bonds with everything."

I scratched Raven's ear as I remembered the strange sensation that'd filled me when her mist had reached out. "So, what are the chances of a wogle bonding with a student?"

"Slim to none. We studied them last year. There hasn't been a documented case of wogle bonding in years."

"Oh." My face fell. Had I been mistaken last night?

He leaned closer, squeezing my knee. "Something wrong?"

"I don't know. Just being silly, I guess." Then, deciding it couldn't hurt to tell him, I recounted every detail of my encounter with Raven. When I got to the part about her eyes glowing and how her mist had blanketed me, Aran's mouth was wide open.

"Strewth, Alina! Are you telling me you've actually bonded with a wogle?" He shook his head in disbelief. "I haven't bonded with so much as a slug, yet you've got the rarest bond in demon history?" He let out a low, impressed whistle.

"It's not like I did anything. Raven just found me, and then it all happened quickly."

"That's how it works. Bonding doesn't need you to fight a dragon or anything—all it needs is you being a certain kind of person. Shadow faun sense your essence, who you are at your core, and what you can provide in exchange for their bond. Make no mistake—Raven sees something special in you."

"I don't get it," I said, chewing it over. "I'm average at most of my classes. I'm pretty sure Professor Spark is going to fail my astral sight assignment. What could I possibly offer Raven?"

Aran thought about it for a moment. "What abilities does she have?"

I shrugged. "Shouldn't I be asking you that? You're the one who studied wogles."

Scooting nearer, Aran extended his hand to Raven. She sniffed it before leaping onto his lap. "A wogle's power is unique to each bond. Some demons get essence enhancements. Others gain access to additional elemental powers—Aeria demons wielding Terre, Cryore demons controlling Faezre. Have you noticed any changes inside?"

I shook my head. "Nothing."

"It's still early. They'll come. And, as your boyfriend, I expect to be the first to know."

A slow smile crept across my face. "My boyfriend?"

He didn't look away from his playful tussle with Raven. "Of course. Couldn't let a woman like you go around unspoken for."

As his words washed over me, it struck me how swiftly life could transform. In a matter of a month, I'd gone from a soul-crushing job at Taco Express to attending an academy where I learned all types of weird and wonderful magic. I'd bonded with the most extraordinary creature I never knew existed and was now dating the kindest—*and* sexiest—man on campus. Sure, I'd also nearly been lured into a world filled with evil demons by Nester, almost had a portion of my soul destroyed by Eben, and had almost been killed by a jealous ex-girlfriend. But what did they matter in the grand scheme of things?

Chapter 31

Chapter Thirty-One

It was with a heavy heart and rumbling stomach that Aran and I said goodbye to the hidden glade around lunch. The magical haven had offered a much-needed respite from all the craziness, but I couldn't put my life on hold any longer. I had a study session with Oliver and Anya in the library after lunch, followed by an evening in the village with CJ, Zach, and Ava for some fondue and wine tasting.

We stepped out of the woods and spotted a group of students huddled around the firepit.

"Alina!" Stanley cried, leaping to his feet. He rushed forward and wrapped me in a spine-crushing hug. "I thought you was dead!"

"Why?" I breathed, fearing my ribs would crack.

He dropped me and looked at me as though I were a difficult math question. "Because . . . the battle?"

I turned to Aran, confused. Was he talking about my fight with Sophia? Had news really spread so quickly?

Aran's face was serious. "What battle?"

Ricci, a fourth year, stepped forward, his face animated. "Didn't you hear? The Reavers infiltrated Astaroth last night! Broke through the gate, they did. Triggered the alarm, which warned the Frostfires. Turns out there was an epic battle."

My nails dug into Aran's arm. I waited for them to let me in on the joke, but they didn't crack. "Are you sure it was the Reavers?"

Ricci nodded. "Didn't believe it when I first heard. But then word got round. Chatter from Raphael kids who reckon they heard it over the bridge. Said they saw flashes that lit up the sky." He whistled. "I believe it now. Reavers got through the gate. Not sure what for. Some think they were just drunk and having fun, but that doesn't make sense to me. Dying's never been much of a laugh."

No, they weren't drunk. This was no spontaneous journey from the bar. They were after someone to join their army, someone with more than one power. Someone to help them reopen the Shadowgates to Earth. I moved closer to Aran, my throat going dry. Over the past few weeks, I hadn't given the Reavers much thought. They were a distant threat, not on Cronix. I'd believed I had time. It seemed I was wrong.

"Kingston reckons he overheard Professor Devon saying they were on a scouting mission," said Stanley.

"Kingston's a fool," said Kate. "They were searching for something. Some sort of weapon."

Stanley shook his head. "What weapon would Astaroth have?"

The embers spluttered, sending a bright-orange spark into the air.

I looked between them. "I don't get it . . . Why were you worried about me? I mean, Aran wasn't here, either—"

"Alina Rose!" a voice called from the château. I spun to find Maviir striding forward from the rear entrance. She hobbled on one leg, and her white hair hung in disarray.

"Because of her," said Ricci. "She's been looking for you all morning. Stormed in before sunrise, if you can believe it. Caused a ruckus.

Not many people could help her, seeing how wildly drunk they still were."

I watched the Aeria Kinesis professor approach with growing apprehension. Her wrinkles were bottomless, and her eyes were glazed and red. Mud splatters stained her green coat, and cigarette ash trailed down to her trousers.

"My dear child!" she said, squeezing me in a hug nearly as tight as Stanley's. "Bless the heavens, you're safe!" She smelled of sweat, smoke, and gin. "I feared, after last night, that you'd . . . No, I won't say it. Christ, you've caused quite a commotion this morning. We searched high and low after the battle . . . We feared they'd taken you."

Her speech was slurred, and she wasn't really making much sense. Nothing since I'd left the glade made much sense. Had she been drinking the whole night?

"I, well . . . I spent the night with Aran."

Her eyes flicked to his. "Yes, yes, good choice, but you could've let us know. We've been scouring the entire academy for you." She straightened her collar. "You must come with me, dear. We have questions." Her talon-like fingers gripped my wrist and pulled me away.

"I'm coming, too," Aran said, following.

"No, you're not, Mr. May."

"I won't sit back while you interrogate her."

She hastened her steps despite her limp. "Then don't sit. I suggest cleaning the leaves from your hair and brushing your teeth."

"I won't cause any trouble. I just want to make sure she's alright."

A rush of gratitude filled me at having him by my side. Apart from Georgie, Dustin, and CJ, few people in my life had ever stood up for me. But I couldn't have him getting involved with this mess. Not with the Reavers. I dug my heels in, jolting Maviir to a standstill.

"I'll be fine," I said to Aran. "Take a shower and get some rest. I'll be back before you know it."

He hesitated, glancing at Maviir. "You sure?"

"Positive." I kissed him on the cheek.

Maviir groaned. "Well, that was sickly. Come along, child. Time is short."

I squeezed Aran's hands, then followed Maviir along the riverside path.

For a while, we walked in silence, my mind a jumble. What would the Reavers have done if they'd caught me? Would they hold me up in some demon cell? Torture me into compliance? A cold shudder rolled through me at the thought.

A voice penetrated my mind. *Stand down, everyone. I've found her. She's safe and, surprisingly enough, uninjured.*

I still couldn't understand exactly what was happening. Why did Maviir assume I was in the fight? Who was she taking me to, and what questions did they have? And now that they knew I was safe, why couldn't they simply let me get some rest? Some food? Heck, I hadn't eaten since yesterday's lunch.

It soon became clear that none of these questions would be answered by Maviir. We reached the bridge and climbed into a waiting buggy. Empty beer cans littered the floor, and an ashtray brimmed with cigarette butts. She slammed her foot on the pedal, and we sped across the grounds, past the rose hedge where Sophia had attacked me, and beyond the cafeteria. We eventually skidded to a halt outside a classroom. Although it was Sunday, the campus felt oddly quiet. The few people I spotted outside moved in tight clusters, as if fearful of being alone in the open.

We entered the room, and I immediately noticed two things. First, it appeared the entire faculty was there, standing in stony silence.

Second, there were a handful of people dressed in the same icy-blue military uniforms I'd seen when I first arrived from Lafayette.

They all glanced up as we entered.

A portly man in a brown suit and horrendous mustache hurried forward and grasped my hand in both of his. "You're a savior," he panted, his watery eyes searching mine. "Never in my life . . . Intruders! Quite right to say I did not see that coming."

"Let her breathe, Baxter," a voice rumbled. It was a man in uniform. His scowl was almost as striking as the razor-sharp creases in his shirt-sleeves.

Baxter released my hands, his cheeks reddening. "It's Mayor Baxter," he muttered, retreating from the burly soldier. "Charmed, Miss Alina."

The uniformed man closed the gap to me. "We meet again, young lady. Name's Lieutenant Colonel Veston."

I stared at him, positive I'd never seen him before in my life. "I think you're mistaking me with someone else."

He studied me, expression tight. "You don't remember?"

"She's experiencing some form of amnesia," Maviir said, lighting her cigarette.

"Heavens," breathed Henri, the ever-dramatic Demon History professor. "She should be at the medical center!"

I was quickly losing patience. "I'm fine. I don't have amnesia. Are you going to tell me why you've dragged me here?"

Harper pushed off the desk, revealing a tear in his tweed jacket. "What do you remember?"

"How's she supposed to know that?" asked Audrey from her seat three rows back. She fixed her hawklike gaze on me. "Reavers breached Little Peak's gate at three thirty this morning. They forced their way into Astaroth on a hunting trip. All indications point to you as being the trophy."

Some of the professors gasped at her choice of words, but I nodded, having already figured this out. "How?"

"How what?" asked Henri.

"When I was brought here, the gate had to be opened from this side. How did they get in?"

A slight tug on Audrey's lips told me I'd asked the right question.

"Yes, yes, precisely—how indeed!" said Mayor Baxter, puffing out his chest. "I shall personally launch an investigation into this—"

"Investigate," growled Veston. "But you'll find no more details than those I've already disclosed. My soldiers were incapacitated, Miss Rose, caught by surprise—"

"Aha!" cried Baxter as if he'd caught Veston in a lie. "How could they be caught by surprise when the gate must be activated from their control room? Surely, you have people staffing the controls?"

"Because," Veston said through gritted teeth, "someone on Cronix neutralized them."

Baxter cast a bemused look at everyone. "Attacked by someone on Cronix? Unlikely, old chap. I believe you have a black sheep in your flock, and they activated the gate while the rest of your soldiers were drinking or gambling or some other nefarious activity." He glanced around smugly as if he had single-handedly cracked the case.

Harper cleared his throat. "What are you suggesting, Veston? That demons from Little Peak seized control of the gate and smuggled in the enemy?"

Veston opened his mouth to respond, but it was Audrey who spoke first.

"This was the work of students."

Stunned silence followed this revelation. My mind raced to Sophia. After seeing her rage firsthand, would it be too far-fetched to imagine her siding with the Reavers to get rid of me?

Laughter echoed in my head.

Sophia? Kali mused. *Trust me, you won't need to worry about that princess anymore. Just wait until you see her.*

Audrey continued before I could respond. "The Reavers sent a boy to Astaroth at the beginning of term to find a way to bring Alina to them. We found him with *The Scripture of Demons' Dominion*. He tried to rip Alina's soul and imprison it in a lizard for easier transportation—"

Baxter's eyes bulged. "A lizard? Of all the despicable things!" He dabbed at his brow with a handkerchief. "Could they not find a more . . . dignified creature to shuttle a soul? A cat, perhaps?"

Audrey stared at the mayor before disregarding him completely. "They planted a spy here before, so it would be foolish to assume they don't have more agents at work in Astaroth."

"The boy deserved what he got and more," said Veston. "Blown to bits, I heard."

"He wasn't a bad kid," I blurted, refusing to let Eben's memory go undefended. "They took advantage of him. He was just overly trusting."

"Seems like he wasn't the only one who was overly trusting," Baxter said. "Trusting a Reaver, Miss Rose? You really should learn to read people."

I liked him less and less with each syllable.

Wasn't a bad kid? Kali asked. *You remember that after he tried to force me into a lizard, which we really should discuss with a therapist, he tried to bury me for good?*

Zip it! I snapped, having no patience for her. I looked at Audrey, the window light illuminating the thousands of rune tattoos covering her skin. "Why am I here? I'm not suffering from some kind of amnesia. I know exactly where I was last night."

"A love tryst with the May kid," Maviir explained to the others, a cigarette hanging from her lip.

I didn't deny it. "So, if you're not going to tell me what's going on, I'm going to get some rest."

"It's wasted on you," Audrey said, standing. Her eyes bored into mine as she walked down the aisle. "All that power locked in your body, but your mind's too weak to wield it. We were losing last night, fighting an uphill battle against a horde of beelzebubs. I know you haven't studied lesser demons yet, but trust me, they're about as enjoyable as a serrated blade to the kidney. We wouldn't be here right now if it weren't for your intervention."

"How many times do I need to tell you I wasn't there?" I snapped. I didn't care what she thought of me. I didn't care about lesser demons. I didn't care about any of this. All I wanted was food—

But the beelzebubs were cool, Kali said with a laugh.

How would you know what they were . . . I trailed off as a terrible thought formed. No. She wouldn't. She *couldn't*. A numbness trickled down my spine, and I knew it in my heart that she had. *Kali—what did you do?*

Ding! Ding! Ding! she exclaimed. *And we have a winner! Took you long enough. To be frank, you're not the sharpest tool in the shed.*

My body? You stole my body? I felt violated. How often had this happened before? What other midnight escapades had she dragged me into? The thought made me sick. I'd never feel safe sleeping again.

Relax, said Kali, *this was the first time. And I didn't take your body—I took ours. What's yours is mine. Except for your IQ. You can keep that.*

I clenched my fists. *You can't just do that—*

Harper cleared his throat. I looked up to find everyone watching me.

I arranged my face to make it look like I wasn't arguing with a voice inside my head. "Okay, the battle. Right. Fill me in?"

"We were hard-pressed, losing ground by the second," said Harper, examining me closely. "But, just as all hope seemed lost, a fireball exploded in their ranks, wiping out their fodder—"

"Lit the night sky like a sun," said Veston with admiration. "Never seen anything like it. Truly powerful."

"We only managed to drive them back through the Shadowgate because of you," said Harper.

I looked down at my hands. Had they killed again? Had they ended more lives? I swallowed, then shook my head. No. That wasn't me. I couldn't accept responsibility for someone else's actions, even if it was my body that executed them. In fact, I found I hardly cared at all about the whole ordeal. Sure, the Reavers' arrival on campus wasn't ideal, but what could I do about that? My more pressing concern was figuring out how to prevent Kali from taking over the next time I slept.

"So, I saved the day," I said. "Excellent. Can I go to lunch now?"

"No," said Baxter, moving to bar the door as if he feared I'd make a run for it. "First, we need to make sure this never happens again. Security, Veston. I want it bolstered and then some. Poor form, man, allowing Reavers to slip through on your watch. I expect you to implement the necessary adjustments at the gate."

Had Harper not hurried to block Veston's path, Veston looked ready to strangle the mayor.

"And, uh, we must set an example with these renegade students," continued Baxter, trying to regain composure while adding some distance between him and the angry Frostfire.

"Excellent idea," sneered Audrey. "Identify them for me, and I'll have them shackled faster than you can wipe your ass."

His face turned a deep shade of red. "Well, now, I hardly think it's the mayor's responsibility to identify culprits—"

"It isn't," said Audrey. "Just as it isn't your job to tell Colonel Veston how to manage his regiment. So, if you don't mind, kindly shut up."

Baxter spluttered, looking like he was having a stroke.

When no coherent words emerged, Harper clapped his hands together. "Unless I'm mistaken, that's all we need from young Alina. If there are no objections, I'd like to escort her out." The room fell silent, and Harper smiled. "Perfect. This way, please."

All they needed me for? They hadn't needed me at all! It had been a waste of my time. I moved toward the door but stopped when Veston blocked my way. "Lass, if you ever tire of the academy, our troops would be honored to have you."

"For heaven's sake!" Audrey snapped. "Read the room. This isn't a recruitment drive."

Veston paid her no mind. "You're welcome at the barracks anytime. I'd be glad to show you around."

"That sounds fun," I said. It didn't sound fun at all. A cheeseburger sounded fun. Sleep sounded fun. Aran sounded fun.

Once outside, Harper closed the door and managed a strained smile. "I know it's a lot to take in. But I wanted to say I'm proud of how you handled yourself. Not just last night, but in there today. You've come a long way since we first met."

I didn't know how to respond. Praise was not something I was accustomed to, especially for something I hadn't done. "Thanks."

"Please, indulge me and consider an old man's advice. You have incredible power, as we've seen multiple times. But don't assume you're safe. Reavers are cunning by nature and will stop at nothing to get you. You are their future, and we're just beginning to see their desperation. I dread what they might do next. Please, be careful. Take no risks."

Maybe it was my exhaustion or the fact that I'd reached my limit for the day, but I was tired of being treated like a child. "I'm always careful. I don't need you to remind me of it. Is that all?"

Chapter Thirty-Two

Eager to get as far away from the classroom as possible, I hurried back past the library, my mind buzzing with the morning's events. I was desperate for a hot shower and the normalcy of some biscuits and gravy. But, more than that, I was annoyed. Not only at being dragged away from Aran before I was ready, but at Kali.

So you waited until I was asleep before stealing control? I asked, trying to keep my face neutral but feeling like I was about to explode.

I was bored, she said. *And it's not like you would've said yes.*

Of course I wouldn't! Every time you take over, you leave me to clean up the pieces. I'm sick of it.

She laughed, and if it were possible, I would have whacked her right in the eye.

You'll be singing a different tune when you see it, she said.

I hesitated midstep. *See what?*

That.

I stopped by the cafeteria and looked around. The last lingering students were trickling out, their chatter hushed.

The one in the hat, she prompted.

And then I saw. Frozen on a path to our left was a person staring straight at us. Her mouth hung open, eyes wide like she'd been crying a lot. The cap she wore was out of place on her, and it took me a second to recognize who it was.

Sophia stammered and took a step back, her hands trembling before her as though not knowing whether to fight or run. But then she squeaked and dashed back the way she'd come, not slowing until she reached the strip of shops. She disappeared into Alfio's.

You're welcome, Kali said smugly.

What did you do? I asked, my stomach twisting.

Not much. Just set her hair on fire.

My mouth dropped open. *Kali! What the heck?*

Oh, calm down. It was a controlled burn. I didn't hurt her. Physically, I mean. But she looks like a rabid fox now. She sounded like a kid who'd just earned a gold star in class.

I wanted to be angry at her, to tell her it was a disgusting thing to do. But my resentment from last night still burned strong. My ankle throbbed and my shoulder was stiff. I squeezed my lips together but couldn't stop a smile from tugging at the corners. Sophia had tried to kill me, after all.

Thought you would like that, Kali said. *At least now you don't have to worry about her jumping you anymore.*

I walked back to Michael. *What if you've made a powerful enemy?*

Powerful? The only thing powerful about that woman is her booty. Damn! And it's not like she didn't already hate us.

Kali!

Don't worry, I would never go there. Attempted murder is kinda a red flag for me. Besides, it wouldn't matter if she were the strongest person at the academy. After I stumbled across the invasion last night, I know none of those idiots have half as much of what we've got. You should have seen me, Alina. I was on fire. Literally.

Yes, I should have seen you, I said. *I should have been there.*

How long you going to hold a grudge for? It's boring.

I entered my cabin to find Aran waiting for me on my bed. He jumped up and hurried to me.

"You alright? What did they want?"

I'd rehearsed this conversation a dozen times in my head. It didn't make it any easier. "We'd better sit down." I guided him back to the bed, and we sat side by side, our knees brushing each other. Each of my words was chosen with care. I told him about the Reavers, about how they believed my three powers could help them open the Shadowgates to Earth. I spoke about the retrieval mission they'd launched, and the professors' "mistaken" identification of me at the battle.

What I neglected to tell him about was Kali, the narcissistic jerk in my head. I felt this detail was a straw too large for the camel.

Aran listened in silence, his fingers woven between mine. His eyes never left my face, studying me as I laid it all out. When I finished, he exhaled a long, shaky breath.

"I—I don't know what to say. That's a lot. I'm sorry it's happening to you. How do you feel?"

I collapsed back onto my pillow. "Honestly, not too bad. I mean, I understand they want me, but I guess I've just got other things to worry about."

"Other things? Alina, what could be more important than demon poachers?"

I knew he wouldn't get it. "Well, there's the next flag fall game, for a start. Then I have CJ's birthday; I want to throw the best party she's ever had. And Audrey gave us a ridiculously long assignment on the detriments of using talismans in battle. Don't look at me like that—I'm swamped."

"You're not like most girls, huh?" he said, lying down beside me.

"Not even close."

"Well, if you're too busy to worry about your own life, I guess I'll have to do it for you. You said Audrey suspects students let the demons through the gate? That means we can't trust anyone. From now on, I don't want you walking around campus by yourself—"

I snorted. "Bit over the top, don't you think—"

"I'll be your escort as much as I can—"

"Come to think of it, I see your point of view."

"At least until this is all sorted out. And when I can't, find one of your friends to go with you. CJ's great. She really cares."

I should have protested, should have insisted that I didn't need babysitting. But the thrill of spending more time with him was too great. My personal bodyguard who I could kiss. My personal bodyguard who I could, well, hide-the-snake with, as Dustin called it.

In the end, I offered a half-hearted argument, then agreed.

His commitment to the new role was admirable, as was his diligence. His first duty as bodyguard took him into the shower with me, then into bed.

The new week came with a crispness in the air that hinted at the coming winter. The mountain peaks were dusted with a white blanket, and the academy lawns glinted with sleet in the early morning. Students wore woolly coats, their breaths steaming in front of them.

In the attack's wake, new academy rules had been set in place. The first was a strict seven-o'clock curfew. Anyone outside their château grounds after-hours was stripped of certain privileges, such as access to Little Peak or the shops. This made planning CJ's party significantly more difficult, as she had friends in all the châteaux, forcing me to get creative with location options.

The second rule mandated that all students were never to travel alone. This brought a smug grin to Aran's face, and he never missed an opportunity to remind me he'd been right.

Despite drowning in homework, flag fall practice, and my library sessions, I carved out a few precious hours for some private moments with Aran. We returned to his secret stream, reenacting our first night together. These thrilling moments were often finished by me calling Raven to our side. Watching Aran and her wrestle together made my heart swell. There was something about seeing a man and a dog—or dog-thingy—playing together that sparked a warmth inside me.

To my relief, Sophia and her minions avoided me like the plague. On the odd occasion that we bumped into each other—her attempts at trying to make berets fashionable was hard to miss—a look of terror gripped her, and she would hurry away. Though this suited me just fine, I couldn't help feeling guilty when I saw how miserable she was.

The days rolled into weeks, a blur of over-the-top security and intensive classes. Before I knew it, the next flag fall game had arrived, bringing with it a fresh wave of stress. What if it was a repeat of the last game, where I stood there like a stunned mullet, unable to call any Faezre at all? Conversely, what if I sent someone to the hospital again? Sure, Zane had healed up fine, but what if the next person wasn't so lucky?

I had paced up and down the locker room, trying to calm the worry that twisted inside me like a snake, until Ava dragged me onto the field. It had been terraformed into an icy landscape. Towering spires and glacial crevices ringed a frozen lake, and an island was set amid the snowdrifts. A scattering of waystations dotted the area, meaning the team that reached the island first would gain a massive benefit.

At the ref's signal, we charged down our mound, fur coats pulled tightly over our leathers. Kali, to my surprise, cooperated better than expected. She did what I asked of her, conjuring her fire with restraint, ensuring no one was in danger. I even surrendered control to her for a while, despite her enthusiasm for hugging Ava after each point scored.

In the end, we won comfortably against Raphael. There were no charred bodies, no grim reminders of losing control. In fact, the magnitude of our power pleasantly impressed me.

The locker room buzzed with celebration after the game, but I couldn't hang around. Time was already running out to finish setting up CJ's party.

"Come on, just one beer," Isabella pressed, looking far too young to even legally smell booze. "It's tradition."

"The little girl is right," said Stanley. "The team wins, the team drinks."

"Have one for me," I said, quickly grabbing my bag from the locker. "And I'll have one with you all at the party. You're coming, right?"

"If you're there, I'm there," said Ava.

Yeah, you are, Kali said creepily. I ignored her.

"Great. It starts at eight."

Oliver, Anya, and a handful of their friends from Gabriel waited for me outside. There was no time to change or freshen up as we needed to reach our secret party location as quickly as possible.

"This is genius," Anya exclaimed as she stepped onto the platform at the Perch. The mist from the waterfall rose in the air, creating a natural curtain of secrecy. "No way we'll be caught breaking curfew."

Though I was proud of coming up with the location, worry gnawed at me at the risk we took. If the professors discovered us, they could revoke my flag fall privilege—a consequence that was too terrible to face. But I wanted to make CJ's day as special as I could.

Oliver pulled a gold balloon from the box and stretched it. "Won't it look suspicious if a bunch of students head up here? I mean, the professors aren't exactly dumb, are they?"

"You worry too much," Anya said. "That's why we have these." She pulled out a folded piece of paper that was a photocopy of a map I'd drawn.

"You're crazy if you think everyone's going to follow the map," Oliver said.

Though it was rudimentary, it showed the network of tunnels beneath Astaroth. It marked the best routes from all the châteaux to the Perch. Aran and I had spent days planning it and were certain we would be fine as long as the tunnels weren't being watched.

The frantic rush to transform the Perch began. By six thirty, it was unrecognizable, with fairy lights twinkling between the trees, casting a warm glow over kegs of beer. A DJ booth sat at the edge of the waterfall, and hundreds of gold and silver balloons drifted overhead. Anya had sourced a variety of drinking games, but Oliver was disgruntled at the lack of any Pokémon-themed activities. The space was dotted with fire barrels to ward off the night chill.

We took a step back to admire our handiwork. Despite my exhaustion, a sense of satisfaction welled up inside me.

"You've done so well," a girl called Kirra said, pouring a beer. "CJ will love it."

"I hope so," I said, trying to ignore the nervous fluttering in my stomach. "You don't think it's too . . . basic?"

"Absolutely not. There's nothing basic about a fairytale party." She took a sip. "Well, not one that looks like this."

I glanced at my watch, and my heart jumped. "I'm late! Oh, heavens—I need to get changed. Can you handle things here?"

Kirra threw her arm around a keg. "I'm sure we'll manage."

I hurried back to Michael with a few other girls, our faces smudged with dirt and wet with sweat. CJ was nowhere to be found. Marie, a girl two bunks down, said she'd wandered off with Morgan. I rolled my eyes, hoping she wasn't falling for him again. She could do so much better.

After a quick shower, I slipped into the figure-hugging red dress CJ had picked out for me. She'd assured me it accentuated my best features, but wearing it made me feel like I was playing dress-up.

Marie gasped when she saw me. "You look stunning!"

"Are you sure?" I said, turning in front of the mirror.

"Aren't you?"

"I don't know . . . I kind of feel like someone else."

"Well, you shouldn't—that dress was made for you."

I fidgeted with the hem. "Do you think Aran will like it?"

Marie pulled my hands away and squeezed them. "He'll forget his own name when he sees you."

Sometime later, as we made our way through the tunnels to the forest below the Perch, a nervous excitement found me. For whatever reason, I couldn't shake the feeling that tonight, even though the party was for CJ, there was something special in store for Aran and me. It'd only been two weeks since the hidden glade, but I felt we'd been together a lifetime. Now, dressed in my nicest gown, I wanted to tell him how much he meant to me and, more importantly, wanted to hear how much I meant to him.

I checked my phone again and was happy to see it was only a little after eight. Aran had sneaked into Little Peak to deliver a package, so I'd have at least an hour of drinking to calm my nerves before he arrived.

The Perch was pumping. We climbed out of the tunnels to music and the sound of laughter. My breath hitched as I saw the large crowd of people gathered around the tables. They smiled and laughed and looked like they were having the best time.

Someone crashed into me, almost knocking me off my feet.

"Oh, Alina!" CJ cried, wrapping her arms around me and rocking from side to side. "I love it! The party—you've gone to so much effort!" She let go and gasped when she saw my outfit. "Damn! I knew you would rock that dress, but wow! Go on, give us a spin."

I laughed and performed a twirl. "This old thing? Just something I threw on."

"If I didn't have my eyes on someone else, I'd take you home myself," she said.

This was the first I'd heard of it. "What someone else?"

"Never you mind," she said mysteriously, hooking her arm through mine. "Come on, let me get you a drink!"

And she did. The first, the second, the third—tequila, Jäger, Fireball. It wasn't long before a warmth crept from my chest to my legs, piloting me to the dance floor. The Perch became so crowded that I was half worried the cliff would crumble into the valley below.

As I poured another beer, watching CJ chat with Oliver, I felt an overwhelming affection for her. Oliver was more interested in games than socializing, which meant he wasn't the most talkative person. But CJ had this extraordinary ability to connect with everyone—a skill that I admired her for.

It was only when I caught sight of the time—dangerously close to eleven—that I really felt Aran's absence. There was still no sign of him. What if he'd decided not to come? What if something had happened to him? Or what if he was too tired after his trip to the village? Was all of it—the dress, the makeup—for nothing?

I quickly downed my beer and poured a whiskey and soda. I was on the verge of texting him, but stopped myself. CJ always said to not seem too available. The last thing I wanted was for Aran to think I was desperate. He'd promised he would come, and I had to believe he would. He knew how much the night meant to me—

A sudden memory resurfaced. Aran, sitting in the bar with a woman who was most certainly not his girlfriend. Their whispered argument, and the anger in his eyes when he realized I'd seen him. He'd said I'd caught him doing something he wasn't proud of.

I downed my drink and poured another.

"So much alcohol for such a small person," said Stanley, sidling up to the liquor table beside me.

"Just trying to keep up with you," I said, slurring slightly.

"No one can keep up with me. Watch." He picked up the bottle of Fireball and upended it into his mouth. Great bubbles gulped to the top as he drank almost a quarter of it. He slammed it back down on the table without a wince. "See? Like water."

"That's cute," I said.

"Not cute," he protested. "Amazing."

I found someone's full beer on the table and grabbed it. "No. This is amazing." I chugged it in one, fighting down the froth bubbling up my throat.

He blew a low whistle. "Let's call it a tie."

With each minute that passed, my disappointment at Aran's absence deepened, and with it, a sadness took hold. Try as I might, I couldn't shake the feeling that he was meeting with someone else in the village. Some other girl. I mean, it would be a perfect time to do it. No students were allowed outside their château grounds, so there was no chance he'd be caught.

When midnight arrived, I was stupidly drunk. The world was a blurry mess, and my limbs had stopped listening to me. I stumbled to the liquor table and poured another whiskey. I raised it to my lips but spilled some down the front of my dress, which was no longer as clean as it had been hours earlier.

"Whoopsie," I said, lifting the cup again. A hand on my shoulder made me pause.

Aran?

I spun to find Oliver.

"Oh," I said. "It's you."

His gaze drifted down to my stained dress. "I was thinking maybe we should get some fresh air?"

I shook my head. "But we're already outside."

"Please?"

I didn't want to leave the party. But what if he had news about Aran? That cheating scumbag Aran. Aran, who I thought I loved. My throat burned at the thought. Nodding, I took his offered arm, leaning on it heavily as he helped me through the crowd. People stared as we passed, but Oliver didn't seem to mind.

"It's alright," he said softly.

At first, I wondered what was alright, but then I realized I was crying.

"Thanks," I said, hating how slurred my voice sounded. "I don't deserve a friend like you."

He led me out of the party and down the forest path, walking slowly enough for me to stumble beside him. We were silent for a long while. "It doesn't fix anything," he said. "The booze, I mean. It causes more pain than it heals."

"I don't use it to heal pain. I use it to hide it. It works."

We passed the ruins of a crumbling stone building. "No," he said softly. "All you do is offload it onto those who care about you."

What was he going on about? "Have you even been drunk before?"

"No."

"So, you don't really know what you're missing?"

"My mom's been drunk before," he said after a moment. "She used to drink a lot. Most of the time, she'd drink in our lounge room with all her friends. I can still smell the smoke and beer. Hear the shouting." He kicked a stone down the path. "Her mood never got better with alcohol. She got angry. Angry at the world. Angry at life. Angry at us. Joe and I—that's my older brother—would hide in our room. We'd use our bed as a barricade to block the door. Sometimes it worked. Sometimes it didn't. In the morning, Mom would always apologize. At night, she'd always find something to be sorry about."

As he spoke, all thoughts of Aran evaporated, leaving me horrified at the way I'd acted. I stopped and turned to face him. "Oh, Oliver, I'm sorry—"

He brushed my comment aside. "I'm not after sympathy. It's been a while since Mom's been angry, and she won't ever be angry again. But I've seen the way you drink. I don't know . . . I guess I'm worried."

I pulled him into a tight hug. "Thank you. For caring. I suppose I have a few things to sort out." I released him and looked down at my dress, disgusted. "But for now, I think I need some sleep. Be a gentleman and walk me home?"

A smile lit his face. "I can do that." He took my arm in his and led me away.

We hadn't walked for more than a minute when I heard a familiar voice ahead. I sucked in a breath, not believing it.

"That's Aran," I said. Releasing Oliver's hand, I stumbled around the bend and toward the stone bridge. Two silhouettes were outlined in the darkness. One was him, and one was . . . *CJ?*

I stopped in my tracks.

He's done it before, a voice inside me whispered. It wasn't Kali but the echo of my own deepest fears. *He did it in Little Peak.*

"No," I breathed. Aran wasn't like that. He wouldn't do that to me.

Yet, as I watched, CJ reached out and pulled him into a hug that stole the light from my world.

Chapter Thirty-Three

The forest grew dull and bleak, the sound of rushing water fading into the distance as the ground churned beneath my feet. I was stuck in place, staring at the bridge as I struggled to breathe. How could this happen? How could CJ betray me like this? How could Aran? When I finally managed a breath, tears blurred my vision.

When they broke apart, Aran said something that made CJ giggle, then draped an arm over her shoulders.

Together, they crossed the bridge.

My chin trembled. I had just witnessed my worst fears unfold. I was indispensable. I'd given him my whole heart, and he'd tossed it away like it was yesterday's trash.

The sound of their laughter did something to me. I snapped. A tide of rage washed away my grief, and as I balled my fists I knew I couldn't let this stand. CJ could have anyone—any student, any professor, just anyone. Yet, she'd chosen my man. Didn't our friendship mean anything to her? I mean, heck, I'd just spent the last few weeks planning her birthday party.

My jaw clenched as I strode toward them, bursts of angry light popping at the edge of my vision. They'd hurt me, and I'd be damned if I didn't let them know it. "I don't know why I'm surprised," I thundered, taking satisfaction as they jumped. "You two together. Always together."

Aran's face broke into a grin when he saw me, but it quickly fell into a look of concern. "Hey, babe, sorry I'm late—"

"I'll deal with you later," I said, eyes blazing into CJ's. My ears rang, drowning out all other sounds except for the pounding of my heartbeat. "How could you do this to me? You were like a sister."

Her stupid eyebrows shot up in surprise. She looked back at Aran, and a small smile played on her lips. "Babes, it's not what it looks like—"

"It's always what it looks like with you," I said, raising my voice. "They're just numbers, aren't they? All the boys? Just a way to make you feel special." Any sluggishness I had from the booze evaporated, leaving me as sharp as a tack.

Aran stepped between CJ and me. "Listen, if you stop chucking a wobbly for a second, I'll explain—"

But CJ barged past him. She stormed across the bridge until we met on the bank of the stream. "All the boys?" Her voice was dangerous but I couldn't care less. "What does that mean?"

"Exactly what you think," I said. "This boy, that boy, any boy, my boy. You're just a . . . just a—"

"Just a what?"

"Just a slut!"

The word came out before I'd even considered it. It hung between us, heavy, echoing in the chilly night.

Pain filled her eyes as she drew her brows together. "It's nice to know how you really think."

Instant regret filled me. "I . . . I didn't mean that."

She shot her hands forward and a blast of wind caught me in the chest, knocking me into the stream. "And I didn't mean that. Cool off, Alina."

My skin burned from the cold. I stumbled to my feet, spluttering and slipping on the slick stones. By the time I'd wiped water from my eyes, CJ had disappeared along the path.

I screamed. Anger, hate, self-pity—all of it tore through me. I was pathetic. Drunk. What had I done in life to become so worthless to people?

I floundered to the bank, shaking like crazy, and brushed aside the helping hands of Aran and Oliver. I looked into Aran's eyes, and my heart shattered.

"Alina, please . . ." he started, reaching for me again.

My throat burned. I turned away from him, the man I'd loved, and crossed the bridge, tears spilling down my cheeks.

"Please, let's talk about this," he said, falling into step beside me.

"Talk to CJ."

"Listen to me—"

I quickened my pace, needing to be alone. Why had I let myself fall for him? I knew he was bad news the moment I laid eyes on him. All the signs were there, but I'd ignored them, a slave to my own desire. I reached down through my drunk haze and felt Kali's power. A wall of flames erupted behind me.

"It's not safe to be alone," Aran yelled, the fire muffling his words. "Damn it, Alina! They're after you!"

His warning was wasted. I didn't care what happened to me. They couldn't hurt me in the way he and CJ just had. No one could.

I hurried down the mountain until I reached the forest outskirts, the campus shops in sight. I waited until I caught my breath, then started across the lawns for Michael. Being caught after curfew was the last thing on my mind. I didn't care about anything other than curling up in my bed and crying myself to sleep.

"Alina?" a voice called from the darkness.

I spun to spot a figure detaching from the shadows of Alfio's Pizzeria. As it crossed under a streetlamp, I recognized it as Morgan. A group lingered by the building behind him.

He reached me and his eyes widened as he took in my messy hair and wet dress. He settled on my face, which I imagined was streaked with mascara.

"Shit, Alina. What happened to you?" He removed his black shirt and dabbed my eyes. "Are you alright?"

"Fine," I said, pulling away, but a fresh wave of tears spilled and I couldn't hold it in any longer. "Oh, I don't know. Everything's a mess." I broke down, sobbing uncontrollably, and allowed him to pull me into a hug, squeezing me against his chest.

"Oh, darling," he breathed, rubbing my shoulders. "It's going to be alright."

I should have hated his touch. Recoiled from it. But in my despair, I found it comforting. No, it was more than that. A part of me felt a sick justice that it was Morgan hugging me. The guy CJ had hooked up with was holding me against his bare chest, his hard muscles pressing against my wet body.

"I hate seeing you like this," he said, pulling back to peer into my eyes. "Whatever happened, I know you're a good person and probably didn't deserve it. Do you want me to sort someone out for you?"

I shook my head. Morgan pounding on Aran was the last thing I needed. "No . . . Thank you, though." He was warm against me. A stabilizing rock. He smelled nice, like vanilla. I wasn't sure why that surprised me.

"Well, then, chin up, Firecracker. Things will look better in the morning." Bathed in the lamplight, Morgan's chest looked twice as thick as normal. He was undeniably handsome. I could see why CJ found him attractive.

I swallowed and wiped my nose. "I'll be fine. Just need sleep."

A ghost of a smile played across his lips when I looked into his eyes. "Sometimes a good distraction helps with unnecessary feelings." His gaze drifted down my body, taking in the wet dress that clung to me. His eyes lingered on my breasts for a moment before settling on my lips.

My breathing quickened. Why shouldn't I? CJ had. Aran had. An eye for an eye. With careless regard for consequence, my skin prickling with danger, I edged in just a fraction, and tilted my face closer to his.

He understood the invitation. He snaked one hand behind my head and pulled me in. His lips were pleasantly soft, his tongue careful, and I was unable to stop myself from pressing into him. I needed a distraction, anything to stop me thinking about what had happened at the bridge. Morgan was that distraction.

What the fuck are you doing? Kali's voice rang in my mind. It was distorted and wobbly.

Her words shattered Morgan's spell. I pulled back, eyes widening as I realized what I'd done.

"Alina?" He looked confused. "What's wrong?"

I stepped away, horrified. "I—I have to go," I stammered. I whirled around and ran, my head spinning as I passed the library. I didn't see another person, and only slowed when I reached the edge of Michael's forest, wheezing and out of breath.

Have you lost your mind? Kali demanded, her voice stronger. *Morgan? Of all the slimeballs you could've hooked up with, you choose him?*

I stumbled through the underbrush, branches clawing at me. *They deserved it. Both of them. I hate them. I'll never talk to them again.*

Them? Them who? Because by kissing Morgan, the only person you're hurting is yourself.

Aran and CJ! You saw what they did.

How can I see anything when you drink enough to drown a fish? Every time you lift a damn bottle to your lips, you bury me deeper down until I can't see a damned thing.

My foot hit a tree root and I stumbled, almost falling over. *Aran cheated on me with CJ.*

There was a long pause, and then laughter rang out in my head.

You think this is funny? I demanded.

Poor, simple Alina. You really think that's true?

I saw it with my own eyes!

What?

Huh?

What did you see?

They were hugging—

Listen, I think Aran is a nob, I won't lie. A nob with a shitty accent who is too good-looking to be trustworthy. But he's a sappy nob with a shitty accent, and not a cheater. I've seen the way he looks at you. I've felt the way he loves you—which is sick on so many levels. He's not cheating. Whatever you think you saw, you didn't.

I readied a rebuttal, sifting through her words to find a weakness in her argument, but there weren't any cracks. *I know what I saw. And what about all the other times they'd been together? Laughing and touching? It's not how friends act.*

How about you and Oliver?

That's different, I started, but my words trailed off as I realized it wasn't different at all. A tightness gripped my chest as understanding settled in, and I crumpled to my knees. The ground spun as my stomach constricted and I vomited uncontrollably. Wave after wave racked my body as though trying to rid me of the bitter truth I'd swallowed.

When my throat burned and nothing else came out, I sat back, breathless, miserable, and splattered with muck. I no longer knew what I believed.

Kali?

I'm here.

I've really messed things up, haven't I? I slowly forced myself to my feet and staggered toward my cabin.

Nothing that can't be undone in time. But you've got a lot of apologizing to do.

Will they forgive me?

You're a good person. They'll forgive you.

When I reached to the cabin, the only thing I wanted to do was dive headfirst into bed, but Kali insisted I shower, drink a bottle of water, and eat some leftover pasta.

When I finally laid my head down on my pillow, I didn't feel nearly as anxious about the following day as I would have if Kali hadn't been there to calm me down.

Thanks, I thought, my mind retreating into the darkness.

I'm always here for you.

Chapter Thirty-Four

Was I dying?

The pain of a thousand angry wasps stung my brain, dragging me back to consciousness. My stomach rolled in sickening waves, threatening to spill what little I had left in it, and my tongue was drier than the Sahara.

With effort, I opened my eyes and squinted against the light stabbing through the curtains. Judging by the sun's position, morning had already given way to the afternoon. Groaning, I tried to lift my head, but quickly gave up when the room swirled around me. I closed my eyes.

In the darkness, memories trickled in. At first, they came slowly: the flag fall game, organizing the party, the red dress. Then, in a brutal rush, each horrifying detail bombarded my mind. My insides withered. How could I have said that to CJ? How could I have kissed Morgan? How could I have believed Aran would do anything to hurt me?

Hot tears trickled down my cheeks. I couldn't face them ever again. I wanted to stay cocooned in my bed until I rotted, but even that wasn't an option, not when CJ lived right above me. Panic bubbled up making my breaths come in short, erratic bursts as the room closed in on me.

Just breathe, Kali's voice came through soothingly. *It's not the end of the world. Everyone makes poor decisions when drinking. It's a part of life. They'll understand.*

I wanted to believe her, to think I could smooth it over, but what I'd done . . . I wouldn't blame anyone if they never spoke to me again.

What do I do now? Would you . . . would you handle it for me? I know it's a lot to ask, but I'm desperate.

Kali didn't reply immediately. *I don't think that's a good idea.*

She'd never refused control before.

It's not that I don't want to help, she added. *I just think it'll be better for you if you take responsibility for this.*

How? How do I get them to forgive me?

One step at a time. If CJ's sleeping above us now, speak to her. Let her understand what was going on in your mind. Apologize, like, a million times. Women love that stuff. If she's out already, then freshen up. Do your hair, grab a solid breakfast, and maybe get some chocolates or something.

I wiped my nose, feeling slightly more hopeful. *She does love chocolate.*

They're for us—you need to put some meat on these bones. Plus, they make you feel good inside. Now, up you get. Shower.

Climbing out of bed was one of the hardest things I'd ever done. Not only because my body ached like it'd been caught in a war zone, but because the prospect of facing CJ and her reaction would make everything painfully real. She must hate me for the name I called her. But how would she react when she found out about the kiss with Morgan?

I mustered my courage and, with growing dread, planted my feet and stood.

Her bunk was empty, bed neatly made.

"She didn't come home last night," a voice said behind me. Marie and Kirra had entered the cabin, each holding a steaming cup of coffee.

"Not surprised," mumbled Kirra, just loud enough for me to hear.

"Kirra!" Marie hushed her.

"You saw what she did to them," Kirra continued, her eyes narrowing. "Someone needs to say something."

Any hope that my confrontation with CJ might remain a secret was swiftly extinguished. "Saw?" I asked. As drunk as I'd been, I was certain there hadn't been anyone else in the forest when I'd stumbled upon CJ and Aran.

Marie's mouth popped open. "Oh, Alina, I'm so sorry. You don't know? Check your socials. But maybe sit down first."

A chill swept through me. I fumbled for my phone and unlocked it with trembling fingers.

Two hundred and seventy-two new messages.

I collapsed onto my bed, eyes widening as I skimmed through them. Cruel comments suggesting I should die. People telling me I was pathetic. Selfish. One guy even sent his phone number, asking to be my next victim. With each message, my horror intensified at the sheer nastiness.

It took me a moment to uncover the cause of all the animosity. When I did, I was so disgusted that I flung my phone across the bed as if a spider had suddenly appeared on it.

It was a photograph, taken last night, near Alfio's Pizzeria. Morgan and I were locked in a kiss.

I stared at the phone at the foot of the bed, paralyzed. Then thick tears spilled down my cheeks and my shoulders heaved as I melted into a sobbing heap.

Marie sat beside me, pulling my head onto her shoulder. “Never mind all those jerks. They’re just jealous. Fix it with CJ and Aran. They’re the ones who matter.”

I nodded, a whimpering sound escaping my lips, but I couldn’t form words.

Kirra grabbed a coat from her locker, then stood at the door. “Coming, Marie? We don’t want to be late for sledding.”

Marie pulled away, gently wiping the tears from my cheeks. “Give them some time. Things will get better.”

They left, and I was alone.

How hot is Kirra when she’s angry?

Not completely alone. Kali was gratingly cheerful.

For my birthday, I want you to let me try my chances with her, she said.

My walls crashed down and I jumped to my feet, fists clenched. It wasn’t fair. None of it. I stormed into the bathroom and jabbed a finger at my reflection.

It was you! I snapped. *You kissed Morgan last night!*

Kali snorted. *In case you’ve forgotten—I’m not attracted to men.*

You planted the seed! I said, not caring how delusional I sounded. I was desperate. I couldn’t be the villain. I wouldn’t be. *You told me to take what I wanted!*

So, you took Morgan? Talk about low standards.

No—I took revenge!

Ah, there it is, she countered. *I never once suggested you do anything of the sort. You need to take responsibility for your life. Don't go back to being the weak Alina from Breaux Bridge. You've come so far.*

Can't you see you're tearing me apart? I thought if I gave you room to breathe, you'd stop hurting me. I was wrong. I'm better off without you.

Her essence swelled. *Tearing you apart? TEARING YOU APART? I've done nothing but help you the entire time we've been here! If it weren't for me, YOU would be a pathetic shell of a demon. YOU would have no friends. YOU would be the outcast.*

I shrank from her rage, caught off-balance by her ferocity.

Want to see where you'd be without me? she surged on. *Fine. Hope you like it.*

Like a balloon deflating, she withdrew, shrinking until she was nothing more than a quivering spot.

And then, all at once, that spot vanished.

I felt it like a slap in the face. *Good! I hope you don't come back!*

I studied my reflection in the mirror. My nostrils flared wildly, and dark circles hugged my eyes. I looked hollow, a broken shell. I turned away in disgust and left the bathroom to sit cross-legged on my bed, staring at my phone for what seemed to be an eternity. Then, in a trance, I picked it up, navigated the menus, and pressed call.

The phone rang six times and was answered on the seventh.

"What?" His voice sounded as dead as I felt.

"I'm so sorry," I gushed. "I didn't mean to—I thought you and CJ were . . . I don't know. It sounds stupid now, but I didn't mean for it to happen. I mean, Morgan? I must have been pretty drunk, huh?"

The line was silent.

"Aran?"

"I'm glad you did it," he said, his words hitting me like a blow to my chest. "I was falling for you, Alina. The pain I'm in now is nothing compared to what it would've been down the track. Thanks for showing your true colors early enough to spare me that heartache."

"No, it's not like that! I like you, Aran. I . . . I love you!" The word tumbled out of my mouth before I could catch it.

There was a long pause as I held my breath.

"Funny. I feel nothing for you."

The line went dead.

My throat constricted. I couldn't take it any longer. I was tired of always screwing up, always making a mess of myself. I leaped to my feet and bolted from the cabin, not caring what I looked like. People lounging by the fire wolf whistled as I sprinted into the forest, not stopping until I found a secluded thicket of pine trees to shelter under. My chest heaved as I collapsed into a fetal position, crying like a lost child.

At some point during the day, Raven found me. Sensing my distress, she snuggled up in my arms, purring softly.

By late afternoon, I'd gathered the courage to message CJ and explain everything. Her response was instant.

Apparently our friendship meant more to me than it did to you. Goodbye, Alina.

It wasn't until the sun had set and the biting chill of the wind became unbearable that I trudged back to my cabin. Craving solitude, I hung a sheet between CJ's bed and mine, creating a makeshift barrier to shut out the rest of the world. Then, lying down, I tried to ignore the thousands of terrible thoughts I had about myself.

The bunk shook at ten thirty as CJ climbed into bed. Muffled sobs filtered down from above, tearing me in two. I wanted to talk to her, to apologize and admit I was an idiot. But I couldn't. I was a coward, too frightened to fight for those I cared about.

I didn't sleep a wink that night. My mind was quick to supply me with cruel scenarios of what might unfold the following day.

The next morning, I stayed hidden in bed until the rest of the cabin had left for breakfast. I dressed, hiding behind the high fur hood of my jacket, and made my way to the cafeteria. I felt like a fresh inmate walking to their cell. People gawked at me and whispered behind their hands. No one approached to verbalize the words they'd sent the day before. I suppose it was true that a keyboard turned someone from a tadpole to a toad. I loaded my takeaway box with sandwiches and made my way into the blistering wind to eat at an empty table.

"Ignore them," said a voice from over my shoulder. I looked up and nearly burst into tears when I saw Oliver. "Things will settle eventually." He sat.

"Eventually can be a long time," I said.

"But it will come." There was a rigidity in his voice, and it took me a moment to understand why.

"What I did, you know, with Morgan . . . it wasn't planned. It was terrible and wrong and I'm an idiot, but I don't have feelings for him like that. He's not my type."

He polished an apple on his shirt, not meeting my eyes. "What's your type?"

"I don't know. Kind. Gentle. Somewhat nerdy."

A timid smile found his face. It was like a burst of sunshine on a cloudy day. "You're describing me."

"Well, you in a few years, maybe."

"It will come."

"Eventually." I took a bite of my sandwich.

"I sent you a message yesterday," he said, dropping his apple to start eating his pho. "You didn't reply."

I winced. "I had to log out of everything. The notifications were making me crazy. Whoever took the photo really screwed me."

He arched his eyebrows. "Don't you know? It was Sophia. I think when she saw you kissing Morgan, she just lost it."

My sandwich slipped from my grip. Wasn't it enough that she'd almost killed me? She was such a . . . I let the thought die. I was the one who'd messed up. Everything I was going through was because of me, not her.

The first class was with Audrey. We were to practice temporary tattoos and symbols. Ordinarily, I would've been thrilled to tattoo a piece of cardboard—I'd always enjoyed doodling—but when the class was divided into pairs and I was forced to team up with Audrey because no one wanted me, any pleasure I could've found in it was sucked away.

"Follow the curve!" Audrey snapped for the third time in three minutes. I was tracing a pattern already drawn on the board but struggled to stay within the lines. "What's wrong with you today? Are you drunk?"

"No, it's just—"

"So, you have less talent than a five-year-old with crayons?"

I clenched my jaw.

"Oh, for fuck's sake—stop that! Why are you having a meltdown?" She snatched the tattoo gun from my grip. "Look at me, girl, and listen. You have an entire legion of demons that wants to use you as fodder in their war, and you're here, moping over a *boy*? You need to reassess your priorities. Have a good hard look at the things you want in life. If you're content to live as a pawn in the hands of the Reavers, by all means, keep neglecting your studies. If you think you're safe because you have some Faezre ability, then you're gravely delusional. Even demons from Fernyre fear them."

"I don't think that at all—"

"Good, then you're not entirely stupid. I saw it on your face at the first flag fall game. You have no control over that fire soul inside you. You couldn't summon a spark if they didn't want you to. And you don't always have control of your body."

"I do—"

"I'm not as witless as the rest of the professors at this academy. I know that wasn't you fighting the Reavers at the gate. It was this Faezre soul. Now, let me ask you this—what happens if this other soul decides to align with the enemy? What if they grow weary of conforming to your lifestyle, of being second fiddle? What if they amass so much power that you're helpless to defy their wishes? You need to come up with answers, and fast, because two soldiers mysteriously vanished from the gate on Saturday night. The enemy is making calculated advances, girl. And you're dangerously close to being checkmated."

I froze as she spoke. The Reavers had returned already? I had been wandering the grounds drunk that night, all by myself. They could have snatched me up without any effort at all.

"I'll get it under control," I said, sounding more confident than I felt. The reality of the situation was sobering, considering Kali and I weren't on speaking terms.

"You'd better," said Audrey, dropping the tattoo gun onto the bench with a clatter. "For the sake of everyone left on Earth. If you fail in this, their world will crumble. Stop hiding from this other soul and learn to work with it." She turned on her heel and strode away, the sound of her heavy boots echoing over the buzz of tattoo guns.

She was right. If the Reavers captured me and lured Kali to their side, did I have any chance of stopping her? For so long, I'd tried to drown her out with booze and drugs. What if that was no longer the right thing to do?

Unless she came out of hiding, there would be no way of finding out.

Chapter Thirty-Five

As the days passed, my status as public enemy number one became increasingly clear. Once the first wave of gossip died down, everyone fell silent around me, and though it wasn't obvious at first, before long I found myself sitting solo more often than not. I understood why everyone acted this way. Their love for Aran and CJ, and their shock that someone—particularly a girl from Louisiana who already had too much power—could hurt them so much made them angry. I got that, but I didn't like it.

Another factor was Sophia. She'd rediscovered her courage and was on a relentless campaign to ruin any chance I had of happiness. It was a success.

While I sank deeper into despair, Morgan basked in the attention. People chastised me while celebrating him. The double standard of it made me sick. Now he wolf whistled every time he saw me, and everyone laughed. It was all I could do to not scream.

My anxiety and depression returned, and I lapsed into old habits. I sneaked vodka into classes, reaching a stage where I was drunk more often than not. This haze made it difficult to speak to Kali. Despite my promise to Audrey that I'd fix things before she could be used as a weapon against us, Kali had become no more substantial than a horrible memory.

So I drank even more.

The next step in my downward spiral was to resign from the flag fall team. Nobody wanted to see me play. Nobody wanted to see me, period. Much to my dismay, Aran refused to let me quit. He insisted I owed it to Michael to help win the championship. He said this icily, and I knew he wanted me gone more than anyone. But he had no real say on who was on the team. Morgan would never give up his most valuable player.

This resulted in flag fall practice nights becoming the most painful periods of my new life. Aran refused to talk with me outside team training, and while the rest of the team wasn't overtly nasty, they were noticeably distant.

The only thing that kept me from giving up and running back to Breaux Bridge was the fear of what that meant for Earth. If I failed, everyone died—or whatever the Reavers did to them. If only the Reavers knew how pathetic I was, maybe they'd stop coming for me. My days blurred into weeks in an endless run of waking with skull-splitting hangovers and drifting to sleep in a boozy fog.

It was during a fierce thunderstorm, with wild winds and relentless rains, that someone shook me awake. I groaned and rolled over, my head pounding. The person didn't leave.

"Damn it, Alina," they said. "What are you doing?"

"Sleeping," I slurred, my hand floundering beneath the tangled mess of sheets, searching for the familiar shape of the vodka bottle.

Loud footsteps sounded as whomever it was stomped away.

Peace.

Just as I was drifting back to sleep, a shock of ice-cold water slammed against my face. I bolted upright, sputtering, my pulse thudding in my ears. I swiped the freezing droplets from my eyes. "What the heck . . ."

My voice faded into a stunned whisper. "Oh," I finished, staring at the empty bucket clutched in CJ's hand. Though we shared a bunk, she hadn't uttered a word to me since our falling-out.

She stormed to my closet and threw it open. "Your match starts in an hour, and you're still sleeping?" She rummaged through my clothes.

It took a moment for her words to sink in. Understanding hit me like a freight train. "Crap!" I lurched out of bed, head spinning. "My alarm didn't go off."

"Normal people don't need alarms at lunchtime on a Saturday."

I shook my head to try and clear the remnants of sleep. "Never been accused of being normal."

She helped me dress, steadying me when I teetered. "You're going to get yourself killed out there—you can't even stand straight." She stepped back and sighed, her gaze taking in my pathetic state. She guided me toward a chair by the crackling fire. "Sit."

I did as I was told, and she stood behind me. Pain stabbed at my scalp as she took a brush to my hair, yanking at a stubborn knot. Why was she helping? She hated me after everything I'd done. How long had it been? Two weeks? Three? I couldn't make sense of it.

She worked in silence, and in some ways that hurt even more.

"I'm sorry," I burst out, blinking back tears. "I—I miss you."

She brushed harder.

I turned to face her. "CJ?"

She wrinkled her nose and stepped back. "Jesus, Alina!" She hurried into the bathroom and returned with a tube of toothpaste. She shoved my head back and, as I opened my mouth to protest, squeezed a glop onto my tongue. I gagged before forcing it down.

"You smell worse than at the Choosing," she said, resuming her attack on my hair.

"Good times, huh?"

In her reflection in the mirror above the mantle, I saw her lips press into a tight line, but there was a twitch in one corner. Had she almost smiled? I clung to that possibility, desperate for any sign that she might not hate me as much as I hated myself.

Her face smoothed over, becoming as unreadable as stone. Seemingly satisfied with my hair, she tossed the brush aside and jammed gloves onto my hands. "Get moving or you'll be late, and everyone will hate you even more."

Sheets of rain fell from a moody sky. The ground, now covered in a layer of water, squelched underfoot. I conjured an air umbrella and staggered to the cliff path. My insides churned with weeks of alcohol abuse.

By the time I entered the locker room, the stadium was packed and Aran was pacing frantically. His face flooded with relief when he saw me. Then he scowled. "About bloody time."

I murmured an apology, moving to stand beside Stanley as Aran launched into his pep talk, rushed because of the ticking clock. My mind was only half present, the other half still left somewhere in bed.

The match, a muddy and bloody affair, was one of the most grueling battles I'd fought. They had terraformed the ground into a giant, half-drowned maze. It was cardio central, with an unhealthy amount of running—something my struggling body did not appreciate. I vomited three times before the final whistle blew. We'd won, but I was dead on my feet. The roar of the crowd echoed around us, and I allowed myself the illusion that, among all the cheers, there might be someone rooting for me.

As I trudged back down the tunnel, drenched and muddied, I realized my hangover was gone, replaced by some foreign sensation—an emotion distant from the self-loathing I'd grown used to. It wasn't pride, not quite. But the edge of my disgust had been softened somewhat.

"Ripper effort, everyone," Aran said, passing around celebratory beers. "Not a bad way to start the year—three wins—our best yet."

"Hudson's been holding us back," said Trix, toasting with her beer. "Getting rid of him was the best thing you did."

Aran stopped in front of me. "No. Alina has brought us forward." He handed me my beer, and though he didn't so much as smile, I felt like he was extending an olive branch. I wasn't foolish enough to think he'd forgiven me, his emotions were likely running high after the win, but it felt good all the same.

"Who's up for an after-party?" Elias asked, pausing in front of the mirror.

Aran sat on a bench and removed a boot. He upended it and a stream of water cascaded to the floor. "Only if you promise to keep your clothes on this time."

"Only if you promise not to feed me tequila."

"Where are we thinking?" asked Zach.

"The Shack," Aran said without hesitation.

Elias, in the middle of snapping a selfie, froze. "There's a damn typhoon tearing it up outside, and you want to go to the Shack?"

Aran shrugged. "We always end up swimming in the lake anyway. Bottoms up!" He downed his beer, then crushed the can and dropped it in the trash bin. "Attendance is compulsory. No exceptions."

I looked at him like a shy girl waiting for an invitation to a cool kid's party. *No exceptions?*

His eyes locked on mine. "Everyone." A moment passed, then he grinned at Ava. "Well, except you. Not sure how you missed that waypoint."

The lightness that filled me was too much to contain. I beamed, not caring how pathetic I looked. I wanted to laugh, to scream, to cry. I wanted to do everything all at once and not care who saw. It was as though the clouds had parted above, and I felt the sun for the first time in years.

In the end, I cracked my beer and took a sip.

"Alina?" a voice called from the tunnel.

CJ stood at the entrance. She'd never set foot in the locker room, even when we'd been friends. I stared at her, beer frozen at my lips.

"Let's chat," she said.

My insides fell into chaos—hope and fear and everything in between. "Sure." I didn't know what else to say. She was going to speak to me twice in one day? Was I dreaming?

"Don't be late," Ava shouted as I left the room.

We ambled down the tunnel in awkward silence, our footsteps ringing around us. It wasn't until we'd exited the stadium and the clamor of the excited crowd faded that she finally spoke.

"It killed me to see how miserable you've been," she said as we passed the sandpit. "But, babe, you need to understand how much you hurt me—"

"I do," I blurted. "Trust me, I do. I never meant it. You were my best friend. I . . . I was an insecure idiot. Everyone loves you. All the girls, all the guys. It's like I'm some sort of swamp creature in comparison." All my thoughts knotted around each other, coming out in one tangled mess. "When I saw you with Aran . . . in my muddled mind, I forced a connection when there was none. I got jealous over nothing. I don't know. I guess what I'm trying to say is, I'm sorry."

She stared ahead. "That's what hurts. It seems like no matter what I do, I'll always be judged on my looks. Back home, none of the lasses could see past their own insecurities to truly like me. Always scared I'd take their man when I had my chance. But, honey, that's not me. They drove me away even though I was nothing but nice to them. I suppose that's why I get along better with lads. They don't hate like women do."

We stopped at the boundary of the forest. She turned to me, her hair whipping around her face. "I'd never go after Aran. I'd never betray you like that. That's what really cuts—that you believed I could. I thought you knew me better."

"I do! I was drunk and stupid and didn't think . . ." I stopped, forcing a deep breath. "I know it's not a justification. Being wasted doesn't fix what I did. That's my shadow to fight, my own demons."

A flicker of a smile passed over her face. "How many demons do you want?"

I stared at that smile, blinking away tears. It was beautiful. "Oliver says I gotta catch 'em all."

In a moment too perfect for words, she pulled me into a hug.

"That night, on the bridge," she began, "I told Aran how lucky he was to have you. I said that you were the kindest and most genuine person I knew." She pulled back. "Kinda ate those words after it. But now . . . now I stand by it."

Movement over her shoulder caught my eye. While most students made their way to the Shack, a handful had broken away and headed in our direction. My happiness spluttered. It was Morgan, Hudson, and two of their friends.

I grabbed CJ's hand and pulled her into the forest, my boots sliding in the mud. "Let's take the scenic route to the lake."

"Someone's thirsty," CJ said, trotting to keep up. "What's the rush?"

"There's a stink in the air." Passing the first trees, I glanced back. They were closing the gap in long strides.

"What does that wanker want?" CJ asked, her eyes narrowing as she spotted him.

I started to jog. "Let's not stick around to find out."

The pines grew tightly in this part of the forest, and with the storm above, it was dark and ominous. We hurried along the slippery trail, weaving around gnarled roots and over moss-laden rocks. Unease swirled in my gut. Why would Morgan want to see us now, after everything that had happened? Surely, he must know that I wanted nothing to do with him. But then again, he was a guy, so he probably thought I was just being coy.

The path led us to a narrow, almost hidden passageway flanked by towering stone outcrops. I breathed a little easier, thinking we'd lost them. But then, as I relaxed, we rounded a bend and he appeared in front of us.

The sheer stone walls on either side of him cast him in shadow. His self-satisfied smirk made my skin crawl. It was the grin of someone who thought himself too clever, always one step ahead. A guy from Uriel stood beside him: Carlos the Creep—it was a name well earned.

"Now, now, ladies," Morgan said, stepping into the pathway, arms spread wide. "You know how much I love it when you play hard to get."

Yep. As stupid as he looks.

"Hard . . ." CJ mused. "Easier said than done, right? How's the Viagra working for you?"

Carlos snorted, trying to hold in a laugh, but Morgan's smile dipped. He flashed his eyes at me. "Hello, darling. It's been a minute. Gotta say, you in your leathers out there, kicking ass . . . sexiest thing I've seen in years." He let his gaze drift down my body, and I shivered. "Really shows how much you've changed since the Choosing, doesn't it? You were timid, fragile, a liability. I didn't need Aran to warn me off you to know you didn't belong in Michael. Funny how life works out, isn't it? I didn't want you, but Michael took you. Aran didn't want you, but he took you. I guess we're all just suckers for an outcast story."

It felt like he'd stabbed me in the chest. A memory flickered in my mind, an image of Aran and Morgan as I stepped into the arena that first time. Had Aran really warned him not to pick me? The betrayal stung more than I could have thought. Sure, Aran hadn't owed me anything back then, but after spending an hour together, couldn't he have just kept his mouth shut?

"Yeah, hilarious," I said, trying to wear a blank face as my emotions ran riot. "Always a blast running into you, but we're late for the after-party."

I turned to leave but froze when I saw Hudson and a stocky girl named Breanna blocking our path. If Hudson's eyes could murder, I'd be an obituary already. CJ's hand squeezed mine.

"So, what's the plan?" she asked, turning back to Morgan. "Trying to frighten us into a gang bang? Gotten over your performance anxiety?"

Morgan's smile twisted, his eyes narrowing dangerously. Something was off about him. He took a slow, stalking step forward.

"You know, it's all kinda funny, isn't it?" he said as lightning flashed overhead. "The things we can laugh about after enough time has passed. As a kid, I grew up on stale bread and water. Bet you didn't know that, huh? I hated it, but now . . . now, I can laugh. They were the good days. Sometimes, we only ate what the streets provided." His boots sloshed in the mud as he took another step. "It was such a marvelous way to keep the weight off. Oh, the silver linings we found in our dear deadbeat dad."

A chill crawled up my neck, making my hair stand on end. Why was he telling us this? I glanced over my shoulder. Hudson and Breanna were creeping in.

"I'm sorry that happened to you," I said. "No kid deserves to go through that—"

"Kids laughed at me at school," he continued as though he hadn't heard me. "Teachers, too. For the clothes I wore and the way I smelled. For where I lived and the nits in my hair. One day, after the bell, some of the older kids invited me to play. It was the happiest moment of my life. I thought I was finally going to have friends. It was all I ever wanted, more than food and a clean shirt. You know what happened?" He was now only a handful of paces away, his smile widening into a terrifying grin. "They lured me into an alley behind the bus stop, stripped me naked, and forced me into a dress. I couldn't understand why my friends would do that to me. They told me I should be thankful—that the dress was brand new, and no one had ever worn it, unlike the ratty clothes I dressed in. Not wanting to walk home naked, I sprinted back in that pretty red dress. My dear old man beat the seven shades out of me before I had a chance to explain. That was his love language, you see. Physical touch. He liked to let his fists do the talking."

CJ's hand trembled in my grip. Or was it me shaking? "Kids can be cruel sometimes," I said, checking over my shoulder again, wishing we hadn't wandered off alone. We needed help. *Kali?* I tried.

No answer.

"Ain't that the truth," Morgan said. "But I've done well for myself since I started my new life at Astaroth. Much better than most. I've built a successful business, meaning I haven't had to eat bread or wear dresses since. What did you think of my merchandise?"

His question caught me off guard. I racked my brain but couldn't understand what he was going on about. "I've never bought anything from you."

"No, but our buddy did. What was his name? Eben?"

It took a moment to understand what he was implying. "The pill?" The drug that sent my mind and body reeling during the exorcism.

"Of course, highly illegal. Selling drugs, that is. And, well, the exorcism, too. I still can't believe that was the best plan he could come up with. Taking you back in a gecko? Pretty funny." He shook his head, chuckling. "I guess you think I'm a scumbag for selling NetherNectar. But I've never forced anyone to take them. I'm guilt free. I simply supply what others demand. Being broke ain't all it's cracked up to be, so we gotta do what we gotta do. Your boy knows that. Yes, young, sweet Aran May plays the part of a prince in white armor. But that armor is built from ivory. Carved from the shady deals he does with his little pets. Some places he sells them to . . ." He shuddered dramatically. "Fighting dens, underground labs, bile farms. I mean, there are people who argue that he belongs behind bars. How he sleeps at night, I'll never know." He took a step closer. "But here we are."

I wanted to argue, to defend Aran, but what did I know about his business? Sure, some students had their pets on campus, but what about the deliveries outside of Astaroth? What homes did those animals find? I didn't believe Morgan about fighting pits and bile farms, but I couldn't shake off the apprehension that filled me.

"Alright, you've had your fun," I said, fighting the tremble in my voice. "Can we go now? People are expecting us." I tried to move past him, but he skipped into my path.

"Yes. People *are* expecting you." He inclined his head, looking like he waited for me to catch onto some joke.

And then it hit. Fragmented memories came to mind, piecing together like a jigsaw puzzle. Eben's urgent voice echoed—*they are already here*. Audrey's certainty that students had let Reavers through the gate. The terrifying way he acted now. It all made a horrifying sense.

Kali! I screamed, stumbling back a step. *Kali, it's Morgan!*

Her silence was deafening.

"Oh, yes, there it is," Morgan said. "You know, don't you? It took longer than I expected. I thought you would've pieced it all together when the guards vanished from the gate. You saw us that night, remember? Or maybe you enjoyed our little pash too much to question why we were out after curfew. Why we weren't at CJ's birthday." He chuckled. "Tell you what, it's a good thing you're hot, because your brain lags."

CJ looked from me to Morgan. "I . . . I don't understand. What do the guards have to do with anything?"

I couldn't tear my gaze away from Morgan. "Reavers are after me. They think I can help them reopen the Shadowgates to Earth. That's why the attack happened. And . . . and Morgan couldn't care less, could you? You'd be happy if the Reavers destroyed Earth, right? Punishment for what you had to go through as a kid."

He shrugged. "More or less. Though I would feel a kind of way if something happened to Metallica." He looked at his watch. "Now, if you'll kindly come with me, the gate should open right about . . ." His voice trailed off as he tilted his head to one side, listening.

I heard it, too. From around the mountain, distant cries echoed over the pounding rain. Screams and shouts.

Morgan straightened, dusting the water from his shoulders with the back of his hands. "It's begun." He cocked one arm and looked at me pointedly. "Come along, little Alina. Let's not make a fuss."

My mind raced, scrambling for an escape. "You're crazy."

"Maybe," he said, wiggling his offered arm. "But if you want to save this academy and everyone in it, then you won't resist. The Reavers won't stop until you're on Noverna. Are you willing to let them run loose around here? Terrible idea."

Of course I didn't want anyone to get hurt. But how could I just hand myself over? They'd force me to help them open the gates to Earth. What would happen then? How many people would die? I shook my head. Surrender wasn't an option.

"I'm sorry you had a shit childhood," I said, fingers curling into fists at my side. "But that's not an excuse to be an asshole." I punched my hands forward, unleashing the full fury of my Terre power. The ground surged up in a wave, hurtling toward Morgan and Carlos. It crashed into them, flinging them into the air. Carlos hit the wall with a crack, but Morgan landed on his feet and sliced a fist through the air. The earth beneath us transformed into a roiling sea of soil and stone as it obeyed him.

I stumbled to one knee as a thunderous roar of colliding air currents filled the ravine. CJ was locked in battle with Hudson and Breanna. I spread my arms wide, fingers splayed, and my wet hair whipped around my face as I released a torrent of pressurized air at Morgan.

But he was viper quick, conjuring a towering shield of stone that easily deflected my attack.

KALI! I screamed, leaping to my feet as the ground ceased its violent waves. *I need you!*

"Look out!" CJ shouted. She threw herself at me, knocking me aside as a scorching jet of air slashed the space where I'd just stood.

I staggered to my feet, my heart pounding, and faced the others. Hudson hovered above us, and Breanna had taken up a position on the outcrop. Morgan, still smiling, crept in. Carlos, I saw with satisfaction, had blood trickling from his nose.

CJ and I stood back-to-back, bracing for their attack. I gulped down breaths, sweat stinging my eyes.

KALI! I cried. Our chance of survival dwindled by the second without her flames.

With a lurch, the ground beneath me gave way and swallowed me up to my knees. It hardened around my arms before I could pull free, locking me in its stony grip. The crushing weight of it fired pain through my joints. I cried out, falling forward.

CJ, also trapped, squirmed behind me.

I reached out with my Terre power, willing the ground to reliquefy. But as I hooked onto the stone, it ignored me.

"Harper was right—you're strong for a fledgling," Morgan said as he circled, aiming one clenched fist at each of us. "But you've got a long way to go before you play in the big leagues." He stopped in front of me. "We could've done this the easy way. I know it's hard to believe, but I don't want to hurt either of you."

Hudson appeared at his side, blood trickling from a cut above his eye. It mixed with rain and streamed down his face. He leaned in low, his hot breath washing over me. "There's no Aran here to save you this time." He reared his foot and aimed at my face.

I flinched, helpless to protect myself. But as I stiffened for the impact, Morgan shoulder-charged him, knocking him to the ground.

"No one lays a finger on them!" he growled.

Hudson picked himself up and angrily swiped the mud from his jacket. "That bitch stole my flag fall position!"

"You should have been stronger," Morgan said. "Stop crying and get to the gate. Bring back a section of Reavers to help take her in. Don't waste time—I don't want her escaping again."

Chapter Thirty-Six

Hudson's face was murder as he blasted into the air and disappeared through the storm above, his wake stirring the falling rain. Morgan did not watch him leave, but kept his eyes locked on me, fists extended, holding CJ and I captive in our stone prison.

I strained against the ground, every nerve screaming as I sought an escape, but my Terre power was nothing compared to Morgan's. The stone only obeyed him.

"You don't have to do this," I pleaded, pain radiating up my arms. "We can still fix things—it's not too late."

He leaned back against the wall and smiled. "How will that make me rich?"

"It won't," said CJ, twisting to glare at him. Like me, she was caught up to her waist in solid stone, both hands trapped by her side. "But it won't make you a murdering asshole, either."

"You'll sing a different tune when I'm lounging in my mansion or jetting off in my private plane. You'll come crawling back, begging for forgiveness for the names you've slandered me with. And hey, if you're still a looker, maybe I'll throw you a bone. But you'll have some making up to do."

"I'd rather get back together with an old tampon than get back with you."

An explosion erupted from the direction of the library. The ground shuddered, vibrating through my bones. The Reavers were close. I looked at CJ, and the fear in her eyes told me she knew it too. It was checkmate. There was nothing I could do to escape. The Reavers would come and take me away. My lips trembled and, as I tried to swallow, the lump in my throat grew. A wave of overwhelming hopelessness filled my chest, and I slumped forward, defeated.

Then something shifted inside me. A spark of electricity crackled in the pit of my stomach. It was a strange sensation that branched in all directions. My veins surged, energizing every muscle, every sinew. I inhaled sharply as this power swelled, demanding to be unleashed.

Morgan kicked off the wall, his gaze snapping to something behind me. "What the fuck?"

I craned my neck to see what he stared at. A small black figure sat on the precipice, eyes locked on Morgan, wings flares.

"Raven!" I cried. "Run! Get out of here while you can." But she ignored me and launched from the ledge and swooped into the ravine to land in front of me. She crouched low, tail flicking, and growled at Morgan as though daring him to take another step.

"Just when I thought the day couldn't be any more profitable," Morgan said. "A wogle! Damn—I've wanted one forever . . ." His voice trailed off into a confused whisper. He stared at his fists, which he shook like they were broken appliances. "Huh? How . . . ?"

Like tuning an old radio through heavy static, my Terre power spluttered back to life. I erupted into action, calling the stone to liquefy once more and sweeping my fists through it like water. Molten earth flew as my hands burst free. I snapped them forward, blasting a jet stream at Morgan. This time, he was not quick enough. The gust smacked him in his stomach, catapulting him into the rocky wall. He hit it with a thud and fell to the ground, not moving.

Carlos and Breanna burst into action, firing volleys of air and stone at us. But CJ and I now had one each and confronted them head-on. She called an updraft to intercept the attacks and send them soaring overhead, and I clapped my palms together, catching the air around the pair and squeezed it in my grip. The force slammed them into each other, and they fell in a tangle of limbs. When they tried to rise, CJ pinned them down with a relentless torrent of wind. They squirmed, fighting its hold.

"Who needs a knight in shining armor when you've got us two, hey babes?" CJ said, her face alive.

A hesitant laugh escaped me, a release of nervous energy. We'd done it. We'd survived, against all odds. My hair was plastered to my face and my breath came in wild gasps. We were alive.

A high-pitched whistle cut my laugh short. Something heavy clipped my shoulder, spinning me to the ground. Agony raced down my arm, my nerves catching fire. I groaned, shaking off the dizziness, and forced myself to my knees.

Morgan stood where we'd left him, his fists extended toward me. His face was twisted into a nasty, satisfied scowl. I blinked away the bright spots, trying to understand what had happened. Then he nodded to a nearby rock, and his lips turned into a sneer.

It was almost the size of my bedside table, and it hadn't been there before. He must have launched it at me. But why was he grinning? My gaze drifted to the base, and I noticed a horrifying detail that turned my world upside down. The ground seemed to lurch from under my feet, and my strangled scream echoed through the canyon.

A tiny black paw.

It was barely visible from beneath the rock, delicate and helpless. Wisps of purple smoke curled around it, fading rapidly. My insides shredded to pieces as I drew breath and screamed again, my stomach squeezing everything out of me. Raven. My sweet Raven. She couldn't be . . . But as my scream died, the purple smoke faded, and the paw was gone.

"Whoops," Morgan said.

A switch flipped inside me. Despair mutated into a ferocious rage. It seized my thoughts, my body, my essence and lit a fire in them. I turned my bleary vision back to Morgan. He was the bastard who'd . . . who'd . . . I couldn't think it.

His hands moved in a familiar pattern, preparing to launch another stone.

To take another life.

I wouldn't let that happen.

I roared, tears streaming from my eyes, and gripped the rocky wall behind him with my Terre. I demanded it bend to my will, to obey only me. Stone shrieked in protest as I yanked with all my rage, and it caved to my command.

Morgan's eyes widened as he spun to face the rockslide. His arms flung across his body in an X as he tried to ward off the surge that bore down on him. In that fleeting moment, I imagined I heard his scream, louder even than the crashing rocks.

I didn't lower my arms until I was certain.

Morgan was dead.

"Alina!" CJ cried. "Help!"

I turned to see Carlos and Breanna regaining their feet, winning the battle against CJ's gust.

They were just as guilty as Morgan.

I flicked my wrists. Shards of stone ripped from the walls on both sides of them and shot forward. I didn't care about the crunch that followed as the bodies fell limp. I didn't care about CJ's horrified gasp.

I didn't care.

I sank to my knees in front of the stone that had buried Raven. Numbly, I summoned a gust to lift it. There was no blood. No sign of the wogle. The purple smoke had faded, leaving only the echoing silence of her memory.

I threw my head back and wailed, the force of my anguish tearing from my throat. My lungs wrung out every shred of air, my cry dwindling to a feeble whimper, and I crumpled forward. My shoulders shook with gut-wrenching sobs.

CJ wrapped her arms around me, whispering into my ear. Her words barely registered as memories of Raven haunted me. She'd been there for me every time I needed her over the last month. If it hadn't been for her, I wouldn't have survived. And now she was gone.

An explosion boomed through the air, making CJ jump. Reavers were nearby. Just beyond the tree line.

Ice-cold fury coursed through my veins. They were the true monsters. They started this nightmare. They killed Eben. Raven. I would make them pay. I didn't care if I was hurt, or even killed—with their dying breath, they would regret what they'd done.

I shoved hot tears from my eyes and stood.

"We have to get you out of here," CJ said.

"No."

I called the wind, and a gust hoisted me into the air, carrying me out of the ravine and above the whipping trees. CJ followed, but unlike me, she couldn't control the stormy gale and was tossed about.

"I know you're hurt, babes, but please think about this. The Reavers are after you."

I didn't answer. The sky slashed at my eyes as I soared higher, rain pelting me like bullets. The campus was a sea of chaos.

Demons wearing crimson armor streaked across the academy like a locust horde, scarring the land I loved. They must be the Reavers. They wore winged helmets that fell into a mane of black feathers around their necks. Their jet-black capes billowed behind them, made of darkness. I'd heard of this material. It granted them the ability to dissolve into shadows, letting them merge with the night.

The grounds writhed under their control, splitting apart to form gaping wounds in the once manicured grass. Trees that had stood tall were now splintered and used as projectiles. A conjured fog rolled through the grounds, and, darting from it, grotesque forms shrieked like hyenas. Their hideous bodies were a blend of bears and bugs, their armored exoskeletons clattering with each movement. They were beelzebubs.

The roiling heavens had their own battle. Swirls of darkened mists merged with bursts of ghoul-green flames as both sides took to their talismans and tattoos for power. Black lightning sizzled through the storm as if the sky itself had ruptured.

Through the carnage, something caught my eye that set my blood on fire. It wasn't just professors and Frostfires who fought back fiercely; students filled the scattered ranks. And though they had the numbers, they were overwhelmed before the Reavers' aggression. They couldn't last.

I turned to CJ and saw the fear in her eyes. "Get to Little Peak and bring back everyone who can help," I ordered. "Fly over the mountain—the gate is no longer safe."

"You're barmy if you think I'm leaving you behind," she said, her wild curls thrashing around her face.

"They're coming for me, CJ. They won't hesitate to kill you if you get in the way. We can only win if we have help."

"I didn't sweat through twelve Krav Maga courses so I could hide in some village."

I opened my mouth to say that was the stupidest thing she'd ever said, when a voice cried out over the roar of the battle: "There she is!"

A Reaver beside the shops pointed at me. As if an unseen command had been broadcast to all of them, the crimson army swiveled their heads skyward and locked their gaze on me.

"That's creepy," said CJ. I didn't disagree.

But they did not attack. After a second, they returned to their skirmishes.

"Maybe you're not as popular as we thought?" CJ said.

"Wouldn't bank on that. Look." A lone figure rocketed from the ground and was on a collision course with us. Unlike the other Reavers, he wore no armor, no helmet, and was without the shadowy cape. He was dressed entirely in black, his long hair trailing behind him like a comet's tail.

I lifted my hands, setting my hooks in the air around me, ready to call on it when needed. But as the distance between us closed and his features became clear, a jolt of recognition stopped me from following through. I lowered my hands in disbelief.

He stopped a short distance away, a small smile on his beautiful pale face. "Hello, Alina."

I raised my hands again, snapping out of my stupor. "You," I growled. "This all started with you."

"No. This started long before we met."

"Liar. You've been after me since Lafayette. You sent Eben!" My voice rose with every word.

He floated closer. "I was against that. He was too young to be involved in this." His gaze drifted over the battle-ravaged ground below where a near constant stream of cries funneled up. "Look around, Alina. Look at the chaos and destruction. We need to put an end to this, and you can help. Stand with us. Save Astaroth."

I stared at him in disbelief. "I'll never be a pawn in your war."

"Even to save the ones you love?"

"And sacrifice everyone on Earth—"

"Fuck, Alina!" He threw his hands in the air in frustration. "How can you be so blind? They're feeding you lies, twisting the narrative to keep you in the dark. The truth isn't hidden, you just need to be willing to see it."

The way he spoke, with such conviction, made me hesitate. There was no trace of deceit in his eyes, no flicker of doubt. He truly believed his words. But it didn't fit together in my mind. How could their brutal actions be justified? "So, what, you're telling me you won't use me to help unlock the gates to Earth?"

His arms fell to his sides, and he chuckled sadly. "I imagine they told you we plan to destroy Earth when we get there? Have you asked yourself why we would fight so hard for a world only to destroy it? Where's the logic in that? Think, Alina. Make it make sense."

I stumbled for an answer. I didn't know enough about this war to answer, but what I did know was the Reavers were hurting people I cared about. I couldn't let that happen any longer.

Before I could reply, CJ cut in with her characteristic bluntness: "You're nuttier than squirrel shit—you understand that, right?"

Nester's lips pressed tight. "This is a private conversation." With a small flick of his finger, he unleashed a blast of wind that sent her spiraling through the sky, back over the forest.

"Stop!" I shouted, gathering my essence, preparing to fight.

Nester lowered his hand. "This is between you and me. Interruptions are going to draw this out and more people are going to get killed. I'm not here to hurt anyone. I'm here to save you from making the worst decision of your life."

"I didn't need saving in Lafayette, and I'll be damned if I need it now." My eyes raced over the battles taking place all around us. "If you're being honest, if you're not the monster they say you are, then call off your henchmen. These students have done nothing to you."

His gaze bore into mine, searching for something. I held it stubbornly. Eventually, he gave a curt nod. "I'll order a cease-fire if you agree to talk to me with an open mind. Listen to the things I say and form your own conclusions. If you still don't like it, then I—"

An icy-blue chain shot through the air and coiled around his ankle. His eyes widened, then he was violently yanked down. For a moment, it looked like he would crash into the ground, but he regained control and slowed just enough to save his life. The collision was still brutal and splattered mud everywhere, but after a moment, he groaned and rolled onto his back.

I stared, shocked by the suddenness of it all. Despite him being the enemy, he had raised enough questions to have me second-guessing myself. No one at Astaroth had ever explained why the Reavers wanted to destroy Earth. That was suspicious. I'd read enough books to understand that no one was wholly evil. No one wanted to see the world burn for the sake of it. So, what was the good in the Reavers?

Eben. Eben was the good. And if one soul was good on Noverna, why couldn't there be more?

I shot a glance over my shoulder to confirm CJ was safe—she now flew back toward me—then dropped to the ground, landing beside Nester.

He struggled to sit, the chain now slack by his ankle. But a group of Frostfires were sprinting toward us, led by Veston, who gripped a glowing talisman with the energy chain attached to it.

"Swear it," I demanded, crouching beside Nester, facing the charge.

He winced as he pushed himself unsteadily to his feet. "Swear what?"

"You'll stop this fight if I talk to you!"

The Frostfires closed in rapidly. The rage twisting Veston's face, along with the blood staining his blue armor, didn't hint at any readiness for conversation.

"On my life," he said.

It was enough for me.

I stepped in front of the charging soldiers, arms flung wide. "Wait!" I cried. "Please, there's another way!"

They didn't break their charge. Veston returned his talisman to his pocket, erasing the chain. He pulled free another artifact that shimmered with an icy-blue hue. From its glow, a serrated blade of what looked like pure ice burst forth.

"Get out of the way," Nester growled, eying them with contempt. "I can take them."

More soldiers called their own blades. Panic set in as I looked around helplessly. They would kill Nester before he could end the battle.

A sharp pop echoed behind me. I spun to find Audrey had appeared. She wore the same rune-engraved black leather suit that she'd worn the night she'd collected me from Earth. Many talismans hung around her neck, and her fingers were laden with rings. She lifted a hand and pressed her lips to one ring. When she shot it forward, a jet of purple energy erupted from her finger.

The Frostfires, caught midstride, tried to dodge, but the attack gripped them all. Their limbs locked, and they collapsed onto the earth like statues, their magical blades dissipating into nothingness.

"You . . . you just attacked our own soldiers," I said numbly, tearing my gaze from their prone bodies to look at her.

"How observant," she said coldly. Her gaze fell on Nester, and something remarkable happened: her hard face softened. She hesitated, then stepped forward, her hand slowly rising to caress Nester's cheek, fingers trembling.

"My baby," she whispered.

He flinched, then took her hand in his, but didn't pull it away.

I staggered back a step, dazed. *Baby?* What the heck was going on? Was Audrey the one who . . . Could she be a traitor like Morgan? The thought horrified me. How deep did it all go?

"You can't call me that," Nester said, voice pained. "Not anymore."

"Please . . . I didn't have a choice. I had to find a way to save you."

His eyes lingered on her talismans and runes. Slowly, he pressed a finger against a tattoo on her neck. Smoke rose from his touch. "It seems you're doing everything to destroy me. It hurts to look at the tattoos, at what they mean. And the talismans you've chosen . . . My soul burns just to be near you." He withdrew his hand.

"I'll get rid of them. All of them. Nester, listen to me. We can go back—it's not too late. We can give up this madness and live a normal life again. No more wars. No more death. Don't you want that? Don't you miss it?"

I looked from one to the other, stunned into silence. Audrey and Nester were once, what, lovers? But . . . gross! She had to be at least twenty years older than him.

"Madness?" Nester echoed quietly. He shook his head. "You never understood what was happening around you. Running back to Earth and burying our heads in the sand won't fix the atrocities that are being inflicted on demons." He looked at me. "She is the answer. She holds the power to set things right, more than you or anyone here can believe."

Tears now streamed down Audrey's face. She stepped closer, clasping his hands in hers. "You know I love you forever and always. But you're wrong. Sweetie, you're wrong." She sniffled. "I can't let you go through with this." Her hands twisted abruptly, and Nester howled as a glowing gold light appeared around his wrists, binding him like handcuffs. Smoke rose from his flailing arms.

"I'm sorry," Audrey whispered, quick-stepping away. "I love you." She turned and dashed at me, seizing my hand.

A dizzying sensation overtook me, my stomach lurching as the world swirled. It felt like I was falling, but my feet never left the ground. It was all over in a moment, but when my insides settled, I was no longer by the shops but inside Audrey's sterile living room, the smell of bleach stinging my nose.

Audrey leaned her forehead against the wall. "Damn it!" She pounded it with her palm. "His stubbornness will be the end of him!"

Suddenly weary beyond anything I'd ever felt, I sank onto the hard sofa, my mind trapped on the battlefield. How many people had been killed? How many students? Where was Aran? Oliver?

A gut-wrenching image surfaced in my mind—a stone crushing a small black paw. My throat constricted. Away from the fight, I let my guard down and suffered all the emotions I'd held at bay.

Dead.

Raven was dead.

I had been too weak to save her.

Audrey's room swam in my tears. How many others would fall because of my weakness?

Chapter Thirty-Seven

It was in that cold, uninviting room that my mind drifted apart. Murderers were at the academy, and it was all my fault. I could have stopped it. I could have surrendered, and Astaroth would be safe. I could have done a lot of things, but I'd failed everyone.

A sharp pain exploded across my cheek, rocking me from the impact and dragging me from my mind. I touched my burning skin in disbelief, staring up at Audrey whose hand was raised as if ready to strike again.

"Enough!" she snapped. "They're here, picking us clean like vultures, and you're *crying*?" She threw her hands up. "I should have let Nester take you back on Earth and be done with this whole damn mess."

I recoiled from her. It wasn't like I'd begged to be rescued, to be dragged into some crazy world filled with demons. None of this was my choice.

"What do you want me to do?" I asked. "March down there and hand myself over on a silver platter? Sacrifice myself for Astaroth?" A tightness squeezed my lungs. "Tell me and I'll do it. I can't make this decision on my own."

"What I want is for you to stop being so damn pathetic. If I had a sliver of your power, a mere whisper, this would be over. Don't you see how strong you are?"

"I'm not—"

"You are! Damn it, girl—there hasn't been another demon in history with as much potential. Never. Yet you choose to hide this gift as if it were a disease. Why? Where's the inferno you used during your first flag fall game? Where's the flaming missiles you launched at the battle of the gate? You were born for this moment."

"I wasn't," I protested, tears splashing onto my lap. "I was born cursed—"

"Rubbish! You're here for a reason. Where's that fucking power?"

"It's not mine!" I said, snapping, wanting to bury my fists in her stupid face. "It never was! I don't decide when to use it—it's all up to her. And she doesn't care if we live or die. She doesn't care about me at all!" I sat back, breathing heavily, aware of how unhinged I must sound, but not giving a damn.

She stared at me for a long moment before closing her mouth and clearing her throat. "Her?"

I nodded.

She exhaled slowly and uncurled her fingers, not flinching as an explosion sounded nearby. Her eyes locked on mine as she lowered herself onto a dining chair. "Why won't she help? It's her body, too. She doesn't want to live?"

That was the question I couldn't understand. How could she still hold a grudge after all these weeks? "I don't know." I lowered my gaze to my rain-soaked leathers.

"I see." She rose from her chair and exited the room, returning shortly with a picture frame clutched to her chest. The image faced her, shielding its contents from view. "I understand your hatred for this other soul. There was a time, many years ago, when we were the same. Filled with anger. I didn't stop at hating one demon, though—I despised them all. But in a terrible twist of fate, it was only them who could help me. I was forced to apply to Astaroth, but learning is hard when you're consumed with fury. I failed repeatedly, all because I couldn't listen through my anger." She pulled the frame away from her chest and glanced at it. A sad smile crossed her lips.

I stared at her. There was a battle being fought right outside, people dying, and she wanted to chat about the past? "Audrey, we have to help—"

"Eventually," she pushed on, ignoring me, "I became desperate enough to let go of my emotions. Only then did I truly learn everything the academy offered. I threw myself to the demons, surrendering to their influence, and came out the other side more powerful than I could have imagined." She traced a finger along the edge of the frame, the lines on her face deepening. "But this story all began long before that, with the birth of my son." Her voice was softer than before. "He was the most precious thing I'd ever known. Full of laughter and joy. His father died before he was born, so it was just the two of us. He was my world."

A memory surfaced: the picture in her office of the laughing boy who'd seemed so familiar. A pang of sympathy fluttered in my chest as her eyes reddened.

"They offered him a position at the academy when he was fourteen. I hated them for trying to take away my boy, but he insisted on going. At the end of the year, he was changed. There was a darkness in him, a shadow that hadn't been there before. Sure, he kept his kindness, but this other side of him, it scared me. I didn't want him to go back. I told him we would move, find somewhere they couldn't reach us. But he refused, saying I couldn't stop him from returning. He was right. I had no more power to hold him back than to stop a bullet in midflight." She held the frame to her chest and studied me. "How much do you know about the birth mothers of demon souls?"

Something tore through the air outside, whistling like a torpedo. "Audrey . . . the battle—"

"Demon's cradle, they call us. When a mother gives birth to a ripped soul, darkness touches them, and an unintentional transfer of power occurs at the moment of ripping. This power was my bargaining chip. I begged Astaroth to accept me, to train me to fight, all so I could help my son."

I sat in stunned silence. She wasn't a demon? But . . . I'd seen her use essence with my own eyes. I searched my memories for any times she'd manipulated the elements but came up blank. Every time she showed power, it came from somewhere else: a talisman, ring, necklace, or tattoo.

With dozens of questions spinning in my head, I grabbed the first one I could. "Why did you need to learn to fight?"

"To kill." She handed me the photograph. It was the one I remembered. "They were brainwashing my boy, and I had to stop them. He didn't go to Astaroth. The Reavers took him to Sevit on Noverna."

Something in my mind clicked and I lifted the picture until it was inches from my face and stared at it in disbelief. How had I not figured it out sooner? I must've been completely blind.

"Nester?" I whispered, taking in the pale, laughing boy.

"Yes."

It explained everything. Why Audrey hadn't hurt Nester in Lafayette. Why, instead of obliterating him moments ago, she'd simply shackled him. It even explained why she was so bitter all the time.

She took back the photo. "This might be my last lesson to you—I hope you learn it better than my runes training. Just as I had to, you must open yourself up entirely. Bury any fear, anger, resentment you have and accept this other demon of yours. Only by fighting together can you truly fight at all." She clasped her hands at her front. "Together, as one. Do you understand?"

Sure, I understood, but she didn't understand that I had no control over the situation. Kali was missing, and no matter how hard I'd tried to find her, she hadn't resurfaced.

A crash of thunder boomed, making me jump.

"Alina?" she pressed. "Demons are swarming through the Shadowgate as we speak. The academy won't hold much longer. Reavers will obliterate every student unless you do something. I've seen what you're capable of. I believe in you. It's time you believed in yourself."

I looked out the window, mind whirling. I wanted to help. More than anything, I wanted to go out there and fight these bastards. But without Kali . . .

Desperate times call for desperate measures, a voice cut through my thoughts.

My eyes snapped back to Audrey. Seeing my astonished look, she raised her eyebrows in question. I nodded, then spoke to Kali for the first time in weeks.

I'm sorry! I said. *I've been a complete idiot. You didn't deserve any of that—*

What I didn't deserve was being forced to lock lips with Morgan. That was repugnant, but we'll deal with compensation later. I'm not sure if you noticed, but we're short on time.

Did you . . . did you hear everything Audrey said?

Unfortunately.

I've got a plan. It's a little out there, but—

If it's anything like your flag fall strategies, it might be worth a shot.

What if we merge our consciousness? Like, share control so we can use both our powers at the same time?

Kali didn't answer immediately. *You've been drinking again, haven't you?*

No, Kali, listen—

Then you've lost your mind. We'd tear ourselves in two before we left the room.

I took a deep breath. *I know we've never tried anything like this before. It's always been one in control, the other sidelined. But think about it—your Faezre with my Aeria . . . together we would be unstoppable.*

I felt her wavering. *We would be catastrophic.*

Invincible. They'd write books about us.

There was a long pause. *I'm not much of a reader. But for your sake, I'm willing to give it a shot. If this all goes down the toilet like I think it will, it's on you. What do you need me to do?*

What did I need her to do? It wasn't like I had some blueprint to follow. I pushed ahead anyway. *Open your mind, feel for my energy. Try to match it. Instead of pushing against me, try to join me here.* After all the mind-control exercises, this seemed the most logical path.

Kali emerged from the depths of our body, a surging power, her presence solidifying. The first tendrils of her consciousness reached up and wrapped around mine. It was disorienting—sweet and sour clashing together—and my mind reactively tried to force her back, to bury her where she couldn't hurt me. I caught myself and brought my urges under control, allowing her to reset.

Moments passed, minutes perhaps, but gradually, with sweat beading into my eyes, our souls harmonized, blending for seconds before we vibrated apart. I'd slipped up again, reflexively fighting for control. Kali, to her credit, whispered words of encouragement, setting my subconscious mind at ease.

Bit by bit, like a well-used rocking chair settling in place, we found a balance where we both shared command of our body. It was strange. I wasn't wholly in control or forced to be a passenger. My thoughts were no longer my own—in fact, I no longer had thoughts; *we* had thoughts. Where mine began and hers ended was a blur.

Despite our success, or because of it, the same all-consuming urge for booze found us. It was Alina's old knee-jerk reaction to wash Machina away before she caused any damage. Our gaze wandered toward the gin bottles on Audrey's mantle, and it was all we could do to not run over there and drain their contents. But things had changed. We would never again survive on a cocktail of meds and alcohol or use it to fix a problem that only needed understanding. A problem buried was not a problem solved. The power to set our life straight rested in us. Not booze. Not Big Pharma. It was us; it always had been.

We stood, ignoring the now constant explosions outside, and lifted our left hand. A gust of wind circled above our palm. Our right hand rose, and a sphere of fire materialized.

Audrey sprang to her feet, slapping her hands together. "Yes! Yes, girl—that's it!"

Our muscles thrummed with new power. It was as though, with Kali and I both at the helm, our essence had doubled, and with it surged limitlessness energy. We stared at the liquor, revulsion coursing through us. Our wind and flames vanished as we extended two fingers toward the bar and fired a volley of icy missiles at the bottles, blasting them to shards that fizzed and smoked.

Our amazement registered briefly at the debut of our ice power. Deep down, we'd known it was possible since the exorcism. Our mother was a Cryore demon, our father a Faezre. Still, to feel it swell within us left us hungry to see what we were capable of.

We turned back to Audrey to find her watching us with tightened lips. "Save him. He's not beyond help."

"If we can."

Outside, we summoned a wind to carry us above the trees, giving us a view of the devastation below. The academy lay in ruins, fallen into a mess of muck and rubble. The beautiful buildings we'd once loved were fractured victims of the battle. Reavers clashed with pockets of fighters: students, teachers, and the Frostfires in their icy blue. Among them was an unfamiliar group wearing olive uniforms. They must be some sort of military asset. In the few heartbeats we watched, they teleported, shifted into gaseous forms, and even cast spheres of darkness at the Reavers, showing their proficiency.

Despite the added soldiers to our ranks, the Reavers were overpowering us. Every passing moment saw them push us back. Our heart pounded against our chest as the grim truth of the situation settled in. Our forces would be obliterated if they remained divided; they needed a leader to bring them together and turn the tide.

They needed an Architect.

Our gaze raced across the grounds, zeroing in on two clusters of defenders encircled by Reavers, their backs against the library walls. A howling line of beelzebubs prevented the two groups from joining forces. Their combined strength would be formidable if we could merge them.

We shot forward, our mind racing to think of a way to unite them. As we drew closer, a familiar figure stood out from the crowd, wearing black leather and a red-and-green cape. Our heart skipped as Aran fought to organize his disjointed group of students, fending off the flanking Reavers that threatened to overwhelm them. A winding trail of upturned earth cut through the beelzebub line. It was a weak point in their formation. If we could widen the fracture . . .

We reached out telepathically with Aran's group. *You're going to be overrun if you stay there,* we projected. *When I give the signal, take the path to the right!*

Aran's head swiveled as he searched for us. His eyes settled on the slim trail through the beelzebubs, and he gave a thumbs up before relaying orders to his team. After a brief pause, they turned, readying themselves for a desperate push.

We channeled our essence into a volley of flaming arrows and fired them at the bearlike demons blocking the path. Their horrendous screams pierced the air as the projectiles crashed through them, erupting on contact. The remaining demons scattered, leaving a clear path open. Aran's group erupted in cheers and surged forward, sprinting toward the newly opened escape route.

A shrill whistle pulled us back from the battle. We whipped around and barely had time to register the cabin wall hurtling toward us. Instinctively, we crossed our arms over our chest and thrust them forward. A wave of essence spewed from our palms, forming an impenetrable shield of crackling flames that devoured the wall. Instead of being crushed beneath splintering timber, a warm, smoky breeze billowed against our face.

Our eyes locked on the Reavers responsible for the attack. We raised our fists above our head, and then, with a twist of our wrists, the ground beneath their feet quaked and split open. The rift gaped like a maw, swallowing them whole. We dragged our fists to our chest and the ground heaved and then collided; sealing shut with a thunderous clap.

We shrugged off the remorse that followed. They deserved to die. They killed Raven. They killed Eben. We had to stop them from killing again.

Our work was far from over. We shot at another group of defenders who struggled to hold off a frenzied group of Reavers. We reached out with our mind and projected a mental image of the path they needed to take to reach Aran's larger group. They acted at once, and we provided covering fire. We didn't hang around to celebrate as the two groups merged but left in search of the next stragglers.

What next? Aran's voice echoed through the fog of battle. We found him staring up at us, waiting for our orders.

Searching through the chaos, we picked out three clusters of defenders scattered across the grounds. One was a solid crew of olive demons, doing a good job of pushing back the wave of Reavers. The other two groups? Not so much. They were on their last legs, barely holding ground against the onslaught. With the Reavers' crimson armor and black helmets dominating the landscape, things were grim. There was no way we could defeat them all. A part of us wanted to collapse, to give in to the weight of it all. But as we fought off the overwhelming resignation, we noticed something in the chaos: a pattern to the Reavers' assault. They weren't as unstoppable as they looked but were a bunch of smaller groups acting independently. They were not unified or coordinated but operated without any shared strategy.

That's when it hit us. We didn't need to be the strongest to beat them; we needed to be the smartest. It wasn't a fight—it was a giant game of chess.

No, not chess, we realized.

Flag fall.

Send twenty of your team to the hill by the medical center, we instructed, hoping our rushed words made sense to Aran. *Draw the Reavers away from the rest.*

We waved our fist, and an entrance to the tunnels appeared beside Aran.

Take everyone else underground. When the Reavers are lured into the ravine, take the ridge and give them hell. You'll have them burning at both ends. Even from the distance, we spotted the smile splitting Aran's face. His hair was drenched with rain, and mud covered his leathers.

I knew there was a reason I liked you, he said. *If we make it out of this, you're Michael's new Architect.*

The battlefield was no longer anarchy, but one large pattern. It was a game, and we knew all the plays.

We watched from above as our strategy unfolded, each move calculated and executed perfectly. Slowly, the tide turned, and we made ground. Most of our forces were now joined as one large army.

We'd captured our flag.

From then on, we called the shots, devising strategies formed from watching countless hours of flag fall games. Reavers fell in the dozens.

They'd killed Raven.

They'd killed Eben.

We had no pity.

Soon, most of Astaroth's professors had joined our ranks. Audrey had returned to the battle, her runes and talismans wreaking havoc among the enemy. Harper was an unstoppable force. Our heart leaped when we saw CJ among our fighters. We even spotted both Oliver and Anya with a ragtag group of Gabriel students.

Together, we pushed back, forcing them across the bridge and up the hill toward the gate. We had them retreating, scrambling back to whatever hell they'd crawled out from.

We ordered our army to stop on the far side of the bridge. The Reavers, having withdrawn further up the hill, had the high ground advantage, and we didn't want our forces to rush in there blind.

The storm pelted us as we landed in front of our army. This was our first time seeing up close the toll the battle had taken on them. From above, they were pieces on a game board. On the ground, the reality was totally different. Rain dripped from faces heavy with exhaustion, and they leaned on one another for support, waiting for the next orders. Many bled, and some were too weak to stand, so sat in the mud.

Aran detached himself from the group and strode toward us. Despite the condition of his battered leathers, his grin remained as infectious as ever. "Ripper day for some flag fall practice."

Unable to contain ourselves, we threw our arms around his neck, hugging him tightly. When we broke apart, we took a moment to study him. His eyes were glazed with fatigue, and he leaned heavily on one side looking on the brink of collapse. They all did. They couldn't go on much longer.

"We need to wrap this up," we said.

"Best idea I've heard all day. Let's do it before dinner, if possible. I'm starving."

Though already dark from the storm, what little light there had been was seeping away, plunging the world into a shadow. The Reavers and their capes would favor the night.

We shifted our gaze back up the hill to where they regrouped. "The ground is against us," we said. "Guess that's why they call it fighting an uphill battle. Any suggestions?"

Aran watched them for a moment. Like us, they licked their wounds and didn't seem eager to fight again just yet. "We need to shut the Shadowgate."

"And trap them here with us? No, we need to drive them out."

"If we close the gate now, we cut off their reinforcements. Every second it stays open adds more enemies for us to face."

The gate's obelisk was barely visible through the trees, its purple mist glowing. Trapping a horde of desperate Reavers didn't seem like a great strategy, but we had no other ideas.

"How do we close the gate?" we asked.

He shrugged. "Planning takes all the fun out of winging it."

"You don't know?"

"Can't be that hard, right? Closing a magical portal to another world can't be much different from closing a cattle gate."

"You're joking, right? Tell me you're joking. Aran?"

He sighed. "The Darkwell is on the roof. I reckon if we destroy that, the gate won't work."

"Darkwell?"

"It powers the gate. Kinda drains essence from a demon and feeds the portal. Take that out, and no more gate. Simple."

Nothing about it sounded simple at all. "And after it's shut, all we have to do is fend off hundreds of Reavers who are trapped here, fighting for their lives?"

"All before dinner, remember?"

We sagged under the weight of it all and looked over Astaroth's army. "Do you think they can manage one last push?"

"What choice do they have?"

Chapter Thirty-Eight

The sky erupted in a tremendous roar that echoed through the mountainside, sending flashes of lightning clawing across the heavens. A wave of torrential rain fell, shielding the world behind its hazy veil, obscuring the gate's obelisk.

Aran's firm grip on our hands brought us back from the turbulent skies to find his eyes searching ours. "You're the best Architect I've ever seen. Get me to the gate, and I'll sort out the Darkwell. Before dinner, if you don't mind." His gaze held ours for a heartbeat longer before he rejoined the others.

As the expectant eyes of the defenders watched us, the adrenaline that'd once coursed through our veins leached away, leaving a knot in our stomach. What if we let them down? What if we made the wrong call and hurt them?

What if they died?

Old Alina would have fallen into that voice. Given it power and reasoning. But we had changed over these last months, grown to believe in ourself. It wasn't only the flag fall success that'd done it, but every friend, every class, every experience Astaroth had given us had shaped us into a stronger person.

We tossed the doubt aside. Failure wasn't an option. Everyone here—the students, professors, even the Frostfires—they needed us to be more than just brave; they needed us to be a leader.

We needed them to give it everything they had.

We straightened against the rain, and lifted our gaze to the sky, summoning wind to propel us over the ranks. When we spoke, our voice boomed above the storm.

"In life, there are some things that belong together, like biscuits and gravy, and folks don't bat an eye," we shouted, trying to instill the same confidence and passion that Aran does with his flag fall speeches. "I can't say that me leading y'all is as natural as that. I'd love to tell a story about some grand destiny or prophecy pointing my way, but that'd be stretching the truth. I'm just a girl from Louisiana who's been caught up in this mess."

A ripple swept through them, and we felt their doubt. It was easy to imagine the higher-ranking Frostfires, or even the professors, questioning why they should take orders from us. We pressed on before they voiced their concerns.

"Yet, despite all odds, here I am," we continued, raising our voice over the stirring unrest. "I stand with you all, ready to fight, ready to defend every one of you. To save Astaroth and our loved ones back home." Murmurs rolled through them. "We've been to hell and back, but we're still standing. That's not luck, that's not fate. That's because we have something those Reavers don't—spirit!"

We swept above them, our eyes locking onto theirs. "Use that to overpower your exhaustion. One final push, that's all I'm asking. Fight like demons and get me to the gate. I'll handle the rest. Let's show those bastards what we're made of!"

Their roar shattered the sky, a wave that echoed through the mountains, banishing any doubt we had. We could do this. We could send them home. We could win.

We spun back to the Reavers, squinting through the downpour. They marshaled their forces into a formidable line of ghastly figures. The gate compound stood higher up the hill behind them, glowing eerily.

We reached out with our mind and connected everyone below, linking them together like a spider's web. This was the moment that would make or break us, the moment that the fates of the worlds rested, teetering uncertainly.

Ready...

We summoned a curtain of mist from the muddy ground to conceal our strike and waited as it drifted between the two armies.

CHARGE!

Everyone leaped forward, bellowing war cries that shook the ground. They called their powers and sent boulders and debris hurtling through the mist, cleaving thick lines through the Reavers' formation. The Reavers responded quickly, summoning air shields and stone barriers to repel the missiles.

We joined the battle, unleashing a whirlwind of ice shards into their midst. We were uncertain whether the idea to combine Aeria with Cryore came from Kali or from Alina, but the chaos it caused tore a path right through their center. Aran spearheaded our side through the mist and into the newly formed breach, Frostfires and the olive-clothed soldiers hot on his heels.

Once the Reavers' line had fractured, they crumbled before our eyes. They gave ground, sprinting back up the hill. A triumphant roar erupted from our defenders as they gave chase, rounding them up to the gate.

Yes! That's it! we cried, pumping our fists in the air, our breath catching as disbelief threatened to overwhelm us. The nightmare was coming to an end. They couldn't bounce back against our fury—

The Reavers reached the compound entrance and came to an abrupt stop. In eerie harmony, they turned to face us. And then they laughed.

It was like a cold knife had punctured our chest. Something was wrong.

Wait! we cried. *It's a trap—*

Our desperate plea, lost in the chaos, was unheard by the charging Frostfires who'd overtaken Aran. The instant the first soldier reached the compound, a massive boulder from above smashed upon her, crumpling her under its weight. The advance of those behind skidded to a halt, and as if in slow motion, the boulder stirred, revealing a truth too terrible to comprehend.

Retreat! we screamed. *Get back to Astaroth!*

It hadn't been a boulder that'd killed her; it was the monstrous fist of a Terre golem that'd been sheltering behind the compound's walls. It leaped out from hiding, landing with a ground-shaking thud that sent shock waves rolling down the hill, knocking people off their feet. It towered at least twenty feet high, its body a mountain of stone fused together to form a horrifying humanoid beast.

Do not retreat! Aran's urgent voice resonated in our mind. *There's no coming back if we do. I'll distract it while you sort out the Darkwell.*

We stared at the monster, our strength slipping away in the face of its sheer power. Never, not in any of the flag fall games we'd watched, had we seen one so big. So raw and destructive. There was no fighting that thing.

The golem seized a nearby military jeep and hurled it at the terrified defenders as they scrambled back down the slope. It was going to hit dozens of them.

We stabbed our hands forward, fingers splaying and cupping the air. The wind bent, redirecting the car's path so it veered off course and crashed down the mountainside instead.

I'll handle the golem, we said to Aran, knowing our only chance at winning was to take it out. *Our plan stays the same. You close the gate—*

Like hell, he said. *I'm not letting you go near that thing!*

You don't have a choice.

We launched at the beast, streaking through the sky like a comet. Reavers hurled stones and uprooted trees in our path, but the fusion of Alina's and Kali's soul granted us heightened essence manipulation. We easily dodged their lumbering assaults, our focus locked on the golem's eyeless face.

Its head swiveled to track us, and as we neared, it slapped its palms together, firing a shock wave that scrambled the air. The attack tossed us about like a rag doll, and we were unable to grip the wind to slow our spiraling fall. Eventually, the wave passed, and we righted ourself, rage taking root. This fucker was ours.

We clenched our fists and called to the mountain, pulling at it with all our combined strength. We grunted with effort, our muscles straining. If we could get the rocks to crumble around the golem, it would fall to the valley floor.

Not a pebble moved.

Just as with Morgan in the ravine, the earth refused our power. This beast ruled the ridge.

But manipulating stone was not our only trick.

We twisted to dodge a boulder the golem had launched our way and channeled our essence through our fingertips. A tornado spun to life, drawing breath from the gale-force winds. It tore toward the monster and crashed into its side with the shriek of a hurricane.

We may as well have puffed our cheeks and blew for all the good it did. Not phased at all, the golem uprooted a tree and held it like a javelin, aiming at a group of students down the hill.

"Shit!" We doubled back, and with an arc of one hand, the tree erupted into white-hot flames, crackling in the monster's grip. With the fingers of the other hand, we sent a gust of wind to carry the embers into the golem's face, hoping to find any weakness in its armor. Once again, it was oblivious to the attack.

Drifting to a halt, we scooped the rain from our eyes and stared at the swamp bastard with growing hopelessness. How could we win against such a monstrosity? Nothing we did was powerful enough to even make it flinch. Maybe if everyone attacked at the same time . . . But no. A quick glance was all it took to see everyone was already busy trying not to die. The Reavers had rallied and repelled our assault, protecting the gate as though their lives depended on it.

As the situation pressed in on us, any hope we had of winning faded. But in the darkness loomed a memory.

Raven's smiling face, her playfulness, her loyalty.

This golem was the creation of those pricks who'd taken away our beautiful wogle. A fire ignited within our core. Determination replaced despair. We were not only fighting for survival but for revenge. No matter the cost, no matter the odds, we would not give up.

Aran needed a clear path to the gate, and it was on us to give it to him. We had to lure it away from the compound at all costs. As the beast tore another tree from the ground and took aim, we shot in to steal its attention. It roared and swung at us, and it took every ounce of agility to dodge its wild arms. We dipped and darted around its cumbersome limbs, drawing its focus—and its wrath—and like the world's deadliest game of tag, we baited it into a chase.

"That's it, you stupid brute," we said, flying just out of reach. But luring it was the easy part. Demolishing it was another thing altogether. We thought back to high school geology. Rocks could be melted, but we doubted our Faezre could reach the heat needed. Erosion wore stone away, but that took centuries.

Unless . . .

A crazy idea formed. Ahead lay a lake cradled in the foothills surrounding Little Peak. If we could draw the golem there . . . If we could use the water to our advantage . . .

It was nuts, maybe even impossible, but it was something.

Despite our fading energy, we forced ourself to continue. Bit by bit, the beast followed, one pounding footstep after the other. It screeched with fury, and its arms were a windmill of death.

When we neared the lake, we chanced a glance at the compound. It was anarchy. We spotted him through the confusion—a figure in black leather dashing along the top of the walls, heading for the roof. A pack of demons surrounded the glowing purple obelisk. There was no way for him to break through them. Every fiber in our being wanted to abandon this battle and fly back to help him. But if we didn't take out this beast, who would?

We shot over the surface of the lake, sending up spray in our wake. In the middle, we pooled all our essence into building a waterspout. It towered upward, spiraling wildly, a force of nature barely under our control. Simultaneously managing the spout and our flight strained our powers to their limit, leaving us vulnerable to the golem's brutal onslaught, but it was a risk we had to take.

We sent the waterspout careening into the golem's stony belly with an enormous crash. The force jetted water into every crevice, penetrating it to its core and achieving what the storm hadn't: drenching its internal joints where the stone was bound by essence.

The golem was unfazed by the attack, and that was okay. We flew back at it, fingers splayed on our left hand, creating a gust of wind. The thumb and forefinger on our right hand formed a V, and the air in that wind froze as it washed over the beast. Frost formed on stone, and from inside, a crackling sounded, like an ice tray being emptied. It grew into a roar as the expanding ice splintered the rocky armor. Sheets of stone crumbled from the body, falling in mounds as the bulk of its size reduced.

The beast wasn't crippled, but our strategy had worked.

Things turned sour in the blink of an eye. With agility we hadn't expected from the creature, it swung its fist in a wide arc, dislodging a jagged shard from the motion. It hurtled at us.

We started to turn but weren't quick enough. It struck our arm, igniting searing pain at the point of impact. We cried out, losing control of our flight, and crashed into the soggy earth at the lake's edge. Our protective leathers, no match for the missile, had a gaping hole in the shoulder with blood oozing out. Our world spun.

A victorious roar echoed through the air, shaking the ground as the golem charged. We gingerly regained our feet, arm dangling by our side, and used one hand to summon a gust of wind. We rode it away, narrowly avoiding a swinging fist.

We needed room to breathe, to formulate a new plan. Fuck, we needed morphine and sleep, but there was fat chance of that happening. Unsteady from only having one working arm, we flew toward the compound, hoping to recruit some of those olive-clad soldiers to help.

But as we approached, our eyes were drawn to the Darkwell. Aran had single-handedly dispatched some of the Reavers who'd guarded it, but he was locked in a fierce battle with Hudson. Fresh from combat, Hudson hurled everything he had at Aran, whose essence was visibly failing. He was on his back foot, retreating toward the edge of the flat roof where a stairwell led to the compound floor.

Reavers stormed up those stairs, about to attack Aran from behind.

Our heart went cold. We tried to summon a wall of fire between Aran and the Reavers but stopped as we started to fall. With only one hand, it took all our concentration to stay airborne.

"Aran!" we shouted, watching on helplessly.

As the Reavers neared the top of the stairs, a second figure swooped onto the roof, setting themselves between Aran and the rushing enemy.

Our mouth dropped open as we recognized the person. Wasn't she one of them? Why was she helping him?

As the Reavers crested the stairwell, Sophia blasted them with wind, knocking all three back over the edge where they crashed to the ground.

A cry of pain yanked our attention to the compound entrance. A throng of Frostfires and students forced their way in, squeezing between the half-closed gate to get to the Reavers.

Through the chaos, we spotted two people we recognized. CJ fought a Reaver, her face a mask of grim determination, with Zach battling by her side. A prone body lay at their feet. A figure dressed in a bright-yellow shirt.

A Pokémon shirt.

That sight trapped us for a long time. *No.* He was only a kid. Our lips quivered as the cold reality made our gut cramp. Bitter tears clouded our vision, bringing with it a paralyzing numbness. He was too young. They were all too young.

A wave of crimson-armored Reavers charged at CJ. Our breathing grew ragged as fire blazed through our bones. We faced them and swept our good arm forward. An inferno crashed over them, and they fell, dead before they could scream.

We would kill them all before they could hurt anyone else.

We turned to the approaching golem and, with a burst of energy, fired out of the compound and flashed past it, narrowly dodging its flailing fist. At the lake's edge, we channeled our essence to summon another waterspout. This one was mightier, more intense, than the first. We sent it smashing into the rock monster as it followed. Before it'd taken its next step, we blasted it with an icy wind, freezing the water instantly. First, we heard the crack, then the crumble. The golem's foot splintered to nothingness, and it collapsed to its knee.

We called another spout. And another. By the time the third frost came, the golem was little more than a writhing mound of rubble. We shot back to the compound.

Most of the remaining Reavers were fleeing through the gate. With the destruction of their monster, they knew they stood no chance.

But the battle for the Darkwell still raged. As long as the gate remained open, the Reavers could return, and if they came with another golem, we would not win.

Sophia, accompanied by several Frostfires, fought to reach the Darkwell, but a group of stubborn Reavers had fortified their position, battling in a ring around the purple obelisk. Aran was not on the roof. A moment of blind panic filled us until we spotted him on the ground, his back against a wall, nursing an arm. He looked in pain, but he was alive. That was more than we could have hoped for.

We touched down on the roof, our gaze drawn to the skeletal Reaver clinging to the Darkwell. His withered skin glowed purple, and wafts of smoke rose from his head. He trembled on his knees, seemingly trapped in his own hold of the device. A stench of charred flesh filled the air.

A figure landed opposite us, drawing our gaze. His hair was blacker than aces, and his face, showing the shiny signs of an old burn, was caked with blood. His eyes blazed.

Slowly, he extended a hand toward us.

Chapter Thirty-Nine

Nester loomed before us, a grim sight with a grisly gash running down his cheek. Waterlogged hair clung to his face as his broad shoulders rose and fell heavily with each breath. Despite his clear weariness, a fierce determination lingered in eyes.

We were beyond exhausted, our essence depleted to nothing. We could not win this fight if it came to blows. This was a task for the Frostfires. We glanced over the edge of the roof to where a large number of them still fought, but we did not move.

A part of us wanted to understand Nester's side of the story. How could he be so certain his side was right? That the demons on Cronix were the real villains? The way he'd spoken earlier, the conviction in his voice, had stirred something in us; a need to know.

A part of us wanted to roast him to ash and spit in the dust of his charred remains.

Caught in an internal battle, we hesitated, one hand raised, the other firmly by our side.

"Come with us," he yelled, his voice barely audible over the storm's fury. "It's not too late. Let me show you the truth."

Burn him, a part of us thought. *Melt him into a bubbling puddle.*

Our palm turned toward him.

No! cried the other part. We shook our head, bringing our hand under control. We would hear him out. His side has lost. All he has left are words.

We dispelled the essence we'd gathered and took a small step forward. "Stay here with us," we countered. "You can mend this. Fix it all by exposing the Reavers' plans. Help us."

He laughed bitterly. "They would have my heart on ice by dawn. I never much enjoyed the cold." His eyes flicked toward the gate, and we knew he was calculating his escape.

"There are people here who still care about you. Your mother—"

"Doesn't know what she wants." His eyes snapped back to ours. "She thinks she can live a quiet life after seeing this. The absolute power these worlds have. How can anyone sleep at night, knowing they turned their back on so many?" His face tightened as Frostfires landed on the roof and joined the battle for the Darkwell. The gate would close soon.

"Forgive me," he said, "but there's not enough time to explain things here." He whipped his arm forward and hurled a disk of air at us.

It all happened so quickly. We threw ourselves to the side, narrowly avoiding the attack, but the rough landing jolted our injured shoulder. Waves of pain shot through our body making our vision swim. We lifted our uninjured arm and shot a blast of frigid air at him.

Nester dodged the attack with an effortless sidestep, but the pooled water on the rooftop transformed into a sheet of ice beneath his feet. He lost his footing and would have fallen if he hadn't summoned an updraft to sweep him above the ice. His right hand closed in front of him, and a gust of wind squeezed around us like an invisible fist, lifting us from the rooftop.

We fought against the hold, but Nester was too strong. With bone-chilling clarity, we realized our destination, and blind terror seized us. "No!" we screamed. "Nester, you can't! Please don't do this!"

He ignored our plea, drifting ahead of us toward the smoking purple portal, silhouetted against its light.

It couldn't end like this. Not now. Not after everything we'd been through. CJ, Aran . . . they needed us. We couldn't give up, we had to fight, to finish this. We took a deep breath. *Feel for the wind. Set our hooks. We've done it before. Come on . . . fight back . . .*

Warmth flowed through our muscles as we snatched hold of Nester's wind and fought to redirect its flow. At first, it remained stubbornly deaf to our calls. But, as we gritted our teeth and dug deeper, desperate, our momentum slowed until we drifted to a stop at the edge of the roof. It took Nester a moment to understand he no longer had control.

"Damn it, Alina!" he snapped, his hair whipping wildly around his face. "Just let me show you—you need to know what side you're really fighting for!" He lashed out, firing a gale that slammed into us, knocking us from the sky to the concrete and stealing the air from our lungs. Our vision swooned as our head cracked against the hard surface.

Before we could cry out, a gust flipped us onto our back. We gasped for breath, clawing at our throat, but nothing came. It was as if Nester had sucked away the oxygen.

"Stop resisting!" he cried from above. "I don't want to hurt you!"

The crushing grip around our lungs gave way, and we gulped in a rush of sweet air. It flowed through our veins, energizing our muscles and clearing our vision. In a desperate attempt to ward him off, we threw our hands forward and unleashed a maelstrom of fire. The flames soared high into the sky, their brilliant light casting a shadow that darkened the heavens. The fire's roar drowned out all else, and the heat dried our eyes.

Nester was engulfed, the inferno catapulting him through the air. When he crashed to the rooftop, he skidded a dozen feet before coming to a stop near the edge, smoke wafting from his skin, raindrops sizzling on impact.

We stared at him for a moment, too drained, too stunned, to move. Eventually, we climbed to our wobbly legs, mind numb as we tried to process what we saw. Nester was . . . he was gone. Dead. Our body shook as we stepped closer, eyes locked on the lifeless form. We'd killed him.

God, we'd killed so many.

A lump formed in our throat, making it impossible to swallow.

Voices swirled around us; our name called in the distance. They were whispers compared to our pounding heart. We shut them out, lost in what we had done.

Nester was dead.

Each step closer made that reality more undeniable. The talismans around his wrists smoked, and his hair was half burned away, revealing charred skin.

A shrill wail shattered the air. *"Nester!"*

We turned as Audrey crested the top of the stairs, horror carving lines into her face. "My baby! Please, not my son!" Her legs gave out, and she stumbled forward, eyes glazed and wild.

Our world crashed around us. What had we done? We were . . . we were monsters. Our hands trembled as we watched Audrey's distress with unblinking eyes.

Audrey suddenly stiffened, her eyes widening on something over our shoulder. "Watch out!"

Our breath caught. We spun to find Nester on his feet, his scorched face twisted in an expression that chilled our blood.

He was smiling.

A disturbance rippled above us. We glanced upward as a boulder plummeted from the storm-laden clouds.

Shock rooted us to the spot as we realized it would crush us. An image of Aran flickered through our mind, his disarming smile; the dimples that went on forever; our times in the stream. Ava made an appearance too, in her flag fall outfit, twirling her long bangs around a finger.

Something hit us from behind, sending us sprawling onto the concrete as a deafening crash rattled our teeth. We lifted our head and saw the boulder embedded in the roof exactly where we'd been standing. Audrey stood before it, watching us with surprise, her hands raised. She must have pushed us out of the way.

It wasn't until we got to our knees that we realized it wasn't surprise on her face. It was confusion. She blinked, her face cloudy, before her gaze fell on Nester, and a loving smile found her lips.

"My boy"—her voice trembled, a fragile whisper—"are you finally home?" Tears streamed down her cheeks, yet her expression was one of relief, like she'd finally lain down in a comfy bed after a long day at work.

Then, one by one, her talismans of protection shattered. Each explosion created a cloud of purple smoke that hung in the air. In a moment of horror, her body ruptured from within. Blood gushed out in a crimson tide as she crumpled, beyond recognition.

We stared, frozen, as gradual understanding crept in. With it came a devastating numbness. The boulder had hit her. Her talismans had absorbed the impact, but it was too great for them to hold. Audrey died saving us.

We sank back to the ground, our legs unable to support us anymore.

"No," Nester cried. *"No!"* He ran past us, skidding to a stop at Audrey's side. His anguished cries filled the air, seeping into our soul. "I'm sorry, Mom," he whispered, his trembling hands brushing Audrey's hair as though trying to coax her back to life. "You're okay. It's okay. You'll be fine . . . Please, Mom—stop it. I'll go back with you. I swear, I'll go. Let's go now, come on."

Audrey did not answer.

How much time passed with Nester like that, we didn't know. But when he finally rose, his face was hardened with grief. He locked his eyes on us.

"You did this," he said, voice wavering on the edge of a sob. "She would still be alive if you had listened." His fists tightened, the knuckles turning white. "Before this is over, you will understand what you have done. I promise you that. You will know, and you will be haunted by it every night you close your eyes."

He summoned a gust to carry him through the Shadowgate.

The fight for the Darkwell was ending, but we were deaf to it. We stared at Audrey, blinking rivers of tears, not caring if the Reavers attacked us.

Our souls disentangled in a dizzying blur. I was Alina once more. She was Kali.

Rest now, Kali said as she lowered me into the darkness. *It's okay, I've got it from here. Don't worry. Just sleep awhile.*

I sank into the abyss.

Chapter Forty

On this brisk morning, only a handful of brave people sat in the outdoor area of the Alpine Owl café in Little Peak. Winter had not just knocked on the door but had barged in with all its frosty might. Most customers chose the comforting warmth inside, flocking to the tables nestled beside the large, crackling hearth.

I preferred the quiet outside, despite the frosty gusts nipping at my cheeks. There was a sense of solitude that came with it, a space to breathe and think. I settled into the comfy chair, steam rising from my cup of coffee.

The view was breathtaking. Majestic mountains frosted in snow towered over the town, their peaks glistening in the morning sunlight. They caught me in their beauty, their timeless power grounding me in the moment.

They served as a reminder of the resilience of nature, its ability to weather the harshest of storms and still stand tall, still be beautiful. Though slightly uncomfortable to sit in the cold, these days, it was the perspective I needed, one that calmed my thoughts, making the burden of recent events more bearable.

The tension in my shoulders eased as I cradled my mug and stared at the peaks. I couldn't escape my problems entirely, but, for now, I was grateful for this moment of peace.

My gaze settled on the white page in front of me. Where was I supposed to start? The moment they'd collected me from Earth? No. It all began long before then, at the time of my birth, as it did for any student at Astaroth. The ripping of souls.

I took the pen and hovered over the paper. The cool breeze tossed my hair about, tickling my face. I sighed and set the pen back down. It was no use.

The academy's counselor had suggested this exercise, putting thoughts into words, writing my story onto paper. It was supposed to help manage my whirlwind of emotions. An idea made more bearable given my interest in writing.

I wasn't convinced. How would revisiting the battle help wrangle my inner demons? But the idea of composing a book was appealing enough that I hadn't dismissed the idea outright.

Whatever you do, Kali's voice interrupted, *skip the part about how you were in the hospital for a week. Refusing to talk to anyone—wildly embarrassing.*

I smiled. Sometimes, while at ease, I forgot she was with me. *I blame that on you.*

Me? You must be crazy.

I winced. *Maybe.*

She paused. *I didn't mean that. I meant crazy as in . . . well . . . you know what I meant.*

I knew what she meant. I also knew that perhaps there was truth in what she didn't mean. Sixty-four students had died on that day. How many had fallen because of the commands I'd given? How many families mourned their lost children because of my decisions—

It's not your fault, Kali said firmly. You saved millions of lives. *Not just on Cronix, but on Earth, too. You're a hero, Alina. Don't think twice about it.*

I nodded but found it hard to agree. The Reavers had only been there for me. The violence could have been avoided if I had surrendered without resisting.

On Cronix, Kali corrected. *Earth would've been screwed.*

I took a sip.

A golden eagle soared high, floating on the updraft to scan the land below. Since our rocky beginnings in Breaux Bridge, Kali and I had come a long way. She'd stopped taking over unannounced, and my constant companion—anxiety—had all but faded to memory. We'd learned to share our body, finding a balance that worked for us both. Although it wasn't a bed of roses—Kali's brazen flirting with Ava was a thorn—there were unexpected perks. Being a silent observer in our body allowed me to experience things I'd never have thought of trying. Ice climbing a frozen waterfall, dog sledding, paragliding, and ice fishing were now adventures imprinted firmly in my memory, opportunities I was grateful for.

That wasn't to say Kali and I were dandy. We had our differences—small ones, like Kali's fondness for donuts at breakfast, and more significant ones, such as my feelings for Aran, which left a sour taste in her mouth. However, I'd be forever in Kali's debt for the way she'd stepped in after the battle. I was emotionally devastated, traumatized, and numb. But Kali helped pick up the pieces and painstakingly glued me back together. She coaxed me out of the hospital bed that I'd confined myself in for far too long. She encouraged me to take care of myself, to venture out into the world, though at a slower pace. An 80 percent solution, she'd said, promising to work on the remaining 20 over time. I wouldn't have made it without her support. I owed her my life.

Well, half of it, at least.

The hospital had been full while I was there, the beds packed with injured students. I couldn't imagine how they had the strength to pick themselves up and march out of there on their own feet, especially given some of their injuries. I smiled, remembering Oliver. He hadn't hung around long. He'd made a great escape the following morning, complaining about hospital food. He returned a few hours later with a bag filled with cafeteria pastries, which he handed out to everyone "suffering" through the medical center rations. The resilience of kids.

No. Oliver could hardly be called a kid anymore. He had changed, matured after the battle. I hadn't seen him playing his game consoles, or even wearing his Pokémon shirt, since that day.

A group of Frostfires strode by, drawing my gaze away from the eagle. Since the attack, the task force had significantly ramped up their presence at the gate. I couldn't understand why they hadn't taken such action sooner. Perhaps all the devastation could've been avoided if they hadn't grossly underestimated the Reavers.

I've already explained this, Kali said, and I felt her anger toward them. *There's a traitor in their ranks. Not one of these henchmen, but someone calling the shots. Nothing else explains it.*

A hand covered my eyes from behind. "Guess who."

I grinned. "Judging by the smell, someone who's spent the night in a zoo?"

"Close," said Aran, leaning in to kiss my cheek. "But it was a château in an academy for demons. Far worse creatures live there, and the stench is twice as bad." He eased himself into the chair opposite me, massaging his right arm. His gaze drifted to my blank page, his lips tightening. It was a fleeting expression, but one I didn't miss. He'd been my pillar of support and wanted me to pen this book almost as much as the counselor did.

Not wanting to get into a discussion about it, I feigned annoyance. "You're late," I said, forcing my eyes to remain on his face, to not let them wander down.

He clumsily flipped open the menu. "Had a last-minute delivery to Icedale. The place is breathtaking. There's this massive ice formation in the town center that glows red. They say it's from the time of ancient power. Personally, I think it resembles a giant's . . . well, you get the idea."

"Delivery? I thought you were done with the trade business." After I'd regained my strength, I'd confronted him about his animals. Morgan's words had played on my mind, unsettling me. Though Aran had laughed off the accusations, assuring me he'd never once sold his animals to bad homes or "bile farms," it wasn't enough to put my fears to bed. In the end, he told me he would reevaluate his business model. Since then, his cages had been empty.

Kendra, Raphael's leader, was less than thrilled with this development. It turned out she'd partnered with Aran to help deliver his animals around the mountains. It had been a rocky pairing from the get-go, as they'd spent more time arguing about expansion than working together. Kendra saw the demand was there and wanted to bring in more animals, but Aran was adamant they couldn't juggle any more while still ensuring the animals were treated kindly. This was the argument I'd caught in Little Peak, the one where I'd assumed they were having a romance.

I shook my head at the thought, thinking it ridiculous that I ever could have thought Aran was a cheater.

"This one was a rescue," he said, flashing that irresistible grin my way. "Promise. It was a bandicoot named Barney. Ridiculous name, I agree, but a cute critter. Anyway—Icedale, we should visit. It's just an hour and a half by train . . ." His voice trailed off as he flagged down a server. "Whiskey on the rocks. Ta."

The server raised an eyebrow. "Starting early?"

"It's five o'clock somewhere."

"I suppose it is." He turned to me. "Care for a stiffer drink, too?"

I shook my head, fighting back a feeling of unease. He wasn't drinking for the enjoyment of it, but to hide. To numb the pain. I knew where that road led, and it wasn't anywhere good. But every time I broached the subject, it irritated him, and he would storm away.

Noticing my gaze on his arm, he hastily moved it out of sight, draping a blanket over himself. "Bloody chilly today," he said, trying to sound casual, but his effort to hide the arm made my heart ache. I wanted to reassure him that no one was judging. That I loved him just the way he was. But mentioning it caused such pain in his eyes that it tore me in two.

No. I wouldn't put him through that this morning. Not yet. I cleared my throat and redirected my gaze toward the towering peaks. "Looking forward to practice tomorrow? It'll be good to get back into the swing of things."

"I'm not going."

"Oh? You're taking the day off? If this is about another delivery—"

"It's not," he said quickly. "And I'm not taking the day off. I'm taking the year off."

His words drifted in the chilly air. "What? No, Aran, I won't let you—"

"It's not your decision to make."

"The team needs you. *I* need you." I clasped his hand. "You can't abandon us. It's like . . . it's like taking the wheels from a car."

He snorted, bitter amusement in his eyes. "Good analogy. Taking the hand off a captain is a better one." His gaze drifted away for a moment, and when it returned to me, his expression told me his mind was made up. "You're a better Architect than I could ever be. You've shown that time and again. There's no place left for me on the team. I can't exactly be down on the field, fumbling around. No, listen—this decision was hard enough to make. Don't make it harder."

The server reappeared with Aran's drink. He accepted it and ordered another before the server could make his retreat. As he took a swig, the flickering outdoor heaters reflecting off his hazel eyes, I had the haunting realization of the enormous divide that'd grown between the man he used to be and the man he'd become. I wanted to bridge that gap, to help him find a way back to his former self. But at that moment, it was still too raw for him to let me in. I had to bide my time. I couldn't imagine what it was like to have a hand pulverized beyond repair. But then to have it amputated? That stuff left a mark. Some marks needed time for the person to grow around them. Only then could the healing truly begin.

I shook off my thoughts and forced myself to focus on the mountains again. Aran would be alright, he just needed time and patience. I had both.

As I took in the jagged peaks, a stirring thought gripped me. In life, there were some things that just belonged together. A shadow faun and its demon, Michael and its all-night parties, and nobody was going to catch a flag fall game without ending up at the Shack.

But it was the things that belonged together, yet were destined to part, that could crumble a person like corn bread between heavy fingers.

A mother and her son.

A man and his hand.

In such moments of separation, I found comfort in knowing that something extraordinary had existed. That two things had created something remarkable, even if it was fleeting. Life needed that bittersweetness to make it rich and full. It was the reminder we needed to cherish what we had, to hold those we loved, and to love with all our might while we had our chance.

I learned this the long way.

But I learned it all the same.

Thank you for taking the time to read my work. If it resonated with you, please consider leaving a review on Amazon Your support means the world to me and helps others discover the book!

www.ingramcontent.com/pod-product-compliance
Lightning Source LLC
Chambersburg PA
CBHW020306030826
48979CB00029B/2277/J

* 9 7 8 0 9 7 5 6 6 1 5 4 3 *